Mixed-Up Mysteries

Camp Club Girls

Print ISBN 978-1-62416-727-0

eBook Editions:
Adobe Digital Edition (.epub) 978-1-62836-313-5
Kindle and MobiPocket Edition (.prc) 978-1-62836-314-2

Published by Barbour Publishing, Inc., P.O. Box 719, Uhrichsville, Ohio 44683,
www.barbourbooks.com

Our mission is to publish and distribute inspirational products offering exceptional value and biblical encouragement to the masses.

 Member of the
Evangelical Christian
Publishers Association

Printed in the United States of America.
Bethany Press International, Bloomington, MN 55438; November 2013; D10004212

Mixed-Up Mysteries

Camp Club Girls

3 STORIES IN ONE

BARBOUR
PUBLISHING

Contents

Camp Club Girls

Elizabeth's
Amarillo Adventure

Renae Brumbaugh

The Mystery Marbles

"Elizabeth! Come quick! My grandmother has lost her marbles!"

Elizabeth held the phone out from her ear, trying to understand what her friend was saying. "Megan, what are you talking about? I thought your grandmother was dead!"

"She is! Listen, you've got to get down here right now." Megan hung up the phone, leaving Elizabeth baffled.

Elizabeth replaced the phone on its base and dashed out the door. As an afterthought, she stepped back inside and grabbed a letter off the entryway table. Cramming it in her back pocket, she called out, "Mom, I'm going to see Megan—I'll be back in a little while!" She slipped her helmet on, jumped on her bike, and headed down the driveway.

"Wait!" her mother cried, and Elizabeth slammed on her brakes. The screen door squeaked as Mrs. Anderson stepped onto the porch, drying a coffee mug with a white dish towel. "I thought Megan was at work."

"She is, but she gets her break at 2:30. That was her on the phone, and she wants me to come," Elizabeth said, adjusting her helmet.

Mrs. Anderson continued drying the mug and looked at her daughter a moment. "Okay, but be careful crossing streets, and come straight back here after Megan's break is over."

"Yes, ma'am," Elizabeth called as she lunged her bike forward. She practically flew the four blocks to the restaurant. If it hadn't been for the pesky stops she had to make at the intersections, she could have made it in half the time. But safety first.

Within minutes, she parked her bicycle next to her friend's scooter near the back entrance. Going to the front of the restaurant, she pushed open the heavy door. The restaurant seemed black compared to the bright Texas sunlight. It took her a moment to adjust her vision, and she looked around.

Jean Louise, the head waitress, greeted her with a wink. "You're just in time, girly. Megan just sat down at her usual table," she drawled.

"Thanks," Elizabeth told her. She sidled through the mixture of cowboys and tourists who were the customers at the Big Texan Steak Ranch.

"What took you so long?" Megan asked as she stood to greet her friend.

Elizabeth slid into the booth and said, "I got here as fast as I could. What's up with your grandmother?"

"I have no idea. Jean Louise is telling me some crazy story about my grandmother and some marbles and us being rich or something. That's all I know. And since you're the mystery girl, I called you."

Elizabeth didn't know what to say. Sure, she had helped solve mysteries with the Camp Club Girls, but she was surprised Megan would even remember that.

Megan leaned her chin on her hands then. "I'm exhausted. We've been busier than usual today. I've washed more dishes today than I have in my entire life! I'm just too tired to try to solve a mystery."

Elizabeth grinned. "Yeah, but just think of all that cash you'll have when you collect your first paycheck!"

Megan put her head on the table and moaned. "All I can think about right now is my tired back." After a few seconds, she sat up and added, "But it will be nice to be able to buy my saxophone. I know Mom can't afford it, and I don't want to ask her. But I really want to be in the band."

Jean Louise set a tall glass of iced tea in front of Megan. "What'll ya have?" she asked Elizabeth.

"Oh, nothing. I just—"

"Nonsense. It's on the house. Just tell me what you want," the tall redheaded waitress said around her gum.

Elizabeth paused, realizing the woman wouldn't take no for an answer. "I'll have a root beer," she said politely.

Jean Louise winked and said, "One root beer, coming up!"

Megan sat up and smiled at her friend. "I'm sorry. I haven't even asked about your day."

Megan and Elizabeth had grown up more like sisters than next-door neighbors. Though Megan was a year and a half older, she and Elizabeth had played together, walked to school together, and gone to church together for as long as they could remember.

Elizabeth pulled the letter from her back pocket and slid it across the table. "It's from my friend McKenzie. I told you about her—from camp? She's the one from Montana, the one who has horses. She's wanted to visit Texas, and she's finally going to. Her family is coming here to Amarillo for their vacation! She's coming to visit!"

Megan opened the envelope and pulled out the pages. She

skimmed the contents of the letter and then handed it back to Elizabeth. "That's great, Beth, really. I'm excited for you."

Both girls sat silently for a moment.

"And I promise to act excited, as soon as I have slept about forty hours," Megan continued with a yawn.

Just then, Jean Louise appeared with the root beer and two oversize pieces of apple pie topped with enormous scoops of ice cream. "Here ya go," she said.

Both girls perked up at the sight of the pie. "Wow! Thanks, Jean Louise!" they told her.

"Awww, hush up now. No need to thank me. You've earned that and more. You just eat and enjoy your break," she told Megan. She turned to go, then changed her mind. "So what are you going to do about that special tip?"

Megan, whose mouth was poised for her first juicy bite of pie, stopped. "Well, actually, that's why I called Elizabeth. She's good at solving these kinds of things."

The waitress turned to Elizabeth. "So you'll help her solve this mystery, huh?"

"I'm not sure," said Elizabeth. "First I need to know more about those marbles."

"Shhhhh!" Jean Louise looked around her, as if not wanting anyone to overhear. "Honey, we need to talk. But not here. These walls have ears. Why don't you two head over to my place after work today?"

Megan nodded, and the waitress moved to take an order from the next table. "So can you come?" the girl asked.

Elizabeth thought a moment. "I'll have to ask my mom. I'm supposed to stay with James while Mom and Dad go to a meeting at church, but maybe he can go with them."

"Okay. Meet me at the back door if you can," Megan told

her. The girls finished their pie and drinks without much further conversation. Elizabeth was still thinking about this new mystery, and Megan was just too tired to talk.

●—●—●

Mrs. Anderson stood in her kitchen, looking between Elizabeth and six-year-old James, who were both talking.

"Megan wants me to go with her to Jean Louise's house at six," Elizabeth told her mother.

"Elizabeth promised she would watch me tonight, Mom! I want her to stay with me," James interrupted his sister.

"I know I said I'd watch him, but I think this is really important to Megan," Elizabeth continued. "Something about a special tip and her grandmother."

"But I wanted Beth to help me finish my Lego airplane. It's more fun when she helps me," James urged. "Make her stay with me. . .please!"

Elizabeth held in an exasperated sigh. She loved James. She just didn't like being his full-time playmate. She needed her space, and he didn't want to give it to her.

Mrs. Anderson looked at Elizabeth, then at James. "I don't think Elizabeth promised you anything, James. I asked her to stay with you tonight, and she agreed. But Josh's mom called earlier and is bringing Josh with her tonight, so you'll have a playmate."

James's face brightened as he said, "Cool! I'll go pack my toys so we can play!"

"You may take two toys, and that's it!" Mrs. Anderson called after him. Then she looked at her daughter.

Elizabeth slowly released her breath. She was off the hook with James, but she still didn't have permission to go with Megan.

"Is this Jean Louise Wilson, the waitress at the Big Texan?" her mother asked.

"Yes, ma'am. She's the tall lady with red hair. She gave us free pie today."

"I know her. She's nice," her mother said. She stood, clearly trying to make up her mind. "Okay, but you need to leave her house by seven thirty. I want you home before dark. And you girls stay together. If we're not home by the time you get back, go to Megan's house with her. We should be back around eight."

Elizabeth gave her mother a tight hug. "Oh, thank you, thank you, thank you! You're the best mom in the world!" She kissed her mother's cheek and ran to her room.

At 5:58 p.m., Elizabeth sat on the back stoop of the Big Texan Steak Ranch waiting for her friend. At 6:01 p.m., the back door opened, and Megan stepped outside and collapsed next to her friend.

"I'm not sure what I've gotten myself into," Megan told her. "Washing dishes here is a lot harder than washing dishes at home. They just keep coming and coming, and I can never get caught up!"

"I'll bet you'll get faster the more you do it," Elizabeth encouraged her. "Besides, just think of the free pie!"

"Speaking of free pie, the cook sent these home with me," Megan answered, nodding toward two pie-sized boxes. "We'll never eat all of this, so one of them is going to your house."

"I won't argue," Elizabeth told her. "Should we drop them off before we go to Jean Louise's?"

"That's a good idea," Megan answered, and Elizabeth took the boxes from her.

"I walked, so I'll carry them. Then we can ride our bikes from home."

Soon the girls were bicycling through town, toward a section of small but well-kept hundred-year-old homes. They found the address the waitress had given them and rang the doorbell.

Jean Louise answered the door wearing cutoff jeans and a trendy T-shirt. It was an outfit that Elizabeth expected to see on a much younger person, but it looked good on the red-haired lady. The woman smacked her gum and said, "Come on in, y'all. I just made some fresh sweet tea. And if you're hungry, I have some leftover fried chicken. You'll have to eat it cold, but that's how I like it."

The girls would have preferred to skip the tea and jump straight to the mystery, but they didn't want to be rude.

"I'll have some tea, thanks," said Megan. Elizabeth nodded that she'd have the same.

The two girls sat in the tidy, old-fashioned living room. A collection of salt and pepper shakers lined the mantel, and a pink porcelain teapot shaped like a pig rested on a tray on the coffee table. They could hear Jean Louise singing with a popular country-and-western song that was playing on an antique radio in the corner.

The older woman handed them the tea and placed a couple of pig-shaped coasters on the coffee table. She turned the radio down and sat across from them in a green overstuffed chair. "Megan, were you serious when you said you didn't know anything about a special tip?" she asked.

Megan set her tea down and answered, "Jean Louise, I still don't know what you're talking about. My grandmother died when my mother was a little girl."

The woman looked at her, as if deciding what she should say. "I don't mean to be nosy, honey, but why are you working as a dishwasher? Is money tight for you all?"

Megan blushed but held her head high. "We do okay. We're not rich, but we always have what we need."

Jean Louise shifted in her chair. "Well, darlin', with that tip your grandmother got, you should have everything you need, everything you want, and then some."

Elizabeth sipped her tea and remained quiet.

"Jean Louise, you're not making any sense," Megan said to the woman.

The woman looked out the window, then back at Megan. "You're really not kidding, are you? You don't know anything about the marbles."

"Jean Louise, please tell me what in the world you're talking about," Megan responded.

"Oh, honey. Some rich fella was head over heels in love with Emily Marie—your grandma. I remember it like it was yesterday. I was just a young teenager myself, and the whole thing was so romantic. Your grandma and my mama were best friends, and I used to hang out at the restaurant after school, till my mama got off work. This fella came in once a week or so, and he'd always sit at the same table in your grandma's section. Then he started coming several times a week. Before long, he was visiting the restaurant every day, ordering nothing more than coffee or tea. But he always left her a twenty-dollar tip. He was smitten.

"Then one day, he gave her this bag of marbles. They were the prettiest things you ever saw! There was a red one and a blue one and a green one, just about every color of the rainbow. There must have been a dozen of them in that bag.

But the prettiest one was crystal clear."

She paused and looked out the window, as if remembering.

Megan interrupted her silence and said, "So the special tip was a bag of marbles?"

Jean Louise slowly brought her gaze to Megan. "Honey, those weren't just any old marbles. But hold your horses. Let me finish the story."

The two girls leaned forward, their eyes glued on the sassy waitress.

"So the fella gives Emily Marie this bag of marbles and tells her to keep them in a safe place. He tells her he wants to take care of her, and he knows these marbles will give her and her children a comfortable future.

"Well, at first she didn't know what to say. After all, you can buy a bag of marbles at any old five-and-dime store. But she didn't want to offend him, so she just said, 'Thank you.'

"Then she started to pour them out on the table, but he stopped her. He pulled her toward him and whispered something in her ear. I remember it plain as day. I was sitting at the table across from them. I was eavesdropping, even though I knew I wasn't supposed to. Your grandma was such a pretty lady, and I used to watch her all the time."

She shifted, and the sofa squeaked. Elizabeth had a pretty good guess what Megan was thinking. They both wanted the woman to get on with the story.

The squeaking seemed to draw Jean Louise back to the present. She laughed. "Oh, listen to me, chasin' rabbits. Anyway, when that man whispered in your grandma's ear, she turned white! She looked at the bag in her hands. Her hands started shaking and she tried to give it back to him, but he wouldn't take it. He kept saying, 'They're yours. I've already put them in your name. The paperwork is all there.' Then she sat down in the booth with the man. That was against the rules, but she did it anyway. Just sat right down and started crying and telling him thank you over and over again.

"He kept telling her, 'Don't cry. I want to take care of you!' I thought he was going to ask her to marry him, right then and there. But a whole bunch of cowboys came in, and your grandma had to get back to work."

She looked at the girls as if she had finished her story.

Elizabeth and Megan looked at each other, then back at Jean Louise. In unison, they nearly yelled, "What was so special about the marbles?"

Jean Louise looked surprised. "Oh, I forgot that part, didn't I? Silly me. I'll tell you that right now. But first, would you like some more tea?"

CHAPTER 2

Camp Club Girls on the Case

The girls responded in unison, "No, thank you!"

But Jean Louise didn't take the hint. She leaned forward, picked up her own glass, and said, "I'll just get myself some, then. I'll be right back." She went into the kitchen while Megan and Elizabeth sat on the couch. They shared confused looks, but neither girl spoke a word. An old Oak Ridge Boys song played softly on the radio.

After a moment, Jean Louise sauntered back into the living room. "Sorry to keep you waiting. I know you're anxious to hear about those marbles. But to be perfectly honest, I'm having second thoughts about telling you all this. Maybe your mama is the one I should talk to, Megan."

Megan told her, "My mama and I tell each other everything anyway. But she's working overtime this week, so you probably won't be able to get in touch with her for a few days."

"Your mama was just a little girl when all this happened," said Jean Louise. She sipped her tea, as if considering her next words. Finally she said, "Okay, I'll tell you. But don't go spreading this around. Tell your mama, of course, but don't talk about it to all your little friends." She glanced at Elizabeth.

"I won't tell a soul, unless Megan wants me to," Elizabeth responded.

Megan said, "Our lips are sealed."

Finally, the woman said, "The marbles were formed out of priceless gemstones. The red one was a ruby, the blue one a sapphire, and the clear one. . .a diamond!"

The two girls looked at each other wide-eyed and then stood to their feet and squealed. "We're rich! We're rich!" Megan sang as she hopped up and down.

The older woman let the girls have a moment before she interrupted them. "Not so fast, Megan. If you're so rich, why is your mama working so much overtime? Why are you working as a dishwasher so you can buy a band instrument?"

Surprised, Megan looked at the waitress. "How did you know that?" she asked.

"I already told you I'm an eavesdropper!" Jean Louise said with a laugh. Then she grew serious. "There's one more thing you need to know. The reason I thought about those marbles after all these years is because a man came into the restaurant the other day asking questions."

"What kinds of questions?" asked Elizabeth, shifting into her detective mode.

"He asked to see the restaurant manager. He wanted to know if anybody knew anything about some marbles that were given to a waitress there, years ago. Of course the manager didn't know anything. We've had so many managers since that time. And your grandma never told anyone except my mama about them."

"I wonder who would be looking for them after all this time?" asked Megan.

Jean Louise snorted. "Honey, plenty o' folks will be looking for them if they know they're missing!"

Soon the girls thanked their hostess and started home.

"What should we do?" asked Megan.

"I don't know. This is your mystery, not mine. I promised Jean Louise I'd stay out of it, remember?"

"No, you didn't. You promised not to tell anybody about it. That doesn't mean you can't help me solve the mystery," her friend said.

"I don't know, Megan. This one seems over my head. I wouldn't know where to begin," Elizabeth told her.

"Come on, Beth, you've got to help me. You're the one with all the sleuthing experience," Megan urged.

Elizabeth remained quiet, as if thinking it over. "Well. . . okay! I'll do it! But first thing, we need to let your mom know what's going on."

"Okay. I'll tell her as soon as—oh, wait! She works late tonight, and I have to be at work early tomorrow. I won't even see her until tomorrow night. But I'll tell her as soon as I can, I promise."

"It's a deal," Elizabeth told her. "Meanwhile, I'll do an Internet search on gemstone marbles and see what I can come up with."

The girls were almost home, and Elizabeth could see her parents' van parked in the driveway. She looked at her watch—7:25. *It must have been a short meeting.*

"I'll see you tomorrow, Beth," Megan called as she headed toward her front door. "Join me on my break again tomorrow. We can talk about what you find on the Internet!"

"See you then," Elizabeth called back, and climbed the front steps.

●—■—●

Later that night, Elizabeth sat at the family computer searching for information on the marbles. Her mother put the finishing touches on the now gleaming kitchen and laid a fresh dish towel on the counter.

"What are you looking at?" Mrs. Anderson asked, laying a gentle hand on Elizabeth's shoulder.

"Oh, I'm just helping Megan with a project. Do you need the computer?" Elizabeth asked her mother.

"No, I'm going to bed now. Don't stay up too late, okay?" She kissed her daughter on the cheek and headed toward the back of the house. Then she called over her shoulder, "Your dad will be home in a little while, though, and you know he'll want to check his e-mail."

Elizabeth laughed. Her father taught Bible classes at the local seminary. He often got e-mails from his students, asking about their assignments. He enjoyed his job, and he loved helping his students understand the Bible better. To him, that was as exciting as a carnival would have been for Elizabeth.

She typed into the search engine *Precious gemstone marbles* and waited to see what appeared. Before long, she had links to museums and fine jewelers all over the world. There was a link for birthstone marbles, precious gemstones, forever gemstones, tigereye marbles. . .but nothing related to Amarillo, Texas.

If only I could send an SOS to the Camp Club Girls. Elizabeth thought of her friends from summer camp. *But I promised Jean Louise I'd keep my mouth shut.* She was in the middle of another search when a flag popped up in the bottom corner of her screen. HORSEGIRL96 WANTS TO CHAT, the message read.

Elizabeth recognized McKenzie's online name and clicked on the flag.

Did you get my letter? McKenzie typed.

Elizabeth: *Yes! I'm so excited!*

McKenzie: *Me too. I can't wait to see you.*

Elizabeth: *What day will you be here?*

McKenzie: *Next Tuesday.*

Elizabeth smiled. She couldn't wait to see her friend. Then she had an idea.

Elizabeth: *Do you think your parents will let you stay at my house while you're here?*

McKenzie: *That sounds like fun! I'll ask and e-mail you tomorrow. Maybe you can stay at the hotel with me some, too.*

Elizabeth: *Okay, I'll ask. Talk to you later.*

McKenzie: *Bye.*

Elizabeth was smiling at the computer screen when her dad walked in. "Hey, Bethy-bug! What are you so happy about?"

She stood and hugged her father. "Hi, Daddy! Guess what? McKenzie's coming to visit. She and her family will be in Amarillo next Tuesday!"

"That's great news, Sparky," he said, using one of his many pet names for her. "Why don't you see if she can sleep over while she's in town?"

Elizabeth giggled. "I already asked her. She's supposed to let me know tomorrow."

Mr. Anderson walked over to the computer and sat down. "What's all this about gemstones you've pulled up?"

Elizabeth had to think quickly. She didn't want to break her promise, but she wasn't going to lie, either. "Oh, just some research I'm doing for Megan."

"You're a good friend, Elizabeth, and an all-around great gal. Just like your mama. 'A wife of noble character who can find? She is worth far more than rubies,' Proverbs 31:10. Tell Megan the real gem is your mama," he said.

Elizabeth smiled. Her parents were kind of sappy sometimes, always holding hands and kissing. It was embarrassing at times, but it was cute.

"I'll tell her, Daddy," she said, and kissed him on top of his head. "Good night."

●—●—●

At 2:33 p.m. the next day, Elizabeth pushed open the saloon-style doors of the Big Texan Steak Ranch and looked around. Megan was already sitting at her table. Two tall iced drinks and two big slices of pie were there, too.

Elizabeth tossed her blond hair over her shoulders as she slid into the booth. Megan looked worn-out.

"I don't know how long I can keep this up!" she moaned. "I'm not sure I was created for hard physical labor."

Elizabeth chuckled. She remembered how tired she had been at camp, after she and her friends had to do kitchen duty for a few days. "You can do it. Hang in there," she encouraged.

Megan leaned forward. "So did you find out anything about the marbles?" she whispered.

"Not a thing. I did an Internet search, but nothing linked any gemstone marbles to Amarillo. I didn't have time to look at much. I'll keep trying."

"Why don't you get all your Camp Detective Club Friends, or whatever y'all called yourselves, to help?" Megan asked.

"Camp Club Girls," Elizabeth corrected. "I thought about that, but we promised Jean Louise to keep it hush-hush."

"Well, we don't need to talk about it to people around

here. But as long as you trust your friends, I trust them."

Elizabeth sighed with relief. This would be so much easier if her friends helped her. "Okay," she said. "I'll send out an e-mail tonight, and we'll see what we can come up with. You're still going to talk to your mom tonight, aren't you?"

"I hope so. As much as she's been working lately, I hardly see her. And when I do see her, she can barely stand up, she's so tired. I'm not sure how to break it to her that her mother lost her marbles," she said.

Elizabeth giggled and thought about the situation. It sure would be nice if Megan's mom didn't have to work so hard. Her dad had been killed a few years ago in a car accident, and things had been tough for their family since then. "I don't know about you, but I'm about to die if I don't start eating this pie! What is it today? Chocolate?" she asked.

"I think so," said Megan without much enthusiasm. But then she took a bite and perked up right away. "Oh, this is *so* good!"

"I wonder if they'd hire me and let me work for pie," Elizabeth said. Both girls giggled and finished their pie in no time.

Just then, Jean Louise stopped by the table and bent down to their level. "You girls had better get crackin' on that marble mystery. That man was snooping around here again this morning, asking more questions."

The two girls looked at each other in surprise. Yes, they definitely needed to get crackin'.

● — ● — ●

Elizabeth typed into the subject line of the e-mail: NEW MYSTERY; NEED HELP! She then moved her cursor to the body of the e-mail and began typing the whole story. She ended it with, "I don't know where to begin. Please help!"

She paused and said a little prayer before hitting the SEND button. *Lord, You know Megan and her mother haven't had an easy life. These gemstones could really help them. Please help us find them.*

There. She sent the e-mail and sat staring at the blank screen. She knew it would only be a matter of minutes before someone answered her.

Since summer camp had ended, the six Camp Club Girls had conspired to solve several mysteries. Elizabeth had traveled to DC and helped her friend Sydney uncover a plot to assassinate the president! The other girls had been busy as well, using the sleuthing skills they had honed at camp to solve their own hometown mysteries. They were becoming quite the team, and Elizabeth knew she could count on them to offer helpful suggestions in this new case. The miracles of e-mail, text messaging, and Internet research had allowed them to keep in close contact, from Alex in California to Sydney in Washington DC. Sure enough, just minutes after she sent her message, the red flag popped up. It was Bailey.

Gemstones? How exciting! Your friend will be rich! Wow, I wish I were there. You should check the local jewelers and see if anyone in your area sells gemstone marbles.

Elizabeth smiled. She missed Bailey, the youngest of their gang. Bailey was always excited about everything. Period. Elizabeth typed back, *Great idea. Thanks, Bales!*

Just then, another red flag showed that Alexis was online.

Why doesn't your friend snoop around the restaurant and see if there are any hiding places there? She can act like she's cleaning or something. Tell her to try tapping on the walls. Nancy Drew is always tapping on walls to see if they are hollow.

A third red flag popped up, and it was Sydney.

Sounds to me like you need to investigate Megan's grandmother's death. It's suspicious to me that she died just days after receiving the jewels.

Elizabeth felt her heart beating faster. This was getting more and more exciting. She typed the words, *Thanks, y'all. This will really help me get started. I'll keep you posted.*

She signed off the computer and walked to the front porch. She would wait there until Megan got home.

●—●—●

An hour later, the two girls sat on Elizabeth's front steps sipping the fresh lemonade Mrs. Anderson had brought out to them. "How much do you know about your grandmother's death?" asked Elizabeth. She had already shared the suggestions she'd received from her friends.

"Only that it was an accident. She was hit by a car."

"Are you sure it was an accident?" Elizabeth prodded.

Megan gave her an exasperated look. "I don't know, Elizabeth. I wasn't there."

Elizabeth giggled. "Oh, yeah. Sorry. But how can we find out more?"

"We can ask my mom. But she doesn't like to talk about it. She loves talking about her mother. But when it comes to talking about her death, she clams up."

"What about Jean Louise?" Elizabeth asked. "She knew your grandmother. Maybe she can tell us more."

Megan's face brightened. "That's a great idea! Why didn't I think of that?"

"Because you're not an experienced detective like I am," Elizabeth teased.

They heard the phone ring, and a moment later Elizabeth's mother called out, "Elizabeth, it's for you! It's your friend McKenzie calling, so hurry!"

Elizabeth went into the house, but Megan kept her seat.

"Hello? McKenzie?" Elizabeth spoke excitedly into the phone.

"It's me! I've been working outside, and I just now checked my e-mail. I asked my parents, and the answer is yes! I can stay with you some while we're there. But they said if it's okay with you and your parents, you can stay some with me at the motel. We're staying at the Big Texan, because of their horse hotel. Isn't that cool, a horse hotel?"

"McKenzie, that's perfect! Did you read my other e-mail?"

"I just skimmed it. I was so excited about staying with you, I went straight to ask my parents, and then I called you. I figured you could fill me in on the phone."

"Well, Megan works at the Big Texan Steak Ranch! That is the same restaurant her grandmother worked at, when she got the marbles. We may want to stay at the Big Texan as much as possible so we can snoop around."

"Oh, this will be awesome! I was already excited about seeing you, but now we'll get to solve a mystery while I'm there! I can't wait," she gushed into the phone.

The girls said their good-byes with promises to e-mail

later in the evening. Then Elizabeth returned to the porch.

"Guess what?" she asked Megan.

"Ummm, let me guess. McKenzie and her family are staying at the Big Texan, and you'll stay with her while she's here."

Elizabeth grinned. "I guess I did talk kind of loud. But I'm excited! I still have to ask my parents, though."

Just then, Megan's mom pulled into the driveway. She cleaned houses in the wealthy part of town. She also cleaned rooms for several local hotels, including the Big Texan.

"Are you going to tell her what's going on?" Elizabeth asked.

"I guess it's now or never," said Megan. "Why don't you come with me? You can fix Mama some pie and iced tea while I break the news."

The Charming Stranger

The girls walked across the driveway, and Megan hugged her mother. The woman's hair was falling out of its pretty clasp, and she had tired circles under her eyes. Still, she was beautiful.

Before Megan's parents had met, Ruby Smith had been Miss Amarillo. As small children, Elizabeth and Megan had enjoyed hiding under her bed and watching her experiment with different hairstyles or shades of lipstick. Once, she had fixed her hair in crazy crooked braids and put cold cream all over her face. Then she had said in a loud voice, "I think I'm ready. I sure wish Megan and Elizabeth were here to tell me how I look!"

The girls had burst into a fit of giggles. Mrs. Smith had coaxed them from under the bed and given them makeovers. But now, things were different. She didn't even wear makeup anymore.

"Hi, girls," she said, offering an exhausted smile. "How are y'all today?"

"We're great, Mama," Megan responded. "Here, let me carry your bag. Come on in and sit down. I need to talk to you."

Elizabeth followed them into the house and walked into the kitchen. She felt as comfortable here as she did in her own kitchen. Pulling three glasses out of the cabinet, she filled them with ice. She figured she'd let Megan and her mom have some privacy.

She poured sweet tea from a pitcher in the refrigerator and transferred three slices of chocolate pie from the box to small plates. She found forks and napkins. Then she listened to see if Megan had told her mother the news yet.

"Megan, what are you talking about?" Mrs. Smith asked her.

"Mom, I'm telling you, we're rich! We just don't know where our treasure is."

" 'For where your treasure is, there your heart will be also,' " Mrs. Smith quoted Matthew 6:21.

Megan paused. "Mom, this is serious. Some man gave Grandma some priceless gemstone marbles. We have to find out what happened to them!"

Though Megan had never met her grandmother, she still referred to her as "Grandma." She told Elizabeth once that she liked imagining what the woman was like.

Mrs. Smith yawned. "Elizabeth, what's taking you so long, child? I thought you were fixin' us some tea!"

Elizabeth appeared with the tea tray.

"Look at you!" The woman smiled. "Before ya know it, you'll be working at the restaurant with Megan. How did you girls grow up so fast?"

Megan looked frustrated. Her mother clearly didn't understand how important the gemstones were. "Mom, aren't you going to try to find out more about the marbles?"

Mrs. Smith took a bite of her pie and then leaned back. "Megan, honey, that sounds like a wonderful story. But if any lost jewels existed, we would have heard about them long before now. If this little story makes you happy, and you want to go hunting these marbles, go right ahead. I'm tired, and I don't have room in my life right now for fairy tales." Then, seeing Megan's disappointed look, she sighed. "I'll tell you what. I'll call your uncle Jack and see if he knows anything. I was only nine, but he was fifteen. Maybe he remembers something I don't. But then I don't want to hear any more about it. I—I don't like to think about that time."

Megan leaned over her mother's chair, hugged her, and then sat back down. The three finished their pie and tea, and Elizabeth excused herself. "Thank you for the refreshments. I'd better get home now. I'll see you tomorrow, Megan."

Megan waved good-bye, and Elizabeth let herself out. She could tell her friend was disappointed. But Mrs. Smith's disinterest might not be a bad thing. The woman had experienced a lot of discouragement in her life. It might be better not to get her hopes up.

"Those who hope in the Lord will renew their strength." Elizabeth thought of the verse she had known for years. *Lord,* she prayed, *Mrs. Smith could use some hope and some strength. Please help us find those jewels.*

●—●—●

The next couple of days passed quickly as Elizabeth continued to research the gemstones. She found several more dealers, but nothing about stolen or missing marbles. She was glad when Tuesday rolled around, and she sat waiting by the phone. McKenzie was supposed to call when she arrived at the Big Texan Motel.

Elizabeth jumped when the phone finally rang. "Hello?"

"Beth, it's Mac. We're here!"

Elizabeth squealed. "I'll be there in ten minutes!" she told her friend, and nearly hung up before she asked for the room number.

"I'm in room 34, right in front of this big, funny-shaped pool," McKenzie told her.

Elizabeth stopped in her tracks. "Mac, surely you know that pool is in the shape of Texas."

McKenzie giggled. "I know. I just wanted to hear what you'd say to me. I've heard you Texans are very proud of your state."

"It's only the best place on God's green earth!" Elizabeth said.

"Well, that may be true, but I haven't seen much green yet. You didn't tell me you live in the desert!" McKenzie teased.

Elizabeth laughed. "I'll see you in ten—no, in five minutes!"

She kissed her mother on the cheek. Mom had invited Mac and her family for dinner, and was planning to stop by the motel later to introduce herself.

Elizabeth was almost out the door when James called, "I want to come!"

"That's not a bad idea," Mrs. Anderson said. "Elizabeth, James has been cooped up in this house all day. Would you take him with you? I'll be there in less than thirty minutes to get him."

Elizabeth sighed. "Come on, little brother."

James lunged at her, squeezing her. "Thank you, Bettyboo! You are the best sister in the world."

Elizabeth hugged him back and said, "You won't think that if you keep calling me Bettyboo!"

James giggled and ran out the door ahead of her. "Bettyboo, Bettyboo, Bettyboo!"

Elizabeth took off after him. Some days she didn't know

whether to hug her little brother or clobber him.

An hour later, she and McKenzie sat by the large, Texas-shaped pool sipping sodas, while Mrs. Anderson visited with Mr. and Mrs. Phillips. James and McKenzie's eight-year-old brother, Evan, sat on the edge of the pool splashing their feet in the water and using a paper cup as a boat.

"So when do I get to meet Megan?" Mac asked. "Is there any more news on the marbles?"

"We'll walk down to the restaurant in a few minutes. Her break isn't for another half hour. We've hit a dead end with the marbles. Her mother just isn't interested in finding out about them. She thinks it's a fairy tale."

McKenzie thought about that. "I guess she doesn't remember anything about the man or the marbles. I wonder if there is anybody else we can ask."

"I guess we can talk to Jean Louise some more, but I think she's told us all she knows," said Elizabeth.

The two girls leaned back in their lounge chairs, sipped their drinks, and thought about the mystery.

●—●—●

A little while later, the girls pushed open the doors of the restaurant and adjusted their vision.

"Well, look who's here!" Jean Louise greeted them in her nasal twang. "You must be here to see Megs. I think her usual table is open, and she'll be out in a few."

"Megs?" McKenzie whispered as they walked through the restaurant.

"That's Jean Louise. Megs is a pet name for Megan. Watch out. She has a pet name for everyone, and I'm sure she'll come up with something for you, too."

McKenzie smiled. "What does she call you?"

After a pause, Elizabeth giggled. "Liza Jane. She sings a song about 'Li'l Liza Jane' to me."

Just then, Megan slid into the booth next to Elizabeth. "Hi! You must be McKenzie." She reached out her hand.

McKenzie returned the handshake. "And you must be Megan."

They were interrupted by Jean Louise, smacking her gum. "I see you've added a new person to your club," she said. "How ya doin', Red?"

McKenzie smiled at the reference to her hair.

"McKenzie and Elizabeth are experienced mystery-solvers. They're going to help me find out about the—" Megan started to say.

"Shhhh!" Jean Louise snapped. She leaned forward. "I thought I told you to keep this quiet."

McKenzie looked confused.

Megan told her, "It's okay, Jean Louise. McKenzie is Elizabeth's friend, and I trust her. Besides, she's not from around here. She'll be gone in a few days."

Jean Louise eyed Mac with suspicion, but then her gaze softened. "Well, what's done is done. But you need to hush up. The man who has been nosing around is sitting right over there."

The three girls turned, trying to get a look at the man in the cowboy boots. His long legs stuck awkwardly from under the table, and he looked a bit like a giant at a tea party.

"Turn around!" Jean Louise whispered. "I thought you girls were supposed to be detectives. You don't want him to know you're staring at him!"

The girls whipped back around in their seats. "Oh, yeah, she's right," said Mac. "Elizabeth, you have the best angle. Tell us what you see."

"Well, uh, he looks about my dad's age, and he's having a cheeseburger and french fries," she said.

"Who cares what he's eating?" Megan whispered.

Jean Louise rolled her eyes. "Look, girls, why don't you wait until he gets up to leave. Then you can get a better look. For now, just hold your horses. I'll bring you some leftover pecan pie." She turned to leave.

"Jean Louise," called Elizabeth.

The woman turned back around, and Elizabeth continued. "Is there any more you can tell us, or anyone else we can talk to?"

Jean Louise cocked one hip and rested her notepad there. "I've told you girls all I know, and nobody else was around back then, except my—hey! Why don't I take you girls to meet my mama? She would love the company, and Megan, she would just love to meet you. She loved your grandma so much. It nearly broke her heart when she died."

The girls perked up at the idea. "That sounds great," Megan answered. "When can we go?"

"You're off tomorrow, aren't you? Why don't we go about ten o'clock in the morning. Meet me here, and I'll drive you over." She looked at the other two girls. "Since y'all are in on this, too, you're welcome to come if your parents agree." With that, the woman moved to another table to refill some iced tea glasses.

Elizabeth continued to discreetly eye the cowboy. "That is one tall man," she said. "Did y'all see how long his legs are?"

Just then, the man looked directly at Elizabeth and smiled. Had he heard her? She quickly looked away, then back. He winked at her!

She could feel the heat rising to her cheeks. Then she giggled.

"What? What are you laughing at?" the other two asked her.

"He winked at me!" she whispered. They all leaned to look at the man, who was now walking toward the cash register. His head nearly brushed against the ceiling fans, and he had to duck around the longhorn chandeliers.

"Let's follow him," Mac whispered. She and Elizabeth stood to leave.

"Wait! I'm not through with my shift!" Megan called.

Just then, Jean Louise showed up with their pie. "You're not leaving before you have this, are you?"

Elizabeth and McKenzie looked at each other, then at the man. "Can you put it in a box for us? We'll be back for it later!" Elizabeth told her, and they followed the man. "Thanks, Jean Louise!" she called over her shoulder.

Megan and Jean Louise stared openmouthed after the two girls. "Apparently they're serious about this detective business," said Megan.

Out in the sunlight, the girls looked to the right and the left. They barely caught sight of the tall man in the cowboy hat as he turned the corner. They followed quickly, trying to act casual.

As they turned the corner, they crashed into James. Mrs. Anderson was a few steps behind him.

"Beth! McKenzie's daddy is going to let me ride a horse! Mama's taking me home now to get my boots and cowboy hat!"

Elizabeth and McKenzie peered over Mrs. Anderson's shoulder at the tall man. He was going, going. . .gone.

"I thought you two were going to sit with Megan during her break. That was a short break," the woman said.

"Well, we. . .uh," Elizabeth stammered.

James jumped up and down. "Do ya want to ride horses with me, Beth?"

McKenzie jumped in. "That will be fun, James. We'll meet you at the stables in a little while."

Mrs. Anderson and James waved and continued toward the parking lot. The girls went in the opposite direction, trying to determine where the man had turned.

"He could have turned here at the ice machines, or up there, or. . .it's no use. We lost him," Elizabeth said.

"Well, since he walked toward the rooms, he's probably a guest here. Maybe we should hang out here today and see if he turns up again," McKenzie replied.

"Sounds like a plan to me."

Later that afternoon, the two Camp Club Girls leaned on the railing of the Big Texan Horse Hotel. Evan waited patiently as Mr. Phillips led James, dressed in red hat and boots, on a black-and-white-spotted pony. "Giddyup! Look, Beth! I'm a cowboy!"

McKenzie laughed. "Your brother sure is cute!"

Elizabeth smiled. "Yeah, I guess he's okay, as far as brothers go." She waved at James as he rode by.

Sue Anderson and Jen Phillips sat on a long bench in the shade, talking.

Elizabeth continued, "I can't wait for you to meet my dad."

"Aren't we all going to your house for dinner tonight?" McKenzie questioned.

"That's the plan. Dad's going to cook out. We'll have hamburgers and hot dogs. Mom even got a watermelon."

"Yummm! I love watermelon," McKenzie said. They

both waved at James again. Neither noticed the tall shadow that appeared beside them until Mr. Phillips looked up and smiled.

"You've got a couple of mighty fine-lookin' cowboys there," said the man, gesturing to Evan and James.

"Yep. Cowboys in training, anyway," said Mr. Phillips, helping James down from the pony. When both boys were safely out of the paddock, McKenzie's dad held out his hand. "Dan Phillips," he said.

"I'm Mark Jacobs," said the man, and the two shook hands.

"Is one of these horses yours?" asked Mr. Phillips.

The man pointed to a gorgeous brown-and-white quarter horse. "That's Lucy. She's one of the best horses I've ever owned. I'm going to miss her."

"You're getting rid of her?" Phillips asked.

"Yep. I'm here for the rodeo this weekend. I'm riding in it. But this rodeo life is getting tiresome, and I'm looking to retire. I want to buy a little spread of land about ten miles from here, but I need to sell all my stock to do it. I'm also waiting for a few other things to fall into place."

Elizabeth and McKenzie looked at one another, wide-eyed.

Phillips looked at Lucy. "Would she be any good on a ranch?" he asked.

"Oh, definitely. She was bred for ranching. Like I said, she's one of the best horses I've worked with," the man said.

"I've been looking to buy another horse for my ranch. We live in Montana. I may be interested in buying her when you finally get ready to sell. Of course, I'd like to see her in action," Mr. Phillips told him.

"Why don't you come watch the rodeo tomorrow night? Bring your whole family. I have a box reserved, but nobody to fill it," the man said.

Elizabeth and McKenzie made frantic eye contact but remained quiet.

Mr. Phillips and Mr. Jacobs began walking toward where the two women sat in the shade. Mr. Phillips introduced the ladies, then told them, "Mark here has invited us to be his guests at the rodeo."

"All of you," Mr. Jacobs said, looking at Elizabeth's mom. "Bring your families. I've got about a dozen seats just waiting to be filled."

"That is very kind of you," Mrs. Anderson replied. "Why don't you join us at our house this evening? We're having a cookout. When Robert, my husband, starts grilling, he goes a little overboard, and we usually have enough food to feed an army!"

Jacobs laughed. "He sounds like my kind of man. I'd love to join you. I'm on the road most of the time, and I don't get many home-cooked meals."

Elizabeth didn't know if this was a good development or a bad one.

Mr. Phillips noticed the girls and motioned to them. "Girls, this is Mr. Jacobs. Mark, this is my daughter, McKenzie, and her friend Elizabeth."

"I. . .uh. . .it's a pleasure to meet you, sir." Elizabeth held out her hand. McKenzie followed suit.

"I believe I saw these young ladies at the restaurant." The man smiled.

The men turned toward the bench where the two women were seated and continued their conversation.

"What are we going to do?" McKenzie whispered.

"What do you mean?" Elizabeth whispered back.

"Well, this man clearly is a crook. I can't let my dad do business with him! And we certainly don't want him coming to your house!"

"What makes you think he's a crook?" Elizabeth asked, though she had the same idea about the man.

"Just look at him! He's way too handsome to be honest," McKenzie whispered frantically. "Look at that smile. He's just oozing with charm. That can't be real."

The girls stared at the tall, good-looking cowboy who looked like he had just ridden into town straight from a movie set. At that moment, the man turned and saw them looking at him. He winked!

A Peek into the Past

Elizabeth and McKenzie looked at one another in shock but remained quiet. They weren't sure what to make of this development.

Mrs. Anderson smiled. "It's settled then. You can come over with the Phillips family. We'll see you all around seven?"

The adults agreed to the time, and Elizabeth's mother stood to leave. "I'd better get going so I can prepare our feast! Elizabeth, are you coming home with me, or would you like to stay awhile longer?"

"Oh, I'll stay here if that's okay. McKenzie and I really need to talk to Megan."

Mrs. Anderson looked at her. "You're not distracting Megan from her work, are you? I wouldn't want her to get in trouble."

"No, ma'am. That's why we're waiting here until she gets off."

"Well, be sure to invite Megan and her mother for dinner," Mrs. Anderson said. She took James by the hand and bid the group good-bye.

The two girls walked casually around the stables, pretending to look at horses.

"What should we do?" asked McKenzie.

"I think we should stay close and see what happens," said Elizabeth.

"But now he's coming to your house! He'll know where you live!" McKenzie continued.

"So?" Elizabeth said.

"So I just don't like the idea of the man we're trying to investigate getting so close to you and your family," McKenzie told her.

"Look," Elizabeth said. "We don't have any reason to believe he's dangerous. We only think he knows something about the gemstones. I think we should just play dumb and see if he brings up the marbles."

After a moment, McKenzie nodded. "Okay. But this feels strange to me."

The two girls stopped a few steps from the stall where the cowboy and McKenzie's dad were talking horse talk.

"McKenzie here is a horse expert in her own right," her dad said, inviting the girls into the conversation.

McKenzie blushed and smiled. "I try," she said modestly.

"She'll take over the ranch for me one day, if she wants." Her dad smiled proudly at her. "She could probably do it right now."

The cowboy smiled. "It's always good to have someone around who knows their business," he said. Then he reached out and shook Mr. Phillips's hand and tipped his hat to the girls. "I have some other business I need to tend to, but I'll look forward to seeing you all at dinner," he said. And with that, his long, lanky legs carried him across the stables, around the corner, and out of sight.

• — • — •

The girls spent the next couple of hours sitting by the pool and looking at the different horses. Elizabeth enjoyed seeing the Big Texan from a tourist's point of view. She had lived in Amarillo all her life and had never stayed at the motel. It was fun.

At 4:00 p.m., they went to the motel lobby. McKenzie had noticed a computer available to the motel guests. They wanted to check their e-mail and see if there were any more tips from the other Camp Club Girls. After waiting for two other people, they signed on.

Sure enough, there was a message from Kate.

Biscuit was sniffing around in the car today, and he found my reader pen! I've been looking all over for that thing. But it got me thinking. . . I wonder if Emily Marie hid the marbles in her car somewhere. What happened to her car after she died?

"That's a good question. Let's go ask Megan. If she doesn't know, maybe Jean Louise will know something," suggested Elizabeth.

They headed to the restaurant. Megan wasn't scheduled to get off until 4:30, but they were hoping to eat their forgotten pie while they waited. Jean Louise met them at the door.

"Well, well. If it isn't Sherlock Holmes and Watson," she said with a smile. "Did you track down the cowboy?"

The girls laughed. "Actually, he found us," Elizabeth told her. "It's been an interesting afternoon."

Jean Louise seated them, then brought their pie, all nestled in white Styrofoam containers. "Here ya go," she said. The restaurant was busy, and she didn't stay to chat.

Twenty minutes later, Megan joined them at the booth. "Tell me everything," she said.

"We will. But first, do you have any idea what happened to your grandmother's car after she died?"

Megan thought for a moment. "No, but my Uncle Jack will know. He's a mechanic, and Mom says he's always been interested in cars."

"Let's go see him right now!" exclaimed McKenzie.

"That will be hard. He lives in Houston," Megan said. "But I can call him."

The girls leaned their heads together, whispering and planning for the next half hour.

●—●—●

That evening, Elizabeth's backyard was filled with laughter and the scent of grilling hamburgers. James and Evan ran around playing cowboys and Indians, and Mr. Jacobs pretended to get shot in the crossfire. The man seemed to enjoy children, and moved back and forth between playing with the boys and helping Mr. Anderson flip burgers.

Elizabeth was inside filling red plastic cups with iced tea. She had left McKenzie sitting near the men in case anything was said about the jewels. She looked out the window at her friend, who looked bored. The last bit of conversation Elizabeth had heard was about football.

"You did invite Megan and her mom, didn't you?" Mrs. Anderson asked Elizabeth.

"Yes, ma'am. Megan said her mom gets home tonight around seven thirty, so they'll be a little late."

Mrs. Anderson looked out the side window toward the Smiths' house. "I sure wish she didn't have to work so hard. I wish we could do something more for them," she said.

"We're actually working on that," said Elizabeth without thinking.

"What do you mean?" her mother asked.

Catching herself, Elizabeth thought quickly. "Oh, just that Megan is working now, earning some extra money. She also makes straight A's in school, and in a few years she'll probably get a full scholarship to some college."

Mrs. Anderson ran a gentle hand across Elizabeth's hair. "That's nice, dear." Then the woman held open the screen door with her backside, and the two joined the party, delivering iced tea to their guests.

A short time later, Megan arrived with her mother. When Mrs. Smith was introduced to Mr. Jacobs, the cowboy stood and took her hand. "It's a pleasure to meet you, Ruby. You add a whole new loveliness to your name," he said.

Mrs. Smith smiled and blushed, and the three girls looked at one another in alarm. What did that cowboy think he was doing? Did he know about the jewels and Megan's mother?

They continued to watch the interaction between Ruby and Mr. Jacobs throughout the evening. Those two didn't talk much, but their eyes kept wandering to each other. Finally, Megan whispered, "We need to have an emergency meeting in your room. Now!"

The three girls excused themselves. As soon as Elizabeth's door was closed, Megan burst into a chain of broken sentences that showed her anxiety but didn't really make much sense.

"What in the—who does he think—and my mother! I've never seen her—she used to flirt with my dad but—of all people! I've wanted her to start dating—but not like this!

Not with that no-good, sweet-talkin', connivin', manipulatin' cowboy!"

"Whoa, calm down, Megs." Elizabeth put her arm around her friend. "She's not dating anyone. Sure, there were some sparks out there. But let's face it. She'll probably never see him again after tonight. Unless. . ."

"Unless what?" Megan and McKenzie asked in unison.

Elizabeth paused. If the looks on their faces were any indication, her two friends were thinking exactly what she was thinking. "Unless he knows the jewels were given to your grandmother. Do you think he's traced them to your mother somehow?"

"How could he? My mother didn't know about them until the other day. And she doesn't even care about them."

"She may not care about them, but he doesn't know that," said McKenzie.

The three girls moved Elizabeth's pink ruffled curtains to the side and peered at the group in the backyard. Cowboy had moved his lawn chair closer to Megan's mother, and the two looked engrossed in conversation.

"We'd better get out there. Now!" exclaimed Megan.

"Not just yet," McKenzie interrupted. "First, tell us if you had a chance to call your uncle."

Megan kept peering out the window as she answered. "Oh, yeah. I called him this afternoon. He doesn't know anything about any marbles. He said the car stayed impounded for a couple of years while they investigated the accident. After that, he took it apart and sold it piece by piece. They needed the money. But if there were any marbles hidden in the car, he would have found them."

McKenzie let out a disappointed sigh. "I was just sure

that's where they were."

The sound of Mrs. Smith's laughter floated through the window, and Megan said, "That does it. I've gotta get that cowboy away from my mother."

"Yep. And we'd better get crackin' on this mystery, before your mother really gets hurt," said Elizabeth.

●━━●━━●

The cookout ended around 10:30, but had seemed much longer. The girls did all they could to interrupt the conversations between Megan's mom and the cowboy, but the man was not easily deterred. This gave the three sleuths even more reason to think he was up to something shady.

They spent the night in Elizabeth's room and were awakened early the next morning with the sounds of humming from Megan's driveway. Megan sat up in her sleeping bag and peered out the window to see her mother leaving for work.

"My mother hasn't sounded like that in a long time," she said.

Elizabeth rolled over and propped her head on her elbow. "She really misses your dad, doesn't she?"

"Yeah," Megan answered softly. "So do I."

They were interrupted by James. "Who wants breakfast?" he asked, opening the door without knocking.

Elizabeth squealed, "Shut the door! James, you know you're not allowed in here without permission!"

He backed out and shut the door. "Sorry, Beth. But Mama wants to know who wants breakfast."

"I do," called all three girls in unison.

"Little brothers. . . ," muttered Elizabeth, and her friends chuckled. The three girls dressed quickly and dashed to the kitchen, where Mrs. Anderson had left toaster pastries, fruit, orange juice, and milk. James had already eaten, so they had the kitchen to themselves.

"We're supposed to meet Jean Louise at the restaurant at nine forty-five so she can drive us to her mother's house. Did you check with your mom, Elizabeth?" asked Megan.

"Mom," called Elizabeth around a mouthful of toaster pastry.

Mrs. Anderson popped her head around the corner from the laundry room. "Don't talk with your mouth full, dear."

Elizabeth swallowed her food and wiped her mouth with her napkin. "Sorry. May I please go with Jean Louise this morning to meet her mother? Megan's coming, too, and McKenzie is going to ask her parents."

Mrs. Anderson smiled. "I think that sounds lovely. I'm glad to hear you girls are doing something constructive with your time. It reminds me of James 1:27."

Megan and McKenzie looked at Elizabeth after Mrs. Anderson went back to her laundry. "James 1:27?" Megan asked.

" 'Religion that God our Father accepts as pure and faultless is this: to look after orphans and widows in their distress and to keep oneself from being polluted by the world,' " Elizabeth quoted.

The other two listened in stunned silence. "How do you do that?" asked McKenzie. "I know a lot of Bible verses, but you're like a walking encyclopedia!"

Elizabeth smiled. "I don't know. I've just heard them all my life."

"Well, we're not exactly going to see this woman because she's in distress," said Megan. "So I'm not sure this visit will count."

"Maybe not, but I'll bet she'll enjoy our visit anyway! Hopefully we'll get some information we can use," replied Elizabeth. "We've got to find those jewels before the cowboy does."

A short time later, having gained permission from McKenzie's parents, the three girls slid into Jean Louise's red convertible sports car.

"This is a cool car!" McKenzie exclaimed.

"Thank you," said the waitress.

The girls enjoyed the ride, laughing as their hair—blond, brunette, and auburn—flapped in the wind.

They arrived at Shady Acres Retirement Community a short time later, and Jean Louise led them through the well-kept apartment complex. She knocked and then used her key to open the door. "Mama!" she called. "We're here. I brought the girls I told you about."

A small, white-haired woman appeared, using a walker. Her eyes were bright, and she wore a cheerful smile. "Come in, come in!" she said. "I've been looking forward to this."

They entered the small, well-kept apartment and smelled something delicious. Jean Louise wasted no time in introducing the girls one by one. "And this, ladies, is my mother, Mrs. Wilson."

"It's a pleasure to meet you, Mrs. Wilson," the girls said politely.

"Sit down," she gestured, and moved slowly to stand in front of Megan. "Except you. I want you to stand here and let me look at you."

Megan smiled a bit uncomfortably while the woman looked her over, head to toe. Then she reached out a gentle hand and touched Megan's hair, then her face. "Such a beautiful girl. You're the spitting image of Emily Marie."

McKenzie looked questioningly at Elizabeth.

"Megan's grandmother," Elizabeth whispered, and the redhead nodded.

"Your grandmother would have been so proud of you," the woman continued. "She was my best friend, you know. A real jewel. Your mother and your uncle Jack were her world. She would have loved watching you grow up."

Then she gestured for Megan to sit down before taking a seat herself. She turned to her daughter. "Jean Louise, I made some lemon bars for these girls, and there is lemonade in the refrigerator. Would you get them, please?"

"Yes, ma'am." The woman moved swiftly to obey her elderly mother.

"I hope you didn't go to any trouble, Mrs. Wilson," Elizabeth said.

The woman responded by waving her hand in the air, as if any such talk was nonsense. Elizabeth liked this woman.

"I understand you have some questions for me," she said, keeping her eyes on Megan.

"Yes, ma'am," Megan said. "Jean Louise told us about some marbles, but I don't know anything about them, and neither does my mother."

The woman smiled. "Oh, the marbles. I remember that day so well. Emily Marie came walking into the break room at the restaurant, white as a sheet. She closed the door, and it was just the two of us. Then she pulled out a little white cloth sack and poured out the contents on the table in front of me. They were marbles, and they were the prettiest things I had ever seen."

She paused, as if remembering, then continued. " 'They're

real,' she told me.

" 'Real marbles?' I asked. I was confused. Of course they were real marbles.

" 'Real gemstones,' she said, and plopped down in front of me. 'Foster gave them to me.'

"Now, Foster was the tall, handsome cowboy who had taken a shine to Emily Marie. He wasn't from around here, but he came through town a lot on business. He began to have more and more business in Amarillo, but no one was fooled. He came to town to see your grandma. She was a beautiful woman." Mrs. Wilson pushed her hair back from her face.

"I was speechless. I had never seen anything like the marbles in front of me. I picked up the emerald and held it up to the light. Then we both started giggling like schoolgirls."

Elizabeth smiled at the image.

The woman paused as Jean Louise brought in the refreshments and placed them on the coffee table. "Keep going, Mama. Don't stop on my account," Jean Louise said.

The woman leaned back in her chair with a smile. "After our giggles were under control, I held up the ruby. 'Won't this make a nice gift for your little Ruby one day?' I asked her.

"She looked at me like I'd gone crazy. 'I can't keep them!' she said.

" 'Why in the world not?' I asked her.

" 'It's too much. It would be different if Foster and I were engaged, but we're not.'

" 'Oh, you will be,' I told her. 'I've seen the way he looks at you. And I've seen the way you look at him. You'll be married before the year is out.'

"When I said that, Emily blushed four shades of red. But

she was smiling. 'Maybe so,' she said.

" 'Besides,' I told her. 'You can't give them back. He'll think you're rejecting him.'

"She sat quietly, looking at those jewels long after my break was over. I covered for her for a while. I knew she needed some time to think. Finally, she joined me back on the floor, waiting tables like nothing had happened."

"What happened to Foster? Was he still there?" Elizabeth asked.

"No, I don't know where he had disappeared to. But he was back later that evening. And before the night was over, Emily Marie was the happiest woman alive."

CHAPTER 5

The Journals

The girls leaned forward, drinking in every word the elderly woman spoke. It seemed more like the makings of a romance movie than a real story.

The woman paused and looked directly at Megan. "At closing time, Foster showed up again, wanting to talk to Emily Marie. They sat in one of the booths while I cleaned up. I tried to give them privacy and turned on the jukebox to a slow country song. But even over the music, I could hear bits and pieces of the conversation.

" 'Emily Marie, you must know how I feel about you. You must see it in my eyes,' he told her. The whole thing was quite romantic. 'I want to spend the rest of my life with you. I'm going to sell my ranch in Colorado and move down here, and we can get married. That is, if you'll have me,' he said.

"There she was, tears streaming down her cheeks. 'But Foster, I have my two kids to think about,' she said.

" 'I know I haven't met Ruby and Jack yet, but I promise I'll love them like my very own. I know things have been hard on you since your husband died. Let me rescue you,' he begged.

"Well, at that point I left the room. I figured the cleanup could wait. Emily Marie and I were best friends, and I had watched her struggle to make ends meet since Paul died. It looked to be a fairy-tale ending for her," Mrs. Wilson said as she leaned back in her chair.

The room was silent, except for the tick-ticking of the old grandfather clock in the corner. Finally, Megan broke the silence. "It sounds like my mom and my grandma had a lot in common. . . ."

Elizabeth reached over and squeezed her friend's hand.

"So what happened next?" Elizabeth asked.

Mrs. Wilson frowned. "The next few days are hard to talk about. I prefer to remember my friend in that moment, her face shining with joy."

The three girls remained silent. They didn't want to push the woman or be disrespectful, but they needed more information.

Jean Louise rescued them. "Mama, Megan wants to find out what happened to the marbles. Is there any more you can tell her?"

The woman looked at Megan again and smiled, a sad kind of smile. Then she pulled herself up with her walker and started toward her bedroom. Jean Louise helped her mother, leaving the three girls alone in the living room.

"Why did she leave like that?" McKenzie whispered.

"I don't know, but it looks like she's our only hope for more information. We've got to find out what happened next," whispered Elizabeth.

Megan remained quiet, and Elizabeth put her arm around her friend. "This is hard for you, isn't it?" she asked.

"Not really. I mean, I never knew my grandmother. It's just strange that she and my mother were both young widows."

The girls heard the walker approaching and ended their

whispered conversation. Jean Louise followed her mother, carrying several old notebooks. She handed them to Megan.

Mrs. Wilson was seated once again and took a moment to get settled. "These are my journals from that time. The whole story should be there, from the time Foster began coming to the restaurant, until. . ."

Megan looked at the books. It seemed she had just been handed her own treasure.

"You take them home and read them," the woman told her. "I hope they'll help you find what you're looking for."

Megan placed the journals on the coffee table in front of her, then walked to Mrs. Wilson's chair. She leaned over and hugged the woman. "Thank you so much," she said.

The old woman patted her on the shoulder, then wiped a tear from her wrinkled cheek. "You're welcome, my dear. You are more than welcome."

•—•—•

Back at the Big Texan, Megan had to report for work. "Here," she told Elizabeth, handing her the journals. "We can't afford to waste any time. Y'all start reading through these and see what you can find."

Elizabeth and McKenzie spent the better part of the morning by the Texas-shaped pool, reading through the yellowed pages and looking for clues. Much of what they found was insignificant—Mrs. Wilson's thoughts about her husband, her children, her job, even the price of groceries. Finally, McKenzie sat up in her lounge chair and said, "I found it! Listen to this: 'A man has been visiting the restaurant regularly and is obviously smitten with Emily Marie. He seems like a kind man. I hope she gives him a chance; she's been so sad since Paul died.' "

Elizabeth read over her friend's shoulder. "Jackpot!" she cried. "Now we have our starting point. Let's keep reading."

McKenzie wiped the sweat from her brow. "Okay," she said, "but can we continue this in the restaurant? I'm burning up out here, and I'm starving!"

"Me, too," agreed Elizabeth.

They gathered the journals and headed toward the restaurant. Passing the stables, they noticed a regal-looking horse across the paddock. "Wow, what a beauty," said McKenzie. "Let's get a closer look."

They were about halfway there when they heard a man's voice. It was Mr. Jacobs, leaning against the stable and talking on his cell phone. The girls shrank into the shadows of one of the stalls and remained silent.

"Yes, that's right," he said. "There were twelve marbles in a variety of gemstones. I tracked them to Amarillo, but it's been thirty years since anyone has seen or heard of them. They just vanished."

Jacobs began pacing in agitation. "I don't know how a set of priceless gemstone marbles can simply disappear. Surely somebody has to know something about them."

The man paused again and then said, "I've got to find those marbles. I'm tired of all this rodeo business, never spending more than a week in the same place. I'm ready to settle down and live the good life, and those marbles will help me do it."

More silence, and then he said, "Okay. Let me know what you find out. I'll keep asking questions here." The man shut his cell phone and strode out of the stables and toward the motel rooms.

"Whoa," said McKenzie. "That proves he's a crook."

"Not necessarily. But it does sound suspicious," said Elizabeth. "One thing is for sure. We're running out of time. We've got to locate those marbles before he does."

●—●—●

The girls kept their noses buried in the journals for the rest of the afternoon. The entries about Emily Marie were sporadic, interspersed with entries about housework and life as a waitress. It was like a treasure hunt—wading through the boring stuff to find the jewels.

Elizabeth liked the way Mrs. Wilson ended each journal entry with a one-sentence prayer. She felt she knew the old woman's heart better from those sentence prayers than from the actual journal entries.

Finally, after hours of searching, she found the following entry:

It seems that Foster, humble as he is, is very wealthy.

Tonight he gave Emily Marie a bag of marbles. But these aren't just any marbles, they're priceless gemstones!

The paperwork is even there—they're in her name. She wasn't sure if she should keep such a gift, and fretted all evening. But after the restaurant closed, he showed up again and asked her to marry him!

Of course she accepted. But they won't make their plans known until he gets to know her children. He is a wonderful man, and I know he will be a good father to Ruby and Jack.

He's leaving town tonight. He told her to keep the marbles in a safe place, and he'll help her set up a safe-deposit box for them when he returns. She'll

*worry herself to death, carrying around something so
priceless.*

*We talked about hiding them in the restaurant,
but for tonight, she took them home. I'll bet she looks
at them all night long.*

*Dear Father, please bless Emily Marie and her
children with Your goodness. Amen.*

"That's it! They're hidden in the restaurant!" shouted
McKenzie.

Elizabeth shut the book and stood to stretch. Her eyes
were tired from reading. "Maybe. Just like Alex suggested.
But she could have gone ahead and put them in the bank,
too. Why don't we head over and tell Megan what we've
found. Maybe she can start snooping around."

"Yeah, and maybe we can get some more of that pie!"
McKenzie added.

●━━●━━●

Later that night, the group sat in the stands at the Greater
Amarillo Livestock Show and Rodeo. Mr. Jacobs had
generously given them his entire section of box seats. "I'd
love to have someone cheering for me," he'd said with a smile.
His eyes had rested on Megan's mom.

James and Evan sat two rows in front of the girls,
exclaiming over the horses and making their own plans to
be cowboys someday. Elizabeth was glad that, for now, her
brother had a distraction.

Ruby Smith sat with the ladies making small talk, and
the two dads seemed absorbed in a conversation about the
Old Testament book of Isaiah. The three girls, satisfied they
wouldn't be overheard, huddled together.

"So did you find anything?" whispered McKenzie.

"No," answered Megan. "I need more information. I have no idea where to begin. I did examine the floorboards in the kitchen area, but I couldn't find any loose ones. I'm just not good at this detective business like the two of you are."

Elizabeth patted her friend on the knee. "You'll be fine. We just need to find more clues. We're not even sure they're at the restaurant. She might have put them in the bank or something. Do you think you can ask your mom if your grandma left any accounts open?"

"I've never heard her talk about any accounts. It seems that anything like that would have been closed out long ago. But I'll ask Mom tonight," Megan said.

"Ask Mom what?" Ruby Smith asked. The girls were surprised to find that she'd moved down and was now sitting directly behind them. Her hair was fixed in a new way, and she was wearing makeup.

"You look pretty tonight, Mom," Megan said. Mrs. Smith smiled.

"What did you want to ask me?" the woman persisted.

Megan smiled sheepishly. "You remember those jewels I talked to you about? We're still trying to find them."

Surprisingly, Mrs. Smith laughed. "Well, I'm afraid you're going on a wild-goose chase. But go ahead, ask me anything."

"Did Grandma leave any bank accounts open?" Megan asked. "We're wondering if she might have stored the marbles in an account somewhere."

"Oh, you mean like in a safe-deposit box?" Mrs. Smith responded.

Elizabeth jumped in. "Exactly! Did your mother leave behind any kind of safe-deposit box?"

Mrs. Smith shook her head. "Not that I know of. But come to think of it, my grandmother did mention a small checking account. She never touched it. She said she wanted to leave it for me and Jack someday. It's still there."

"Bingo!" McKenzie shouted with excitement. "We've found the—"

Elizabeth clapped a hand over her friend's mouth. "Let's not announce it to the whole world," she said.

"Oh, yeah, sorry!" McKenzie whispered. "I tend to get a little excited."

The others chuckled good-naturedly. "It's okay," said Megan. "It is pretty exciting."

Mrs. Smith continued, "I have some business at the bank tomorrow anyway. I'll ask about the checking account. And since this is official mystery business, would you girls like to come with me? I'll take you all for ice cream afterwards."

The girls nodded, and Mrs. Smith returned to sit with the ladies.

Megan looked a little stunned, and Elizabeth asked, "What's wrong?"

"Who was that woman?" she asked.

Elizabeth turned and looked at Megan's mom, not sure how to respond to the question.

"My mom is fixing her hair, wearing makeup, coming to the rodeo. . .she's *smiling*! What has gotten into her?"

Elizabeth's and McKenzie's eyes swung to the handsome cowboy, sitting tall on a horse and getting ready to enter the arena.

No one answered Megan's question, but the looks of concern stayed on their faces for the rest of the evening.

●━━●━━●

The next morning, Elizabeth and McKenzie stared gloomily out the window of the Phillipses' motel room. Rain poured down outside.

"I guess we won't do much sightseeing today," said McKenzie.

Elizabeth leaned over and lifted the stack of journals from the bedside table. "Well, as long as we're stuck here, we might as well read some more. Megan has to be at work at ten a.m., but she was going to come early and do some more snooping," she said, looking at her watch.

"Not snooping—*investigating*," McKenzie corrected her friend.

Elizabeth chuckled. "Same thing," she said. "But *investigating* does sound more official, doesn't it?"

The girls settled in, sharing the same journal page, skimming for more clues. Before long, they found what they were looking for.

Emily Marie might go ahead and put the jewels in a safe-deposit box. She thought about doing it today, but it was late when she got off work, and the banks were already closed. Carrying around something so valuable is making her as nervous as a cat in a room full of rockers.

She's anxious to put them in a safe place.

She was headed to work a party at the Cadillac Ranch this evening. She said the pay is good and the tips are even better. She tried to get me to go with her, but I was just too tired tonight. I told her I'd go with her next time.

McKenzie shut the book and hopped from the bed. "There you have it. She deposited the jewels. What time is Megan's mom taking us to the bank today?"

"I think at three thirty, when Megan gets off work. Why don't we walk to the restaurant and see if she's there yet?"

The two sleuths quickly headed toward the Big Texan Steak Ranch, staying close to the buildings to keep from getting wet. They rushed through the swinging saloon-style doors, straight into a plaid cowboy shirt. Leaning their necks back, they looked up, up, up to see the owner of the shirt. It was Mr. Jacobs.

"Good mornin', ladies," he said, and tipped his big white cowboy hat. True to form, he winked at them before he strode out the door.

The girls didn't know whether to be angry or giggle. "I wish he didn't look so much like a movie star," McKenzie said.

"Why?" Elizabeth asked.

"Because it would be a lot easier not to like him," she replied seriously.

Just then, Jean Louise appeared. "What is it with you early birds this morning?" she asked. "Megan's already been here for twenty minutes, cleaning every nook and cranny of the supply room. She's not even clocked in yet."

The two girls looked at each other and then at the red-haired waitress. "Um, could we, uh. . . ," Elizabeth stammered.

"Go on back," she said, pointing the way. "But if the manager catches you, she may put you to work."

The girls dashed through the kitchen area to the dark storage room. They pushed open the door, and Megan gasped.

"You scared me!" she whispered, looking guilty. "Quick, close the door!"

The Costumes

The girls entered the small room and shut the door behind them. Megan was on her knees, surrounded by cans of tomato paste. She held a dust rag in her hand and appeared to be cleaning the bottom shelf.

"Look at this," she said.

The girls leaned forward, but the dim lighting made it difficult to see. "Isn't there a better light in here?" Elizabeth asked.

"One of the bulbs is burned out," Megan told her. "But you can still see if you look close enough."

McKenzie got down on her knees and examined the wall where Megan was cleaning. Elizabeth bent low and looked over her shoulder. Sure enough, there was a square break in the paneling, just large enough for a small teenage girl to crawl through.

"Do you think it's a secret passageway?" McKenzie asked.

"I don't know what it is. I haven't been able to get it open. There are a couple of screws, but I need a screwdriver. Do you think the marbles could be hidden here?"

"That's what we were coming to talk to you about," Elizabeth told Megan. "We read in the journal that Emily Marie was planning to put the marbles in a safe-deposit box at the bank. We may be wasting our time here."

Megan looked at Elizabeth, then McKenzie, her mouth hanging open. "You mean I've been breaking my back in here for nothing?" she said.

McKenzie chuckled. "Well, look on the bright side. Just think how impressed your boss will be that you spent your free time cleaning out the supply room."

The three girls returned the cans to the lower shelf and left the small room.

"It's time for me to clock in," said Megan, looking at her watch. "I'll see you both this afternoon. Maybe we'll actually find the marbles!"

Elizabeth and McKenzie left the kitchen and spotted the Phillips family at a corner table in the restaurant. "Come on," McKenzie said. "Let's join them. I'm starved!"

"Me, too," agreed Elizabeth.

Before long they were each devouring a tall stack of pancakes, drenched in syrup and covered with whipped cream. Outside the window, the sun peeked through the clouds. The rain had stopped.

As they ate, Mr. and Mrs. Phillips asked, "So what do you want to do today?"

The girls both shrugged their shoulders and kept eating. They were having fun as long as they were together.

"I'd like to go shopping," said Mrs. Phillips. "I saw some little boutiques a few blocks over."

Evan groaned, and Mr. Phillips shifted in his seat. "Why don't you girls go shopping, and Evan and I will hang out here with the horses and the cowboys?" the man suggested.

The girls nodded, and before long, the three females headed toward Amarillo's shopping district.

In and out of shops they went, looking at Texas-shaped handbags encrusted with rhinestones, flashy cowgirl boots and hats, and western wear in all colors and sizes. Before they knew it, two hours had passed.

They were on their way back to the motel when McKenzie spotted a fun-looking thrift shop. "Oh, I want to see what they have in there, Mom," she said.

"I want to run across the street to the post office and get some stamps," Mrs. Phillips said, waving a handful of postcards. "Why don't you two go over there, and I'll meet you after I mail these."

The girls entered the old store and were thrilled at the endless racks of vintage clothing, hats, and scarves. McKenzie wasted no time trying on a dark pair of sunglasses, an oversize hat, and a feather boa.

Elizabeth laughed at her friend's outfit and then spotted a large cardboard box filled with wigs. Within moments, she was a brunette with long, messy curls.

The girls giggled as they tried an array of wigs, scarves, and jewelry. They were completely unrecognizable when the bell over the door jangled. The two looked toward the entrance expecting to find Mrs. Phillips. Instead, Mark Jacobs walked toward them, a serious look on his face.

They froze. What in the world could a cowboy like Mr. Jacobs want in a girlie thrift shop like this? The man nodded at the girls but kept walking. He didn't recognize them!

He approached the counter and asked to speak to the shop's owner. The clerk went to the back of the store and returned with an elegant, gray-haired woman.

"How may I help you?" she asked.

The cowboy introduced himself, then asked, "How long have you owned this shop?"

"Oh, I inherited this business from my grandparents. This little shop has been in our family since it opened, over forty years ago," she told him.

"I'm trying to track down a rare set of marbles," he said. "The last record I can find of them is here in Amarillo, about thirty years ago. I heard they were given to a poor waitress. I'm wondering if she sold them."

Elizabeth and McKenzie moved a little closer to the counter. They pretended to be looking at some jewelry, and the two adults paid no attention to them.

"Marbles? I don't recall any unusual marbles. Every now and then we've bought little toys like that, but we sell them pretty quickly. Usually to a young mother who is in here shopping," she told him.

"Oh, these marbles weren't toys. I'm sure the woman wouldn't have sold them cheaply. They were very valuable," he told her.

The woman thought a moment, wrinkling her brow in concentration. "No, I'm sorry. I don't recall anything like that."

Mr. Jacobs looked disappointed. He tipped his hat to the woman, thanked her, and headed out the door.

The girls stared after him, mouths hanging open, when the clerk startled them. "Can I help you find something?"

Elizabeth and McKenzie began taking off their costumes and returning them to the proper places. "Oh, no thank you. We were just having a little fun. This is a great shop you have," Elizabeth told her.

The bell jangled again as Mrs. Phillips walked through the door.

"Are you ready, girls?" she asked.

"Yes, ma'am," they called, and left the store. They wanted to discuss the scene they'd just witnessed, but that conversation would have to wait.

Back at the motel, Elizabeth and McKenzie exchanged frustrated looks. They hadn't found a moment of privacy since they were at the shop. First they had stopped at Dairy Queen for hamburgers. Then Mrs. Phillips had asked the girls to entertain Evan for a while.

They were about to meet Megan when the phone rang. "It's for you, Elizabeth," said Mr. Phillips. It was her mom.

"Hi, baby. Are you having fun?" Mrs. Anderson asked.

"Yes, ma'am. We've been busy today."

"That's good. Listen, I know Ruby is taking you to the bank, and then for ice cream. After that, why don't you swing back by the hotel and pick up Evan? I've already talked to the Phillipses about this. You all can spend the evening over here so McKenzie's parents can have a date."

Elizabeth groaned inwardly but said only, "Yes, ma'am." Evan was a nice kid, but two little boys could put a real wrench in their sleuthing plans. After hanging up, she shared the news with McKenzie, who did groan. Loudly.

Mr. and Mrs. Phillips looked at the girls and chuckled.

With a wave, the two girls finally escaped to the restaurant. When the door shut behind them, they began their frantic whispers.

"Can you believe that man? Calling Megan's grandmother a 'poor waitress,' like she was some charity case. And who does he think he is, anyway? It's none of his business!" McKenzie said.

"Well, technically, she was a poor waitress. But we know the rest of the story, and he doesn't. I wonder how he knows that much, though," Elizabeth responded. The sun had disappeared behind some more gray clouds, and the storm threatened to return.

Rounding the corner, they found Megan and her mom waiting for them. Mrs. Smith was dressed in her maid's uniform. Her hair was coming out of its clip, and she wore no makeup. Still, Elizabeth thought she looked more like a runway model than a maid.

"Hop in, everyone. The quicker we get to the bank, the quicker we can hit The Marble Slab," said the woman, referring to the popular ice cream shop.

All three girls climbed into the backseat of the old sedan, and Ruby Smith laughed. "I feel like a chauffeur," she told them.

On the way to the bank, McKenzie and Elizabeth whispered to Megan, telling her about the event in the thrift shop.

They were interrupted by Mrs. Smith. "Am I supposed to be hearing this?" she asked. "Because I can hear almost every word you are saying. Something about a tall cowboy in a girlie thrift store? That must have been a funny sight."

The girls laughed nervously but stopped talking. They didn't want Mrs. Smith to know about Mr. Jacobs. Not yet, anyway.

They pulled into the bank parking lot, slid out of the car, and went inside the old building. "You all wait here while I make my deposits," Mrs. Smith told them, gesturing to a long bench. "After that, I have an appointment with Mr. Sanders, the bank's vice president. Megan, you can come with me and tell him what you've heard."

The girls took a seat and waited as Mrs. Smith approached the teller. A few minutes later, she joined the girls on the bench.

Before long, a balding man approached. "Hello, Ruby," he said. "This is a lovely group you have with you."

Ruby smiled and introduced the girls, and then she and Megan entered the office to the left of the bench. The door was pushed shut, but it bounced open just a crack.

Elizabeth and McKenzie scooted closer to the door, hoping to hear the conversation. They heard bits and pieces and knew Megan would fill them in on the details later. Still, they strained to catch the words being spoken.

Mrs. Smith's voice was soft and sweet. They heard, ". . .my mother. . .bank account. . .curious. . ."

Then the banker's voice, "Yes. . .did leave. . .lovely woman. . .still open. . . interest. . ."

They heard Mrs. Smith's voice again, "Megan. . .rumors. . . safe-deposit box. . ."

Megan added something to the conversation, but the girls couldn't make out the words. Didn't she know to speak up when her friends were eavesdropping?

There was a shuffling of some papers, then a faint noise. Was he typing on a computer?

The banker's voice came back. "No. . .record. . .safe deposit. . .nothing. . ."

There was a scooting of chairs, and the two girls on the bench slid to their original positions. The door opened, and Mr. Sanders shook Mrs. Smith's hand. "I'm sorry I couldn't help you more," he said. "Good day, ladies."

Megan looked disappointed, and Mrs. Smith patted her

on the back. "It would have been nice to have found those mysterious marbles. But we've done fine without them, haven't we? We don't need a hidden treasure. I have all the treasure I need in you, sweet girl."

Megan smiled at her mother and gave her a hug. But Elizabeth knew this wasn't the end of the search. The group headed out the door. The mystery would have to wait; it was time for ice cream.

●—●—●

Back at Elizabeth's house, the girls shut the door to her bedroom. The young detectives were ready to talk seriously.

"Tell me again what happened at the thrift shop," Megan said.

Elizabeth and McKenzie took turns telling the story, and Megan laughed out loud when she heard about the costumes. "I wish I had been there!" she said. "I can just see you two, all decked out in sunglasses and wigs. You must have looked ridiculous!"

"Actually, we looked pretty good," said Elizabeth.

McKenzie giggled. "Um, Elizabeth, I hate to tell you this, but that black wig did not look good on you! You definitely can't pull it off like Hannah Montana can. I think you need to stay a blond," she said.

Elizabeth laughed. "Come to think of it, your freckles did look rather out of place with that yellow wig. And those tiny little sunglasses!"

"Well, you looked like a demented movie star with those huge things you were wearing!"

All three girls were on the floor now, laughing at the silliness of it all.

Before they could get any further in the story, they heard a thud on Elizabeth's door. Then another, and another. Elizabeth got up and opened her door, only to have a miniature car crash into her ankle. "Ouch!" she cried.

James and Evan sat on the floor at the end of the hallway, with Matchbox cars lined up in front of them. "Sorry, Beth. We're racing," said James.

Elizabeth sighed a heavy sigh. "Why can't you do that in your bedroom?" she asked her brother.

"Because there's not enough space," he told her matter-of-factly. She stepped to his doorway and saw what he meant. Toys were scattered across every inch of the floor.

"You'd better clean up that mess before Mom sees," she told him.

James looked crestfallen. "But that will take too long," he said. "I want to race with Evan."

Elizabeth felt a wave of compassion for her little brother. He really was a good kid, even if he was annoying at times. "I'll tell you what. You and Evan pick up your toys, and then we'll sit with you in the driveway so you can race out there."

James looked at his sister as if she were his hero. He wasn't allowed in the front yard without supervision, but he loved to race his cars up and down the long driveway.

Just then, a loud clap of thunder startled them all. James's face fell, and he said, "We can't. It's raining."

Sure enough, it looked like the heavens had opened up. Lightning flashed, rain poured in heavy sheets, and water gushed off the sidewalks and into the gutters.

Another loud crash of thunder was followed by a pop, and everything went black.

The girls squealed and huddled together.

James and Evan stayed seated at the end of the hallway.

Through the dark, they heard Evan's voice saying, "This is so cool!"

Then James said, "Hey, let's race cars in the dark!"

A moment later, Elizabeth yelped in pain. Another flash of lightning revealed that a Hot Wheels car had crashed into her ankle. Again. "James, cut that out!"

"Sorry, Beth," he said. She shut her door, leaving the boys in the black hallway.

The three girls gathered at the window to watch the show. Thunder clapped. A fierce wind forced the trees to sway into unnatural positions. Somewhere in the distance a car alarm went off. The whole scene was scary and fascinating.

Suddenly a pair of headlights pulled into Megan's driveway, behind her mom's car. They shut off, and all was black again.

"I wonder who that could be," Megan said.

They peered through the darkness, trying to catch a glimpse of the unknown guest. A flash of lightning revealed a tall dark figure in a cowboy hat, heading for Megan's porch.

Through the Hole in the Wall

The three girls gasped. They peered through the darkness, hoping to catch another glimpse of the man.

"What in the world is he doing here?" asked McKenzie.

"I don't know, but my mom is alone. We've got to do something!" said Megan.

"I'll grab my flashlight. Megan, you unlock my window. We'll crawl through and stay hidden until we can figure out what's going on." Elizabeth felt around in the dark, pulling open the drawer to her bedside table. Locating the flashlight, she clicked it on and returned to the window, which was now wide open. Wind and rain gushed through, getting her curtains all wet.

The three girls slipped through the window, and Elizabeth pulled it shut behind her. She would have a lot of explaining to do if her parents found the wet room, but this was important. Ruby was in danger.

The girls ran, staying low to the ground. *Pow!* Rain soaked their skin. *Crash!* A flash of lightning revealed an empty porch. Mr. Jacobs's truck was still parked in the driveway.

"Come on!" Megan called out. Through the window, Ruby appeared to be lighting candles. Soon their soft glow gave light for the girls to see what was going on.

Jacobs spoke, but they couldn't hear the words. Ruby laughed. Then Mr. Jacobs began moving around the house with the flashlight!

"He's looking for the marbles," McKenzie said.

"But why is she letting him?" asked Elizabeth. "That doesn't make sense."

"Somebody has to stop him," said Megan. She stood and pushed open her front door.

Ruby Smith was startled. "Megan? What are you doing out in this weather? I thought you were at Elizabeth's house!"

Elizabeth and McKenzie appeared in the doorway. The girls shivered like puppies fresh from a bath, dripping water all over the hardwood floor.

"Oh my goodness! Girls, get in here. Let me find you some towels." Ruby pulled the girls inside and shut the door behind them.

Mr. Jacobs appeared from the hallway. "What on earth? Girls, are you okay?"

Ruby picked up a candle and brushed past Mr. Jacobs into the hallway. She returned with an armload of thick, fluffy towels. Each girl took one and dried herself. Suddenly there was a loud *pop!* and the electricity returned.

The house lit up, and the television began broadcasting the Home and Garden Network, Ruby's favorite. Weather updates scrolled across the bottom of the screen.

Ruby stood, hands on hips, looking at the girls. Finally, her eyes rested on Megan. "Explain yourself, young lady. Why would you go running around in a storm like this? You could have gotten struck by lightning!"

Elizabeth and McKenzie looked at their sopping shoes. Megan lifted her chin and said, "We were worried about you,

Mama. We were in Elizabeth's room, and we saw a strange car pull into the driveway, and. . ." Her eyes flashed to Mr. Jacobs. "And we saw a man coming onto our porch."

Mr. Jacobs stepped forward. "Well, now, that would be scary. That was very brave of you to come and check on your mother. I'm sorry. I never meant to frighten anyone."

Megan held the man's eyes, as if waiting for an explanation. She was usually very respectful to her elders. But she was also very protective of her mother.

Jacobs continued. "I was driving a couple of blocks from here when the power went out. I thought of you and your mama here by yourselves. I thought I'd come check on you." The man shifted his cowboy hat from one hand to the other, then back again. He looked nervous.

Megan held his eyes but said nothing. Elizabeth and McKenzie watched the scene. The electric clock on the side table flashed on and off, on and off.

Mr. Jacobs said, "Well, it looks like everyone is okay, so I guess I'll head back to the motel. Sorry to have frightened you girls."

Ruby held out her arm in protest. "Oh, don't go before I can fix you a cup of coffee. You're soaking wet! Here, take a towel."

The man smiled gently at Ruby and said, "Aww, no, ma'am. I'll be fine. But thank you." With that, he tipped his hat to her and left.

Ruby Smith's eyes swung to the girls standing in front of her, landing on her daughter. "Let's get you three warmed up. Then you have some tall talkin' to do."

The girls followed the woman into the kitchen and sat around the oak table as Mrs. Smith made hot cocoa. While the water was boiling, she picked up the phone and dialed. "Sue? This is Ruby. The girls are at my house. I just wanted you to know they're safe. . . . No, they haven't explained themselves yet. We're getting to that. . . . Okay, I'll see one of you in a minute."

Elizabeth groaned inwardly. How would she explain sneaking out the window? It hadn't seemed like a bad idea at the time. But now it was going to be hard to defend.

Moments later, there was a knock at the door, and Ruby rushed to let Robert Anderson in. He didn't look happy. "Elizabeth, what were you thinking? The boys said you sneaked out your window! And in a storm? That's not like you at all. Explain, young lady."

Elizabeth took a deep breath and sent a desperate plea to heaven. "We weren't trying to be bad. We just got scared, and the electricity was off, and then we saw Mr. Jacobs coming toward the porch, and we knew Megan's mom was here by herself, and—"

"Wait a minute," interrupted Ruby. "You knew it was Mr. Jacobs? It sounded to me like you thought he was a stranger!"

Megan answered. "Mom, we thought it might be Mr. Jacobs, but we didn't know for sure. And there's more. We don't trust him."

The two adults looked at each other and then at the girls. Elizabeth's dad sat down and leaned forward. "We've got all night. Start talking."

The girls remained silent, not knowing where to begin. Finally, Elizabeth and Megan began pouring out the story from beginning to end, one pausing as the other jumped in, back and forth like a tennis match. McKenzie added a detail here and there.

The two adults looked at the girls, stunned. "So you've been trying to solve a mystery?" asked Mr. Anderson.

The girls nodded. Elizabeth's dad leaned back in his chair, and a great belly laugh erupted that continued for several minutes. The girls weren't sure how to respond.

Mrs. Smith chuckled, too, but she appeared to be laughing more at her neighbor than at the situation.

Finally, the man pulled himself together and gave Elizabeth a stern look. "I'm glad you wanted to help Megan's mom. But what you did was foolish. First of all, it is never okay to sneak out your window, unless something dangerous is inside the house, like a fire. Second, it is never okay to go running around in a storm. You all could have been seriously hurt. Third, it was foolish of you to think you could save Mrs. Smith from any man. You should have come to me immediately."

Elizabeth looked at her father. She hated disappointing him. "I'm sorry, Daddy."

"You're forgiven," he said. "But you still have to be punished. I'm not going to ground you while McKenzie is here. But when the Phillipses' vacation is over, you're going to be seeing a lot of the inside of our house."

◆—◆

Later that night, McKenzie and Elizabeth lay awake whispering. Their room at the Big Texan had a small living area with a pullout bed, which gave the girls some privacy.

"Did you notice that my dad and Megan's mom weren't concerned about Mr. Jacobs?" Elizabeth asked.

"Yeah, I did," whispered McKenzie. "Your dad thought the whole thing was funny."

"My dad has a good sense about people. But the fact that

Mr. Jacobs is looking for the marbles is strange," she said. "Maybe we should just come out and ask him about it."

McKenzie thought. "No. He clearly has plans for those marbles. But Megan and her mom could use the money. I'm still not sure I trust him."

"Me neither," replied Elizabeth. "We have to find those marbles before he does."

The girls were quiet for a few minutes. Then McKenzie rolled to face her friend. "Hey, Elizabeth. . .since the marbles never made it to the bank, I wonder if they really are hidden at the restaurant."

"I was thinking that, too. We'll go there first thing in the morning," she said sleepily.

———•—•———

The two sleuths were awake and dressed before dawn the next morning. They walked to the restaurant, which was open early for breakfast. A waitress they'd never seen before seated them, and the girls studied the menu.

"We need to get into that supply closet," said Elizabeth, her eyes scanning the walls and floor planks. "That secret panel seems like the perfect hiding place."

"What time does Megan come in?" asked McKenzie.

Elizabeth's eyes focused on someone behind McKenzie, and a grin spread across her face. "Right now," she said.

McKenzie turned to find Megan walking toward them. "I see we all had the same idea," she said. "I think we need to check that supply closet again."

Elizabeth scooted over in the booth to make room for her friend. "Did you and your mom talk any more last night?" she asked.

"Yeah. I ended up sleeping in her bed and we talked for a

long time. She does think it's weird that Mr. Jacobs is looking for the marbles. She promised to keep her distance from him," Megan told them.

The other two girls observed something in Megan's attitude that seemed. . .not quite right. "You don't seem happy," said McKenzie.

Megan let out a heavy sigh. "It's just that my mom's been through so much. I wasn't thrilled when Mr. Jacobs flirted with her. But he made her smile! She was singing and humming. For the last few days, she's seemed happier. I just hate that he's a fake."

Elizabeth thought about that. "He might not be a fake. My dad doesn't have a problem with him, and you know my dad. He's pretty good about figuring people out," she said.

"Maybe so, Elizabeth, but he's definitely after those marbles. We can't let him find them before we do," McKenzie said.

"I have a feeling that when we find the marbles, we'll find out the answers to a lot of our questions about Mr. Jacobs," McKenzie told them.

After a moment, Megan stood and said, "Well, we won't find them sitting in this booth. Let's get started. Come with me."

The girls followed their friend through the restaurant, into the kitchen area, and to the supply room. The early morning manager, a friendly-looking woman in her early fifties, said, "You're here early, Megan!"

"Uh, yes, Mrs. Edgar. I really want to get that supply closet cleaned out. My friends have volunteered to help."

The woman gave them a strange look, but smiled. "Interesting. I suppose it's a better way to spend your time than sitting in front of the television. It's good to see young people with a sense of responsibility. Have fun!"

The girls entered the supply closet, and Megan flipped on the dim light. "I guess I'll have to fix that light myself," she said, grabbing a stepladder. "McKenzie, could you hand me one of those bulbs behind you?"

McKenzie did as she was asked. Elizabeth got on her hands and knees. She moved the tomato cans away from the hidden panel.

"Megan, do you know where a Phillips screwdriver is?" she asked.

"Well, I know where a Phillips is," Megan responded, and she and McKenzie laughed. It took a moment for Elizabeth to catch on to the joke about McKenzie's last name, but when she did, she laughed, too. After a few minutes, the lightbulb was changed. Elizabeth was on her stomach unscrewing the panel in the wall. When the last screw was loose, the panel was removed to reveal a small square.

Elizabeth reached inside and felt around but found nothing. "This hole goes pretty far back. One of us will have to go in with a flashlight."

The three girls stood looking at each other, trying to decide who was least likely to get stuck. All three were slim but had different shapes and builds. Finally, McKenzie and Megan said in unison, "Elizabeth is the skinniest."

"Hey!" Elizabeth said, then looked down at her long arms and legs. "Okay, I guess I'm skinny. But so are y'all."

"Slim, yes. String beans? No. You're the only string bean in the bunch," said Megan.

Elizabeth sighed good-naturedly. "I knew I should have gotten three scoops of ice cream yesterday. . . ," she muttered. "Where is Kate when we need her?"

McKenzie laughed at the memory of their tiny camp friend. Kate had made them all look like giants.

Megan got a flashlight from the office, and Elizabeth shimmied into the opening. The beam from the light revealed years of accumulated dust, a crack in the concrete floor, and a few dead bugs. There was even an old label from a green bean can, which looked as if it had been there for decades. "Cool!" Elizabeth called out, examining the label.

"What did you find?" asked Megan.

"This old green bean label must be older than our parents!" she called.

Megan and McKenzie shared exasperated looks. "The marbles, Elizabeth! Stay focused," Megan called out.

Mrs. Edgar pushed the door open and poked her head in. "Megan, dear, since you're here early, why don't you clock in? We're shorthanded this morning. I may let you try waitressing."

Megan and McKenzie jumped and turned to block the pair of legs sticking out of the wall.

"Yes, ma'am," Megan said.

"Pronto," the woman said, shooing the two girls out of the supply room. "I thought there were three of you," she questioned.

Suddenly a loud crash came from the kitchen, followed by a yelp. "Jesse, how many times do I have to tell you to wear oven mitts?" Mrs. Edgar said to a young man across the room. She closed the door, leaving Megan and McKenzie wondering what to do next. The woman called over her shoulder, "Megan, show your friend out of the kitchen. Too many people are back here as it is. Then go sign in and report to the waitress's station."

CHAPTER
8

Trapped!

Elizabeth heard the muffled voices. She tried to draw her feet up into the hole, but something caught on her blue jeans. She was trapped! She couldn't wiggle backward or forward.

The voices faded, and she heard a loud crash, followed by the click of a door. Somehow she knew she'd been left alone. She tried to shine her flashlight to find what was catching her jeans, but she couldn't wiggle her body that way in the tight space. She finally gave up and decided to wait.

Lord, what have I gotten myself into? she prayed silently into the darkness. *What will my dad say? He'll tell me I should have known better than to go crawling around in holes in buildings. But Lord, we have to find those marbles! Please help us.*

Elizabeth made herself as comfortable as possible and waited. After a while, she shined her light on the green bean label. Not very interesting.

She heard a sound above her head like running water. Shining her light, she tilted her head backward to find pipes. Water pipes. *So that's the reason for the panel. To let the plumber work on the pipes.*

"I wish I had a book or something," she whispered. Then it dawned on her. The journals! In their excitement to solve the mystery, she and McKenzie had abandoned Mrs. Wilson's journals. But what if there was more?

How could we have been so blind? Elizabeth mentally berated herself for jumping to conclusions and not reading the journals at least to the end of Emily Marie's story. Her mind raced with the possibilities of those journals when she heard another click. She felt two hands on her ankles.

"Hello?" she called in a soft voice. "Who's there?"

Through the darkness, she heard a familiar twang. "What have you gotten yourself into? Gracious sakes alive, girl! Here, your jeans are caught. Be still, now. Okay, I'm gonna pull."

After a few tugs from behind, Elizabeth was able to back herself out of the hole. She sat up, looked into Jean Louise's face, and sighed with relief. "Oh, Jean Louise! Am I glad to see you! I was scared I was going to—"

"You should be whipped, young lady! What kind of stunt do you think you're pulling? Why, there could be rats in those walls, or loose wires. . ."

Elizabeth shuddered. She hadn't considered those possibilities.

"And you could have been arrested for breaking and entering. You have no business being back here!" the woman continued.

Elizabeth blinked back tears. "I—I'm sorry, Jean Louise. We were only—"

The woman grabbed her and hugged her. "Now don't you start crying. I'm just glad you're okay. You'd better be thankful I was on duty! When the girls told me what y'all were up to, I just about died. I've got to get back. Come on, now, dust yourself off. And no more crawling around in holes, ya hear me?"

Elizabeth nodded and promised. Jean Louise pushed open the supply room door. When the coast was clear, the two headed out of the kitchen.

Out front, Megan was frantically taking orders. When she saw Elizabeth, she smiled but continued her work. Mac was waiting on a bench near the entrance and stood when she saw her friend. Without a word, the two girls headed back to the motel room.

◆—◆—◆

Several hours later, Elizabeth and McKenzie were stretched out by the Texas-shaped pool. Elizabeth read aloud from Mrs. Wilson's journal while McKenzie listened. They were determined to read to the end of the story this time.

Dear God, I can't believe this is happening. Why Emily Marie? Why now? Lord, You knew her car was going to break down. You knew she would be out alone after dark. Why couldn't You have stopped this from happening?

Oh, I'm not blaming You, Lord. It just doesn't make any sense. She's got those two precious children, and now Foster. Why did that car have to hit her?

If only I had gone with her, like she asked. Maybe then, none of this would have happened. Oh, God, please let her be okay. It doesn't look good.

I sat with her tonight, Lord. She talked a lot, but she didn't make much sense. She kept asking about her babies, and then saying something about the big blue fin. She's hallucinating, Lord. I tried to hold her hand and comfort her. But she just kept telling me to look under the fin.

The next few pages told of Emily Marie's death and funeral. After that, the journal entries ended until nearly a year later, but nothing more was said about Emily Marie.

The girls thumbed back through the pages, trying to find something more that would help them. But it was no use. They found no more hidden clues.

McKenzie sat up in her lounge chair. "The big blue fin," she said. "What a strange thing to say."

Then, as if reading one another's mind, they both started talking at once. "The fish! Isn't there a—"

"A big fish! In the restaurant!"

"Yeah, it's hanging on that back wall! It's a—a swordfish or something!"

"A blue marlin, I think the sign said!"

The girls looked at each other, excitement flashing in their eyes, and started for the restaurant. They were halfway there when they realized they were wearing their swimsuits.

They practically ran back to their room and changed, and were at the restaurant in no time.

Jean Louise greeted them at the door. "Well, well. If it isn't Bonnie and Clyde."

Elizabeth laughed at the comment, then leaned over and whispered, "We think we may have found the marbles."

Jean Louise's eyes grew wide, and Elizabeth continued. "Can you seat us at that table under the big fish? Your mom put something in her journal about a blue fin."

The waitress looked skeptical but led them through the restaurant. "That fish has been hanging there since I can remember. Just don't go crawling through any more holes in the wall without telling me first. I don't want to be bailing you kids out of jail."

The girls laughed and took their seats. They were thrilled to be sitting right beneath the fish, and felt certain this would be the end of their search.

They examined the fish closely. McKenzie lightly tapped the wall under the fish, but stopped when the people next to them looked at her curiously.

Elizabeth picked up the crisp linen napkin from the table. She dropped it on the floor. Crawling under the table to retrieve it, she examined the wall and floor. Suddenly she felt a tap on her shoulder. Turning to find Jean Louise's white work shoes, Elizabeth scrambled out from under the table. She banged her head.

"Ouch!" she cried.

Jean Louise showed little sympathy. "Elizabeth Anderson, I don't know what I'm going to do with you."

"But Jean Lou—"

"Don't 'But Jean Louise' me! You'll get in big trouble if you don't stop poking around." The woman sighed and placed her hands on her hips. "I'll tell you what. The restaurant closes at ten p.m. If you can be here then, I'll let you look to your heart's content. I'll even help you. But you have to leave well enough alone while the customers are here."

Elizabeth jumped from her seat and hugged the woman. "Oh, thank you, Jean Louise! You're my hero! I just know we're going to find the—"

"Shhh! Not so loud. You never know who might be listening." She gestured toward the opposite corner of the restaurant, and they noticed Mr. Jacobs for the first time. He was looking at them strangely. When they made eye contact, he waved.

Elizabeth sat back in her seat. "Okay. We'll meet you

here at closing time," she said. The woman left them, and McKenzie and Elizabeth leaned their heads together, trying to decide whether the marbles would end up being in the floor or the wall.

"Just think. We may be sitting on them right now," McKenzie said.

Elizabeth's eyes grew round. "They could be in the booth! What if she pulled the stuffing out of one of the benches and put them in there?"

"They've probably replaced the benches since then," McKenzie told her. Their eyes grew wide at the thought. They pushed it aside and decided to deal with that possibility when the time came.

●—●—●

Back at the motel room, Mr. and Mrs. Phillips were looking at travel brochures. "We only have a few days left in our vacation, and we want to make the most of them. There's a water park, a cowboy museum, and the famous Cadillac Ranch," said Mr. Phillips.

"There's also an outlet mall I'd like to visit, and a zoo," added Mrs. Phillips. "What are you all interested in?"

"Water park!" shouted McKenzie.

"Cadillac Ranch!" shouted Evan.

Elizabeth remained quiet.

Mrs. Phillips placed the brochures for the water park and the Cadillac Ranch to one side. "That nice man, Mr. Jacobs, offered to take us back to the rodeo grounds and let us see the livestock up close. There's also a fair with the rodeo," she said while reading over some of the brochures. "We'll probably go there this afternoon."

"Cool!" said Evan. "Do you think he'll let me ride a bull?"

"No, but you might be able to ride a real rodeo horse," his father told him.

"Dad, are you going to buy that horse from him?" McKenzie asked.

"I'm thinking about it. He seems pretty anxious to sell. Says he wants to buy a house near here. But he's not sure what will happen until some inheritance of his comes through."

"Inheritance?" McKenzie and Elizabeth asked at once.

"Yeah, apparently his uncle left behind some priceless. . . marbles or something. But they've disappeared. Jacobs is trying to track them down."

Elizabeth stood and grabbed McKenzie by the arm. "I just remembered something I wanted to look at down at the gift shop," she said.

"Okay, girls. Stay close," said Mrs. Phillips.

As soon as the door closed behind them, McKenzie looked at Elizabeth questioningly.

"I have an idea. We've been skirting around Mr. Jacobs, trying to go behind his back. But since he's so interested in those marbles, why don't we go straight to him?"

McKenzie's eyes grew wide. "You mean just come out and ask him?"

"No. I have a plan," Elizabeth told her friend. They headed to the gift shop, where they purchased sidewalk chalk and a bag of marbles.

A half hour later, the two young detectives sat on the sidewalk near Mr. Jacobs's room, casually playing a game of marbles. Elizabeth had drawn a large circle using the sidewalk chalk, and the two girls took turns thumping their shooter marbles, trying to knock the other's marbles out of the circle.

They were absorbed in the game and didn't notice when the door behind them quietly opened and shut.

McKenzie noticed the embroidered cowboy boots first. They were behind Elizabeth, who was concentrating on which angle to shoot her marbles. McKenzie's eyes followed the long legs up, up, up, until she looked into the amused eyes of Mr. Jacobs.

"You know, if you shoot to the left, it will ricochet and knock out the marbles on the right," he said.

Elizabeth nearly jumped out of her skin, even though she'd expected him. "Oh, hi, Mr. Jacobs!" she told him after she regained her composure. "Are we in your way? We're sorry."

"Oh, no, not at all," the man told her. "I love a good game of marbles." He eyed the colorful balls with interest.

The two shifted into sleuth mode. "Really? Are you a marble expert?" McKenzie asked the man.

He stepped off the curb and sat on the sidewalk next to them. "I guess you could say that. I've played marbles since I was a little boy."

"Really? Not too many people play the game anymore. Did someone special teach you how?" Elizabeth asked.

"Yep," said the cowboy. "My uncle. He was more like a father to me than anything. He never married or had children, but he loved me like I was his son."

"Really?" Elizabeth probed. Her plan was working perfectly. "Do you still see him a lot?"

"Unfortunately, no," he said. "He passed away about a year ago. But he had a soft spot in his heart for Amarillo. Never told me why, though. I suspect he fell in love here. He never talked much about the time he spent here. But whenever he mentioned Amarillo, he got a distant look in his eyes."

The girls remained quiet and let the man talk.

"I really miss him. I've decided to settle here, since he seemed to love the place so much."

"What was your uncle's name?" Elizabeth asked. Just then, Evan rounded the corner.

"McKenzie, Mama says to come. We're going to the fair," the boy told his sister.

Mr. Jacobs stood up and said, "I need to be going, too. Nice talking with you girls." And with that, he left.

The girls gathered up their marbles as Evan watched. "Those are cool," he said. "Where did you get them?"

Elizabeth replaced the colorful round balls into their drawstring pouch and handed them to Evan. "Here you go. I got them at the gift shop, but you can have them," she told him.

"Cool! Thanks, Elizabeth!" he said.

The three of them walked back to the Phillipses' motel room, where McKenzie's parents were waiting. "Elizabeth, call your mom and ask if it's okay if we pick up James. He'd probably enjoy a day at the fair, don't you think?" Mrs. Phillips asked.

A short time later, the four Phillipses and the two younger Andersons were oohing and aahing over the sights at the fair. Elizabeth and Evan held dripping ice cream cones, while McKenzie and James opted for cotton candy.

They rode the Ferris wheel and held their arms high during the roller coaster ride. While they walked along a row of games, James spotted the balloon darts. He wasn't looking at the balloons, however.

"Look, Beth! Look at those cool cars! I need one of those for my collection!" He tugged at his sister's arm as he pointed.

Elizabeth looked at the row of model cars lined up as prizes. "Do you think you can pop three balloons?" Elizabeth asked him.

"I don't know, but I'll sure try!" the boy said. Elizabeth gave her brother a ticket, and James handed it to the man behind the counter.

While he was trying to pop the balloons, McKenzie leaned over and whispered, "It's getting late. We need to get back to the motel before ten so we can find the marbles."

Elizabeth couldn't hear her friend over the noise of the fair. "What?" she asked.

McKenzie repeated herself a little louder, but Elizabeth still couldn't hear. Finally, McKenzie ended up nearly shouting, "We've got to get back to the restaurant so we can look for the marbles!"

At that moment, Elizabeth spotted a tall flash of cowboy hat disappearing around the corner. She pointed, but the person was gone. "Was that—" Her question died. She decided she must be seeing things.

James popped one balloon but missed the other two. He was disappointed, and Elizabeth draped her arm over his shoulder. "It's okay, li'l brother. Come on. I see the house of mirrors. You'll love that!"

The four young people offered their tickets and entered. "We'll meet you at the exit," Mr. Phillips told them.

Inside, they giggled at the distorted images of themselves, some tall and wavy, others short and bumpy. They decided to chase each other through the maze, and before long, they were laughing and hollering. Each time they thought they'd caught one of the others, it turned out to be an image in the mirror!

Elizabeth began to see flashes of that cowboy hat again. Each time she focused on the image, it was gone. But then there it was again, in the corner of her eye.

She told herself not to panic, but concentrated on finding the others. What in the world would Mr. Jacobs be doing in the house of mirrors? Was he shadowing them?

The Man in the Mirrors

"Hey y'all, I think we need to go. Everyone head for the exit," she called.

The others laughed. "Aww, you're not giving up that easily, are you?" called Evan.

Stay calm. Figure out how to get everyone out of here, away from that creepy cowboy, Elizabeth told herself. *Please, God, help.*

Then she had an idea. "I'll race you! The last one to the exit is a rotten egg!" she called.

Within moments, she heard footsteps and hoots of laughter as the other three dashed to the exit. But then there was a thud, and the sound of something rolling on the floor. The marbles! Evan had kept them in his pocket!

"Oh no! My marbles!" Elizabeth heard Evan calling out. She could see the images of marbles rolling on the floor but couldn't find them. Before long, she saw Evan's reflection. But everywhere she turned were more reflections. Where was the real thing?

"Here, let me help you with that," came a deep voice. Elizabeth looked, and there was that cowboy hat, attached to Mr. Jacobs! And there he was again, and again, and again.

She had to find the real Evan and protect him from the real Mr. Jacobs!

She stood up, closed her eyes, and just listened to the voices, to the sounds of the marbles on the floor. Without opening her eyes, she turned toward the sound.

Holding her arms in front of her, she slowly began to walk, letting the sounds guide her. Before she knew it, she bumped into something. Opening her eyes, she looked directly down on a cowboy hat, sitting on top of Jacobs's head. The man was on his hands and knees, examining a handful of marbles. Evan was next to him, gathering more of the round balls.

"Here, let me help you," Elizabeth said, trying to keep her voice calm. Her heart was pounding, and she felt sure the others could hear its loud thud. Still, she kept her composure, knelt, and began searching.

"Hello, Elizabeth," said Mr. Jacobs.

Elizabeth forced herself not to look directly at the man. She tried to watch him in the mirrors as she looked for more marbles. "It's funny to see you here, Mr. Jacobs," Elizabeth said.

The man chuckled. "Aww, I'm just a big kid at heart. I love these fairs. I was supposed to meet Dan at the rodeo, to let him look at Lucy. But I thought I'd wander around the fair for a while first. Then I spotted you all over at the balloon darts. I've got something for your brother, by the way. I saw you kids come in here and thought I'd try to catch up with you."

Elizabeth turned to look at the man. "If I didn't know better, I'd think you were following us," she said.

The cowboy chuckled. Was that a nervous laugh? "Well, I was starting to think you were following me," he said.

Elizabeth averted her eyes and called out to her friends again. "Meet everyone at the exit!" She stood but found herself at a loss for which way to turn. *I really need to do something about my sense of direction, or lack of it,* she thought.

Mr. Jacobs stood and towered over her. Sensing her hesitancy, he said, "Follow me. I'll get you out of here."

Drats! She hated to depend on her prime suspect to get her unlost, but she didn't seem to have much choice. She kept her eyes fixed on the back of his plaid shirt and, before long, stepped into the bright lights of the fairground.

Mr. and Mrs. Phillips laughed when they saw Mr. Jacobs. "You're a brave man," Dan Phillips said.

Mr. Jacobs smiled but didn't make eye contact with anyone. Did he feel guilty about something? He reached into his pocket and pulled out a tiny model car. He handed it to James.

"I saw you trying to win a car, James. I thought you might like to have this," he said.

"Wow, thank you!" said James, a smile lighting his face. "And it's blue, too! My favorite color!"

Elizabeth and McKenzie exchanged glances. As the adults began talking and moving toward the rodeo grounds, the two girls stayed a few steps behind.

"What is he doing here?" Elizabeth whispered.

"He's meeting my dad, and they're going to look at that horse, remember?" McKenzie reminded her.

"Yeah, but it's strange that he seems to be following us. It's like he knows we know something," Elizabeth continued.

"Maybe. But I think it's a good idea for us to stay close to him anyway. We might learn something," McKenzie said.

The girls followed the rest of their group at a safe distance, so they could talk freely without fear of being heard.

"I wish the other Camp Club Girls were here. I think we

need to e-mail them all tonight and see if we can get any more ideas," said McKenzie.

"That's it!" said Elizabeth. "Why didn't I think of that a long time ago? We can get them to help us investigate Mr. Jacobs!" She pulled her cell phone out of her pocket. Scrolling down in her address book, she hit Kate's number.

It was busy.

She moved to Sydney's number. After a couple of rings, Sydney's grandmother answered.

"Hello, Mrs. Washington. This is Elizabeth. How are you?" she asked politely.

"Oh, Elizabeth! What a nice surprise. I'm doing well, and you?"

"I'm fine, thank you, ma'am. May I please speak with Sydney?"

"Oh, she's not here. She's at a Wilderness Club meeting. She'll be back in about an hour or so. Would you like me to have her call you back?"

"Oh, no thank you. I'll just e-mail her. Tell her I'm sorry I missed her."

"She will be so disappointed. I'll tell her you called. You take care now," said the woman.

Elizabeth hung up and then sighed a frustrated sigh. McKenzie watched as she moved the arrow down to Alex's name and number and pressed the button. It rang.

"Hello?" came Alex's voice from the other end of the line.

"Hi, Alex!" Elizabeth said.

"Elizabeth Anderson, is that you?" the girl exclaimed from the other end of the line.

"Yep, it is," replied Elizabeth.

"Is McKenzie with you? She better be. You e-mailed us

all about your new mystery, and then it was like the two of you just dropped off the face of the earth. Haven't you been checking your e-mails?"

Elizabeth was surprised at Alex's scolding. She felt like a child who had gotten caught sneaking a cookie. The truth was, Elizabeth and McKenzie had been too busy to think about e-mailing. "Uh. . .sorry," she said.

"You're forgiven," said Alex. "Now tell me everything! Did you find the jewels? Are Megan and her mother wealthy heiresses? Oh, this is *so* Hollywood! I can see it now. 'Impoverished woman inherits millions!' It will be made into a television movie, I just know it! You'll have your own mystery show. An *iCarly* on the go!"

Elizabeth held the phone away from her ear a bit. McKenzie could hear Alex's excited chatter from a couple of feet away. The two laughed. Same old Alex. She handed the phone to McKenzie, who said hello to her friend, then handed the phone back to Elizabeth.

"We haven't found the marbles yet. And Megan isn't exactly impoverished. But we need your help," she said.

"What can I do?" asked Alex.

"We couldn't find anything in our search for the marbles. But there is this cowboy named Mark Jacobs. He keeps snooping around. We know he's after the marbles, too. He claims to have inherited them from a rich uncle, but I think he's a fraud.

"We know a man named Foster left them to Megan's grandmother before she died. We're still trying to find where she might have hidden them. But can you check out Jacobs for us? And get the others in on the search, too. Mac and I are at the fair now, tailing the cowboy."

"Oh, how exciting! I wish I were there. I'll get right on it. I'll call you back if I find anything."

"Thanks, Alex." The two girls hurried to catch up with the rest of their group.

Mr. Jacobs and Mr. Phillips were talking, and the cowboy led them to a row of stalls where the horses waited to enter the rodeo arena. The announcer said something funny, and the crowd laughed.

"I ride again in about a half hour. Lucy has been a great horse. I hate to sell her, but at least I know she'll be in good hands."

"Tell me again why you're selling her," Mr. Phillips requested, and the girls scooted in closer, pretending to watch the rodeo. Evan and James were on the ground, driving the tiny car through tracks of loose hay.

"I'm ready to retire. The rodeo life is fun, but I want to put down roots somewhere. I don't have any family still living, but Amarillo was always special to my uncle, and I like it here, too. I've found a piece of land with a creek and a nice little house, and I want to settle here. I thought I had a sizable inheritance coming my way, but that doesn't seem to be panning out. So my backup plan has always been to sell my stock and supplies for a down payment."

"So if your inheritance comes through, you may not want to sell her?" asked Mr. Phillips.

Mr. Jacobs paused. "I hope my inheritance comes through, but I'm trying not to count on it. It's a long story," the cowboy said. His voice sounded so sad that Elizabeth couldn't help but look at him. When she did, she was surprised to see him looking at her! She looked away, but it was too late.

McKenzie's dad studied the horse, and Mrs. Phillips was talking to the boys. Jacobs stepped to the railing where the girls were leaning and whispered, "I heard you talking to that waitress at the restaurant about some marbles. What kind of marbles are you looking for?"

Elizabeth couldn't believe her ears. Was the man really questioning her about the marbles? How could she get out of this conversation? Panicked, she looked at McKenzie, but Mac appeared as flustered as she felt.

Suddenly the announcer's voice boomed over the loudspeaker. "We invite all of our young people, ages eight to fourteen, to enter the arena for the pig chase. You might get a little muddy, but you're sure to have a barrel of fun! The first one to catch a baby pig wins $250 cash."

McKenzie grabbed Elizabeth and pulled her into the arena. A woman at the gate attached a number to each contestant's back and instructed them to stand along the railing. Elizabeth looked at her new pink tennis shoes and knew they would never be the same.

"That was a close call," whispered Mac as they waited for the event to begin.

"Tell me about it! The nerve of that man, just coming out and asking me like that!"

"I feel sorry for him," said McKenzie. "He's all alone in the world, and now it looks like he'll have to sell his horse. I'd die if I had to sell mine."

Elizabeth looked at her friend in shock. "Don't tell me you're falling for his sob story! Don't let him fool you." Elizabeth tried to convince herself as much as she tried to convince her friend. Deep down, she shared McKenzie's sympathy. But he had to be a bad guy. He just had to be.

"Yeah, you're probably right," whispered McKenzie.

The gate closed, and the dozens of contestants were instructed to scatter throughout the arena. The announcer's voice said, "In just a moment, six piglets will be released into the arena. Oh, and did I mention they are covered in baby oil? When you hear the gunshot, you do whatever you can to catch one of these pigs. Of course, there will be no hitting or shoving or foul play of any kind, or you'll be disqualified. The first one to successfully catch and hold a pig wins the cash. Are you ready? Get set!"

The sound of a gunshot set the arena into chaos. Piglets raced into the arena, and the contestants sprang into action. The crowd roared with laughter and cheers. For a moment, Elizabeth stood frozen to her spot. She had never done anything like this!

McKenzie, on the other hand, was quite at home. She'd singled out a tiny black-and-white-spotted pig and was trying to corner him. "Elizabeth, don't just stand there! Get moving!" she called out. "I could use a little help!"

Just then, a small pink blur ran over her foot, leaving behind tiny mud prints on her shoes. Elizabeth reached for the creature, but it was too late. She sprang forward to chase the offending animal. She could hear McKenzie calling her name, but Elizabeth had no interest in any other pig. This one had muddied her shoes. He was going to pay.

The pig ran around the arena, Elizabeth close at his heels. He led her through the center of the ring, around the outer edge, and into a mud puddle. In the background, she could hear James calling, "Go, Bettyboo! Go, Bettyboo!"

Suddenly, all of Elizabeth's frustrations took the form of the tiny piglet in front of her. She leaped forward in a stunning show of determination, grabbed the oily little creature, and held him to her chest. She wasn't about to let him escape.

The crowd stood to their feet and roared, and the announcer's voice exclaimed over the loudspeaker, "We have a winner! The pretty little blond, now covered in mud, has caught herself a pig! Folks, did you see her jump? She was determined to win that cash! Congratulations, miss!"

Elizabeth stayed where she was, her jeans soaking in the mud beneath her. She looked up to find McKenzie standing over her, hands on hips and a huge smile on her face.

"Congratulations! I didn't know you had it in you!" Mac told her.

"I didn't either," Elizabeth replied as she gripped the wiggling animal in her arms.

A rodeo official approached and asked her name. The woman then spoke into a cordless microphone, "Our winner is Miss Elizabeth Anderson. Miss Anderson, on behalf of the Amarillo Livestock Show and Rodeo, we would like to present you with this certificate, and a check for $250. Congratulations!" She held out a large manila envelope as the crowd cheered.

Elizabeth still didn't move. She was afraid to let go of the pig, afraid he would escape.

The woman leaned forward and whispered, "You can let go now. You've already won."

Elizabeth laughed, then gave her wiggling bundle a kiss on the head and set him free. The crowd applauded as she stood to her feet and accepted the envelope. The contestants exited the arena, and the two girls were greeted by their group.

"Congratulations, Beth! Did you hear me cheering for you?" asked James.

Elizabeth took a muddy finger and smeared the tip of his nose. "Yes, I did, little brother. And your cheers helped me win!"

"We'd better get you home and out of those muddy clothes, Elizabeth," said Mrs. Phillips.

For the first time, Elizabeth noticed that McKenzie was as clean as a whistle. Not a mark on her, except for a little mud on her shoes. "How did you stay so clean?" she asked her friend.

"I guess I've had a little more experience than you," Mac laughed.

Then Mr. Jacobs clapped her on the back. In the excitement, Elizabeth had forgotten all about him! "That was great, Elizabeth. I have a feeling you're the kind of girl who always does what she sets out to do!"

Elizabeth shifted nervously from one foot to the other and looked at the ground. She wished the man would leave her alone. "Uh, I guess so," she whispered.

The man leaned in and whispered, "Whether it's catching a pig or solving a mystery, huh?"

Elizabeth jerked her head up and looked at him. The man winked at her and tipped his hat to the group. "I'll see you folks later," he said, and walked away.

A Fishy Clue

As they left the fair, the Phillipses stopped at the Andersons' house to drop James off and give Elizabeth a chance to change clothes. Then they returned to the motel, where the girls headed to the restaurant.

It was 9:45 when Jean Louise greeted the girls. There were still a few scattered customers. "Take a seat, girls, and mind your manners till all the customers are gone," the woman told them.

They sat under the blue marlin. "I'm itching to take that thing off the wall and look behind it! I know we'll find the marbles there," said McKenzie.

Elizabeth's eyes lit with excitement. "I do, too. Hey, what if they are actually inside the fish? Maybe it's hollow!"

The girls continued whispering until it looked like the last customer had left. Just as Jean Louise was about to lock the door, it pushed open, and Mr. Jacobs walked in! Had he been looking for them again?

He looked around, tipping his hat to the girls before greeting Jean Louise. "Pardon me, ma'am. I know it's closing time, but could I trouble you for a tall glass of that wonderful iced tea?"

"Why, certainly. I'll get it for you right now," said the waitress.

While he waited, he looked at the girls. "Fancy meeting you here," he said. "What are you girls doing here so late?"

Elizabeth looked like a deer caught in the headlights. She had no idea how to respond.

McKenzie, thinking fast, eyed the grand piano sitting in the corner of the restaurant. "Uh, Elizabeth plays the piano. Since she's spent the week here, with me, she's hardly gotten to practice. So she's going to practice after everyone leaves."

"That's right. Elizabeth's going to play the piano. Here's your tea, sir," said Jean Louise, handing the man a large Styrofoam cup. Megan had followed her out of the kitchen and had a towel draped over her shoulder.

"I see. I'd love to stay and listen. Would you mind?" the man said.

Elizabeth looked at Mac, then at the old piano. Taking a deep breath, she walked across the room and sat at the bench. Mr. Jacobs dropped into one of the booths and watched. *Why won't he just go away?* she thought. *I don't like to play in front of anybody, and especially not sneaky, low-down cowboys!*

She began to play Mozart's Sonata in C, and then transitioned into a praise song. Before long, she became absorbed in her music, and she played nearly flawlessly for the next several minutes. By the time she had finished, she had almost forgotten anyone else was in the room. She was startled by their applause and cheers, and began to blush.

"I'm impressed," said Jacobs. "Not very many people have a gift like that. 'I will sing and make music to the Lord,' Psalm 27:6."

"Thank you," she whispered, and turned back to the keyboard. *Now he's quoting scripture?* Elizabeth had no idea what to make of this man.

He stood to his feet and tipped his hat. "Thank you for the tea, and for the music. Good night, ladies," he told them, and walked out the door.

As soon as he was out of sight, the girls all sighed with relief. "What are we going to do?" Elizabeth asked. "He's following us. He knows we're on to something."

Jean Louise stopped smacking her gum and said, "You do the only thing you can do. You keep looking, and you beat him to the treasure. Come on, ladies. Let's tear this place apart!"

Megan climbed on the table and hefted the large fish off the wall. The four of them examined it but didn't find any secret compartments or hollow spots. They looked at the wall behind the fish. They examined the floor beneath the fish. They even moved all the booths and benches to make sure there was nothing hidden beneath them.

"What if they're hidden in the stuffing of one of the benches?" Elizabeth asked. She was about ready to tear into a bench with a steak knife when Jean Louise stopped her.

"Whoa, there. This furniture gets replaced every ten years or so. If Emily Marie hid the marbles in one of the benches, they are long gone by now."

Frustrated, the girls sank into one of the booths. Megan looked close to tears as she said, "We might as well hang it up. We'll never find those marbles."

Elizabeth wanted to argue, but she was feeling the same way. Then she remembered her prize money.

"Megan, do you know what I did tonight before I came here?" Elizabeth asked.

"I don't know. What?"

"I caught a pig," Elizabeth said with a giggle.

Megan sat up and said, "You did what?" She looked to McKenzie for confirmation.

"She did," Mac told her. "She caught a pig at the Livestock Show and Rodeo, in front of the entire stadium. And she was covered from head to toe in mud!"

"You're kidding!" Megan laughed at the thought. "You mean Miss Perfect, always-keeps-her-room-clean, never-a-hair-out-of-place Elizabeth was covered in mud?"

"Yep. And she won the prize, too," Mac said.

"Really? What was the prize?" asked Megan.

"It's money. Not much, but I already know how I'm going to spend it," said Elizabeth. "I'm going to buy a saxophone."

"A saxophone?" the two girls asked in unison.

"I didn't know you wanted to play the saxophone," said Megan.

"I don't. But I would love to have someone accompany me on the saxophone. Me on the piano. . .you know. A duet," Elizabeth said.

Slowly Megan realized that Elizabeth wanted to purchase her band instrument for her. "Elizabeth, I can't let you do that."

"Why not? It's my money. I'll spend it however I want," Elizabeth told her.

They were interrupted by Jean Louise. "Girls, I promised your parents I'd have you all home before midnight, and it's almost that time now. We'd better go."

They piled into the woman's car, and within minutes they were pulling up to Elizabeth's house where the girls were going to spend the night. They were surprised to see the lights still on. "Thanks, Jean Louise!" they called from the porch. The woman waved and drove away.

Inside, Elizabeth's mom, dad, and brother were in the living room. James was chattering a mile a minute about spooky houses and greasy pigs and somebody losing marbles. Between sentences, he zoomed the tiny blue car through the air.

"Why are y'all still awake?" Elizabeth asked.

"Someone had too much cotton candy." Her mother nodded to James. "Besides, we wanted to make sure you girls made it home safely."

"Can anyone explain to us what the spooky house is?" asked Mr. Anderson. James was still zooming his car around the room.

"Probably the house of mirrors. Evan's marbles spilled out of his pocket while we were in there."

Mr. and Mrs. Anderson burst into laughter. "So that's what he was talking about when he said Evan lost his marbles! We thought Evan had gone crazy!"

The girls giggled, and the adults stood. "There are snacks in the kitchen, girls. Try not to stay up too late. James, it is way past your bedtime. Come on. Into bed you go."

James obeyed, still zooming his tiny blue Cadillac as he headed down the hallway toward his room. "This is the coolest car I've ever seen. Just look at those fins!"

The girls looked at one another in stunned excitement. "Fins!" they all three called out at once. "The Cadillac Ranch!"

●—●—●

Within the next half hour, e-mails were flying. Alexis had contacted the other Camp Club Girls, and they were expecting Elizabeth and McKenzie to be online around midnight.

Elizabeth's fingers clicked away at the keyboard:

We searched the restaurant. No luck. We wonder if the marbles are hidden at the Cadillac Ranch. Did anyone find information on Mark Jacobs?

Bailey: *The only thing I found on your Roy Rogers is that he's an award-winning rodeo rider. I found his picture, too. You're right! He is handsome.*

Elizabeth: *We can't figure the guy out. One minute he's following us and asking questions. Then he quotes scripture. Either he's a really nice guy, or he's a great crook. I guess we'll see what happens at the Cadillac Ranch tomorrow.*

Kate: *Too bad u can't attach a secret spy camera or recorder to him to see what he's doing and saying when you aren't around. That might help.*

Sydney: *What are you going to do? Just go there and start digging? You might get arrested.*

McKenzie took over the keyboard: *Well what else can we do? Any suggestions?*

Alexis: *What led you to the Cadillac Ranch? I thought we were looking for fins or something. I'm confused.*

Mac typed out the events of the evening, including James's exclamation over his car's fins.

McKenzie: *We plan to visit there tomorrow. I guess we'll look around and see what we can find. Maybe we'll have to go back after dark.*

The girls all signed off, promising to do further research and stay in close contact.

During this time, Megan sat quietly at the kitchen table, observing the exchange. "You need to take a shovel with you tomorrow. I'll be working—as usual."

"How can we take a shovel without everyone seeing it?" asked McKenzie.

Elizabeth eyed the pot of geraniums on the kitchen windowsill. "We can't take a full-sized shovel. But I know what we can take." She stood up and walked to the back door. Flipping on the porch light, she stepped outside.

McKenzie and Megan looked at each other and shrugged their shoulders. They could hear Elizabeth rummaging around on the porch. Finally, they heard their friend call out, "Got it!"

Elizabeth walked back into the kitchen holding a garden spade. "It may take us awhile, but this will definitely dig a hole. Trust me. I've dug plenty of holes with this for my mom's garden."

"That's a great idea, Beth, but Sydney is right. We can't just go out there in broad daylight and dig."

The three girls sat drumming their fingers on the table, trying to think of a solution. "We've got to get out there in the evening when there aren't so many tourists. But how?"

Megan sat up straight. "We could ride our bikes. It's only a couple of miles outside of town."

"Do you know how to get there?" Elizabeth asked her.

"Yeah," the older girl answered. "I even know a shortcut from the church."

"Mac can ride my bike, and I'll ride my mom's," said Elizabeth.

"We've just got to figure out a reason to go to the church tomorrow evening, since it's not a church night," said McKenzie.

"That'll be easy," Megan told her. "Elizabeth's family practically lives at the church, anyway."

The girls talked a little longer, but their conversation was interrupted by yawns. Before long, the three young detectives scooted to bed.

The next morning, the girls slept in. The sun was high in the sky by the time Elizabeth woke to a paper airplane landing on her face. She fluttered her eyes and found James staring at her.

"Mama said to get up if you want to go to the Cadillac Ranch. McKenzie's parents will be here in a little while to pick us up."

Elizabeth rolled over and pulled the covers over her head, but James was persistent.

"Mama said if you get up now, she'll make homemade doughnuts. But if you wait too long, you'll only get cereal."

McKenzie popped up from her pallet on the floor.

"Homemade doughnuts? I love doughnuts," she said sleepily.

Megan stirred from her sleeping bag and said, "Tell your mom we'll be there in a minute, James."

James jumped from his spot on Elizabeth's bed, and she heard him padding down the hallway. Groaning, she forced herself to sit up.

The girls looked at each other, each one wanting a hot doughnut, but none wanting to actually leave bed.

McKenzie finally spoke. "Tomorrow is our last full day here. We go home the next day."

Elizabeth groaned and flopped back down in her bed. "I don't want to think about it. I've gotten used to having you around twenty-four hours a day."

"Y'all, we've got to find those marbles," Megan said, rummaging around in her bag and pulling out her toothbrush.

"Let's review the plan. We'll ride our bikes to the church this evening. And you know a shortcut from there to the Cadillac Ranch?" Elizabeth asked.

Megan nodded.

"It sounds like the perfect plan," said McKenzie. "So why do I have a bad feeling about the whole thing?"

"Riding our bikes two miles out of town doesn't sound great to me, either," said Elizabeth. "But sometimes you've just got to do what you've got to do. And we've got to find those marbles before Mr. Jacobs does."

James banged on the door, hollering, "Mama says come now while the doughnuts are hot!"

"We're coming!" Elizabeth called back. Then she said, "Let's just take this one step at a time. We're going out there today. Maybe we'll be able to dig some. Let's see what happens."

Nodding, the girls stood up and followed the smell of fresh, hot doughnuts.

●—●—●

Elizabeth and McKenzie stared at the row of Cadillacs, noses buried in the ground, tails sticking high in the air. "Cadillac Ranch my foot. This is a Cadillac graveyard!" McKenzie said.

Elizabeth giggled. "Who would think of doing such a thing?"

"Apparently, Chip Lord, Hudson Marquez, and Doug Michaels," Mac replied, referring to the brochure she held. "They are supposed to represent the birth and death of the early model Cadillacs, and an era in American culture. They are buried at the same angle as the Great Pyramid of Giza, in Egypt."

"Groovy," responded Elizabeth, and Mac giggled at the old-fashioned word.

The sun glistened off the shiny metal, and the girls shielded their eyes from the glare. Evan and James were already running in and out of the cars, exclaiming over the bright colors and shapes.

"Well, there's the blue one, third from the end," said Elizabeth. "We might as well take a look."

The girls smiled as they passed another group of tourists. "We'll never get to explore with all these people around taking pictures at every turn," whispered McKenzie.

Elizabeth fingered the garden spade in her purse as they approached the blue Cadillac. "I have an idea. Stand in front of me, and I'll kneel down like I'm inspecting the motor. Watch for people, and tell me when anyone is coming."

McKenzie did as she was told, exclaiming loudly over different features of the car every time a tourist walked by. At one point, she even posed for a picture one of them was snapping.

"What are you doing?" Elizabeth asked her.

"Hiding in plain sight," Mac answered.

"Huh?" Elizabeth grunted, confused.

"If it looks like we're trying to hide what we're doing, people will be suspicious. But if we just act like goofy tourists, no one will suspect a thing!" Mac explained.

"Mac, you don't have to act like a goofy tourist. You are one," Elizabeth said with a laugh.

"Just keep digging," ordered Mac, and Elizabeth obeyed.

All of a sudden, she hit something in the dirt. Something hard. "Mac! I think I've found it!" she whispered.

Mrs. Phillips chose that moment to call, "Girls! Come on. We have several more stops to make today."

Mac stiffened and told Elizabeth, "Quick! Cover it up! My mom's coming over here. We'll have to come back tonight."

Elizabeth frantically replaced the dirt in the hole she'd

dug and slipped the spade back into her purse as Mrs. Phillips approached. "You two sure are fascinated with this blue one. Hey look, Elizabeth, it matches your eyes. I'll tell your dad he needs to buy you a blue car one day."

Elizabeth laughed and replied, "A blue *Cadillac*."

Mrs. Phillips chuckled and began moving toward the car. The two secret sleuths took deep breaths, gave one last look over their shoulders at the loose dirt beneath the motor of the car, and followed her.

Danger in the Dark!

That evening, the girls sat in the Andersons' kitchen acting bored. Mrs. Anderson was putting the last dish in the dishwasher.

"I need to get some exercise," said McKenzie. "All this vacationing and lounging around the pool is making me tired."

"Why don't we ride bikes?" Elizabeth asked.

"That sounds great. But I don't have my bicycle here."

"Why don't you ride mine? That is, if my dear mother will let me ride hers," Elizabeth said, smiling at her mom.

Mrs. Anderson smiled. "That sounds like a wonderful idea. It's a beautiful evening for a bike ride."

"I have an idea. Mom, I left my library book at church last Sunday. Can we ride up there to get it?"

"I suppose. Just stay on the back roads. Don't go on the busy streets," she said. "And why don't you ask Megan to go, too. She needs to get out more."

Within minutes, the plan was under way. The three girls rode their bikes the short distance to the church. When Megan led them on a narrow trail behind the church, Elizabeth said, "What about my library book? We need to stop and get it."

"We'll stop on the way back," Megan called over her

shoulder. "Let's get out there while we still have some light. The church doors will still be open till at least ten. I think the senior high teens are having a volleyball tournament or something there tonight."

"This is so exciting," said Mac. "I can't believe we're actually going to find the marbles."

"We *hope* we're going to find the marbles," Elizabeth corrected. "But I do have a good feeling about this. Something was down there this afternoon when I was digging. And that's the last place your grandmother was, Megan, before she got in the car wreck. Remember, she was serving at a party there so it would have been easy for her to step outside and hide them there. "

The bike trail grew bumpy, and tall ears of corn formed a wall on either side of them.

"Uh, Megs, are you sure you know where you're going?" asked Elizabeth.

"Trust me. It's just a little further," she called over her shoulder.

Sure enough, a few minutes later they pulled into a clearing. Ahead of them was the row of cars, half buried in the ground.

"I had no idea this was so close," said Elizabeth.

"Yeah," agreed McKenzie. "It seemed a lot farther in the car today."

"It is farther when you take the main road. That's why they call it a shortcut!"

The girls stowed their bikes in the tall stalks of corn and surveyed the field before them.

With whispers and giggles of excitement, they started digging through their backpacks, pulling out supplies.

"Where's the other flashlight?" whispered Megan.

"I have it," Mac answered, clicking on the beam.

"Turn it off. You'll run the battery down. We don't need it yet," Megan whispered, and McKenzie turned it off.

"I have the spade and another small shovel," whispered Elizabeth. Then, as an afterthought, she asked, "Why are we whispering? No one is around."

The girls giggled nervously. "I don't know. It just feels like we're supposed to be whispering," answered Mac. The three made their way across the country field to where the ten Cadillacs stood with their rear ends sticking in the air.

Stopping in front of the blue one, they found the place where Elizabeth had dug that afternoon.

"Here it is," Mac whispered. "Megan, you've been working all day. You keep watch while Elizabeth and I dig."

"Okay," the sixteen-year-old answered. Something in her face held a look of hope that made her look much younger than the other two. "Please, God, let the marbles be here."

"I'm surprised they don't have more security here," McKenzie said.

"Why? They're just a bunch of junk cars," Elizabeth pointed out.

"But they could still be vandalized," McKenzie said as she started to dig.

"Guess they're not too concerned," Elizabeth said.

Elizabeth and Mac moved the loose dirt to the side and found the hard object Elizabeth had felt earlier. With grunts and groans, they pulled the object out of its resting place.

"A rock," they all three sighed with disappointment.

"Let's keep digging," Elizabeth said, and she and Mac went back to work. They dug and dug, finding nothing.

Finally, sweat dripping down her brow, Elizabeth realized she had a problem.

"Uh, y'all?"

"Yeah?" the other two answered.

"Remember that soda I drank earlier?"

"Yeah?" they answered again.

"Remember the refill?"

"Uh-huh," came the reply.

"I have to go to the bathroom."

Mac giggled, and Megan sighed.

"I really have to go. Now!"

"Well, go! Nobody can see you," Megan told her.

"I'm not going to the bathroom right here! That's disgusting!" Elizabeth said.

"You could go back to where we parked the bikes," Mac suggested. "But then again, that might be too corny!" She laughed at her own joke, and the other girls snickered.

Elizabeth crossed her legs. "It's getting dark," she whispered.

Mac and Megan kept working.

"Will somebody go with me?"

"No," they both responded.

"Here, take the big flashlight. Mac and I will stay here with the smaller one. Hurry back," Megan said, handing her the larger of the two lights.

Elizabeth dashed toward the direction of the bikes. Only she couldn't actually see the bikes, and there were several little trails that led off the field. She didn't know which one to take. Soon, she couldn't wait any longer, and just followed one of the trails a few feet from the opening. Turning around, she could still see her friends' flashlight beam, and knew she could find her way back to them. Shining her light, she found a place that seemed to offer enough privacy and took care of her business.

Suddenly a flash of headlights flooded the area, and she ducked behind the corn. Her breath caught in her throat as she watched the pickup truck pass on the road in front of the cars and saw the silhouette of the driver, wearing a cowboy hat.

Mr. Jacobs!

Had Megan and Mac seen the truck? She had to warn them! But their flashlight beam had disappeared. Where had they gone? Had they seen the headlights, too?

The truck pulled to the side of the road. Its headlights lit up the small gate before they died down. She heard the sound of the truck door opening. Closing. The beam of another flashlight clicked on.

The new flashlight steadily moved toward the row of upturned cars! She watched, not knowing where to go or what to do. Turning around, she realized she was lost. She had no idea where the bikes were. And the sun had disappeared from the horizon.

The night was black, except for her flashlight.

It can't be too far, she thought. *I think I need to go. . . this way.* Staying low behind the cornstalks, she cupped her hand around her flashlight beam. *Maybe this will keep Jacobs from spotting me.*

Dear God, she prayed, *this was a stupid idea. What were we thinking? Riding out here alone at night. . . God, I'm scared. Please be with Megan and Mac and keep them safe. And please help me to find my way back to them!*

She looked toward the old cars. Only one beam of light. She knew by its brightness it belonged to Mr. Jacobs—the girls had kept the tiny light for themselves. "Where are they?" she whispered. Suddenly the clouds shifted. The moon cast a soft glow on the area.

Then, a rustling sound! She put her fist in her mouth to keep from gasping.

"Elizabeth?" Megan's whisper came through the darkness.

"Meg? Where are you? I got turned around, and I can't find the bikes!" Elizabeth whispered back.

A tiny beam of light flickered on and off, and Elizabeth scooted toward it. She saw the shapes of her two friends, and she let out the breath she hadn't known she was holding. Sliding onto her bike, she commanded, "Let's get out of here!"

The girls pedaled faster and faster, away from the Cadillac Ranch, away from danger. Corn husks slapped their faces and ankles. Elizabeth nearly lost her balance on the bumpy trail, but she kept going.

No one said a word until they approached the lights of the church. The only sounds were the tires on the rough road and the girls' heavy breathing.

Elizabeth spoke first. "What happened back there? I was so scared!"

Mac turned around on her seat. "A couple of minutes after you left, we saw the truck's headlights coming up the road. We thought it would just pass, but we turned off our flashlight just in case. Then, when it stopped, we knew we had to get out of there!"

"We hoped you'd be at the bikes when we got there, but I should have known better. How could you have gotten lost? It's a bare field. Nothing's there!" Megan teased her friend.

"You know how easily I get turned around. When I saw him stop the truck, and then I couldn't find y'all, I just about died. I was so scared!"

"So were we!" Megan and Mac replied.

"When we turned our flashlight off, we couldn't see a thing! Then the clouds shifted, and the moon gave us just enough light to find our way back to the bikes. But you weren't there," Megan continued.

Elizabeth felt a warm feeling and knew that God had sent that moonlight as an answer to her prayer. Then she remembered their reason for going out there in the first place. "Did you find the marbles?" she asked.

Megan kept her eyes on the road but said nothing. Mac silently shook her head.

As they turned onto the street that Elizabeth and Megan called home, they were surprised to see five adults standing in the driveway. None of them looked happy.

Elizabeth watched relief cover her mother's face, and she realized they had been out longer than they'd realized.

"Where have you girls been? It got dark half an hour ago! We've been worried sick!" exclaimed Ruby Smith, first hugging her daughter and then giving her a frustrated look.

The other two sets of parents reached for their own daughters. "You girls had better have a good explanation," McKenzie's father told them.

"Why don't we go inside? I have a feeling this is going to take awhile," said Mr. Anderson.

The three girls filed into the living room, followed by the adults. Evan was sound asleep on the sofa, and Elizabeth assumed James was down the hall, in his own bed.

"Let's go in the kitchen. I'll make some coffee," suggested Mrs. Anderson. The adults sat around the table, leaving the three girls to lean against the counter.

"We're ready when you are. Spill it," said Ruby Smith, looking at her daughter.

Megan took a deep breath and said, "Mom, those marbles are real. And Mark Jacobs is after them. He's been looking for them this whole time, and I think he knows they belong to you and Uncle Jack. You work so hard all the time, and I just thought—"

"That's what this is about? Those silly marbles? Megan Rebecca Smith, I ought to tan your hide! That is the most ridiculous—"

"Excuse me, Ruby, but what's this about Mark Jacobs? He seems like a decent man to me," said Mr. Phillips. He looked to McKenzie. "Would you like to tell me what's going on?"

McKenzie looked at her father and said, "I'm sorry, Daddy. But we think he's a con man. Megan's mother inherited some jewels, but she didn't know it. Now Jacobs is trying to get them before she does."

"Jewels?" he asked. "Megan said you were looking for marbles!"

"Hold on a minute," Elizabeth's father interrupted. "I think we'd better back up and start from the beginning. Elizabeth, why don't you start?"

It took a lot of starting and stopping, but eventually the adults were filled in on the entire account. It was late, and the adults decided to withhold judgment until the next day. McKenzie cast Elizabeth a worried look over her shoulder as she stepped onto the front porch.

Megan kept her head down as she followed her mother to their own front door. When everyone was gone, Elizabeth turned to face her parents. She hated the disappointment she read there.

"We'll talk about this in the morning. There is cold pizza in the refrigerator if you're hungry. Get a snack and go to bed," her father told her, and then joined her mother in their own bedroom. She could hear them talking but couldn't make out any words as she poured herself a glass of milk. She tried to drink it, but the knot in her throat made it difficult to swallow. She was about to place the glass back in the refrigerator when she noticed the e-mail light flashing at the bottom of the computer screen.

Sitting at the desk, she opened her inbox. There was a message from Kate. It read:

Did some research. The Cadillac Ranch has moved. Is now in a different location than it was 30 years ago. You're looking in the wrong place.

The next morning, Elizabeth sat at the kitchen table with her parents, listening to the lecture she knew she deserved. "I can't believe you girls rode out there at night, alone. Why didn't you come to us?"

Elizabeth tried to explain. "I know it was a dumb thing to do. I can't even begin to tell you how sorry I am. I know there's no excuse, but I was only thinking of Megan and her mom. They've had such a hard time since Mr. Smith died, and these marbles would help them so much. And I guess I was afraid you wouldn't take the whole thing seriously."

Her mom and dad looked at one another, then back at her. "Maybe you're right. We might not have taken this seriously," her mom said. "We still see you as our little girl, playing make-believe. But Elizabeth, you can always come to us about anything. There's no excuse for what you did last night."

Elizabeth looked at her hands. She was truly sorry for sneaking around behind their backs.

Her dad spoke up then. "First you sneaked out of your window in a storm. Then you go riding off without telling us where you are. At night! Anything could have happened. I know your intentions were good, but that's no excuse for acting foolish. You're grounded to the house for the next two weeks. But we won't start the punishment until after McKenzie goes home. We know you want to spend as much time with her as possible."

Elizabeth scooted her chair back and threw her arms around her parents' necks. "Thank you so much! I promise I'll never do anything like that ever again!" Then, remembering Kate's e-mail, she said, "Uh, Mom and Dad? There's one more thing I need to talk to you about." She shared the latest discovery, only to be interrupted by her father.

"That's right. I had forgotten about them moving the Cadillac Ranch. I know exactly where it used to be."

"Really?" Elizabeth questioned. "Will you take us there?"

He smiled at his daughter and said, "Of course I will. But it's not that simple. The old location was in a huge wheat field. Trying to find your marbles there would be like looking for a needle in a haystack."

"Dad, you do the driving and leave the rest to me," she told him. Sitting down at the computer, she typed *Cadillac Ranch—original location—pictures* into the search engine.

Sure enough, dozens of pictures popped up. Elizabeth knew she was on the brink of discovery when she noticed something. In each of the pictures, the Cadillacs were painted differently. Some of the pictures even had graffiti covering each of the cars. How in the world was she supposed to figure out which one was the blue one?

She let out a groan just as the phone rang. "Hello?" she spoke into the receiver.

"Elizabeth? It's Mac. Are you in as much trouble as I am?"

"I'm grounded for two weeks. But Mom and Dad said it can wait until after you leave."

"That's good. We leave tomorrow, and I'd hate it if we couldn't spend my last day together. But I have bad news."

Elizabeth braced herself for whatever Mac had to say. But she never would have guessed just how bad that news was. . . .

CHAPTER 12

The Best Vacation Ever

"This morning when I woke up, I heard voices outside our door. I peeked out the window, and my dad was out there talking to Mr. Jacobs. And he was showing him the journals."

Elizabeth nearly dropped the phone. "He what?" she croaked. Visions of the tall cowboy riding off into the sunset holding the bag of marbles flashed through her mind. "Why would he do such a thing?"

McKenzie sighed. "He's convinced that Jacobs is a nice guy. Even after hearing the whole story."

Elizabeth took a deep breath. "Well, we can't do anything about it now. But Mac, listen. After y'all left last night, I had an e-mail from Kate. The Cadillac Ranch has changed locations! We weren't even digging at the right site!"

"You're kidding," said McKenzie with a groan. "What will we do?"

"My dad said he'd take us out there today. I've got pictures of where the cars used to be, but they've been painted over the years. I'll do some more research. Do you think your parents will let you come?"

"I don't know. Let me call you back."

"Okay, but hurry. We've got to get there before Mr. Jacobs does," Elizabeth told her.

Within the hour, the Andersons, Phillipses, and Smiths were all squeezed into the Andersons' van. Heavy, dark clouds were moving in, giving a sense of urgency to the situation.

"The storm looks a ways away. I think we can beat it," Mr. Phillips said. Elizabeth's dad started the car, and they headed toward the old Cadillac Ranch.

Elizabeth, McKenzie, and Megan sat in the backseat of the van. Elizabeth had printed some pictures so they could get an idea of the location. She had even found a picture dated close to the time of Emily Marie's death.

"Why are the cars different colors in the pictures?" asked Megan.

"The cars are repainted every so often. Once, they were all painted pink, in support of breast cancer victims. Tourists are allowed—even encouraged—to paint graffiti on the cars, and every so often they are repainted to offer a fresh canvas," Elizabeth told them.

"So we have no way of knowing which car was blue at the time of my grandmother's death?" asked Megan.

"Not really. This picture is dated the same year, and the blue car is the fourth from the right. Look, it's lined up with this telephone pole, and there are two big oak trees in the background, one on either side of it. Hopefully the telephone pole and the trees are still there," Elizabeth said.

Before long, Mr. Anderson stopped the car on the edge of an endless wheat field. "This will be tough," murmured McKenzie.

Everyone piled out of the car, and immediately James and Evan began chasing one another in and out of the rows of wheat.

Elizabeth looked at her father. "How will we ever do this?" she asked him.

"This is your job. Remember, you said all I had to do was drive." Patting her on the shoulder, he whispered, "I have faith in you."

Elizabeth stood a little taller and held the pictures to the horizon. "Okay, girls, it looks like it's up to us. First things first. Let's find these trees."

Before they knew it, everyone was hunting—even James and Evan. The pictures were passed from person to person, with cries of, "There's a tree!" and "Look! There's an electrical pole!"

They were all distracted with their scavenger hunt and didn't notice a beat-up truck pulling up behind them. An old farmer got out and asked, "Can I help you folks with somethin'?"

Mr. Anderson stepped forward and shook the man's hand. "Yes, sir, there is. We're looking for the original location of the Cadillac Ranch."

The man scratched his head and chuckled. "Well, there's not much to see. But I can take you to it if you'd like," he said.

Elizabeth and McKenzie started jumping up and down. "Really? You'll take us to the exact spot?"

The old farmer shook his head and muttered, "Crazy tourists." He got in his truck, rolled down his window, and said, "Follow me."

A crash of thunder sounded, and the group piled in the car just as the first drops of rain started falling from the sky. The man led them to a spot about a half mile up the road and veered off to the left. Rolling the window down, he pointed to a sign, half covered with wheat. It read ORIGINAL

LOCATION OF THE CADILLAC RANCH. Small posts stuck out of the ground to show where each car had stood. The man waved and drove away.

"I don't believe it," Megan whispered.

Thank You, God, Elizabeth prayed silently. *Please let us find the jewels. Marbles. Whatever they are, Lord, please help us find them.*

The three girls climbed out of the van, but the adults didn't want to get wet. Mr. Phillips handed McKenzie a shovel through the open window. They were splattering through the mud when they realized Ruby Smith was on their heels.

"I'm going to help. If those marbles are real, I want to be there when they are found," the woman told them.

Elizabeth smiled, reached into her purse, and handed her the spade.

They located the fourth post from the right and started digging. The rain softened the earth, making the digging easier. And messier.

Thunder continued crashing, but the four females paid no attention. They were so focused on their task that they didn't notice a large pair of mud-covered cowboy boots approaching.

"May I give you a hand?" Mark Jacobs's voice spoke over the sound of the rain.

Startled, Ruby looked up at him and continued digging. The three girls weren't sure how to respond to his presence and stopped what they were doing.

Gently, the man took the large shovel from McKenzie and started digging on the opposite side of the post. His muscles took the shovel deeper into the ground than the girls had been able to dig, and after a couple of scoops, the shovel revealed an old, small tin cash box. Ruby's mouth dropped open, and she looked up at the man.

"I bet this belongs to you," he said.

The woman reached down and took the box from the shovel. Her mud-covered hands shook as she opened it. Inside was a velvet bag. Inside that were some papers and a smaller cloth bag with a drawstring tie.

By this time, Elizabeth's and McKenzie's parents had joined them. No one spoke as Ruby Smith opened the bag her mother had buried so long ago. She emptied its contents into her hands, and twelve of the most beautiful, brightly colored marbles spilled out.

"Oh!" the woman cried. "Oh, Mama!"

Megan knelt in the mud beside her mother and hugged her as they both wept.

The rest of the group decided to give them privacy and headed back to the van. Jacobs turned to go, but Ruby called out, "Wait! I have so many questions. Where are you going?"

The tall cowboy smiled and said, "We'll have plenty of time to talk later. Right now, you enjoy this moment with your daughter and her friends." He tipped his hat and left.

Without warning, the rain stopped and the sun broke through the clouds. The marbles in Ruby's hands cast a brilliant glow on her face as she looked at her daughter. "We're going to be okay," she whispered.

●—●—●

The group sat around the table at the Big Texan Steak Ranch, drinking in the exchange between Ruby Smith and Mark Jacobs. Even Jean Louise, who was their waitress, had broken the rules and pulled a chair up to the table.

"I can't believe Foster Wilson was your uncle. I never met

him, though I do remember Mama talking about a nice man she wanted me and Jack to meet," Ruby told the man sitting across from her.

"It's as much of a surprise to me as it is to you. I always knew Uncle Foster fell in love here in Amarillo. I just never knew the whole story," Mr. Jacobs responded. He looked around the table, and his eyes rested on Elizabeth. "I knew you were on to me, and I'm sorry I made you nervous. When I realized you were after the same thing I was, I just figured you were some detective wannabe. You were always one step ahead of me, though. When I figured out you really knew what you were doing, I began to follow you. Sorry if I scared you."

"That's okay. I'm sorry I thought you were a con m—"

"Elizabeth!" her mother stopped her.

Mr. Jacobs tilted his head back and roared. "It's okay, Sue. She had every right to believe I was a con man."

Everyone laughed this time. Then Ruby spoke again.

"I've given this a lot of thought, Mark, and my brother, Jack, and I have talked about it on the phone. He agrees with me, and I don't want to hear any arguments. There are twelve marbles, and we're going to split them. Jack and I will take six and the other six belong to you," Ruby said.

"Oh no, Ruby, I couldn't, now that I know the whole story. Those were a gift to your mother. I wouldn't dream of taking them," Jacobs replied.

"Now Mark Jacobs, you listen. Your uncle would have wanted you to have them as much as he wanted me to have them. You can argue with me all you want, but I'll get my way. Each marble is worth close to one hundred thousand dollars. We can certainly afford to share them," Ruby argued.

Jacobs opened his mouth, but Ruby cut him off. "Not another word!" she said.

The handsome cowboy leaned back in his chair and grinned. "How do you know what I was going to say?" he asked.

"You were going to argue with me, I know that," the woman told him.

"No, ma'am. I know better than to argue with you; I have the feeling that once your mind is made up, there's no changing it."

"You're right about that," Ruby told him. The two bantered back and forth as if no one else were in the room.

McKenzie nudged Elizabeth under the table, then whispered, "I don't know why she's giving him the marbles. When they get married, they'll belong to both of them."

The two girls giggled. "Let's not rush things," Elizabeth whispered back. "But they do make a nice couple, don't they?"

They turned their attention back to Ruby and the cowboy. "So what were you going to say?" Ruby asked coyly.

Jacobs looked her in the eye and said, "I was going to say that I came here looking for a treasure. I believe I may have found one, whose worth is far more than rubies. And her name. . .is Ruby."

The group applauded, then Jean Louise began taking their orders.

Elizabeth focused her attention on Megan, who was smiling and watching her mother. "You look happy," she told her friend.

Megan turned to Elizabeth and McKenzie. "It just feels so good to see Mom smile. It's been a long time since I've seen her so happy. And it's all thanks to the two of you and the Camp Club Girls."

Elizabeth glanced at Megan's mom, who was laughing at something Jacobs had said. "I'm not sure if we can take the credit for making your mom smile. I think that goes to a certain handsome cowboy," she told her friend.

Megan laughed. "He may have something to do with it, but the sadness is gone from her face. Now she won't have to work so hard all the time. Now she doesn't have to worry as much about paying the bills every month. And I owe it all to the two of you and your excellent sleuthing skills."

"I just wish we didn't have to leave as soon as we finish our lunch here," said McKenzie. Then, reaching into her backpack, she said, "Oh! Before I forget. . .these belong to Jean Louise."

She pulled out the journals. Then she turned again to Megan. "Thank you for letting me help solve the marble mystery. This has been the best vacation ever!"

●—●—●

Elizabeth sat at the kitchen table, chin propped on her hand, flipping through a library book. She loved to read, but reading was all she had done during the past week. One more week, and her grounding would be over.

"Hello, princess. What are you reading?" her father asked as he came into the kitchen.

"It's a book about an Amish girl named Rachel Yoder. I'm a little over halfway through," she told him.

He pulled out a chair and sat down across from her. "Did I ever tell you how proud I am of you?" he asked.

Elizabeth smiled but said nothing. He had told her many times.

"You are like those marbles you found—rare and precious.

I'm proud of you for being so determined to help Megan and her mom," he told her.

"It was kind of fun, looking back on it. Maybe I'll be a detective someday," she said with a laugh.

He leaned forward and rested his arms on the table. "Ruby told me that you offered to use your prize money to buy Megan's band instrument. That was very generous of you."

Elizabeth blushed. She hadn't meant for others to find out. "I didn't need the money, and they did. It was no big deal."

"God loves a cheerful giver, you know," he told her, reaching out to pat her hand.

"I know—2 Corinthians 9:7," she said.

Mr. Anderson smiled at his daughter before standing up and mussing her hair. "Like I said, princess, I'm proud of you. By the way, your computer screen shows that you have e-mail waiting."

Elizabeth wasted no time in moving to the computer and clicking on her e-mail. It was from Alexis, addressed to all the Camp Club Girls.

I'm going to the London Bridge! Did you all know they moved it, and it's not in London anymore? It is at Lake Havasu, Arizona. Isn't that the craziest thing you've ever heard?

My grandmother is going to be a guest speaker at the London Bridge Festival there, at the end of October. And she's invited me to go along! I'm so excited!

Elizabeth read back through the e-mail a couple of times. *Lake Havasu. Lake Havasu.* Why did that name sound familiar?

Suddenly she remembered. "Uh, Dad?" she called over her shoulder. "You know that convention or whatever that you go to at the end of October every year? Isn't that at Lake Havasu, Arizona?"

"Yes, it is. It's during the London Bridge Festival there. Why do you ask?"

Elizabeth felt the excitement mounting inside her. She was almost afraid to ask her next question. "Any chance I could go with you this year?"

"Funny you should ask that. I've been thinking about taking the whole family. I think you'd enjoy it."

Elizabeth lunged from her chair and threw her arms around her father's neck. "Oh, thank you, Daddy! Thank you, thank you, thank you!"

Surprised, he laughed and returned the hug. "Whoa! You're welcome! You want to tell me what this is about?"

"I will in a minute. First I have to e-mail Alexis!"

Camp Club Girls

Sydney's
OUTER
BANKS
BLAST

Sydney's Ghost Story

"It wasn't a UFO," said Sydney Lincoln as she and Bailey walked along the beach. "There's a logical explanation for it."

Bailey Chang disagreed. "I looked out at the ocean at two o'clock this morning, and there it was. It had red flashing lights, and it was hovering over the water. It spun around and around, and then *poof*, it was gone. It was a UFO!"

Sydney bent and picked up some small stones from the sand. "What were you doing up at two o'clock?" she asked as she walked to the water's edge.

"I couldn't sleep in a strange bed," Bailey told her.

Sydney waited a few seconds before skipping a stone across the waves. "I think what you saw was just a coastguard training exercise or something."

"It was a UFO," Bailey insisted. "I'm sure of it."

"I don't believe in UFOs," said Sydney, skipping another stone. "Anyway, I'm glad your parents let you come. Ever since camp, I've wanted to show you the ocean."

Sydney had invited her friend Bailey to spend a week at her grandparents' beach house on the Outer Banks of North Carolina. Sydney loved to escape the activity of her home in Washington DC for the peace and quiet of the long, narrow string of barrier islands that separated the Atlantic Ocean from several sounds off the edge of North Carolina.

Bailey was always willing to accept an invitation to anywhere. She couldn't wait to leave her hometown of Peoria, Illinois, and see the world. Now, in the early morning sunshine, Bailey was getting her first taste of the salty ocean air as she and Sydney walked together through the sand.

"It's not exactly what I expected," Bailey said.

She had imagined that the Atlantic Ocean would look vastly different from the huge Great Lake that bordered her home state. In fact, the ocean *was* very different—much larger and far grander—but just not as different as Bailey had hoped for. She was often disappointed when real life didn't match up to her imagination.

"The ocean sort of looks like Lake Michigan," she said. "Lake Michigan also has waves, and it's so big that you can't see to the other side."

She picked up a handful of sand and let it sift through her fingers. "This beach looks like it's not taken care of. In Chicago, a tractor pulls a machine that combs the sand and keeps it nice and clean. There aren't weeds and stuff sticking up, like here. And they test the water to make sure it's not polluted."

Sydney kicked at the sugar-fine sand with her bare feet.

"Nobody tests the water here," she said. "It's clean. I swim in it all the time." She waded into the ocean a few yards offshore.

"Come on!" she told Bailey. "Check it out."

Bailey hesitated. "What about jellyfish and sharks?" she asked.

"If I see some, I'll introduce you," Sydney said, joking.

Bailey rolled the legs of her khaki pants over her knees. Then she tiptoed into the breakers. All at once, she felt the world between her toes as she imagined thousands of miles between herself and the nearest shore.

Sydney and Bailey had met at Discovery Lake Camp where they bunked in Cabin 12 with four other girls: Alexis Howell from Sacramento, California; Elizabeth Anderson from Amarillo, Texas; McKenzie Phillips from White Sulphur Springs, Montana; and Kate Oliver from Philadelphia, Pennsylvania. The Camp Club Girls, as they called themselves, were the best of friends. They loved to explore, and they'd become quite good at solving mysteries together. When they weren't at summer camp, the girls kept in touch by chatting on their Camp Club Girls website, sending instant messages and e-mails, and even by phone and cell phones.

"I still think it was a UFO," said Bailey, splashing in the water. "I'm sure that it wasn't an airplane, so what else could it be?"

"Oh, I don't know," Sydney answered. She added with a fond grin, "Maybe your imagination?"

As the girls waded and splashed in the water, only one other person was in sight, and he kept a very safe distance away from them.

"Who's that?" Bailey asked, pointing a shell she'd picked up toward the boy.

"I think his name is Drake or something," Sydney said. "He's kind of different. I see him alone on the beach sometimes. But it seems whenever people show up, he just kind of disappears."

"He's about your age, it looks like," Bailey said, squinting to see him better. "Looks like he's kind of cute, too."

"I don't know how anyone can tell if he's cute or not," Sydney said. "He always keeps his head down, digging around in the sand."

"What's he looking for? Shells?" Bailey asked.

"I dunno," Sydney said, shrugging. "It seems whenever he picks up something, it's bigger than shells, though. Some friends of mine who live here all the time, the Kessler twins, say he's a relative of the Wright Brothers. Remember where we drove across the causeway? The Wright Brothers did their famous flying around there."

"Well, that's neat! To be related to the Wright Brothers!" Bailey exclaimed.

Sydney waded out of the ocean and stood on the shore. She watched Bailey scoop water into her hands, smell it, and then carefully stick her tongue in the water.

"It tastes sort of like potatoes boiled in salt water," Bailey observed.

"Whatever you say," Sydney answered. Her wet legs were caked up to her knees with sand, and against her chocolate-colored skin, the sand looked like knee socks. She bent over and brushed it off. "Let's take a walk up the shore," she said.

Bailey hurried out of the water and fell into step alongside her friend. The boy saw them coming, and he walked quickly on ahead of them. After they had gone about a hundred feet along the beach, Bailey's right foot landed on something hard. "Ouch!" she said.

Sydney, who was a few steps ahead, stopped and turned around to see what was the matter. "What's wrong?" she asked. "Crab got your toe?"

Bailey jumped. "Where?"

"Where what?"

"Where's a crab?"

"I didn't see a crab," Sydney answered. "I just wondered if

you got pinched by one."

"No," Bailey told her. "I stepped on something."

Sydney explored the sand where Bailey stood. "Do you have crabs in Lake Michigan?"

"We have crayfish," Bailey answered. "I don't know if they live on the beach or if they're just bait that fishermen leave behind, but I've seen them there a couple of times. They're brown and ugly, and they have big claws. They kind of look like lobsters."

Sydney saw a white bump protruding from the sand. She reached down and pulled it up. It was a long, slender bone, a rib bone, maybe, from a wild animal, or possibly left from a beachfront barbeque. Tiny bits of dried flesh clung to its underside. Sydney held it up and showed it to Bailey. "This is what you stepped on," she said. "It's a bone."

"Eeeewwww!" said Bailey. "Where do you think it came from?"

"Oh, I don't know," Sydney teased. "Maybe from the body of an old sailor who died at sea. They call part of the Outer Banks the Graveyard of the Atlantic, you know."

"Eeeewwww!" Bailey said again. "Are there really dead sailors floating around out there?"

"Oh sure," Sydney said matter-of-factly. "Not to mention the ones from the ghost ship."

Bailey shuddered. "Ghost ship! What ghost ship?"

"The *Carroll A. Deering*," Sydney replied. She tossed the bone into the water and walked on with Bailey at her side.

"The story of the *Carroll A. Deering* is really spooky," Sydney went on. "I don't know if I should tell it to you. You might be too afraid." She looked at Bailey and grinned.

"I will not!" Bailey protested. "I'm not scared of anything."

"Well, okay then," Sydney answered. "But if you can't sleep tonight, don't blame me."

She stopped and picked up a stick at the ocean's edge. Frothy white fingers of water washed across the beach, scrabbling at the firm wet sand. Sydney used the stick to write Beware of UFOs on the gritty, light tan canvas. Then she tossed the stick back to the ocean. The girls walked on, leaving two sets of footprints behind them.

"The *Carroll A. Deering* was a tall ship, a schooner," Sydney began. "Pirates used several types of sailing ships. The ships they used had to be fast and strong. The *Carroll A. Deering* was bigger than most schooners. It had five tall masts with billowy sails—"

"I know exactly what you're talking about," Bailey interrupted. "Those kind of tall ships came to Navy Pier in Chicago last summer. Of course, they weren't old ones. They were only made to look like the old ones. Mom, Dad, my sister, Trina, and I went to check them out. They looked really old, and we even got to sail on one of them out on the lake."

"Cool," said Sydney. "So, since you've been *on* a tall ship, you can imagine what it was like to be a sailor on the *Carroll A. Deering* back in 1921. Imagine that it's the middle of winter. Some coastguardsmen are looking out at the ocean, sort of like we are now. They're about a hundred miles south of here near the Cape Hatteras Lighthouse, down by Diamond Shoals."

"What's that?" asked Bailey. She carefully stepped through the sand watching for bones and other hidden objects.

"What's what?"

"Diamond Shoals."

"It's a bunch of sandbars just off the coast of the Outer Banks, down at the southern end," Sydney replied. "Anyhow, that's where they saw it."

"The ghost ship?" Bailey asked. Just saying the words sent a little shiver up her spine.

"The ghost ship—the *Carroll A. Deering*," Sydney answered. "There she was, half washed up on one of the shoals, with her sails still opened wide and flapping in the wind. The ocean was pushing at her from behind. Her prow, that's the front end of the ship, was scraping against some rocks in the sand. *Scrape. . . scrape. . .*" As Sydney said the words, she brushed the tips of her fingers along the side of Bailey's arm.

"Stop it!" Bailey said. "You're spooking me out."

"I thought nothing scared you," Sydney answered. "Maybe I shouldn't tell you the rest."

A seagull swept over Bailey's head. It dove and snatched a small fish out of the ocean. "Go on," she said tentatively. "I want to hear."

"It was a foggy, cold, misty morning," Sydney continued, "and the sea was rough. The men of the Coast Guard knew it would be really hard getting to the wreck, but they had to, because they knew that the crew was in danger. So they got into their heavy wooden rowboat, and they rowed through the boiling waves toward the shoals."

"But it was the middle of winter," said Bailey.

"So?" Sydney asked.

"You said that the waves were boiling, and if that's true, it was summertime. You're making this up, aren't you?"

"Bailey!" Sydney protested. "It was a figure of speech. The sea was rough. The waves were rolling *like* boiling water. That's all. The ocean never gets hot enough to boil, and this is a true story. You can ask anyone on the Outer Banks, and they'll tell you—it's true."

Bailey stopped in the sand and let the edge of the ocean tickle her toes. "Okay," she conceded.

"So anyway," said Sydney. "They got into their big rowboat, and they rowed out to the *Carroll A. Deering*. When they reached her, they climbed up onto her deck."

"How'd they climb onto it?" Bailey wondered. "Did they have a ladder? Weren't the waves too rough?"

"I don't know. They were the coastguardsmen, and they know how to climb up on decks and stuff." Sydney swatted at a deerfly that landed on her elbow. "And when they got up on the deck, it was eerily quiet except for the waves lapping at the sides of the ship and that awful *scrape. . .scrape. . .*"

Bailey pulled away as Sydney's long fingers reached for her arm.

"Ahoy!" Sydney yelled.

Bailey jumped.

"Did I scare you?"

"I just didn't expect you to yell, that's all," said Bailey. "And why did you?"

"That's what the coast guard yelled," Sydney said. "They stood on the deck, and they yelled, 'Ahoy there! Is anyone here?' But nobody answered. So they searched the deserted deck, and the only sounds they heard were the echoes of their own footsteps."

"Don't forget the waves and the scraping," Bailey interjected.

"And the waves and the scraping," said Sydney. "And after looking around the top deck, they went down into the center of the ship, and then they opened the door to the crew's quarters. And do you know what they found?" Sydney stopped. She looked at Bailey and grinned.

"Stop playing with me," Bailey said. "What did they find?"

"Nobody," said Sydney. "There was no one there. The beds had all been slept in, and everything was shipshape, except that eleven crewmen and their stuff were gone."

"Gone?" Bailey wondered.

"Just like that. Disappeared. Then the coastguardsmen went to check out the galley. There was food standing out like someone had been preparing a meal, only nobody had eaten anything. The table was all set with plates, cups, and silverware, but nothing had been touched. So the men checked out the officers' quarters next. The beds had been slept in, and the officers' boots were on the floor next to their beds, but nobody was there. Their personal stuff was gone and so was the ship's log, the navigating instruments, all of it—gone."

"So where did everybody go?" Bailey asked.

"Nobody knows," Sydney answered. "It's a big mystery around here. It was like they vanished into thin air. The sailors were never found. The shoals are near enough to shore that something should have washed up, if not their bodies, then some of their belongings, but nothing ever did—"

Sydney's story was interrupted by a powerful, rhythmic noise. All at once, a swirling cloud of sand covered Sydney and Bailey as something huge and brown rushed past them.

Bailey screamed. She gripped Sydney's arm. "A horse!" she cried.

In the swirling dust, she saw a muscular brown stallion galloping on ahead of them. Its black mane stood on end as it

147

raced against the wind.

Sydney caught her breath. The horse had frightened her as much as it had Bailey. She wondered if God was having a good laugh, getting even with her for trying to scare Bailey with the ghost story of the *Carroll A. Deering*.

"It's a wild horse," she said. "Probably one of the mustangs."

"What mustangs?" Bailey asked.

"Usually they're not this far south," Sydney told her, "and they don't typically come near people. They're wild horses— they don't belong to anyone. They wander as free as any other wild animal around here. I'm pretty used to seeing them. They've lived on the Outer Banks for at least four hundred years, so people who live here don't pay much attention to them. They're another mystery of the Outer Banks. No one knows for sure how they got here."

"Oh great," said Bailey. "The sailors disappeared and nobody knows where they went. The wild horses showed up, but nobody knows how they got here. And this morning I saw a UFO.

"What kind of a place is this, Sydney? First you tell me a story about a ghost ship, and then a wild horse comes galloping by almost close enough to touch. You know, this sort of reminds me of *The Legend of Sleepy Hollow* where the headless horseman comes dashing out of nowhere."

"You never know," said Sydney. "We might have a headless horseman roaming around here, too. The Outer Banks is loaded with folklore about all kinds of stuff. It's even known for pirates like Captain Kidd, Calico Jack, and Blackbeard. They all walked along this beach once upon a time. Who knows, maybe they still do."

"Do you believe in ghosts?" Bailey asked.

Before Sydney could answer, a small ghost crab popped out of the sand and skittered toward the girls. It stopped briefly and looked at them through two black eyes set atop its head like periscopes sticking up from a submarine.

"Maybe," said Sydney, "and maybe not."

CHAPTER
2

The Disappearing Captain

The girls left the beach and walked to Corolla Village and the Currituck Beach Lighthouse. It was one of Sydney's favorite places, and she wanted to show it to Bailey. Something was wonderfully mysterious about the way the lighthouse rose from the trees and almost touched the sky. Its weathered red bricks sat tightly atop each other, forming rows around and around. The bricks stopped at an iron-framed lookout. The lookout encircled the lantern house, the highest part of the tower. There, inside a giant glass dome, was the powerful beacon of light that swept across ocean and sound.

Not far from the tower, nestled in a grove of trees, was a small lightkeeper's house. It had a steep red roof and white paint. The place was a gift shop where tourists could buy everything from T-shirts to figurines. Its wide front porch was empty but for a pair of old wooden rocking chairs that often rocked alone in the wind.

Bailey and Sydney sat in the chairs looking up at the tower. Bailey nervously sipped the root beer that she'd bought at a little post office and convenience store nearby.

"You have to at least try," Sydney said.

"But I'm afraid of heights," Bailey answered. "You know

that, Syd. In fact, if I could have, I would have walked here from Peoria instead of taking a plane." She swirled the root beer around in its plastic bottle.

"But you got on the airplane, and you got here in one piece," Sydney pointed out. "The next step is to climb to the top of the lighthouse."

Bailey glanced toward a short line of tourists waiting at the entrance. "How tall is it, anyway?"

"Not that tall," Sydney answered. She wrapped a napkin around the bottom of her ice-cream cone and licked the melting vanilla custard as it dribbled down the sides.

"How tall?" Bailey asked again.

"What difference does it make?" said Sydney.

"How tall!" Bailey demanded.

"I think two hundred fourteen steps to the top!"

"That's a lot."

"The Statue of Liberty has three hundred fifty-four steps," Sydney added. "You're always saying you want to go to New York and climb the Statue of Liberty. Think of this as your training. Once you've climbed the lighthouse, Lady Liberty will be a piece of cake."

"I dunno." Bailey sighed.

"And what about the Eiffel Tower?" Sydney went on. "You want to go to Paris and climb the Eiffel Tower. You told me that. And the Eiffel Tower is a whole lot scarier than the Currituck Beach Lighthouse."

"I guess so," Bailey agreed.

By now, Sydney had finished eating her custard and chomped on the cone. "Come on, Bailey," she said. "If you don't face your fears, you'll never climb the Statue of Liberty, or the Eiffel Tower either."

"I suppose you're right," Bailey said. She gulped down the rest of her root beer, got up, and tossed the empty bottle into a trash can. "Let's go."

"Go where?" Sydney answered.

"Let's climb to the top of the lighthouse before I chicken out."

The girls followed a curving brick path to the lighthouse entrance. A small blue sign sat in front of the six concrete steps that led to the front door. It said: PLEASE WAIT HERE TO CLIMB. A family with three boys, all of them younger than Bailey and Sydney, stood waiting in line. The oldest one shoved his little brother and knocked him to the ground.

"Trevor!" his mother shouted. "Why did you push your brother?"

"He called me a name," Trevor said.

"I did not!" said the little brother, getting up and standing next to his mom. "I want to go home."

"Behave!" said the dad.

Just then a gray-haired gentleman came from behind the lighthouse. He walked toward the family, looking as if he'd stepped off a page in a history book. He wore a blue captain's cap, and his face was framed with a neat gray beard. Although the weather was hot, he wore an old-fashioned blue wool officer's coat with shiny brass buttons and a name tag that read CAPTAIN SWAIN.

As Sydney and Bailey watched, the captain stopped in front of the boys. He opened his left fist and showed them four silver coins. "Spanish doubloons," he announced.

The boys gathered to see the treasure in the captain's hand. "Is this your first trip to the Outer Banks?" the captain asked.

"Yeah," the boys answered in unison.

"Then you don't know about the pirates," said the captain.

"What pirates?" Trevor asked. He grabbed Captain Swain's hand and pulled it closer to get a better look at the coins.

The old man smiled and looked Trevor straight in the eyes. "Blackbeard," he whispered.

Trevor stepped back.

"Blackbeard the pirate used to hide out on this very land," the captain said mysteriously. "He and his crew attacked ships at sea, robbed them, and brought their treasures back here to the Outer Banks. And these coins, my little friends, are some of the treasure that Blackbeard stole."

The boys' eyes grew big. They were so busy studying the doubloons that they didn't even notice when a group of visitors left the lighthouse.

"You're up next," Captain Swain told the family. "And when you get to the top, look out in the ocean as far as you can see. Maybe you'll spy Blackbeard's ship."

"Blackbeard doesn't exist," the older boy said. "He died a long time ago, and your coins are probably fakes."

"Trevor!" his mother scolded.

"Now, would I tell a tale?" said the captain. "Sure Blackbeard's dead, but some say his ghost haunts the sea while he and his crew sail on their ghost ship. You know about the ghost ships, don't you?"

The boys shook their heads.

"Then visit the museum down in Hatteras," the captain replied. "Graveyard of the Atlantic, it's called. They'll tell you all about Blackbeard and the ghost ships. You'll find a brochure inside." He pointed to the front door. Then, as the family disappeared into the entrance, Captain Swain turned to the girls. "Aren't you going with your family?" he asked.

"Oh, we're not with them," Sydney replied. "We're next in line."

The captain looked surprised. "How old are you young ladies?"

"Thirteen," said Sydney. She noticed the captain's sparkling blue eyes.

"I'm nine," Bailey announced.

"Oh dear," said the captain. "Young people thirteen and under have to be accompanied by an adult. I'm afraid you won't be able to climb the lighthouse."

Bailey breathed a sigh of relief.

"But I'm *from* here!" Sydney protested. "Well, I'm not actually from here, but my grandparents have a beach house in Corolla Light. I visit them every year."

"Ah, the resort community," said the captain. He shook his head sadly. "I rarely get there. It's too crowded, and there's far too much traffic on the highway. This is the *real* Corolla, you know. This tiny village was here long before Corolla Light or any of the other subdivisions."

"I know," said Sydney, "but can't we please climb the lighthouse? My friend Bailey is trying to overcome her fear of heights."

The captain winked at Bailey. "So you're afraid of heights, are you? Well, we need to do something about that. The view from the top is outstanding. On one side there's the Atlantic Ocean, on the other side Currituck Sound."

Bailey's heart sank. She didn't really want to climb to the top of the lighthouse no matter how beautiful the view.

Captain Swain scratched his beard.

"I'll tell you what," he said. "I'll take you to the top. And, Bailey, you'll be fine. There's nothing to be afraid of. Nothing at all." He looked up at the tower, and Sydney noticed his mouth curl into a wistful smile.

Suddenly the front door burst open. Trevor's little brother scuttled out with his father close behind. "I am *not* being difficult," the boy shouted. "I don't want to climb those curvy steps. They're scary!"

His mother and brothers came out, too.

"Chicken!" Trevor taunted. He stood with his hands on his hips. "I wanted to go to the top, and now you've wrecked everything!"

"Let's go," said Trevor's dad. "I've had enough of this."

The mother grabbed the smaller boy's hand, and the family rushed to the parking lot.

"When justice is done, it brings joy to the righteous but terror to evildoers," said Captain Swain.

"What?" Sydney asked.

"Nothing," replied the captain. "Just God and me talking out loud. Looks like it's our turn to climb."

When they went inside, Bailey noticed how cool and stuffy the lighthouse felt. An ancient brick wall circled them, and the narrow space smelled old. Sunlight streamed through several tall, narrow windows up high. In the center was a green spiral staircase that reminded Bailey of a loosely coiled snake. Its metal stairs went up and up. When Bailey looked to where they led, she felt dizzy. She hesitated, afraid to take the first step.

Captain Swain seemed to know how she felt. " 'I can do all things through Him who strengthens me,' " he said.

Sydney gave him a quizzical look.

"Just God and me talking again," the captain announced.

Sydney knew that Bible verse from camp. It had given her courage when she was afraid.

"I want you to go first, Bailey," said the captain. "Your friend here—what's your name?" he asked, turning to Sydney.

"Sydney Lincoln," Sydney replied.

"Sydney Lincoln and I will be right behind you. We'll take very good care of you all the way. There's nothing to worry about. Absolutely nothing. I climbed these stairs a lot—back in the day."

The captain's voice echoed inside the tower. It seemed to drift all the way to the top and then disappear.

"I'll watch every step you take," Sydney told her. "You'll be fine. I promise."

Tentatively, Bailey put her right foot on the bottom step. She looked down to make sure that her shoes were tied. She didn't need to trip over any loose laces. Then she breathed deeply and whispered, "'I can do all things through Him who strengthens me.'"

She put her left foot on the first step, and then Bailey Chang was on her way. She was ready to conquer her fear of heights and tackle all 214 steps. "One. Two. Three. Four." She counted each step unwaveringly, bravely marching upward. But then she made the mistake of looking down. The stairs weren't solid. They had holes, like Swiss cheese, and when Bailey looked down at the fifty or so stairs she'd already climbed, she felt sick to her stomach. She stopped and Sydney almost tripped over her.

"Bailey! What?" Sydney wondered.

"I can't," Bailey whispered. "I'm afraid."

"Just move!" said Sydney. "This staircase is only wide

enough for one person, and right now you've got us stuck here."

Bailey gripped the railings with both hands. Her feet wouldn't move. She was afraid to look up and afraid to look down. Her mind drifted to a strange place where she imagined she was the main character in a ghost story. She was stuck forever on that one step, an eerie mist that visitors sensed as they climbed to the top. Bailey Chang, Ghost of the Currituck Beach Lighthouse.

"Bailey." The captain's calm voice startled her. She grasped the railings even tighter. "I'm right here with you," he said. "I won't let anything happen to you. We're on our way now. You can do it. Just keep telling yourself that."

Bailey's heart slammed in her chest. Her mouth felt like sandpaper. She couldn't speak.

"Just one step, Bailey," said the captain. "Take one more step."

Bailey's feet moved up to the next step, whether she wanted them to or not.

"That's good," said the captain. "Now, one more."

Bailey felt Sydney close behind her. She decided if she fell backward onto her friend, and Sydney fell, too, the captain was strong enough to catch them both. So Bailey took the next step, and the next, and she kept going. Whenever she got to a landing and one of the tall, narrow windows, Bailey avoided looking out. She wouldn't look down or up either. She just concentrated on one step at a time.

" 'I can do all things through Him who strengthens me,' " she murmured.

As she climbed the last steps, Bailey noticed a small landing and an old wooden door that stood wide open. She couldn't see where it led, but from where she stood Bailey caught a glimpse of blue sky and puffy white clouds on the other side of it. She took the last step to the top and then turned away, refusing to look beyond the door.

"You did it!" Sydney exclaimed. She stepped onto the landing and hugged her friend, but Bailey stood frozen.

"I'm not going out there," Bailey said. "I don't even want to see."

The captain stood between Bailey and the door. "It's your decision," he said. "But someday you might regret that you didn't. You might be sorry that fear got in your way."

Bailey swallowed hard.

"Come on, Bailey," Sydney coaxed. "Do you want to be an old lady telling your grandkids how scared you were? What kind of an example will that set?"

Bailey turned around. Beyond the captain's broad shoulders, she saw nothing but sky and clouds. Then, slowly, Captain Swain stepped aside. Bailey suddenly saw the tops of trees and, in the distance, the Atlantic Ocean. She felt like she was back in the airplane flying over North Carolina. But this time, if she chose to, she could step outside onto a narrow, open platform that was rimmed by a thick iron railing.

The captain stepped outside. "I won't let anything happen to you," he said. "Sydney Lincoln, would you like to join me out here?"

Sydney's heart did a little flutter. She would never admit that she was scared, too. She had never climbed to the top of the lighthouse, and it was higher than she had imagined. Still, she wouldn't make Bailey more afraid than she already was.

Bravely, Sydney stepped through the door. She leaned against the captain and felt his strong arm holding her steady.

"It's not so bad, Bailey," she said, holding on to the railing. "Come on, we'll help you."

The captain held out his hand.

The image of herself as an old woman flashed through Bailey's mind. She heard herself say, "When I was little, I *almost* went out that door."

Bailey took the captain's hand, and then nothing stood between her and the world but the black iron railing. Her stomach churned, but she inched along the lookout with her friends. They rounded the bend. Now, instead of seeing the ocean, they could see the sound—the strip of water between the Outer Banks' island and the shore of North Carolina.

"I knew you could do it, Bailey," said Sydney. "I watched you all the way, and you were really brave. I'm glad I convinced you to do it."

Bailey grabbed Sydney's arm. "Syd," she said. "Where'd the captain go? He was right behind me."

Captain Swain was gone! Just as if he had vanished into thin air!

CHAPTER 3

A Mysterious Mug

"That's odd," said Sydney. "Where is he?"

A strong wind swept across the lighthouse. Sydney noticed Bailey's fingers gripping the railing. She grabbed Bailey's hand, and they carefully walked back to the door. When they got there, a lady whose name tag read MEGHAN was waiting.

"I was wondering if anyone was up here," she said. "I'm closing the lighthouse now. Storms are coming, and it's not safe up here when there's lightning."

The woman led the girls down the curving staircase. It was scarier going down than up because Sydney and Bailey had no choice but to look at their feet and imagine how far they'd fall if they tripped.

To keep her mind off it, Bailey began to talk—she tended to talk a lot whenever she got nervous. "So, do you like working in a lighthouse?" she asked.

"It's fascinating!" Meghan answered. "It's fascinating to go up to the top and see how the ocean changes every day."

"I live like two and a half hours from Lake Michigan," Bailey told her. "And we go there in the summer to the beach and I think the lake looks a lot like the ocean, only it's not as big, and we have perch and trout instead of sharks and jellyfish."

She gulped a breath and went on. "Lake Michigan has fresh water and, of course, the ocean has salt water. This is the first time I've climbed a lighthouse. I'm afraid of heights, you know, but I climbed to the top—"

Sydney interrupted her. "Did you see Captain Swain come down the stairs?"

"Captain Swain? No," said Meghan. "Why?"

"He took us up to the lookout but disappeared. We didn't see him leave. We were wondering where he went." They were almost to the bottom of the stairs now, and Sydney sighed with relief.

"When was this?" the woman asked.

"Just a few minutes ago," said Sydney.

"I didn't see him come downstairs," Meghan replied as they reached the main floor. "As far as that goes, I didn't see him go up either. I must not have been paying attention."

"You weren't here," said Sydney. "When we came in, no one was around."

"That's odd," said Meghan. "I've been here for the past hour or so. I don't know how you got by without me seeing you, unless I was in my office. Did you say this was your first lighthouse visit?"

"It is," Bailey answered. "I'm visiting from Peoria. That's in Illinois."

"You know what?" said the lady. "I have something for you." She went to a desk in a little room nearby and picked up two small cardboard folders. "These are lighthouse passports," she said. She gave one to each of the girls. "You can visit lighthouses all over America and get stickers to put in your passport book. There's already a sticker from this lighthouse inside."

"Wow!" said Bailey. "I'm going to visit every lighthouse and collect all the stickers."

"If you do that, come back here and show me your passport. I'll buy you a cheeseburger," said Meghan.

"It might take me awhile to get them all," Bailey responded.

"Like, years!" Sydney added.

The woman smiled. "I imagine I'll be here."

After the girls left the lighthouse, Sydney pointed at two girls on the other side of Schoolhouse Lane. They were eating ice cream by the Corolla Village Bar-B-Q. "Come on," she told Bailey. "I want you to meet my friends." She led Bailey to a picnic table where the girls were sitting outside the restaurant. "Hi, Carolyn. Hi, Marilyn," said Sydney.

"Hi, Sydney!" the twins answered in unison. The Kessler twins often spoke in unison, Sydney had noticed. They were so much alike that Sydney still had trouble telling them apart, and she had known them for six years. The Kessler family owned a house near Sydney's grandparents' place. She knew they lived there year-round since Mr. Kessler ran a company that made recreational water vehicles and racing boats.

"What are you guys doing here?" Sydney asked.

"Hanging out," they answered together.

"This is my friend Bailey Chang," said Sydney.

"I thought so!" said Marilyn.

"I thought so, too," Carolyn echoed. "You're one of the Camp Club Girls. Sydney talks about you guys all the time."

Bailey slid onto the bench at the picnic table. "Nice to meet you," she said. "We just finished climbing the lighthouse."

"You did!" the girls exclaimed.

"I've lived here since I was five, and I've never climbed it," said Marilyn.

"I haven't either," said Carolyn.

They both looked at Sydney as she slid onto the bench next to Bailey. "Okay, I confess. I hadn't either," she said.

Bailey couldn't believe her ears. "What do you mean, you hadn't either? You acted like you'd climbed it a million times."

"I've always wanted to climb it," Sydney told her. "Would you have gone if I'd acted scared?"

Bailey thought for a second. "Well, no," she conceded. "But I wish I had known."

Two odd-looking bikes were propped against the picnic table. Each had two seats, two sets of handlebars, and two sets of pedals. "Are those your bikes?" Bailey asked the twins.

"They're tandems," said Carolyn.

Marilyn nodded in agreement. "Bicycles built for two." She took a lick of the chocolate ice cream that was melting in her cone.

"How come you *each* have one?" Bailey wondered. "Can't you both just ride on *one*?"

"One of them belongs to our brothers," said Carolyn. "The other one is ours."

"We just dropped them off at a friend's house on the Sound," said Marilyn. "They're spending the night there."

"And we're taking their bike home," Carolyn added. She popped the last bit of ice-cream cone into her mouth and Marilyn did the same with hers. "You can ride back with us if you want to," she said. "We have our brothers' helmets you can wear."

Bailey looked at Sydney, hoping she would agree.

"Okay," Sydney answered. "We probably should get home soon anyway. Gramps said Nate Wright might try to take a cluster balloon flight off the beach this afternoon. That'll be cool to watch."

"Who's going to do what?" Bailey asked. She looked at her reflection in the side-view mirror of one of the tandem bikes and smoothed her jet-black hair.

"Nate Wright is going to do a cluster balloon flight," said Sydney. "He ties a bunch of extra-large helium party balloons to a chair contraption and sails up into the sky. Then he releases the balloons gradually to come back down."

"Why would he want to do that?" Bailey asked.

Carolyn climbed onto the front seat of one of the tandems and put on her helmet. "Mr. Wright's an inventor," she said, pointing for Bailey to get on the back seat.

"Well, sort of," said Marilyn, picking up the other bike and climbing onto the front seat. "He's kind of strange. He's always trying to invent weird ways to get around. Lately he's been experimenting with cluster ballooning."

"Mr. Wright's a distant relative of the Wright brothers," Carolyn explained. "Usually people cluster balloon in the early morning when there's no breeze, but today he's doing it in the afternoon."

"We saw his son on the beach this morning," Sydney said. "What's his name? Drake?"

"Yes, that's Drake Wright, Nate Wright's son," Marilyn said. "He's a beachcomber."

"They call him Digger," said Carolyn.

"He picks up junk along the beach and digs stuff out of the sand. Then he sells it to people who sell it in their shops or use it for crafts. Driftwood and glass floats and old fishing nets and stuff," Marilyn added. "And he hardly ever talks."

Carolyn gave her bike a shove with one foot and then started to pedal. Bailey held tight to the handlebars. She didn't know what to do when the pedals under her feet began to spin.

"Don't try to steer!" Sydney told her. "Just keep your feet on the pedals and help Carolyn push."

Soon the girls were riding down Schoolhouse Lane heading for Corolla Light. They were almost to Highway 12—the two-lane road that was the main road for the Outer Banks—when Sydney's cell phone rang.

"Can we stop for a second?" she asked Marilyn. The twins steered their bikes to the side of the road. Sydney pulled her cell phone out of the pocket of her shorts. She flipped it open. "Hello?"

"Sydney," said a concerned voice that Sydney recognized as her grandfather. "Where are you?"

"We're biking home with the Kessler twins," Sydney answered. "We should be there in about ten minutes."

"Come straight home, and don't stop anywhere," said her grandfather. "A bad storm is coming, and I don't want you girls out in it."

"Okay, Gramps," said Sydney. "We're on our way." She folded the phone and slipped it back into her pocket. "There's a storm coming," she said. "Gramps wants us home."

"The sky does look kind of greenish and black over there," said Bailey, pointing to the right. "Do you guys have tornado warning sirens here?"

"I don't know," Sydney answered. "If they do, I've never heard one."

"Me neither," said Marilyn, steering her bike back onto the road.

"I haven't either. We don't usually have tornadoes here," said Carolyn, following her.

"They go off a lot in Peoria," Bailey said. "Sometimes the sky looks ugly like this, and then we get a tornado warning."

Suddenly a bolt of lightning sliced through the black clouds. *Whoosh!* The wind picked up. The girls pedaled as fast as they could. By the time they got to their street, big droplets of rain started to fall. Then the rain turned into a rushing waterfall that spilled onto the girls' helmets and soaked their clothing. The twins made a perfect turn into Sydney's driveway, and Sydney and Bailey hopped off the bikes. Then the Kesslers sped off toward home.

Sydney's grandparents stood on the upper deck of the beach house. "Hurry!" Gramps called to the girls. "Come on up here."

Sydney ran up the two flights of stairs with Bailey close behind.

Crash! At the sound of thunder, Bailey nearly tripped on the last step. She caught the railing and climbed up onto the covered deck.

Bailey, Sydney, and her grandparents stepped inside the sliding screen doors and watched the storm from the safety of the family room. The fierce purple cloud was right over their heads now. To the south, near the ocean's horizon, the sky was clear and the sun was shining. But north of the beach house, the scene was very different. A long, thin, white tail dropped from the cloud until it met the ocean. It turned brown as it sucked up water.

Bailey screamed. "Oh my goodness! Oh my goodness! It's a tornado!"

"If they're over the water, they're called waterspouts," Sydney's grandmother explained. "Then when they come to land, they're called tornadoes."

Bailey squeezed Sydney's arm.

"It's heading away from us," Sydney said as the cone swept out to sea. "Pretty soon it'll dwindle to nothing."

Gramps added, "We're safe here, but can you imagine being in a sailboat out in the ocean? A decent-sized waterspout could easily drop on one of those and smash a small boat to smithereens. In fact, that *did* happen. There are so many shipwrecks near the Outer Banks that folks have lost count."

"Maybe that's what happened to the sailors on the ghost ship," Sydney suggested. "They got sucked into a water spout."

Bailey watched the long, coiling twister disappear. Beyond it, in the distance, two more waterspouts formed as the ocean carried the storm away. The back edge of the dark cloud passed over the beach house now, and the rain turned to drizzle. Bailey wasn't afraid anymore. She thought the tumbling waves and the waterspouts were awesome.

"Lake Michigan has waterspouts, too," she said as the sun broke through the clouds. "I remember reading about them in current events, but I've never seen one. Very cool, although a bit scary."

"Look over there," said Sydney. The end of a rainbow was barely visible near the beach opposite of where the waterspout had been. Its colors gradually became bright, clear ribbons of red, orange, yellow, green, blue, indigo, and violet.

"See?" said Sydney's grandmother. "God is sending us a message, just like He did to Noah on the ark. He's telling us we don't have to worry about the waterspout. It won't hurt us. A rainbow is God's way of saying, 'I promise.' "

"Let's go stand in the end of it!" Bailey was already out the door and running down the stairs toward the beach. Sydney followed, but by the time they got to where it looked like the rainbow ended, they realized it was out over the ocean.

"You can't touch it," Sydney explained when she caught up with Bailey. "Rainbows are sunlight bouncing off raindrops. I've chased them before, but you can't catch them. They move with the rain."

Bailey looked at her sand-caked feet. "Hey, look!" she said. "I'm wearing sand shoes."

She dropped to her knees and began scooping wet sand into a big pile. "Come on, Syd, let's make a sand castle or something."

Sydney sat near her friend and helped form sand into a mound. "You know, don't you, that the tide will come in and wash it away."

Bailey patted the sand with both hands, sculpting it into a tower. "I don't care," she said. "Building it is the fun part."

"I see something we can use," said Sydney. A cylinder-shaped container was half-buried in the sand nearby. Sydney went to get it. "This'll work," she said. "We can put wet sand in here and mold it into turrets."

The container that Sydney found was a tall, insulated coffee mug. The top was screwed on so tight that she couldn't get it off. She tipped the mug, and water dribbled out of the tiny hole on top. She shook it, and the inside rattled.

"Something's in here," she said. Sydney shook the mug again, but nothing fell out. She shook it harder. Still nothing. Then she peeked into the hole.

"I can't see anything," she said. "This is kind of gross. We should wash it or something." She walked to the water's edge and swished the mug in the ocean. Then, once more, she looked inside. Nothing. She turned the mug upside down and shook it hard and fast.

A beam of light jiggled across the sand!

"Bailey? I think it's glowing!"

"Huh?" said Bailey, who hadn't been paying attention.

"It's glowing. The mug is glowing!" Sydney repeated.

She turned the mug upright. A bright beam of light streamed out of the tiny opening. She put her eye to the opening, but the light was too bright to see what was inside.

Bailey put her hand a few inches above the tiny hole. A small circle of light reflected on the palm of her hand.

"Weird," she said. "What do you think this is?"

"Beats me," Sydney answered. "I've never seen a coffee mug that lights up."

"Me neither," Bailey replied. "Maybe it's not a coffee mug at all. Maybe we've stumbled onto something else."

"Like what?" Sydney asked, handing her the mug.

Bailey sat down and chewed her lip, a nervous habit that she vowed to break. "Like, maybe some sort of secret weapon," she said. "Something the UFO left behind."

"If it were a secret weapon, we'd probably be dead by now," Sydney told her. "Your imagination is getting away from you again."

The girls sat for a few minutes pondering the odd gadget and then—

"Hey, the light went out!" Bailey exclaimed.

UFO!

The object was indeed strange. It seemed to light up only after Bailey or Sydney shook it for a while. Then it cast an eerie glow for about five minutes and went dark. They brought it back to the beach house, and Sydney put it on a metal bookshelf in the guest room. She had the idea that they might try to dissect it later.

When the Camp Club Girls met in their chat room after supper, Sydney told them about the mug.

> Kate: *A coffee mug that glows from the inside? Why would you need it to light up inside?*
> Alexis: *Maybe it's so you can see how much coffee's left.*
> McKenzie: *But you have to shake it to make it light. That doesn't make sense, because if there's hot coffee, you'll get burned when it leaks out of the hole on top.*
> Elizabeth: *I think you can close the hole. My mom's coffee mug has a flippy thing you turn to open and close the hole. Oh, and by the way, the kind of mug you have is a*

travel mug. Some of them aren't supposed
to be submerged in water. At least my
mom's can't.

Sydney: *Maybe it got dropped in the ocean
and the salt water wrecked it or something,
and then it washed up on the beach.*

Bailey took the laptop from Sydney.

Bailey: *Hi, Bettyboo. Hi, everyone else.*

Elizabeth: *You know I don't like being called
Bettyboo.*

Bailey: *Just kidding, Beth. I have a theory
about the mug. It was half buried in the
sand. I don't think it washed up on the
shore. Someone put it there. I think it's
some kind of secret weapon.*

She bit her lip hard and waited for someone to reply.

Alexis: *Something like that happened in one
old alien movie I saw.*

McKenzie: *Why would you think it's a weapon?*

Bailey: *I don't know. It's too creepy to be
anything ordinary.*

She pushed the laptop back to Sydney and went to get the
mug from the bookshelf. She grabbed the handle, but the mug
wouldn't budge.

"Hey," she said. "It's stuck."

"What do you mean?" Sydney asked.

"It's glued to the bookshelf, bozo," said Bailey. "I can't pick it up!"

"Oh for goodness' sake," said Sydney. She set the computer on the twin bed, where they had been cyber-chatting, and she went to help Bailey.

Sydney grasped the mug's handle. Bailey was right. It was stuck. She pulled hard. The mug let loose, almost catapulting her backward.

"See?" said Bailey. She examined the spot where the mug had been. "I don't see any glue or other sticky stuff."

Sydney moved closer to inspect the bare spot. All at once, the mug shot out of her hand and stuck itself to the shelf. "It's a magnet!" Sydney gasped. "Look at this." She yanked the mug away from the metal shelf and then let it fly back. "I didn't notice it when I put the mug here before."

"Way cool!" Bailey squealed.

Sydney hurried back to the laptop to tell the girls. When she looked at the screen, she found a string of messages.

> Alexis: *Syd? Bailey? Where are you?*
> McKenzie: *Hey, did you log off without saying good-bye?*
> Kate: *Where did everybody go?*
> Sydney: *Sorry. Bailey went to get the mug, and we found out it's a magnet! It was stuck to my metal bookshelf.*
> Kate: *DANGER! DANGER! Do not—I repeat—DO NOT put that mug anywhere near the computer.*

Bailey was just about to plop down on the bed next to Sydney with the mug in her hand. "No!" Sydney yelled. She shoved Bailey off the bed and onto the floor.

"Hey!" Bailey protested. She sat there looking startled. "What did you do that for?"

"I'm sorry," said Sydney. "Kate just wrote that the mug is very dangerous—"

Bailey shuddered and flung the coffee mug over her shoulder. It landed somewhere across the room. "What's the matter with it?" she asked nervously.

"You didn't let me finish," said Sydney. "It's dangerous to put it near the computer."

Sydney told the girls what had just happened.

> Alexis: *Well, at least now you know that it's not a bomb. The way you two are messing with it, it would have gone off by now.*

Bailey joined Sydney on the bed. She read what Alex had just written.

> Bailey: *Not funny. Why is it dangerous to put a coffee mug next to a laptop?*
> Kate: *I read a magnet will kill the pixels on your computer screen, so it's best to keep the mug away from it. Can you take a video with your cell phone?*
> Sydney: *No, but I can with my digital camera.*
> Kate: *Good. Stand away from the computer and shoot a video to show us what you do to make it light up.*

Sydney retrieved the mug from a corner of the room.

"You hold it," said Bailey. "I don't want to touch it."

"It won't bite you," Sydney answered. She got her digital camera out of her dresser drawer.

Bailey took the pink camera out of Sydney's hand and turned it on. She switched the button to VIDEO MODE. "All set," she said. "Ready?" Bailey pushed another button and started recording. "The case of the mysterious cup. Take One!"

Sydney held the mug and shook it hard, but nothing happened.

"It stopped recording," said Bailey. "The LCD says OUT OF MEMORY."

"My camera only takes a forty-five-second video," Sydney answered. "Don't start recording as soon as I shake it."

Bailey deleted the first video, and the girls tried again. Sydney shook the mug hard and fast, but again the time ran out before anything happened.

Sydney sighed. "Hang on a minute. I'll shake the mug to see how long it takes to light up." Sydney shook the mug hard, but it wouldn't light. "Bailey, I think you broke it."

"I did not!" Bailey defended herself.

Sydney tried again, but the mug stayed dark.

By the time they returned to the computer, Kate had an idea.

> Kate: *You know, that thing reminded me of my shake flashlight, so while you were away I went on the Internet and looked up how it works.*

McKenzie: *What's a shake flashlight?*

Kate: *Don't you have them in Montana? It looks like a regular flashlight, but it doesn't work on batteries. It has a strong magnet inside. When you shake it, the magnet passes up and down through a coil. That causes the capacitor to charge and the flashlight lights!*

Alexis: *Now you have a perfectly reasonable explanation.*

Bailey: *But there's nothing reasonable about a glowing coffee cup.*

"Mug," Sydney corrected her. It bugged her when people misused words.

Bailey: *In fact, a lot of unreasonable stuff has gone on since I got here last night.*

McKenzie: *Like what?*

Bailey: *I saw strange lights over the water that looked like a UFO. Today I stepped on a bone on the beach and Syd said it might have come from a dead sailor. A lot of them have disappeared around here. Like when a ghost ship washed up on the beach down the coast. The sailors vanished into thin air. Then today we climbed a lighthouse with an old sea captain but he disappeared. Maybe he was a ghost, too.*

Elizabeth: *Bailey, calm down. There are no
ghosts!*

Bailey chewed on her lip as her fingers flew across the keyboard.

Bailey: *There are, too! There's the Holy Ghost.
We learned about Him at camp, and I
heard my pastor talk about Him.*
Elizabeth: *The Holy Ghost is a part of the
Trinity of God. Sure, He's a spirit, and
you can't see Him, but He's not out to get
you. There are no such things as ghosts.*

Bailey said no more. Elizabeth was the oldest of the Camp Club Girls, and she seemed to know everything about God. Sometimes Bailey felt like such a kid when she was around her.

Kate: *So what are you going to do with it?*
Sydney: *I don't know. Throw it in the trash,
I guess.*
Kate: *Gotta go. Biscuit just made a mess,
and I have to clean it.*

It was getting late, and the rest of the girls decided to sign off, too.

Bailey and Sydney's guest room in the beach house was on the second floor. It had two twin beds with matching striped bedspreads and big, fluffy pillows. A white wicker nightstand separated the beds, and it held an alarm clock and a table lamp made out of seashells. The room was painted a soft blue, and instead of one wall, two big sliding glass doors led to a private covered deck that overlooked the ocean. Gramps had said that Bailey and Sydney could sleep out there if they wanted to. It would be like camping, only instead of sleeping in a cabin near Discovery Lake, they would sleep under the stars near the beach. The girls got their sleeping bags and went outside.

"Hey, what's going on down there?" asked Bailey. She leaned over the deck railing to get a better look. Below, children ran around on the beach with plastic buckets and flashlights.

"Ghost crab hunting," said Sydney as she settled into a hammock on one end of the deck.

"Ghost crabs? You mean that ugly thing that we saw on the beach this morning?"

"They're not ugly," Sydney said. "I think they're kind of cute."

"They look like monster white spiders," said Bailey. "Why is everyone trying to catch them?"

Sydney rolled on her side and gazed at the ocean. "Because they're fun to chase," she said. "They pop in and out of their holes so fast you never know when you'll find one. Little kids especially like looking for them."

She paused and watched the moonlight dance across the waves. "They're hard to catch, because they blend in with the sand. Sometimes, if you stay real still and wait, it's like the sand comes alive around your feet. The ghost crabs come up out of their holes all around you, and then they start scurrying sideways, and if you move—even one tiny little bit—*they bite your toes!*" Sydney made a quick grab at Bailey's foot.

Bailey jumped. "Oooh! Don't scare me like that," she said. "I've heard enough ghost stories for one day."

Sydney rolled onto her back and gazed up at the stars. "Like Elizabeth said, Bailey, there's no such things as ghosts."

"Then how do you explain the captain disappearing?" asked Bailey.

"I don't know where the captain went," Sydney said, "but I don't think he was a ghost that just floated off the top of the lighthouse."

Down below, on the beach, children giggled and screamed with delight as they tried to put crabs into plastic buckets.

"Be careful!" a man's voice called in the darkness. "They pinch!"

"Hey, look up there. It's the Big Dipper," Sydney said, changing the subject. She pointed out the constellation to Bailey, and the girls settled down to watch the stars, Sydney in the hammock and Bailey on a mattress on the deck. Soon they were sound asleep.

Bailey had a nightmare. She dreamed that she was climbing the stairs in the lighthouse, and they disappeared beneath her. There was no way down and no way out.

She awoke with a start. The full moon was high in the sky, casting a glow on the water. The beach was deserted, and Bailey had no idea what time it was. She stood and looked out at the sea.

The waves washing up on the beach glowed an eerie blue-green, and she saw what looked like glowing ghost crabs skittering across the sand.

"Sydney!" she whispered. "Wake up!"

Sydney groaned and rubbed her eyes. "What's the matter?"

"Get up!" Bailey demanded. "The ocean is glowing and so are the crabs."

"Huh?" asked Sydney. She sat up wearily and looked at the

beach. "It's just bioluminescence."

"Buy a luma what sense?"

"Bioluminescence," Sydney repeated. "It's a phenomenon caused by phosphorous in the water. On moonlit nights, it makes the waves glow."

"And crabs, too?" Bailey wondered.

"I suppose," said Sydney. "It's nothing to worry about. Go back to sleep." Sydney rolled over, and in no time at all, Bailey heard her breathing heavily.

She felt lonely on the deck with Sydney sleeping. At night, the ocean didn't seem at all like Lake Michigan. The Atlantic was huge, and it held sharks and stingrays and who knows what else. And scorpions and snakes might be nearby. If they were on the beach, they could find their way up to the deck where the girls slept.

Although it was muggy outside, Bailey climbed into her sleeping bag and zipped it up tight. She sat on the deck with her back against the wall, fighting sleep. She worried that if she slept she might have another nightmare.

Dawn was peeking over the ocean when Bailey lifted her head. She had dozed off sitting up and now her back ached. The moonlight had faded, and the ocean was like a black, gaping hole. She thought she heard something on the beach. It was a soft whirring sound, kind of like the blade of a helicopter spinning. It stopped. Then she heard nothing but the waves lapping up on the sand.

Bailey climbed out of her sleeping bag and stood by the railing. Something caught her eye. There, not far offshore, was some sort of flying thing. Bailey could barely make out its shape, but it was the size of a car and covered with blinking, multicolored lights. It moved slowly, hovering above the water.

"Sydney! Wake up!" Bailey commanded. She ran to the hammock and shook her friend awake.

"What!" Sydney exclaimed.

"Get up!" said Bailey. "The UFO is out there!"

Sydney sat up and looked toward the ocean. "Bailey, nothing is there. That story I told you about people seeing things at night? It's just a story. I don't believe there's anything to it."

When Bailey looked toward where the lights had been, she saw they were gone. "Oh, Syd," she gasped. "You have to believe me. Something dreadful is out there."

"I believe you," Sydney said halfheartedly. "Now, forget it, and go back to sleep."

"I won't!" said Bailey. "Look!"

Mysteries on the Beach

"Whoa! What on earth is that?" Sydney exclaimed.

The object was making small, tight circles above the water and darting to and fro. It's blinking lights alternated from red to multicolored, and it didn't make a sound that the girls could hear from their balcony.

"It's not on earth," Bailey answered, "and it's not *from* earth either. It's a UFO! I told you so. I'll go get your grandparents." Bailey started for the sliding glass doors.

"Not yet," said Sydney. "It's probably nothing. Let's go check it out."

She climbed out of the hammock and put on her sandals.

"Are you crazy?" Bailey shrieked.

"Shhhh!" Sydney told her. "You'll wake everybody."

"We are *not* going to check it out," Bailey whispered. "What if the aliens on it abduct us and take us to their planet? No way, Syd!"

But Sydney was already hurrying down the stairs to the beach.

"Don't leave me alone," Bailey begged.

"Then come on," her friend said.

The UFO was just offshore now. The blinking lights faded to black, and the object disappeared into the darkness. Soon a strange whirring came from the water's edge. It turned into a soft *flop flop flop*, sounding like a flat tire on asphalt. Whatever it was had landed on the beach. And it was moving!

Sydney walked toward the noise, but she couldn't see a thing.

The noise stopped.

Bailey had Sydney by the arm now and held her back from going even closer.

Whoof!

A strong puff of hot air hit the girls in the face. Something whizzed past them only a few yards away.

"A wild horse!" Bailey gasped.

"That was no horse," Sydney said.

"Are you sure?" asked Bailey. She loosened her grip.

"I'm sure," said Sydney. "It was going so fast that it's probably to the sound by now."

Sydney decided to run home to get a flashlight. Bailey insisted on coming along. In only moments, the girls returned to the place where whatever it was had rushed past them. Sydney focused the light onto the sand at the water's edge.

"Oh my," she said, "look at that!"

Along the water was a line of strange footprints in the wet sand.

Or were they footprints?

The prints were like big, oval waffles. Their pattern of lines and squares looked like someone had gone along slapping the sand with a tennis racket. The prints came out of the sea and stretched only across the wet sand at the ocean's edge. When they reached the dry part of the sand, they disappeared.

"Bigfoot!" said Bailey. "You know, that gigandamundo

monster that leaves his footprints but is hardly ever seen!"

"There's no such thing as Bigfoot," Sydney said. She crouched down to get a better look.

"And until a few minutes ago, you didn't believe UFOs existed," said Bailey.

She had a point. Sydney had no idea what they had just witnessed. She had no explanation for the strange thing that hovered over the water or for the way that it had rushed past them on the beach without a sound.

As she looked over the ocean, Sydney saw the sun beginning to rise. It painted the sky a beautiful salmon orange and sent diamonds of light dancing across the lavender-colored sea.

"Bailey, go get the camera," Sydney said. "We have to get a picture of these prints before they wash away."

Bailey ran to the beach house. She quickly returned to where Sydney waited. By the time she got there, the water was already lapping at the prints.

Sydney snapped a half dozen shots until the prints had almost disappeared.

"Looking for ghost crabs, Sydney Lincoln?"

A man's deep voice came from behind them.

"Captain Swain!" Bailey exclaimed. "What are you doing here?"

The captain stood in front of them dressed in a crisp blue jogging suit. Sydney noticed it had a coast guard emblem on one sleeve. He had a dog with long black fur, about the size of Kate's dog, Biscuit, by his side.

"McTavish and I are taking our morning walk," the captain replied. "And what brings you girls out so early on this fine summer morning?"

"We saw a UFO," Bailey answered. "And then we went to check it out, but it disappeared. Now there are Bigfoot prints in the sand."

Bailey didn't notice that Sydney was shooting her a look that said, *"Be quiet!"* By now, the footprints had been completely washed away.

" 'So we fix our eyes not on what is seen, but on what is unseen, since what is seen is temporary, but what is unseen is eternal,' " the captain said.

In the back of her mind, Sydney remembered reading those words in her Bible study class at camp, but she wasn't quite sure what they meant.

"Just God and me talking out loud," said the captain. He bent and patted McTavish on the head. The dog wagged its tail, sending sand flying in all directions. "Go play, my boy," the captain said, and McTavish scampered along the water's edge, leaving footprints trailing behind him.

"I thought you said you never come to Corolla Light," Sydney reminded him.

"I said I *rarely* come here," the captain corrected her. "I *never* come here in the daytime when things are busy unless I absolutely have to. Too many tourists! But often in the morning hours, I hear the ocean calling me."

Bailey still wasn't sure about Captain Swain. Something about him was different. He seemed not to fit in with the residents and tourists on the Outer Banks. She imagined him instead in the days of the ghost ships, hoisting the billowing sails and standing at the ship's wheel. He seemed mysterious. From a different time in history.

She decided to come right out and ask: "Are you a—"

"Girls! Breakfast!" Sydney's grandmother stood on the upper deck of the beach house calling to them. "Come on, now."

"We have to go," Sydney said. She and Bailey ran back to the house.

"Who was that man?" Sydney's grandma asked. "And why were you girls on the beach so early?"

"We saw a UFO," Bailey announced. "And we went to check it out, but we didn't find anything but Bigfoot's footprints. And then Captain Swain showed up. I think he's a ghost because yesterday he disappeared into thin air." She looked down at the beach, but the captain was gone.

"See," she said. "He disappeared *again!*"

Sydney looked toward the beach and tried to come up with a logical explanation.

"Did you see where he went, Grandma?" she asked.

Sydney's grandmother looked north and south.

"No," she replied. "But I had my eyes on you and not on the beach. Bailey, UFOs and Bigfoot and ghosts don't exist. Those are all just stories." Her brown eyes twinkled as she smiled at Sydney's friend. "We're so happy to have you here, but we don't want you to be afraid of things that don't exist. We just want you to have fun."

Bailey still wasn't convinced. She had seen the UFO with her own eyes, and she had seen the footprints, too. And those footprints weren't from any animal or human.

"But those things do exist," she whispered to herself. "At least, I think so."

The girls hurried to their room to dress. Sydney quickly e-mailed the photos to the Camp Club Girls, telling them what had happened at the beach that morning. Then she and Bailey dashed to the kitchen table. Grandpa said the mealtime prayer:

"Loving Father, we thank You for this food,
And for all Your blessings to us.
Lord Jesus, come and be our guest,
And take Your place at this table.
Holy Spirit, as this food feeds our bodies,
So we pray You would nourish our souls. Amen."

"Is the Holy Spirit the same as the Holy Ghost?" Bailey asked as she chose a piece of cinnamon bread.

"He is," Gramps answered, scooping some scrambled eggs onto Bailey's plate.

"And He's truly a ghost?" Bailey wondered.

"He's a spirit, Bailey," Gramps answered. "Many things about God are a mystery and beyond what we humans can understand. The Holy Spirit is one of them. He's a part of God, but He isn't a ghost who haunts or hurts people. He's the Helper, the One who guides us through every day. Grandma says you've been seeing things since you got here."

Bailey shook some pepper onto her eggs. She didn't know what to say except that she had seen strange things, and they were real.

"You girls are good at solving mysteries," Sydney's grandfather went on. "I think you've discovered, by now, that when it comes to mysteries there's usually a logical explanation."

Sydney went to the refrigerator and got a slice of American cheese. She put it on top of her scrambled eggs and zapped her meal in the microwave.

"I think it's my fault," she said. "Yesterday I told Bailey about

the ghost ship. Since then, she's been thinking about ghosts."
Sydney carried her eggs back to the table and stuck her fork
into the gooey cheese.

"Ah, the ghost ship," Gramps said. "That's an unsolved
mystery on the Outer Banks. Folks like to make up stories about
it. Somewhere, though, there's the truth about what happened
to those poor missing sailors. You can be sure there's a good
explanation."

Gramps stirred cream into his coffee. "You know, I think
tomorrow I'll take you girls to the Graveyard of the Atlantic
Museum. Then you can learn all about the ghost ship and the
other shipwrecks off the coast."

While the girls continued eating and talking about
shipwrecks, someone knocked on the door and Sydney's
grandmother went to answer it.

In a moment, the Kessler twins walked into the room,
greeting the girls. Grandpa offered them some cinnamon bread,
but they declined.

"Hey, Nate Wright is down at the beach near Tuna Street,
and he's setting up his chair," Marilyn said.

"Digger is starting to blow up the helium balloons," Carolyn
added. "And I thought Bailey might want to see."

"Can we?" Sydney asked her grandparents as she picked up
her plate and Bailey's to carry to the dishwasher.

"Go ahead," Grandma said. "But when he takes off, you
girls stay a safe distance away. I don't want you getting hurt."
Grandma sipped her coffee. "Cluster ballooning is dangerous,
even when it's done the ordinary way, but when Nate does it,
it's even more dangerous. He takes too many risks if you ask me
and is even a bit crazy. And that son of his is an odd duck, too."

Grandma poured a little more creamer into her coffee. "Why, you wouldn't believe the junk that boy picks up on the beach. One day I was near their house in the village, and you should have seen the junk piled up by their equipment shed!"

"One night our dad had to go to the village, and he saw Mr. Wright and Digger welding stuff in their yard," Marilyn said. "The sparks lit up their place like fireworks on the Fourth of July. He said he heard that they get real busy at night moving stuff around in the dark—"

"And using hammers and power saws, too," Carolyn added.

Grandpa buttered a piece of bread for himself. "Nate says he's an inventor, but the only invention I've seen so far is that silly balloon chair. He thinks he can use that idea to someday create travel that's fast, clean, and inexpensive. Can you imagine all of us flying around in chairs tethered to party balloons?"

The girls laughed.

"Let's go," said Sydney. "Are we walking or taking our bikes?"

"Walking," said the twins.

The girls joined a small crowd that had gathered on the beach just off the sandy beach access lane. Nate Wright was checking the chair, adjusting the straps and making sure they were secured. The seat looked like it came from an airplane cockpit. It had lots of instruments and a big joystick.

"It'll never get off the ground," Bailey said. "It'll be too heavy with all that stuff on it."

"No, it won't," said Sydney. "You won't believe your eyes."

An old beat-up school bus was parked at the edge of the beach on the end of the access road. On its side was a hodgepodge of words:

LASERS
LEVITATING
ELEVATING
WRIGHT &
SON
ORIENTEERING
RACING

"What does it all mean?" Bailey asked.

"I guess it advertises things they're working on. I don't really know," said Sydney.

"Why don't we ask them?" said Bailey.

"Because they don't talk to anybody," Sydney replied. "The only time the Wrights say anything is if they think you're getting close enough to get hurt."

Drake Wright, Digger, was on the roof of the bus with a helium tank. One by one, he filled balloons with helium and fastened them to big hooks on top of the bus roof. Each hook held several dozen colorful balloons.

"What's he doing?" asked Bailey.

"He has to have a place to store the balloons until they get attached to the chair," said Marilyn. "So he ties them to the bus, because anything lighter than a bus would lift right off the ground."

"No way!" said Bailey. She took her cell phone out of her pocket and snapped a few pictures. "I'm going to send these to Kate right now," she said. "She'll love this!"

Once Digger had filled all of the balloons, he helped his dad slide the chair to the front of the school bus. Then they chained and locked it to the bumper. Mr. Wright sat down, strapped himself in, and put on a helmet, the kind astronauts wear.

"Now what?" asked Bailey.

"Watch," said Carolyn.

"Watch," Marilyn echoed.

Methodically, Digger carried the balloons from the rooftop to his dad's chair, one bunch at a time. He attached them to special fasteners on the chair frame and the chair soon began to rise.

"Awesome!" Bailey gasped, snapping more pictures.

"You haven't seen anything yet," said Sydney.

When all of the balloons were in place, the chair hovered near the hood of the school bus. It strained to break loose.

"Get back!" Digger yelled at the crowd.

Everyone took several steps backward.

Drake shook his dad's hand and released the chains. The chair shot up into the air like a rocket. It kept soaring up and over the water.

"Oh wow!" said Bailey.

Digger disappeared from sight.

"Where'd he go?" Bailey asked, snapping a few more pictures.

"He's probably gone to get the boat," said Carolyn.

"Mr. Wright can only go so high before the oxygen gets too thin," said Marilyn, "so he has to start popping balloons to slowly come down. When he splashes down in the ocean, Digger will be there to pick him up."

"But Digger has to go down the shore a bit to get the boat in the water," Carolyn explained to the girls. "There's no dock or boat ramp here, and you have to have a boat with some power to withstand the waves."

"He usually flies over the sound side of the Outer Banks," Marilyn said. "That's where most of the smaller boats and jet skis are because the water is calmer."

Bailey's cell phone rang. It was a text message from Kate: READ THE FIRST LETTERS OF EACH WORD ON THE BUS FROM BOTTOM TO TOP. THEY SPELL ROSWELL! K8

"Check it out," Bailey said, handing the phone to Sydney. "What's Roswell?"

Sydney read the message. "Roswell is a town in New Mexico famous for UFOs," she explained. "People think one crashed there years ago."

Pop! Pop-pop! Pop!

As a series of a loud bangs rang over the ocean, the girls wondered about UFOs as they watched Nate Wright's chair fall slowly toward the sea.

Aliens

Dear Syd and Bailey,

Kate e-mailed me about the Wrights and the Roswell connection. How creepy! Do you think that the Wrights are connected with the UFO you saw this morning? I don't know if you've seen the movie Close Encounters of the Third Kind, *but in the movie people tried to make contact with a spaceship by using a code— five musical notes, re-mi-do-do-so. I wonder if that flashlight thing you found on the beach is some sort of signaling device. Do you think the Wrights are trying to communicate with aliens?*

Be careful,
Alex

Alexis's e-mail, marked Highest Priority, was waiting for Sydney and Bailey when they got back from the beach.

"Now do you believe me?" Bailey asked, flopping on her bed in the guest room. "Even Alex thinks we're being invaded by spaceships."

Sydney sat on her bed fidgeting with her cornrows. She was

trying to find a practical explanation.

"I don't know what to believe," she answered. "I mean, Roswell is another unsolved mystery like the ghost ship. According to the story, a UFO crashed in Roswell, in the desert. A rancher found pieces of metal scattered all over his property. He called the authorities and even the army got involved. It was a very big deal back then. They roped off his land and didn't let anyone inside. At first the government said they found pieces of a flying saucer. Later they said that the pieces were from a weather balloon. No one knows for sure, but just like the ghost ship story, rumors have kept going around."

Bailey lay on her bed thinking. She was sure the UFO she saw was not a helicopter, boat, or other ordinary thing. If the Wrights were involved, it would make sense, because they were so different and secretive.

"Hey," said Bailey. "Maybe they're aliens!"

"Huh?" said Sydney.

"Mr. Wright and Digger," Bailey answered. "Maybe their spaceship crashed in the ocean, but they survived. That would explain Drake Digger picking up stuff along the shore. He's picking up pieces of the spaceship!"

Sydney sighed. "Oh, Bailey, your imagination is getting away from you again."

"No, it's not," said Bailey, sitting up on the bed. "At night, when most people are asleep, the Wrights are trying to reconstruct their spaceship from the pieces Drake finds. That's why they're welding and stuff. And meanwhile they're trying to create an alternate vehicle that could go high enough to meet a rescue ship or something. That's why they're experimenting with the cluster balloons. And that thing we found on the beach? Alex is right. It's a signaling device."

"Bailey!" said Sydney.

"And you know what else?" Bailey went on. "I think Captain Swain is one of them. He was on the beach this morning when the UFO was there. He saw the whole thing! *He* knows what that thing was hovering over the ocean, and he knows what scooted past us in the dark. He knows about those footprints, too!"

"Oh, Bailey, stop," said Sydney. "Yesterday you thought the captain was a ghost." She got up from her bed and got the coffee mug from the bookshelf.

"I don't think he's a ghost anymore," said Bailey. "Now I think he's a space alien."

Sydney shook the coffee mug, but nothing happened. She shook it again. Still nothing. Then she tossed it into the wastebasket. It landed with a thud. "Enough of the alien stuff already!" she said. She slid open the glass doors to the deck and went outside.

Bailey screamed at the top of her lungs.

"What's the matter?" Sydney exclaimed, hurrying back inside.

Bailey was sitting on the bed, her knees pulled tight to her chest with her arms wrapped around them. She looked terrified.

"Bailey, what's wrong?" Sydney asked again.

Bailey pointed to the wastebasket. The inside of it was lit with an eerie, flashing light. Sydney looked more closely and saw that it was coming from the hole in the lid of the mug.

This was too weird. For the first time, Sydney believed no logical explanation existed for the mug, the UFO, or any of the other strange things that had been going on. She bent to take the mug out of the trash, but then she stopped.

Better to leave it alone, she thought.

"Count 'em, Syd. Count 'em," said Bailey.

"Count what?" Sydney asked.

"Count the flashes of light," Bailey answered. "One, two, three, four, five. . . One, two, three, four, five. . ."

The mug sent out five quick flashes of light. Then it stopped briefly and sent out five more.

"So?" said Sydney.

"So, remember what Alex said in her e-mail?" Bailey answered. "In the *Close Encounters* movie, the signal was five musical notes. One, two, three, four, five notes. One, two, three, four, five flashes of light. It's a code, Sydney."

Bailey's phone dinged. It was another message from Kate. Bailey read aloud. "BAILEY, DO YOU KNOW ABOUT THE LAKE MICHIGAN TRIANGLE AND THE FOOTPRINTS? IF NOT, LOOK IT UP ONLINE. K8." There was a URL address.

"What's the Lake Michigan Triangle?" Sydney asked.

"Never heard of it," said Bailey. "Let's check it out."

Sydney typed the URL address into the browser window on her computer. An article from a Michigan newspaper appeared on the screen. She read, then explained.

"This says the Lake Michigan Triangle has a history similar to the Bermuda Triangle. The lines of an imaginary triangle run from Ludington, Michigan, down to Benton Harbor, Michigan, then across the lake to Manitowoc, Wisconsin, and back across the lake to Ludington."

"I know where Manitowoc is," Bailey said. "Our family rented a cottage near there one summer."

Sydney continued. "Ships have disappeared inside the triangle. This even says one of them is seen sailing on the lake from time to time, but then disappears."

"Another ghost ship!" said Bailey. "And that's not too far from where I live. Do you know what, Syd? I just remembered something."

"What?" Sydney asked.

"A couple of years ago, there was a report of a UFO over O'Hare International Airport in Chicago. Pilots saw it, and some other people did, too. They said it was shaped like a saucer and spun around slowly, but didn't make any noise. The air traffic controllers couldn't see it on the radar. Then— *zoom!*—it shot straight up into the sky."

"For real?" asked Sydney.

"Really," Bailey answered. "It was in the *Chicago Tribune* and on the TV news, too. Nobody ever found out what it was."

"Check this out," said Sydney, reading the article. "There have also been reports of strange footprints on the beach near the points of the triangle."

Bailey gasped. "Footprints! Syd, maybe those footprints were like the ones we saw this morning. Alien footprints!"

Sydney logged off her browser. "You know, Bailey," she said, "maybe UFOs do exist."

Bailey got up the courage to walk to the wastebasket and peer inside. The flashing light had stopped. Once again, the thing looked like an ordinary travel mug. "So what do we do now?" she asked.

"We put the mug back where we found it," said Sydney. "Then we stay up tonight to see what happens."

At sunset, the girls took the mug to the beach. They tried to find the exact spot in the sand where it had been buried. They put it there and hoped children hunting for ghost crabs would leave it alone. After that, they set up the deck for spying. Sydney hung a pair of binoculars around her neck. Bailey had a mini audio recorder in her pocket, a gift Kate had given her for her birthday. The girls had their digital cameras, flashlights, and a notebook and pencils. Now they only had to wait.

Two hours later, Sydney wrote in the notebook:

> *UFO Log*
> *9 p.m. Kids on beach with flashlights looking*
> *for ghost crabs.*

"Can you see if our mug is still there?" Bailey asked.

"I think so," Sydney answered from a folding chair set up near the hammock. "I can only see when one of the kids shines a flashlight in that direction, but so far, it's there."

Bailey settled into a chair next to Sydney's. She opened a bottle of water and sipped. "So did you talk to Beth while I was in the shower?"

"I did," Sydney answered.

"What did Bettyboo say when you told her what was going on?"

"She already knew about it," said Sydney as she took the cap off her water bottle. "McKenzie heard about it from Kate, and she e-mailed Beth. And don't call her Bettyboo. She hates that."

"What did she think about the UFO?" Bailey asked as she put her feet on the deck railing.

"She doesn't believe in UFOs, and she sure doesn't think the Wrights are aliens. She said we should be careful, and she suggested that we look for a logical explanation instead of thinking about UFOs and spirits." Sydney gulped her water.

"What do you think, Syd?" asked Bailey. "Do you think that God created UFOs?"

Sydney put her feet up on the railing and settled back in her chair. "In my heart of hearts, I don't," she said. "I mean, the Bible says that He created the heavens and the earth and humans and animals, but it doesn't say anything about UFOs."

Bailey looked up at the stars. "I don't want to believe in UFOs and ghosts and stuff, Syd. I don't think that God would create anything bad. But I know what I saw, and I don't see any other explanation for it." She sighed.

"Tomorrow Gramps is taking us to the Graveyard of the Atlantic Museum," said Sydney. "Maybe we'll find some answers there. And do you know what, Bailey? We both need to get some sleep. Otherwise we'll be really tired tomorrow. We should watch the beach in shifts. One of us sleeps while the other one watches."

Sydney wrote in the notebook:

> *Sydney—10 p.m. to midnight*
> *Bailey—midnight to 2 a.m.*
> *Sydney—2 a.m. to 4 a.m.*
> *Bailey—4 a.m. to dawn*

At ten o'clock, Bailey stretched out in the hammock and was soon asleep. Sydney had a hard time staying awake. The beach was deserted except for a couple of four-wheelers heading back up north. She watched the moon dodge in and out of clouds. Besides it, the stars, and an occasional airplane flying above the ocean, nothing was in the sky.

When the little travel alarm clock she'd brought on the deck said 12:00, Sydney wrote in the notebook. *Midnight and all is well.* Then she woke Bailey.

"What time is it?" Bailey groaned.

"It's midnight," Sydney said. "I didn't see anything, and it's your turn. Try hard to stay awake. It's easy to get bored." Sydney and Bailey traded places, and Sydney fell asleep.

At first, Bailey scouted every inch of the beach with the binoculars, but she couldn't see anything in the darkness. There was no sound except the waves rolling up onshore. She tried to occupy her mind by singing songs in her head and reciting scripture verses Elizabeth had taught her. Finally, it was 2 a.m. She wrote in the notebook, *2 a.m. Nothing to report.*

"Syd?" she said, shaking her friend awake. "It's your turn."

Sydney rolled over in the hammock. "Anything?" she sighed, rubbing the sleep from her eyes.

"Nothing," said Bailey. Then the girls again traded places.

By 3:30 a.m., Sydney was ready to give up. She was bored out of her mind sitting on the deck looking at nothing. She felt her chin hit her chest as she fought off sleep. Then, out of the corner of her eye, she saw something. At least, she thought she did. She thought she saw a flash of bright, white light in the ocean. It flashed briefly and then it disappeared. She waited a few minutes, but there was nothing. Then it flashed again. Five quick bursts of light!

"Bailey! Bailey! Get up. I see something," she urgently whispered.

Bailey rolled so fast in the hammock that she almost sent it flying upside down. "What?" she asked, trying to sit up.

"Shhh," Sydney whispered. "Look out there." She pointed at the ocean in front of where they sat. After a few seconds, the light flashed again. Sydney noticed that the bursts of light were sometimes long and sometimes short. "It's a code!" she said.

"See? Sometimes it flashes longer than others. Write it down, Bailey."

Bailey shone her flashlight onto the notebook paper. "Hide under something," Sydney commanded. "They might see your flashlight."

Bailey dodged under the sleeping bag. As Sydney dictated, Bailey wrote:

> *Short short long*
> *Short short short*
> *SS*
> *LS*
> *LSL. . .*

She wrote for what seemed like forever. Then Sydney stopped dictating. "What's going on?" Bailey asked from under the sleeping bag.

Sydney didn't answer.

"Syd?" Bailey asked. Her muscles tightened and her heart began to race.

"It stopped," Sydney said. "I think you can come out now."

Bailey turned off the flashlight and crawled out from under the sleeping bag. "How weird was that?" she asked.

"Pretty weird," Sydney answered. "Did you get it all written down?"

"Every flash of it," said Bailey proudly. "What do you think it means?"

"I don't know," Sydney answered. "I think we should e-mail it to McKenzie. She's good at analyzing things."

It was just past 4:30 a.m. now, and the beach was pitch black.

It was about the same time that Bailey had seen the UFO the morning before. As the girls looked out at the water, nothing was above it but fading stars. In a little while, the sun would come up over the Atlantic, and another day would begin.

"Hey," Sydney whispered. "Listen."

The girls heard footsteps along the wet sand at the edge of the beach. They came from the south and plodded along rhythmically, passing Sydney's grandparents' beach house and then stopping just to the north.

"Did you see?" said an older male voice in the darkness.

"It's Captain Swain!" Bailey gasped.

"I saw," a younger male voice answered. "I didn't put the vehicle in the water. Probably best not to until that girl leaves. At least I got my light back." Suddenly Sydney and Bailey saw their coffee mug flash on and off.

"I think they broke it," said the younger voice.

"That's too bad," said Captain Swain. "We should get out of here before the sun comes up."

Bailey and Sydney sat quietly until they thought the men were gone.

"See?" said Bailey. "The captain is one of them, and they do have a vehicle. I think that they're trying to get back to the Mother Ship, Syd."

"Let's e-mail McKenzie right away," said Sydney. "She won't be up for a few hours, but I know she checks her e-mail first thing in the morning. Maybe she can tell us what the code says before we leave for the museum."

The girls went inside, and Bailey copied the code from her notebook pages to the e-mail document. "There," she said, typing the last *Long short long*. "Let's hope she can figure this out." She hit SEND, and the message flew off through cyberspace. In less than a minute, they got a reply.

> *I'm up. Our horse, Princess, foaled about an hour ago. She had a darling colt that we named Benny. I just came in from the barn. I'll check out your code and e-mail you back.*

As the sun rose, Bailey and Sydney got dressed and packed their backpacks for the drive to Hatteras. After breakfast, just before Gramps went to get his pickup truck, they checked the e-mail. A message was waiting from McKenzie.

> *It's Morse code. It says: I think we're being watched from the Lincoln house. Someone is on the deck with a flashlight.*

Double Trouble

After a long drive down Highway 12 from the top of the Outer
Banks to the bottom, the girls and Gramps stopped at the
museum, ready to stretch their legs.

"It kind of looks like a shipwreck," said Sydney as she
climbed out of her grandfather's truck. She had never been
to the Graveyard of the Atlantic Museum, and she had no
idea what to expect. The front of the building was outlined in
weathered timbers shaped like the hull of a wooden sailing
vessel. The building resembled a long, gray ship. Four porthole
windows protruded from its roof, reminding Sydney of giant
bug eyes.

"I think you'll find some pieces of the ghost ship in here,"
Gramps said as they walked to the front door.

"Pieces?" said Bailey, holding the door for them. "What
happened to the rest of it?"

"It stayed aground on the shoals," said Gramps. "After
weeks and months of the wind and waves pounding against it,
it started to break apart. Then the coast guard dynamited what
was left of it."

"Why did they do that?" Bailey asked.

"Because it was a hazard to ships sailing out there. Most of the pieces ended up on the beach. Some of them floated down here to Hatteras Island and got put in the museum. Look over there. There's the capstan. It was used to haul in the ropes on the ship."

The heavy, rusty metal device of the *Carroll A. Deering* rested in front of them. The top was shaped like a lampshade, and a pole came out of the bottom like a rusty old water pipe.

"Was that really a part of the ship?" Sydney asked.

"Yes," said Gramps. "It's the part that raised and lowered the anchors."

Bailey was busy looking at other pieces in the exhibit. She saw timbers from the hull and also pieces of the ship's boom— the long wooden pole that had held up the sails.

"Can you imagine?" she said. "This thing was on the ship when all of those sailors disappeared." She felt a shiver run down her spine. "It was there when it happened. The wind probably tore the sails off it when it rocked back and forth on the shoals."

Something ran up the side of her arm and made her jump.

"*Scrape. . .scrape. . . ,*" Sydney whispered as her fingers tickled Bailey's shoulder.

"That's not funny!" Bailey protested. "If this thing could talk, it would tell us exactly what happened."

"Interested in the *Carroll A. Deering*, are you?" The museum curator walked toward them. He was a short, older man with a bald head and a happy smile.

Gramps shook his hand. "Travis Lincoln," he introduced himself.

"David Jones," said the curator.

"We'd like to know what really happened to the sailors

on the ghost ship," said Sydney. "They couldn't have just disappeared. There has to be a logical explanation."

Mr. Jones stood with his elbow resting against a glass cabinet that held more artifacts from the ship. "Well," he said, "that depends on who you talk to. What do you girls think?"

"I'm not sure," said Sydney. "A lot of ships have wrecked off the coast around here. But this one seems so mysterious." She looked inside the glass case at a model of the *Carroll A. Deering*.

"I think they were abducted by aliens!" said Bailey. "I'm almost sure of it."

"Aliens," said Mr. Jones. "Why, that's a theory I haven't heard before. What makes you think it was aliens?"

Bailey waited for a few visitors to pass out of earshot before she answered. "Because we've seen them," she said softly. "With our own eyes."

Sydney frowned at Bailey. "We're not sure what we saw," Sydney said. "We saw some strange lights over the ocean the other night and unusual footprints on the beach."

"Big footprints that looked like waffles!" Bailey added. "And then an alien spacecraft whooshed past us on the beach in the dark. It didn't make a sound, but it hit us with a big puff of air."

Gramps looked confused.

"Young lady, you have quite the imagination," said Mr. Jones. "Let's sit down and talk about this. Maybe I can shed some light on what really happened to the crew of the *Carroll A. Deering*."

He led them to a small round table and some chairs. The table held a book about the ghost ship and some brochures about the museum. "Now, tell me. What are your names?"

"Sydney Lincoln."

"Bailey Chang."

"Well, Sydney and Bailey, folks have come up with three *logical* explanations. The first one is that the crew abandoned ship. When the coast guard got to the *Carroll A. Deering*, the rope ladder was hanging over the side, and both lifeboats were gone. Someone had run red flares up the rigging to indicate trouble on board."

"Red flares?" said Sydney. "The lights we saw over the ocean the other night were red."

"And sometimes multicolored and flashing," said Bailey. "Maybe it wasn't a spaceship we saw. Maybe it was the ghost ship!"

"I doubt that, Bailey," said Mr. Jones. "Because what's left of the ghost ship is right here."

"You have a point," Bailey said. "But how about a ghost of the ghost ship?"

Mr. Jones smiled and continued. "Now, if the crew did jump ship, they did it in a big hurry, because the galley was set up for a meal, and everything was left behind. However, the theory of abandonment doesn't add up."

"Why?" Sydney asked.

"Because the men were professional sailors who knew what they were doing. In stormy seas, they would be able to steer the ship away from the shoals, but the evidence shows that they sailed right into them!

"Two days before that they'd sailed past the Cape Lookout Lightship, and a crew member reported to the lightkeeper that they had lost both of their anchors, but they'd gotten through the worst of the storm.

"And something was strange about that. Usually a ship's officer makes the report. But on that day the lightkeeper didn't see an officer on deck with the men. Not the captain or a mate or even an engineer. So the officers might have already been missing by then. And the ship ran aground so near the Hatteras Lighthouse that the crew would have been better off to wait for a rescue than to jump ship. The ship didn't seem to be taking on water or anything."

Bailey nervously folded the pages of a brochure. "So maybe the crew member was a ghost?"

"No," said Mr. Jones. "But the crew member might have been up to no good. The officers might have been tied up on board or thrown overboard or even killed."

Gramps had been listening and looking through the book about the *Carroll A. Deering.* "What's your second theory?" he asked.

"Mutiny," said Mr. Jones.

"What does that mean?" Sydney wondered.

"Mutiny means the sailors take over the ship," said Gramps. "If the sailors didn't like the captain, they sometimes found a way to get rid of him."

"That's right," said Mr. Jones. "Captain Willis Wormell was the captain of the *Carroll A. Deering,* and he and his first mate, a man named McLellan, probably didn't get along. Some folks think there was a mutiny at sea. Something strange must have happened because it should have taken the ship about twelve hours to get from Cape Fear to Cape Lookout, but it took six days!"

"Why so long?" Bailey asked.

"No one knows," Mr. Jones answered. "It's part of the mystery. But some of the ship's charts were found in the wreck.

After the ship got past Cape Fear, none of the entries in the charts were in Captain Wormell's handwriting. Three sets of boots were found in the captain's cabin, but none of them were the captain's. Some folks think he was killed and thrown overboard."

"Was he?" Sydney asked.

"No one knows," said Mr. Jones.

"Boy," Bailey said. "There sure is a lot of stuff that no one knows. So it still could be aliens, right?"

"I doubt it," said the curator. "Plenty of things point to a mutiny, but there's no evidence, and if you know anything about solving a mystery, you know you need evidence."

"Oh, we know that!" said Sydney. "Our group of friends, the Camp Club Girls, have solved several mysteries now."

Gramps smiled. "The girls and their friends from summer camp have quite the reputation for solving mysteries. You wouldn't believe some of the adventures they've had."

"I can only imagine," said Mr. Jones.

"I suppose it could have been mutiny," said Sydney. "But without evidence, we can't make that conclusion. If McLellan killed the officers and the crew, he had to do something with the bodies, and they were never found. Were there any signs of a fight on board?"

"No," said Mr. Jones. "Wormell was a big man and could have put up quite a fight. And *both* lifeboats were missing, and that doesn't make sense if McLellan was the only one left on board."

"That is weird," said Bailey. "But there's not enough evidence in either of those theories to convince me the crew members weren't abducted by aliens."

"Is there evidence to convince you that they *were*?" Sydney asked.

Bailey bit her lower lip. "No," she confessed. "What's the third theory?"

"Pirates," said Mr. Jones.

"Like Blackbeard?" Sydney asked.

"No," Mr. Jones replied. "He died long before then. But pirates still sailed in the sea. One theory is that pirates took over another ship named the *Hewitt*, killed everyone, and then threw a tarp over the ship's nameplate. So, if anyone saw the ship, they wouldn't know which one it was.

"And shortly after the *Carroll A. Deering* passed the Cape Lookout Lightship, another ship sailed by—"

"What's a lightship, anyhow?" Bailey interrupted.

"A lightship is a special ship equipped with a really bright light," said Mr. Jones. "Lightships are used in places where a lighthouse can't be built. They're moored off the coast in places that are dangerous for ships to navigate." He found a picture of a lightship in the book on the table and showed it to the girls.

"Maybe the signals we saw were from a lightship," Bailey said.

"Signals?" said Gramps.

"We think we saw someone flashing a white light in Morse code early this morning," said Sydney. "It was in the ocean straight out from our house at around four o'clock."

"What were you girls doing up at four o'clock?" asked Gramps.

"Watching for UFOs," said Bailey.

"Oh, girls," said Gramps, shaking his head. "There are no such things as UFOs. . . . Mr. Jones, please tell us more about the *Hewitt*."

"Well, that second ship, the one that was following the

Deering, was hailed by the lightship at Cape Lookout. Usually someone on board would shout a report, like the crew member from the *Deering* did. Only this time the ship sailed right on by without reporting. The lightship keeper said he couldn't find a nameplate on the ship, so no one knows, but it could have been the *Hewitt*."

"Another unknown," said Bailey.

"The theory is that pirates killed everyone on the *Hewitt* and then stole the vessel. After that, they attacked the *Deering*, killed its crew, and stole anything valuable. Then they transferred their treasure to the *Hewitt*, steered the *Carroll A. Deering* in the direction of the shoals, and jumped ship."

Sydney was fidgeting with her cornrows again, like she often did when she was thinking. "But what about the bodies of all those sailors? They were never found."

"They never were," Mr. Jones agreed. "And some of their remains would have probably appeared sooner or later."

"Except that we found one of their bones on the beach," said Bailey.

"What?" Gramps exclaimed.

"I stepped on a bone in the sand, and Sydney said it was part of a dead sailor."

"I did not!" said Sydney. "I was telling you a ghost story. The bone was probably left from someone's barbeque lunch."

Mr. Jones chuckled. "It sounds like you girls are having quite the time up there in Corolla."

Sydney remembered what she had been thinking about before Bailey had mentioned the bone. "What happened to the *Hewitt*?" she asked.

"Well," said Mr. Jones, "that's another great mystery. It

disappeared around the same time the *Carroll A. Deering* was found stuck in the shoals. It was never heard from again."

"Another ghost ship!" said Bailey. "It sounds like there's no more evidence to support those theories than mine: I still think they were abducted by aliens."

Mr. Jones sighed. "I guess I can't argue with you, Bailey. But I don't believe in UFOs."

"Me neither," said Gramps.

Bailey looked to Sydney for support.

"I don't know," Sydney said. "We've seen and heard some strange things lately and haven't found any logical explanations."

"You're the Camp Club Girls!" Mr. Jones said. "Be good detectives, and see if you can find an explanation for your UFOs. If nothing else, you'll come up with some good theories. Who knows, maybe fifty years from now, people will discuss your UFO theories the way we just discussed the theories about the *Deering*."

The girls thanked Mr. Jones for his time. Then they went to explore the rest of the museum.

Bailey was excited to see a lighthouse exhibit, including a model of the Cape Hatteras black-and-white-striped lighthouse. She enjoyed looking at the exhibits for each of the lighthouses on the Outer Banks, including the Currituck Beach Lighthouse in Corolla.

"Hey, Kate would be interested in this," said Sydney. "When the lighthouse we climbed was first built, it didn't have electricity. The lighthouse keeper had to rotate the lens at the top of the tower by hand so the light appeared to flash."

Bailey looked at a diagram of the lighthouse showing all of its parts. "If Kate had lived back then, she'd have found some sort of high-tech gadget to make it easier. Hey, if there was no electricity, where did the light come from?"

Sydney read the caption under a picture. "It came from a giant oil lamp," she said. "The lens was rotated with a system of weights, sort of the way a grandfather clock works. The lighthouse keeper or his assistant had to crank the weights by hand every two and a half hours. Look, here's a picture."

Bailey studied the old, yellowed photo of the lighthouse keeper cranking the weights. "Captain Swain!"

"What?" said Sydney.

"It says here, CAPTAIN NATHAN SWAIN ROTATES THE LENS ON THE CURRITUCK BEACH LIGHTHOUSE, 1910. Sydney, that's a picture of him. It's Captain Swain!"

Sydney looked carefully at the photo. "It does sort of look like him," she said, "but it can't be, because this picture was taken one hundred years ago."

"It's him," Bailey insisted. "He's a ghost."

"What are you girls so interested in?" asked Gramps. He had been looking at another exhibit across the room.

"Just this picture of the Currituck Beach lighthouse keeper," said Sydney. "He looks like someone we saw there the other day."

"There's a whole book about the lighthouse keepers over there," said Gramps, pointing across the room. "Maybe you can find him in there."

Bailey and Sydney found the book *Lightkeepers of the Outer Banks* on a table near the exhibits. Sydney looked in the table of contents and found "Currituck Beach Lighthouse." She turned to page 87 and found a list of lightkeepers beginning in 1875. Sydney read them aloud, "Burris, Simmons, Shinnault, Scott, Simpson, Hinnant, another Simmons. . . Here he is—Nathan H.

Swain! He was the lighthouse keeper from 1905 until 1920."

"Is there a picture of him?" Bailey asked, looking over Sydney's shoulder.

"No," she answered. "But there's a footnote." She turned to the back of the book, and there she found a photograph of an old newspaper article, CAPTAIN NATHAN H. SWAIN RETIRES AS KEEPER OF THE CURRITUCK BEACH LIGHTHOUSE.

There was a picture, a close-up of the captain wearing his uniform. Sydney caught her breath. "It's him!"

"Oh my," Bailey said. "He really is a ghost!"

CHAPTER
8

Theories

After their day in Hatteras, the girls were relaxing in their room. Sydney was on the bed studying a photocopy of the Captain Swain article. She even used a magnifying glass to look at his picture better.

"This photo is a little blurry. It sure does look like our captain," she said. "But it can't be the same man."

Bailey sat at the desk painting her fingernails with a light blue nail polish called Gonna Getchu Blue.

"He's a ghost!" she insisted. "That explains why he disappeared at the lighthouse and on the beach the other morning."

"Yeah, but what about *this* morning?" said Sydney. "We heard him talking with that other guy on the beach—"

"The alien," Bailey added, blowing on her nails.

Sydney got up and slid open the glass doors, letting the warm ocean breeze rush into the room. "Think about this, Bailey. You're telling me that a ghost was on the beach this morning, and he was talking to a space alien. Do you know how crazy that sounds?"

Bailey tightened the cap on the nail polish bottle. "Okay, so do you have another explanation? If he's not a ghost, how do you explain that the Captain Swain in the newspaper article

214

isn't the same guy?"

"I don't know yet," said Sydney. "But I'm going to find out." She sat down on the bed and opened her laptop. "I'm going to e-mail the girls everything we know so far, and if we work together we'll get to the bottom of this."

Sydney wrote an e-mail to the Camp Club Girls. She included her list of facts:

1. Before Bailey arrived, there were reports of strange lights over the Atlantic Ocean near the Outer Banks.

2. On Bailey's first night, she saw flashing red lights over the water.

3. The next day, after we climbed the lighthouse, Captain Swain seemed to disappear.

4. That afternoon, we found the mysterious mug on the beach.

5. Early yesterday morning, we saw a UFO. We heard a whirring noise, but then the sound quit. Something rushed past us on the beach with a puff of air. It left waffle-like footprints. Then we ran into Captain Swain on the beach. He seemed to disappear in a hurry again.

6. Later, we went to watch Nate Wright cluster balloon. The words on the Wrights' bus spelled "Roswell" backward.

7. In the afternoon, the mug started flashing, so we put it back on the beach where we found it.

8. *Early this morning, someone out in the ocean was using a flashing light to send Morse code. The message said: "I think we're being watched from the Lincoln house. Someone is on the deck with a flashlight."*

9. *We heard Captain Swain on the beach talking to another guy. The guy said he wasn't going to put the "vehicle" in the water until Bailey left. He also said the mug was his and that we broke it. He took it with him.*

10. *Today we went to the graveyard of the Atlantic Museum. We found an old newspaper article with a picture of a guy named Captain Nathan Swain. He looks just like our Captain Swain. But the picture was taken 100 years ago!*

So, Camp Club Girls, who is this man, and what are the mysterious lights over the ocean?

Sydney and Bailey

Sydney attached a copy of the article with the picture of Captain Swain. "There," she said. "Now we'll see what the girls come up with."

Bailey was looking at her nails. "Do you like this color," she asked, "or should I try Sparkle Me Purple?"

"I like the blue," said Sydney. "You know, I just remembered something. Didn't the captain say he'd climbed the lighthouse before?"

"Yeah," Bailey answered. "He said, 'I climbed these stairs a lot back in the day,' or something like that—which would make sense if he was the lighthouse keeper. I mean, they had to rotate that thingy by hand to make the light work, right? Didn't they have to do that every couple of hours? So he would've climbed those stairs lots of times. He's a ghost, Syd. Admit it."

Sydney sat fidgeting with her cornrows. "Remember what Mr. Jones said? We should rule out all the other theories before we decide that he's a ghost or an alien or a mystery that we can't explain." She picked up Bailey's bottle of blue nail polish and shook it.

"So what's your theory?" asked Bailey.

"Well, I thought that maybe our captain was the son of the man in the article." Sydney opened the bottle and brushed some Gonna Getchu Blue onto her thumbnail. "But then I read the article again, and Captain Nathan Swain only had one child, a daughter named Nellie." She held her right hand out to look at the color.

"Any other theories?" Bailey asked.

"Not yet," said Sydney. "How about you?"

"Maybe he just happens to look exactly like the guy in the photograph and just *happens* to be a captain, too, and just *happens* to have the same last name."

"Are you being sarcastic?" Sydney asked, wiping off the polish.

"Of course I am," said Bailey. "There's maybe room for one coincidence, but not three."

Sydney chose a bottle of pale Tickle Me Pink nail polish and began brushing it onto her nails. She was almost done when her cell phone rang. "Bailey, will you get that, please?" she asked. "My nails are wet."

Bailey got Sydney's phone out of her backpack. "It's a text message from Mac. It says: I'm SETTING UP A GROUP CHAT FOR TONIGHT. WE NEED TO DISCUSS THIS!"

"Great," Sydney said. "We need all the help we can get."

●━━●━━●

When Bailey and Sydney logged into the chat room after supper, the other Camp Club Girls were waiting.

> McKenzie: *We were talking before you got here. Do you know much about your Captain Swain, the one from the lighthouse?*

Sydney and Bailey sat next to each other on Syd's bed.

> Sydney: *No, we didn't really get to know him at all. He walked up the stairs with us and helped Bailey get over her fear of heights. Then, once we were up there, he left, or something, and we didn't see him go.*
>
> McKenzie: *What does he look like?*
>
> Sydney: *He's about as tall as I am and sort of round. He had a gray beard and was dressed like a sea captain. He had on a blue captain's cap and a blue, heavy jacket with shiny buttons.*

"Don't forget about the dog," said Bailey.

> Sydney: *And he has a shaggy black dog about*

the size of Biscuit. Named McTavish.
When we saw the captain on the beach,
he wore a dark blue jogging suit with a
coast guard emblem on the sleeve.

"And he talks about God," Bailey reminded her.

Sydney: *And he talks about God.*
Elizabeth: *What does he say about God?*
Sydney: *He quotes the Bible and says that he*
and God are talking out loud.
Elizabeth: *Then he must be a Christian. And*
I think that's your best reason to believe
that he's not a ghost.

Bailey borrowed the laptop from Sydney.

Bailey: *Why?*
Elizabeth: *Because when Christians die,*
their souls go to heaven. The Bible says
in 2 Corinthians 5:8 that when we're
absent from our bodies, we're present with
the Lord.
McKenzie: *So we know your captain is*
somehow involved with the lights, right?
Bailey: *He had something to do with whoever*
was flashing the Morse code this morning.
But we don't know for sure that he had
anything to do with the strange lights
flashing over the water.

Alexis: *What do you know about the cluster*
ballooning guys, the ones with the Roswell bus?

Bailey looked at Sydney and shrugged her shoulders. She didn't really know much about the Wrights except what she'd heard from Sydney, her grandparents, and the Kessler twins. She gave the laptop back to Sydney.

Sydney carried it over to the desk and turned on a lamp in the room. It was nearly dark outside, and it had begun to rain. Bailey pulled up a chair and joined her.

Sydney: *They're related to the Wright*
Brothers. You remember them, don't you?
They invented the airplane, and they
made their first flight down the coast
from here near Kitty Hawk. Nate is a
distant cousin or something. He has a son
named Drake, but everyone around here
calls him Digger. I think he's around fifteen.
Kate: *How cool is that? You actually* know
relatives of the Wright Brothers!
Sydney: *I don't know them. They keep to*
themselves. The only time anyone sees Mr.
Wright is when he's testing an invention,
and Digger only comes out when no one
else is around or when he's helping his dad.
Elizabeth: *Why do they call him Digger?*

Sydney got up and slid the glass doors closed. It was raining hard now, and the beach was empty. It was too rainy for ghost crab hunting, or anything else for that matter. She sat back at the desk.

Sydney: *Because he picks up junk on the*
beach. I'm not sure what exactly, but it's
usually stuff that washes up on the shore.
The other morning, Bailey and I saw him
stuffing things into his backpack. Some-
times he walks along the water with a
strange cart. He fills it with driftwood and
stuff, but if he sees anyone coming,
he leaves.

Bailey took the computer from Sydney.

Bailey: *I've seen him a couple of times. He's*
kind of cute. He's tall, thin, and tan,
and he has shaggy blond hair. He looks
like a surfer.
McKenzie: *Mmm. What's Mr. Wright like?*
Sydney: *Imagine Santa Claus on a bad day.*
He's older with a sunburned face, a scruffy
white beard, and white hair that hangs over
his collar. He always wears a red baseball
cap and bib overalls.

"And cowboy boots," Bailey added.

Sydney: *And cowboy boots. Mr. Wright is*
an inventor. At least that's what people
say. He doesn't talk much. This summer,
he's experimenting with cluster ballooning
as a green way of transportation.

Elizabeth: *So in the future, we'll all travel in chairs powered by balloons?*

Sydney: *If Mr. Wright has his way.*

Alexis: *I think your captain fits in with the Wrights, but I can't figure out the missing piece. So far, we have a 100-year-old Captain Swain, a younger Captain Swain who looks like him, a kid who picks up junk on the beach, and an inventor who flies in a chair powered by balloons.*

Bailey was busy thinking. She licked her lips and borrowed the laptop from Sydney.

Bailey: *Maybe they're all modern pirates. Mr. Jones, at the museum, said pirates were still around when the ghost ship disappeared. Maybe Nate Wright has invented a flying machine that scopes out ships at sea. Maybe it has a big hook that snatches the cargo. Then he drops it on the beach, and Digger picks it up. I'm still not sure what the ghost captain does, though.*

McKenzie: *Maybe they're divers and scavengers. Divers find old shipwrecks and rummage through them looking for stuff to sell. Aren't there tons of old wrecks off the shores of the Outer Banks?*

The rain was falling harder now. It drummed on the roof

over Sydney and Bailey's room.

"That's the best theory yet," Sydney said to Bailey. "Don't you think so?"

Bailey was chewing her lower lip. "It makes sense," she answered. "But what about the captain? We still don't know who he is, or how he's involved."

> Sydney: *We like your theory, Mac, but how does Captain Swain fit in?*
>
> Kate: *And what about that other guy on the beach, the one the captain was talking to this morning. Do you have any theories about him?*
>
> Elizabeth: *A kid's young voice, or a man's young voice?*
>
> Sydney: *A young man's voice. Lots of boys are around here. It could have been anyone.*
>
> Kate: *Could it have been Digger?*
>
> McKenzie: *I was just going to suggest that.*
>
> Alexis: *I was thinking it, too.*

The rain was pelting the windows in the guest room, and Bailey sat watching the water stream down the panes. "What do you think?" Sydney asked her. "Could the voice we heard on the beach this morning have been Drake Wright?"

"I suppose it could," said Bailey. "The only time I've heard him is when he yelled 'Get back' yesterday morning, and I don't really remember what he sounded like."

Sydney sighed. "Well, that would connect the Wrights with the captain. It's an idea worth exploring."

Sydney: *We're not sure, but it might have
been. We need to investigate.*
Alexis: *The scavenger theory is beginning to
make sense. But we still need to figure out
Captain Swain. Do you know anyone else
who knows him?*

Sydney leaned back in her chair and thought.

Sydney: *I don't know many people in the
village. I only go there when I ride
my bike. I like to get ice cream at a
little restaurant there and hang out by
the lighthouse sometimes. I've never seen
the captain before, but I could ask around
and see if anyone knows him.*

Bailey's face lit up. "Hey," she said. "What about the lighthouse lady?"

"Huh?" Sydney asked.

"You know. The lady who gave us the sticker books. You asked her if she'd seen the captain coming down the stairs, and she said 'Captain Swain.' I remember. She used his name."

Sydney remembered, too. "You're right! She did use his name, didn't she? Then she definitely knows who he is. She's new at the lighthouse this summer, so I didn't even think about her. Good work, Bailey."

Sydney: *Bailey just remembered the lady who
takes care of the lighthouse talked about*

*the captain, so we'll go there tomorrow
and ask her.*

McKenzie: *That's great! If you can find out
about him, you'll be closer to solving the
mystery of the lights over the ocean.*

Elizabeth: *I know he's definitely not the ghost
of Captain Swain. I'll pray tonight that
you find out your beach isn't haunted by
ghosts or being invaded by aliens.*

Alexis: *Keep us posted. Good-bye for now
from Sacramento.*

McKenzie: *And from big sky country.*

Kate: *And from Philly.*

"Well," said Sydney, shutting down her laptop. "It's a good theory that they might be scavenging old shipwrecks." She turned off the desk lamp.

"I guess so," said Bailey. "Maybe the lighthouse lady will have some answers about Captain Swain when we go there tomorrow."

CHAPTER 9

Camp Club Spies

"It's locked," Sydney said. She stood on the lighthouse porch and pulled the door handle. "Maybe storms are coming."

Bailey laid her bike in the grass next to Sydney's and took off her backpack. "I don't think so. I watched the weather this morning. We're in for a bright, sunny day." She threw her backpack on the ground next to Sydney's.

"Everything's still wet from the rain last night," Sydney observed. "There are puddles all over the place."

"And mud," Bailey added. "Look at the mess you're leaving." She pointed to the footprints going up the front steps to the door.

Sydney lifted each foot and checked the bottoms of her tennis shoes. They were wet, but clean. "It's not my mess," she said. "Someone else has been here." She knocked on the lighthouse door, but no one answered.

"The footprints are too big to be the lighthouse lady's," Bailey said. "They're more like boot prints."

Sydney knocked again.

"So now what?" Bailey asked.

"Maybe there's a back door," Sydney replied. She walked down the steps and disappeared around the side of the lighthouse with Bailey close behind.

The lighthouse was attached to a small brick house. The girls discovered that it had no back door. Instead, where a back door would be, the house was connected to the tower. The sides of the house had several tall windows flanked by green shutters. Each narrow window was made up of ten little panes of glass.

"I wish I could look inside," said Sydney. "But the windows are too high." She jumped up, trying to peek in, but still wasn't tall enough.

"Boost me up," said Bailey.

"Huh?"

"Boost me up." Bailey stepped behind Sydney. She grabbed her shoulders and swung her legs around Sydney's hips. Then she stretched her neck to see through the window. "I'm not high enough," she said. Bailey put her feet back on the ground. "Can you boost me up on your shoulders?"

"I can try," said Sydney. She bent over. Bailey climbed onto her shoulders and wrapped her arms around Sydney's neck. Then Sydney stood up and teetered against Bailey's weight. "Can you see anything?" she asked.

"The sun's reflecting off the glass," Bailey answered. "Move me closer."

Sydney took a giant step forward while trying to balance Bailey and keep herself from falling.

Bailey let go of Sydney's neck and rested her hands on each side of the window. She pressed her nose against the glass. The room she was looking at was the office.

"Nobody's in there," she said. "The blue Wait Here to Climb sign is in the middle of the room, so the lighthouse must be closed. Hey, wait. Someone is moving in there. I see a shadow." For a few seconds, Bailey said nothing. Then she pushed herself off Sydney's shoulders and fell to the ground. "Run!" she said. She got up from the ground and scrambled with Sydney toward a grove of trees.

"What did you see?" Sydney asked as they slipped behind a big evergreen tree.

"It was Nate Wright," Bailey answered. "He had a really long chain and was heading for the curvy staircase. I think he might have seen me."

"Shhhh," said Sydney. "Look."

Nate Wright came around the side of the lighthouse. He was dressed in his bib overalls and red cap, and he looked as scruffy as ever. He stopped and looked left and right. Then as the girls watched through the thick, needled branches, he took off his cap, scratched his head, and walked back toward the front of the lighthouse.

"I think he saw you," Sydney whispered. "I think he was looking around for you."

"Yeah, but he has no idea who I am," said Bailey. "Unless he recognized me from when we watched him cluster ballooning on the beach."

"I doubt it. He was too busy to pay any attention to the crowd."

"So now what?" Bailey asked.

"We find a safe place to watch, far enough away, where we can keep our eyes on the front door. There's no other exit from the building."

Bailey stepped out of the grove of trees and began walking toward the lighthouse. Sydney grabbed her arm and pulled her back. "Where are you going?"

"We have to get our bikes and backpacks," said Bailey.

"Not now," Sydney told her. "We should leave them there. Otherwise, he might see us."

Bailey sighed. "But if we leave them, it's a dead giveaway that we're here."

"We have to take that chance," Sydney answered. "Let's double back through these trees. We'll end up on Schoolhouse Road by the Village Bar-B-Q. Then we can cross the street and watch the lighthouse from there."

Bailey followed Sydney through the trees, along a winding footpath, and over to Schoolhouse Road. They made a wide circle to avoid walking close to the lighthouse. Then they found a park bench not far from the lighthouse museum shop. From there, they could see the lighthouse and its front door.

"Look," said Bailey, pointing upward. "He's up on the lookout."

From where the girls sat, Mr. Wright appeared to be a tiny figure. His red baseball cap made him easy to see. His back was to the heavy iron railing, and he seemed to be busy doing something, but they couldn't tell what.

"I wish I had my binoculars," Sydney said. "They're in my backpack."

"No problem," said Bailey. "I'll get them."

Before Sydney could stop her, Bailey was running up the brick path toward the lighthouse door. With lightning speed, she snatched Sydney's bike and backpack. Then she hurried back to Sydney.

"There," she said, handing her the backpack. "Mission accomplished." She laid Sydney's bike on the ground.

Sydney unzipped a deep pocket on the outside of the backpack and pulled out her binoculars. Then she put the eyepiece to her eyes, pointed the lens at the lookout, and focused.

"He's pulling on something," she said. "Wait. It's that chain you saw. He's pulling it through the little doorway that leads out to the lookout. Boy, is it ever long! He's already got a bunch of it lying on the floor up there."

"Why do you think he's doing that?" Bailey asked. She squinted, trying to see.

"Beats me," said Sydney. She handed the binoculars to Bailey.

Just then, a rumble came from Schoolhouse Road. Sydney looked in that direction and saw a man driving a small green tractor. The tractor pulled an open trailer that held a tall wooden crate. The tractor left the road and turned onto the lighthouse grounds. Sydney watched it weave around the trees and onto the path near where they sat. Then she recognized the driver.

"Bailey, turn away!" she hissed.

"What?" asked Bailey.

"Turn and face me, right now!"

The urgency in Sydney's voice made Bailey do as she was told. She put the binoculars on her lap, turned her body sideways on the bench, and looked at Sydney's back.

"Syd, why are we sitting like this?" she asked.

By now the tractor had passed them and was moving toward the front of the lighthouse. Sydney turned and looked at Bailey. "I didn't want him to recognize us," she said.

"Who to recognize us?" Bailey wondered.

"The man driving the tractor was Captain Swain!" said Sydney.

The captain was barely recognizable without his navy blue

clothing. He was dressed in a pair of jeans and a black T-shirt. The only thing that made Sydney sure that it was him was his neat, gray beard and the captain's cap on his head. He drove the tractor to the lighthouse steps and stopped. As the girls watched, Captain Swain walked to the front door, took out a key, and entered.

"Look, he has a key to the lighthouse," said Sydney.

"That's strange," Bailey replied. She handed the binoculars to Sydney. "Why would he have a key? Maybe it's a skeleton key, the kind that opens any old door."

"Hi, Sydney!"

"Hi, Bailey!"

The Kessler twins came from behind them. Each was walking with a tandem bike.

"I didn't know you guys were going to the Village this morning," said Carolyn.

"Me neither," said Marilyn. "What are you doing with those binoculars?"

Sydney wasn't about to tell the Kesslers what was going on. They had a reputation for not being able to keep a secret.

"Sometimes I like bird watching," she said, which was totally true.

"Bird watching!" Marilyn exclaimed.

"Sydney's a nature nut," said Bailey. "At Discovery Lake Camp she was the only camper who knew about every animal in the woods and every bird in the sky. What are you guys doing here?"

"We're going to pick up our brothers," said Carolyn.

"We stopped at the Bar-B-Q first to get root beer," said Marilyn. "Are you guys going to the crab fest tonight?" She rested her bike against the bench where Sydney and Bailey sat.

"What's a crab fest?" Sydney asked. Captain Swain came out of the lighthouse now, and Sydney nudged Bailey with her elbow.

Sydney watched the captain as he unhitched the gate on the trailer. Mr. Wright was still on the lookout, but without using her binoculars Sydney couldn't tell what he was up to.

"So are you going?" said Marilyn.

"Where?" Sydney asked. She was busy watching the captain as he climbed into the trailer and took the straps off the crate.

"To the crab fest!" Marilyn replied.

"Sydney asked you what it is," Carolyn reminded her.

"Oh, yeah," Marilyn said. "The Village is having a crab boil tonight."

"The restaurant is sponsoring it," Carolyn added. "They'll have a big crab dinner—"

"With corn, potatoes, deep-fried onion petals, and homemade cherry pie," said Marilyn.

"And ice cream!" Carolyn said. "And they're having bands and some carnival games. It's to raise money for the lighthouse renovation. That's a good cause, don't you think?" She picked up her tandem and held on to the front handlebars.

"Uh-huh," said Sydney. She noticed that Mr. Wright looked even busier up on the lookout. She nudged Bailey again, and Bailey nudged her back.

"So are you going?" asked Marilyn, picking up her bike.

"I'm not sure yet," said Sydney. "We'll let you know." Her fingers were wrapped around the binoculars in her lap. She couldn't wait to look through them to see what Nate Wright was up to.

"It sounds like fun," Bailey said halfheartedly. "So maybe we'll see you later, then."

"Okay," said Marilyn, hopping onto her bike and shoving off. "See you later!"

Carolyn got onto her bike and followed. "See you later," she echoed.

Sydney sighed with relief. "I'm glad they're gone."

She already had the binoculars to her eyes. "He's lowering the chain down to the captain." Mr. Wright had the big chain wrapped around a heavy wheel-like machine up on the lookout. He was lowering one end of it to Captain Swain, who was standing inside the trailer. Sydney noticed a big hook on the end of the chain.

"What do you think's in the box?" she asked.

"I don't know," Bailey replied. "It's about as tall as I am, so it must be big."

"Too big to carry up that spiral staircase," said Sydney.

Bailey watched. "You know, Syd, I'm wondering where the lighthouse lady is. Do you think she knows what's going on in there?"

"I don't know," Sydney answered. "Captain Swain just hooked the chain onto the crate."

From somewhere above them came the whirring of an engine. Bailey looked up, expecting to see a small plane flying overhead, but nothing was in the sky.

"What's that noise?" she asked.

"It's coming from the lookout," said Sydney as the crate lifted off the trailer and up into the air. "Mr. Wright has a gasoline-powered pulley up there. That's what's making the noise. It's lifting the crate to the top of the lighthouse."

Sydney and Bailey took turns with the binoculars watching the crate rise. Mr. Wright guided it over the top of the railing and set it on the narrow floor. Once it was safely secured, Captain Swain went inside.

"He's going up by Mr. Wright," said Sydney. "Now's a good time to get your bike. You watch, and I'll go this time." She handed the binoculars to Bailey before heading up the narrow brick path. When Sydney got near the door, she heard two men talking inside. She hid next to the porch and listened. One of the voices she recognized as the captain's. The other was the younger voice they'd heard on the beach.

"She's locked up in our equipment shed," said the young man.

"Good," said Captain Swain. "A job well done, Drake, a job well done."

Digger! Sydney thought. *He was on the beach with the captain.*

"I've taken care of all the paperwork," Captain Swain continued. "You won't have to keep it a secret anymore. Tonight I'll help you fix the problem with the rudder. Then you're on your way."

"I'm nervous about people seeing it," Drake answered.

"My boy, an anxious heart weighs a man down," said the captain. "Just me and God talking to you."

Sydney grabbed Bailey's bike and rushed back to the bench. "Drake's in there, too!" she told Bailey. "They have someone locked in their equipment shed!"

"Who?" Bailey asked.

"I don't know," Sydney answered. "Drake said, 'She's locked up safe in our equipment shed.'"

"The lighthouse lady!" Bailey gasped. "They've kidnapped her."

"I didn't think of that," Sydney answered as she laid Bailey's bike on the grass. "Do you really think they've kidnapped her? And why would they do that?"

"What else did they say?" Bailey asked as she handed the binoculars to Sydney.

"Tonight the captain is helping them fix some sort of problem, and then they're leaving. The captain said that after that they'll be on their way." Sydney sat down next to Bailey.

"See," said Bailey. "I *am* right. They're aliens, and Captain Swain is helping them. They're taking the lighthouse lady with them. She's being abducted by aliens!"

Sydney watched while the Wrights and Captain Swain pried open the wooden crate. "Bailey, I still believe that there's a logical explanation for all this. I just don't know what it is yet."

Bailey sighed. "So now what?"

"I think we need to go to the crab fest tonight. We can go to the Wrights' place when it's dark out, and then we can see what's going on."

Up on the lookout, the men were lifting something out of the crate.

"It's a big telescope!" Sydney said as she handed the binoculars to Bailey.

"They're setting it up," Bailey observed. "They're attaching it to the railing up there. Now the captain is looking through it. He's looking out at the ocean." Bailey handed the binoculars back to Sydney. "I think they put it there so they can watch for the Mother Ship tonight."

Sydney didn't even bother to argue with Bailey about the alien idea. Mr. Wright was lowering the chain, and the empty crate dropped to the ground.

"I think they're leaving," said Sydney.

The girls waited to see what would happen next. Mr. Wright and Digger were the first to come out the front door. They walked across the grass to Schoolhouse Road. Then they turned west toward home. The captain came out next. He locked the door behind him and started down the front porch stairs. When he got to the bottom, he stopped.

"Oh no, my backpack!" said Bailey.

Captain Swain picked up the backpack and read the name on its ID tag: BAILEY CHANG. He looked around. Then he set the backpack on the lighthouse steps and drove away on his tractor.

Questions

Sydney's grandparents agreed that the crab fest would be a fun activity for the girls. As they got ready to leave, Bailey flung her backpack over her shoulders.

"At least he didn't take it with him," she said. She was talking about what had happened that morning when Captain Swain saw her backpack by the lighthouse porch.

"I'd feel better if your name wasn't on it," said Sydney. "If Mr. Wright saw you looking through the window and described you to the captain, he might have put two and two together."

"I didn't think of that," Bailey answered.

"Let me check in and see if any of the girls have sent anything," Sydney said.

Sure enough, when she logged on the computer, she found a couple of notes on the private wall of the Camp Club Girls Web site.

> Alexis: *I watched an old TV show today and*
> *it made me think about your problem*
> *with the identity of Captain Swain. On*
> *the show, two grown-up cousins looked so*
> *much alike that they were mistaken for twins.*

Sometimes that happens—a family resemblance may be strong in several people, even if they're not brothers and sisters, or children of the person they look like. We know the original Captain Swain didn't have any sons, so your Captain Swain couldn't be his son. But maybe he's a cousin of the original Captain Swain or something.

Kate: *I've been thinking about Captain Swain, too. Bailey, I'm like Beth—I don't believe in ghosts. And ghosts don't own property—according to the law, no dead people can own property. But I looked on the Internet and found that there's a Captain Swain with the address of Duck, North Carolina. When I Googled Duck, I found out it's just south of Corolla. So it sounds like your Captain Swain is a legitimate resident of the area!*

"Sounds like one mystery is solved, anyway," Sydney said.

"I don't know," Bailey said. "It sounds convincing, but I think I'm going to confront Captain Swain and ask him for myself."

Sydney grinned. Sometimes Bailey was so dramatic!

"Well, come on," Sydney said. "Maybe you'll see him at the crab fest and you can ask him there!"

By the time the girls arrived in Corolla Village, the sun had just set. A crowd had gathered at the Corolla Village Bar-B-Q where glowing paper lanterns were strung from tree to tree. On the front lawn, steam rose from a huge black pot over a fire. Two cooks from the restaurant dumped buckets full of crabs into the boiling water. Then they added Old Bay seasoning, ears of corn, onions, and small new potatoes.

"Yum, that smells good," said Bailey. On a small stage at the edge of the parking lot, the Wild Horse Band was playing a tune. Bailey grabbed Sydney's hands and swung her around in time with the music.

"Woo-hoo! Let's hear it for the crab fest!" Bailey squealed.

As the girls spun, Sydney glimpsed the Kessler twins arriving with their brothers and mom and dad.

"The twins are here," she told Bailey when the music stopped. "We probably have to hang out with them, but we need to get away to investigate the Wrights' place. Listen, don't say anything about what we're up to, okay? They can't keep a secret."

"Have they seen us?" Bailey asked.

"I don't think so," said Sydney.

"Then why don't we go over to the Wrights' now? We can see what's going on and then come back here and hang out with the twins."

Sydney agreed, and soon she and Bailey were walking up Schoolhouse Road in the direction of the sound. When they got to Persimmon Street, they saw a narrow, sandy road marked PRIVATE DRIVE.

"This must be it," said Sydney. She remembered her grandmother saying the Wrights lived on a wooded private road off Persimmon. "Gram knows a potter who lives on this road, and the Wrights' place is just beyond hers. It's at the end of the drive, I think."

The girls turned onto the sandy lane and walked along the edge of the woods.

"I wish we had a flashlight," said Bailey. The only light came from porch lights along the way. The road was barely wide enough for two cars to pass, and it was deserted. Either all the residents were at the crab fest or they were inside their houses.

Bailey noticed that these houses weren't like most others on the Outer Banks. These were old-fashioned, two-story cottages with narrow front porches and gabled roofs. They looked like they had been there forever.

Who-who-whooooo-who-who. A great-horned owl called from a distant tree.

"I feel like I'm back at Discovery Lake Camp," said Bailey. "This place is spooky. It's so dark and deserted. Syd, are you sure you want to do this?"

"Look. Here's the potter's house," said Sydney. At the edge of the road, an old tin mailbox sat atop a lovely statue of a mermaid. The name on the box said WILMA HEISER, POTTERY PLUS.

"The Wrights' place has to be over there." She pointed ahead to a sharp bend in the road.

"Listen!"

A loud rumble came from behind them. Some sort of vehicle had just turned off Persimmon Street and onto the private drive.

"Someone's coming. We have to hide!"

Sydney grabbed Bailey and pulled her behind some tall bushes in the potter's front yard. They could see the road.

Thud-thud. . .thud-thud. . .rumble. . .thud-thud. . .thud-thud. . .

rumble. . . Whatever it was grew closer. It chugged along slowly, its headlights illuminating the sand. Soon the girls saw a big yellow wall. They could almost touch the school bus as it lumbered by, and in the darkness, they could barely make out the words.

LASERS
LEVITATING
ELEVATING
WRIGHT &
SON
ORIENTEERING
RACING

"It's the Roswell bus," Bailey whispered. She and Sydney watched it disappear around the bend at the end of the road. "What do we do now?"

"Let's wait a few minutes," Sydney answered. "Until we're sure they're inside."

Soon the girls heard the sounds of hammering and sawing coming from the Wrights' place. Cautiously, they walked to the bend in the road and, keeping in the cover of the trees, they got close enough to see the Wrights' equipment shed. It was set about fifteen yards away from the grungy old house that Mr. Wright and Digger lived in.

The equipment shed was almost as big as the house, and its heavy front doors were wide open. A shower of sparks rained inside.

"Welding," said Sydney. "They must be working on the whatever-it-is."

An eerie blue glow came from fluorescent lights hanging

from the rafters, and a strong smell of hot steel wafted through the air.

The noise stopped for a few seconds. After a ghostly silence, the inside of the shed went dark.

"Look!" Bailey exclaimed. The shed lit up with flashing lights, first red, and then multicolored. "It's the spaceship. Remember? I said that they were reconstructing their ship from parts Digger found on the beach. Now do you believe me?"

Sydney had to admit that they were looking at something very strange. "Let's get closer so we can see what's going on," she said.

"I wish we had that listening thing Kate has," said Bailey. "You know, that little gadget that lets you hear a conversation from a block away? Then we could know what's happening without having to go right to the building. Syd, do you think they have the lighthouse lady locked up in there?"

"I don't know," her friend replied. "But we're going to find out."

She took Bailey by the hand and they crept along the side of the road, careful to stay in the shadows. A soft whirring sound came from the shed now, and Sydney and Bailey made a wide circle, staying clear of the open doors. Then they tiptoed to the side of the shed, just below the window.

"I don't think it's safe to look inside just yet," Sydney said. "We should listen for a while."

She'd barely gotten the words out when the colored lights stopped and a bright white light started to flash. One, two, three, four, five flashes. Then nothing. One, two, three, four, five more.

"It's that code from *Close Encounters of the Third Kind*!" Bailey whispered. "That's the light we saw in the ocean yesterday morning."

The flashing stopped. For a few seconds, the shed went dark again. Then it was suddenly lit up by the overhead lights and the bluish fluorescent glow.

"Well, the signal lights work fine," the girls heard Digger say. "I wish I could program the other lights to change color so opponents can disguise themselves. It would add more strategy to the battle. Imagine that you're approaching a friendly craft, but when you get there, you find it's an enemy craft disguised as a friend."

The girls sat on the ground beneath the window with their backs pressed against the side of the building. Sydney could hear Bailey breathing fast and heavy. She felt her own muscles growing more tense.

Relax, Syd, she told herself. *Think! There has to be a logical explanation.*

Bailey whispered so softly that Sydney could barely hear her.

"Maybe they're not trying to get home to their planet," she said. "It sounds like they're going to wage war on an enemy spaceship or something. Syd, they're planning a space war!"

"I doubt it, Bailey," Sydney whispered back. "You know at the lighthouse they said something about Captain Swain helping with the rudder. A rudder is part of a boat. Could that be some sort of funky boat?"

"That's a great idea," Mr. Wright boomed out. The girls jumped. Then as he continued, they realized he wasn't talking to them but to Digger. "But if I were you, son, I'd leave the lights alone for now. Save changing the colors for Phase Two. Hit 'em with what you've got. Then, after it takes off, surprise 'em with something even better."

"I guess you're right, Dad," said Digger.

"See? They're planning to strike with some sort of weapon," Bailey whispered. "It probably has to do with that coffee mug thing that we found on the beach."

Sydney was feeling very vulnerable sitting under the window. If anyone came along, they would surely see the girls. She noticed a brown tarp in the grass nearby. Staying close to the ground, she shimmied over and pulled it back to where Bailey sat.

"Here, let's cover up with this," she said, draping it over herself and Bailey.

"The noise problem is fixed now," Mr. Wright was saying. "When these crafts are on the ocean at night, the folks near the beach won't hear them. So there won't be any trouble."

"And I've got the hover fan working fine now," said Digger. "As soon as the craft hits the beach, a blast of air lifts it off the ground, and you can go anywhere without it being heard."

Bailey linked her arm with Sydney's.

"That was the puff of air that we felt on the beach!" she said. "Drake Wright went past us in the dark with that thing just a few yards away from us. Do you think he saw us?"

"I'm almost sure of it," Sydney answered. "Now we know the Wrights are responsible for those strange lights over the water."

"I'm telling you, it's a spacecraft!" Bailey insisted.

The word *hover* brought a picture into Sydney's mind.

"Listen, Bailey!" she exclaimed. "The word *hover*. . .one day at home, I thought I saw something just floating around outside my window. When I looked out, it was a remote-controlled helicopter one of my friends was flying. Do you think this is some sort of remote-controlled device? Like a spaceship-shaped, remote-controlled thing?"

"No. How could they fly it in the dark?" Bailey said.

"I'm going to text Kate," Sydney said, wiggling around to pull the phone out of her pocket. "She'll be able to tell us if it's at least possible."

Sydney had started texting when the sound of a hammer pounding against metal startled the girls. Digger said, "We need to get this rudder fixed. When that's done we can load her up."

The pounding started again.

"See, they do have the lighthouse lady," Bailey said. "I hope she's all right. They're planning to load her onto the spacecraft."

Sydney didn't answer. Her mind was racing, trying to come up with answers for her questions. "*Test the spirits to see whether they are from God.*" She remembered hearing her pastor preach about that in church. As Sydney sat there thinking, she believed more than ever that Mr. Wright and Drake Wright were not space aliens.

"You know, if it's some sort of boat—since rudders are part of boats—they always call boats 'she,' " Sydney explained.

"Cap has the paperwork done and everything is in order," Mr. Wright said. "It's up to you now, son. You have to get it out there for the right person to see. Plenty of investors are vacationing in Corolla and the other subdivisions around here. If you show it around, surely you'll find a backer or two."

"Huh?" Bailey whispered to Sydney under the tarp. "What are they talking about now?"

"Beats me," Sydney answered.

Listen, said a little voice in her head.

"We should just listen," she told Bailey.

"You have to get the word out," Mr. Wright continued. "I'm not going to help you this time, son. If you're going to be successful, you need to get out there with people and show them what you're up to. Why, think about our cousins. Some people thought they were crazy to keep jumping off cliffs with their flying machine, but they didn't let that get to them. They kept at it, and today—"

"But Dad," Digger said, "I don't think I can do it. Besides, I don't mind keeping to myself. I like having time alone to wander and pick up stuff on the beach that we can sell to scrap yards. Last night I found another doubloon for the Cap. He likes giving them to the kids at the lighthouse, you know."

The girls heard a few more strikes of the hammer against metal.

"Are you going to spend the rest of your life selling junk you find on the beach?" Mr. Wright asked his son. "Or are you going to face your fear and live the life God gave you? Remember what the Cap always says."

" 'I can do all things through Him who strengthens me,' " Digger replied.

"That's what Captain Swain said to me when I was afraid to climb the lighthouse," Bailey whispered.

"I know," Sydney answered. "I want to look inside and see what's going on."

"Me, too," Bailey said. "But I'm scared."

The girls stood, still wrapped in the tarp. They dropped it around their shoulders and peeked through the dirty window.

"Oh my." Bailey gasped.

"Awesome," Sydney exclaimed in a whisper.

In the center of the shed sat a vehicle beyond her imagination. It was about the size of a small car, but round. It was painted a soft gray-blue, the color of the ocean on an overcast day. The paint sparkled the way sunlight dances on waves.

In the center of the craft a cockpit was covered with a clear glass bubble. It reminded Sydney of pictures she'd seen in school textbooks of fighter jets. As she watched, Digger climbed into the cockpit and flipped a switch. The flashing colored lights encircled the craft and spun around its middle. Drake Wright sat in the driver's seat and grinned.

"What do you think it is?" Bailey asked.

"I don't know," Sydney replied. "It's not like anything I've seen in my whole life. It's kind of beautiful."

"But scary, too," Bailey added.

"Maybe it wouldn't be if we knew what it was," said Sydney.

A muted *whoosh* came from the craft. It sounded like a choir softly singing "Shhhhhh. . ."

As Bailey and Sydney watched, the machine rose off the ground. It hovered several feet above the floor. Then it slowly began to rotate. It spun around faster and faster, and the girls heard Digger laughing gleefully. Slowly it stopped and dropped gently back to the floor. Drake opened the cover on the cockpit and said, "Well, if it doesn't make it as a water sport, maybe I can market it as a carnival ride."

Mr. Wright chuckled. "You're a Wright, my boy," he said. "You always have a backup plan."

Sydney motioned to Bailey to sit. The girls sank back to the ground and covered themselves with the tarp.

"Now I'm really confused," said Bailey. "I'm not so sure it's a spaceship anymore, are you?"

"I was never sure it was a spaceship," said Sydney. "I just don't know what it is yet."

She started to crawl out from under the tarp again.

"What are you doing now?" Bailey asked.

"Stay put," Sydney answered. She crawled to the window. When she was sure the Wrights had their backs to her, she took several photos of the contraption. Then she climbed back under the tarp.

"I didn't use the flash," she said. "I think it's bright enough in there for the pictures to turn out." She looked at the display on her phone and saw she was right. The photos were clear enough to show the craft in the middle of the equipment shed floor.

"Now what?" Bailey asked.

"I'm texting Kate," Sydney replied. "And sending her these pictures. You know how smart she is about technological stuff. She might know what this is."

SYDNEY: K8 , WE'RE HIDING OUT NEXT TO THE WRIGHTS' EQUIPMENT SHED. LOOK AT THESE PICTURES. THEY'VE BUILT THIS THING. IT HAS FLASHING LIGHTS THAT SPIN AROUND IT. IT CAN HOVER A FEW FEET OFF THE FLOOR AND IT ROTATES REALLY FAST. WHAT IS IT?

Sydney sent the message, flipped her phone closed, and stuck it back in her pocket.

"I don't think the Wrights are aliens," she told Bailey. "It looks like that thing is just another one of their crazy inventions. But what is it?"

"Digger said something about a water sport," said Bailey.

"I don't think a water sport would be remote-controlled," Sydney said reluctantly. "And we'll wait to hear back from Kate, but I think anything that is as big as that would be too heavy to be remote-controlled. . ."

"Unless the battery was as big as a bus!" Bailey said.

"Hmm. Could they have a giant battery in that bus of theirs?" Sydney asked. "Nah. I don't think that's the answer."

"But they talked about battles and enemies. That doesn't fit with any water sport I know of. And what about the lighthouse lady? Where has she disappeared to? And then there's Captain Swain. Who do you think he *really* is? And where is he? Wasn't he supposed to be here helping the Wrights tonight?"

"I'm right here, Bailey Chang," said a voice in the darkness. "And I can answer all of your questions."

Answers

Bailey and Sydney crawled out from under the tarp.

Captain Swain stood in the shadows looking at them. He was still wearing jeans, as he had been that morning, and now he had on a sweatshirt that said NAVY on its front. His captain's cap sat squarely on his head.

"What are you girls doing here?" he asked gently.

"You answer our question first," said Bailey. "Who are you, really?"

"You know who I am, Bailey Chang," said the captain. "I'm Captain Nathan Swain."

"No, you're not!" Sydney answered. "Captain Nathan Swain is dead. We saw his picture in an old paper. He was the lighthouse keeper here about a hundred years ago, so you can't be him unless you're an imposter."

"Or a ghost!" Bailey added.

"Well, I don't think you're a ghost," Sydney said with a smile. "But Captain Nathan Swain, the lighthouse keeper, didn't have any sons, so you can't be his son. But I suspect you're another relative."

The captain smiled. "Kudos. Congratulations to you for figuring it out, Miss Sydney Lincoln. Captain Nathan Swain, the lighthouse keeper, was my uncle," he said. "I resemble him, but I can assure you, Miss Bailey Chang, that I'm *not* his ghost. Now, as far as being an imposter, Sydney Lincoln, I'll admit to that. I sometimes masquerade as my uncle."

"Why?" Sydney asked.

Before the captain could answer, Bailey interrupted.

"If you're for real, why did you disappear when we were at the top of the lighthouse?" She climbed out from the tarp and stood up. "One minute you were there, and then you were gone. And the same thing happened on the beach. You were there walking your dog, we talked to you, and then you disappeared. What's up with that?"

The captain leaned against the side of the equipment shed.

"Bailey, my girl, you have quite the imagination. I'm sorry if you thought I had abandoned you. Once you girls were safe on the lookout, I hurried to an appointment I was already late for. I should have said farewell, at least. I sincerely apologize for being rude." He tipped the brim of his cap. "As for the incident on the beach, McTavish saw a cat and ran off. I ran after him. McTavish is a good boy, you know, but he hates cats and would do harm to one if he caught it. I'm sure by the time you looked for me, I was chasing my dog across the dunes."

The clues were beginning to add up for Sydney. There was no ghost of Captain Nathan Swain, and she was certain the captain wasn't helping the Wrights build a spaceship.

"But you were wearing a captain's uniform at the lighthouse," she said, getting off the ground. "The kind captains wore years and years ago."

"I was acting," said the captain. "I volunteer at the lighthouse where I play the role of Captain Nathan Swain, the lighthouse keeper. When schoolchildren tour, I tell them the story of the lighthouse and about the pirates and shipwrecks of the Outer Banks. In fact, years ago, I *did* work in the lighthouse, helping maintain the beacon up top."

Bailey was beginning to feel a bit foolish for thinking that the captain was a ghost, but she still had some unanswered questions.

"So why were you on the beach yesterday morning with Digger?" she asked. "We heard you talking with him about not putting *the vehicle* in the water until after I went home. What exactly is he up to, and what's that thing in the shed?"

The captain shook his head. "'Let the words of my mouth be acceptable in Your sight, O Lord. . .' Just me and God talking out loud," he said. "I know that folks around here call him Digger, but Drake Wright is the young man's name. And Bailey, before I tell you what young Mr. Wright and I were discussing yesterday morning, why don't you tell me why you girls are hiding here in the dark."

Bailey sighed. She was almost certain her theory about space aliens and space wars was wrong. "We thought. . . well, actually *I* thought the Wrights were space aliens and you were helping them get back to the Mother Ship after their spacecraft crashed into the ocean. I thought Digger, I mean Drake, was picking up pieces of the spacecraft along the beach and that the Wrights were rebuilding it in their equipment shed. And I think they've kidnapped the lighthouse lady. I thought they were going to take her to wherever with them. We're spying on them to find out what's going on."

The captain chuckled. "And you, Miss Lincoln, do you believe in aliens from outer space?"

"I guess I always thought there was a logical explanation," Sydney said. "But I agree with Bailey that a lot of things are happening that just don't add up. Why did you and the Wrights put a telescope on the lighthouse lookout this morning?"

The captain chuckled again. "That telescope is part of the lighthouse renovation. It's there so visitors can view the ocean from the tower. And Bailey Chang, the lighthouse lady—I assume you mean the young woman who works at the lighthouse and is named Meghan Kent, by the way. She's—"

"Wait, don't tell me," Sydney said. "She's just taking a day off and when the Wrights were referring to 'she' they meant their invention."

"Again, cheers to you, Sydney Lincoln," said Captain Swain. "Miss Meghan Kent is on vacation for a few days while some remodeling takes place. People who are vacationing here don't stop to think that sometimes we natives need vacations ourselves!"

The captain paused and smiled at the girls.

"Come on inside," said the captain. "There are a couple of fellows I'd like you to meet."

The girls walked with Captain Swain around the side of the equipment shed and through the open front doors. Drake turned and greeted the captain with a smile, but when he saw the girls, his smile faded. "Oh," he said softly.

Mr. Wright walked toward them wiping his hands on a rose-colored rag.

"Hi, Cap." He greeted his friend with a handshake. "I see you've brought some visitors." His voice held a hint of disapproval, and his blue eyes flashed at Sydney and then at Bailey.

"It's all right, Nate," said the captain. "These are my friends and they can be trusted. This is Sydney Lincoln and Bailey Chang." His right hand swept toward the girls.

"You're the kid who looked at me through the lighthouse window this morning," Mr. Wright said gruffly.

"I'm sorry, Mr. Wright," Bailey apologized.

"The girls have been watching us test Drake's invention, and they're curious to know more about it," the captain said.

Sydney noticed that Drake's face had turned a bright shade of red. He looked shyly down at his feet as he stood next to the mysterious craft. Sydney walked up to him with a smile, "Hi, Drake," she said, extending her hand. "It's very nice to meet you."

Drake Wright looked up, but not directly into Sydney's eyes. He grasped the tips of her fingers, gave them a little shake, and then dropped his hand to his side. "I've seen you around," he mumbled.

"Drake, why don't you tell the girls about the Wright D-94 Wave Smasher?" said the captain. "It's okay to talk about it now. You own the patent. I have the paperwork to prove it."

Drake swallowed hard. He looked more embarrassed than ever.

"Go on, son," Mr. Wright encouraged him. "Tell them what this is."

"Yeah," Bailey said, stroking the shiny blue paint. "We can't wait to know."

When Drake saw Bailey's hand touch the paint on the D-94, he stopped looking embarrassed. "Please don't touch it," he said firmly.

Bailey quickly pulled her hand away and stepped backward. "Why? What's it going to do?"

"It's not going to do anything," Drake answered. He pulled

a rag out of the back pocket of his blue jeans and polished the spot Bailey had touched. "I just finished waxing it."

"Oh," said Bailey.

"So tell us about this," Sydney said. She walked around the craft so she could see it from all sides. "You were talking about a rudder. Let me guess. This is a new form of transportation."

Drake said nothing.

" 'I can do all things through Him who strengthens me,' " Captain Swain said. "Just me and God talking, Drake." He walked over to the young man and put his arm around his shoulder. "Think of this as a rehearsal. Tell them about the next great Wright invention, the one that's destined to change life on the Outer Banks forever."

Drake looked at his feet for a few seconds. Then he took a deep breath and began what sounded like a well-rehearsed speech. "This is a vehicle called the Wright D-94 Wave Smasher. It's a new recreational water vehicle that I've been working on for the past several years. The D-94 is unlike any other recreational water vehicle because it can ride on the water or sail up to thirty feet above it with the flick of a switch. It's built tough enough to withstand a ten-foot wave, and the driver is completely protected in the cockpit, so he won't get hurt or wet."

"Or *she*," Bailey corrected him. "Girls can use it, too, right?"

When Bailey saw Drake's shy smile, she was positive that he fell into the "cute" category.

"Yes, girls can use it, too," Drake answered. "But it's not a toy. It's for professional sportsmen—I mean sports people," he corrected himself.

"So why did you invent it?" Sydney asked.

"Well," Drake went on, "you can travel up and down the

Outer Banks and see all sorts of fun things to do on the water. You can kite sail, hang glide, water ski, kayak, sail a boat. . .there are all kinds of activities. But there's nothing like the D-94. In the daytime, it's a superfast racing boat. You can zoom across the water, leap over waves, and even hover or sail up to thirty feet above the water. In fact, it even works on the beach. You just press a button, and it becomes a hovercraft that rides on a cushion of air, or it can walk on its feet." He pushed a button, and four tennis racket–shaped platforms came out of the bottom of the craft.

"So *you* made those strange footprints and passed us on the beach," said Sydney. "You scared us half to death."

"Sorry about that." Drake smiled. "But I didn't think anyone would be out that early in the morning. I've had to be real careful so no one stole my idea until Cap here got me the patent."

"So you only tested it at night?" Bailey asked.

"Yeah," Drake answered. "But there's a reason for that. That D-94 is not only a daytime recreational water vehicle; it's actually a very expensive game piece."

"Huh?" asked Sydney.

"Well, you see," Drake said, "I've also invented a new water sport." He walked over to one wall of the equipment shed and pointed to a big drawing on a sheet of paper stuck to the wall. "Come over here," he said.

When the girls got closer, they saw the drawing looked like a football field off the shore of the ocean. There were pictures of D-94s positioned on the field and a goal post on either end.

"I don't have a catchy name for it yet," said Drake, "but it's all done with lights. Players compete on teams, and the goal is to get all your D-94s safely into your end zone. You play in the dark on an imaginary field on the ocean. A floating string of lights outlines both end zones. The only other lights are on the D-94s. The lights can be stationary or flashing, and they're used as a way to signal plays to other members of your team."

"Baseball players use hand signals, and in this game, the players use light signals instead," said Sydney.

"Yeah, that's right," Drake said, looking like his confidence was growing.

"Wow, this is so cool!" said Sydney. Just then, her cell phone started to vibrate. She excused herself, flipped open the phone, and found a message from Kate. I THINK IT LOOKS TOO HEAVY TO BE A REMOTE-CONTROL DEVICE. I GOOGLED NATE WRIGHT. HE HAS A REPUTATION FOR CREATIVE FORMS OF TRANSPORTATION, SO I WOULD GUESS THAT IT'S AN EXPERIMENT THAT HAS SOMETHING TO DO WITH THAT. INVENTORS ARE OFTEN HUSH-HUSH UNTIL THEY HAVE THE KINKS OF THEIR EXPERIMENTS WORKED OUT AND UNTIL THEY GET A PATENT. B CAREFUL! K8

Sydney texted back: YOU'RE RIGHT. IT'S A WRIGHT D-94 WAVE SMASHER. MORE LATER.

"Can you imagine how awesome a game would look from the beach?" Bailey asked. "With all those lights scooting around and flying over the water?"

"I can," Sydney answered. "It was pretty exciting when we thought your D-94 was a UFO. People are going to love watching these things at night."

Mr. Wright was standing near his son, grinning. "And Drake here has taken extra-special care to make sure that it runs quietly so it doesn't disturb the residents. They already think we're crazy, you know. They don't get it that some of the craziest-looking ideas might change the world someday."

"Like the Wright Brothers' flying machine," said Bailey.

"That's *right!*" said Captain Swain. Everyone laughed. "Girls," he said with a serious tone. "Always remember: 'Do not judge according to appearance, but judge with righteous judgment.' That's just me and God talking to you," he said.

"You like to quote God, don't you?" said Sydney.

"I do," the captain replied. "His Bible gives me the words, and I just speak them aloud."

"Just like our friend Bettyboo," Bailey answered. "She likes to quote scripture verses, too." She walked over and stood next to Drake. He was about a foot taller than she was, and he had deep brown eyes. She was happy that he finally looked at her instead of down at his feet. "What are your plans for the D-94?" she asked.

Drake clammed up again, and his face turned red. Sydney noticed that he looked very uncomfortable. "Drake, I'm sorry for not getting to know you sooner, and even sorrier that I was suspicious of you and your dad."

"Me, too," Bailey agreed. "I guess I let my imagination get the best of me."

Nate Wright took off his cap and scratched his head. "Imagination isn't a bad thing," he said. "Don't be sorry for letting it go when it wants to run, but remember that you have to rein it in once in a while. Otherwise, it *will* get the best of you."

"I'll remember, Mr. Wright," Bailey said. "So, how about it, Drake, what are you going to do with the D-94?"

Drake sat on some tires stacked in a corner of the shed. "Well," he said. "Dad and the captain think I need to promote it.

You know, get it out there in the ocean in the daytime and show it off. They both think people are living in Corolla Light who have the money to back my invention and get it into the hands of the right people."

"Like companies that build recreational water vehicles and race boats and stuff?" Sydney asked. An idea was beginning to form in her head.

"Yeah, exactly," Drake replied. "Know anybody?"

It was a rhetorical question. He didn't really expect an answer, but Sydney had one for him.

"Mr. Kessler," she said.

"Who?" Mr. Wright asked.

"The Kessler twins' dad," said Sydney. "They have a house near my grandparents' place. Mr. Kessler runs a company that builds race boats and other water vehicles. I'm sure he'd be interested in seeing the Wright D-94 Wave Smasher."

"'God works for the good of those who love Him,'" said Captain Swain, smiling. "Where can we find Mr. Kessler?"

"They're in the Village at the crab fest," said Bailey. "The whole family is there. I think we should all go over there and find them, before the crab boil and all the stuff that goes with it is eaten up."

"And if you want an audience at the beach when you show off your invention, you only have to tell the Kessler twins about it. They're terrible at keeping secrets," said Sydney.

The Wrights washed up in an old sink in the equipment shed while the girls and the captain waited.

"I have a couple more questions, if you don't mind," said Bailey.

"Go ahead," Mr. Wright told her.

"Well, are the words on your bus a secret code?"

"Bailey!" Sydney scolded.

"Why would you even think that?" asked Drake.

Bailey felt a little embarrassed, but she wanted answers. "If you read the first letters of the words backward, they spell *Roswell*, like that place in New Mexico where the spaceship crashed back in 1947. I thought maybe your invention was a UFO."

Drake laughed out loud.

"Okay, call me silly," said Bailey. "But what is that weird coffee mug that lights up inside? We heard you say that it belongs to you. I thought it was an alien weapon."

Drake looked at her wide-eyed. "A what! It's no weapon. It's my idea for a pinhole flashlight that's magnetically powered," he said. "It's another invention I'm working on. I'm hoping someday it'll be a fun thing for kids to use when they go ghost-crab hunting."

"Okay," Bailey said, slapping him on the shoulder. "You've passed the Camp Club Girls' interrogation. You and your dad are definitely *not* from outer space. Now, let's go find the Kesslers."

The Wright D-94 Wave Smasher

Hi, Camp Club Girls.

Well, last night, at the Wrights' equipment shed, we solved the mysteries of the UFO and Captain Swain. The Wrights aren't space aliens, and Captain Swain isn't a ghost.

Drake has invented an awesome water vehicle called the Wright D-94 Wave Smasher (pictures attached). That's what we've seen over the water at night. He's been testing it. It's also what made the footprints on the beach and whooshed by us that day. Captain Swain helped Drake get a patent on it. The D-94 can race like a speedboat, jump waves, and hover or fly about 30 feet over the water. And Drake invented a new water sport to go with it. He doesn't have a name for it yet, but it's played in the dark, and the lights on the vehicle have a lot to do with the strategy of how it's played.

Drake is really shy (Bailey says to tell you he's really cute, too). He was nervous about showing his invention to anyone. We convinced him he has to or else he'll never sell it and become famous like his distant cousins the Wright Brothers. So tonight he'll demonstrate the Wave Smasher at the beach. One of our neighbors runs a company that makes racing boats. I introduced him to Drake last night, and he can't wait to see the D-94 in action. Bailey and I are going to the beach now to watch.

That's all we know. Mystery solved. The only question that's still hanging out there is: What really happened to the sailors on the Carroll A. Deering? *Nobody knows for sure. Maybe you guys can all come here next summer, and we can crack that case together.*

All for now,
Sydney

P.S. from Bailey: I'm really sorry that I called Drake "Digger." The captain said, "Do not judge according to appearances, but judge with righteous judgment." I think Drake Wright and his dad are awesome! Oh, and we forgot to tell you, Captain Swain is the nephew of the Old Captain Swain, the lighthouse keeper. He dresses like the old captain when he volunteers at the lighthouse. Syd says to tell you the lighthouse lady is on vacation. Aliens did not abduct her.

Sydney put her binoculars and cell phone into her backpack, zipped it shut, and slung it over her shoulder. "Let's go," she said to Bailey.

Bailey went into the bathroom to check herself out in the mirror. She smoothed her straight black hair and applied strawberry lip gloss to her thin, pale lips. "Can I use some of your banana-coconut body spray?" she asked Sydney.

"Sure," Sydney agreed.

Bailey spritzed some onto her arms and her neck. "So do you think he's going to buy it?" she asked.

"Who?" Sydney wondered.

"Do you think that the twins' dad is going to buy Drake's idea?"

"I really think he might," Sydney answered. "He sure liked the Wave Smasher when he saw it in the Wrights' equipment shed, and since we gave the twins the job of spreading the word around Corolla, I think people will come out to see it."

Bailey took one last look in the mirror. Then she picked up her backpack and slipped her arms through its straps. "Okay, let's go," she said.

At twilight, the girls walked down the beach to Tuna Street. A crowd was starting to gather. Families spread blankets in the sand and sipped bottles of water. Several big floodlights were there to illuminate the beach, and a small set of bleachers was set up for special guests who might want to buy Drake's invention. The Wrights' bus was parked at the end of the access road. Drake, his dad, and the captain were rolling the D-94 out of a trailer that was hitched onto the back bumper. When Captain Swain saw the girls, he tipped the brim of his cap. "Good evening, young ladies," he said.

"Hi, Captain. Hi, Drake!" Bailey said brightly.

"Hi," Drake responded without looking up.

"A lot of people are here," Sydney said as she noticed more

curious onlookers arriving in cars, on bikes, and on foot. Several men in business suits, looking quite out of place, stood at the end of Tuna Street talking with Mr. Kessler. "I guess Carolyn and Marilyn got busy getting the word out."

"I guess *so*," Drake replied.

Bailey saw that he seemed nervous. "Hey, just imagine you're one of the Wright Brothers," she said. "I'm sure they drew a big crowd with their flying machine. It's your turn now, Drake. Trust me. They'll love you."

The corners of Drake's lips curled into a tiny smile. "I don't want them to love me," he said. "I just want them to love my D-94."

"That, too!" said Bailey.

"My boy," the captain said, "this is your shining moment. I don't think we should just launch the craft without a fanfare. Why, when they launch a ship there are speeches, and sometimes they even smash a bottle on the bow—"

"I don't want anything smashed on my invention!" Drake exclaimed.

"No, no, I didn't mean that." The captain chuckled. "I just think that we should make this an occasion. Do you still have that megaphone in the bus?"

Drake's face turned beet red.

"It's under the driver's seat," Mr. Wright said. "I agree with you, Cap. We should make this special."

Drake gulped. "Do I have to do all the talking? I mean, do I have to tell everybody about my invention?"

"No," said the captain. "I'll introduce you as the inventor and give a brief account of what you are about to show them. I think, for now, we should keep the water sport part to ourselves. That's something that you can discuss privately with Mr. Kessler and his friends. You can meet with them after the demonstration and answer their questions."

The captain went to the bus to get the megaphone.

By now, the crowd was trying to push toward the Wrights to get a better look at the shiny machine. "Get back, please!" Nate Wright shouted. Everyone took a giant step backward. Before long, the beach security team showed up and stretched a line of yellow tape between two posts that they pounded into the sand. They patrolled the line, telling onlookers to stay behind the line. The Kessler twins showed up, and the officers let them through.

"We told security that they'd better get down here," said Carolyn.

"We told them to hurry, because we needed crowd control," Marilyn added. "Tons of people are here already!"

The only time Sydney had seen the beach more packed was on the Fourth of July. "How many people did you tell?" she asked.

"Hundreds!" said Carolyn.

"At least!" added Marilyn. "When we got home from the crab fest last night, we printed up flyers on our computer. We told everyone to come down here at eight o'clock tonight because a UFO was going to be on the beach."

"We used up two big packs of paper—" said Carolyn.

"And a whole black ink cartridge," said Marilyn. "Then we got up early this morning and started putting them in all the mailboxes."

"And after that, we went to the shopping centers," said Carolyn. "And we stuck flyers under the windshield wipers of all the cars in the parking lots."

"But then a guy came out and told us not to do it anymore, so we left," said Marilyn.

Captain Swain stepped out of the bus with the megaphone in his hand. He turned it on and pointed it toward the crowd. "Testing one, two, three, four. Testing." His deep voice boomed across the beach. He turned the megaphone off.

"I thought you didn't like crowds, Captain," Sydney said.

"I don't," the captain replied. "But this is an historical day. Why, once people see the Wrights as serious twenty-first-century inventors, we can only imagine how their inventions will someday change the world."

As twilight faded to darkness, Mr. Kessler and his friends ducked under the yellow tape. The twins' dad wore khaki shorts, a white T-shirt, and flip-flops. His friends were obviously not as prepared for the beach. They had taken off their suit coats, rolled their pants legs above their knees, and were barefoot. "Let's get this show on the road," Mr. Kessler said. "Are you ready, Drake?"

"Yes, sir," Drake replied.

Mr. Kessler and his friends joined several others who were seated on the bleachers.

Bailey was at Drake's side now. She stood on her tiptoes and whispered to him, "You can do it. Just keep repeating to yourself, 'I can do all things through Him who strengthens me.' That's what I did when I climbed the lighthouse."

Drake's face turned redder than ever.

The captain flipped a switch inside the bus, and floodlights wired from the bus turned the beach from darkness to daylight. He then walked to the front of the crowd and stood with the megaphone in his hands. "Ladies and gentlemen, boys and girls, may I please have your undivided attention?"

A hush fell over the crowd.

"I have the great privilege of introducing one of our own, Mr. Drake Wright!" He swept his left hand toward Drake.

Bailey, Sydney, and the twins moved out of the way, leaving Drake by himself next to the Wright D-94 Wave Smasher. They began to clap loudly.

"Let's hear it for Drake!" Bailey shouted. Then everyone on the beach clapped and cheered.

The captain continued, "Drake and his dad, Nate Wright, are well known around Corolla as inventors, and tonight Drake will show you an invention he has worked on tirelessly for the past several years. It is a recreational watercraft unlike anything you have ever seen. As soon as you have watched it in action, you will want a Wright D-94 Wave Smasher of your very own. I won't take up your valuable time explaining the fine points of his amazing invention. I will, instead, let it speak for itself. Drake, my boy, take it away!"

Drake climbed into the cockpit and pulled down the bubble-like cover. He started the engine and the soft whirring sound began. He pushed a button, making the four snowshoe-like feet pop out of the bottom of the vehicle. Then another button raised the D-94 up on its legs. It started walking toward the water, and people in the crowd gasped.

"You haven't seen anything yet, ladies and gentlemen," the captain said. "Prepare to be amazed."

When Drake got within several feet of the water, he let the D-94 lift and hover a few yards above the beach. Then it started rotating.

"It walks. It hovers. It even spins!" the captain announced. "Around and around she goes!"

Drake let his invention spin faster and faster until it looked like a top spinning out of control. The crowd oohed and aahed. Then, slowly, Drake let the craft rotate counterclockwise to a complete stop. He set it down in the ocean, just offshore. The legs and feet folded up into the bottom of the vehicle and it floated.

"How about a game of leapfrog?" the captain asked the crowd.

With the spotlights fixed on his craft, Drake pushed the control stick forward, and the D-94 sailed out to sea, leaping over waves that got in its way. The crowd went wild. Captain Swain flicked a switch, and all the spotlights went dark. "Keep your eyes fixed on the horizon," the captain said. "The best is yet to come."

"Now what?" Carolyn asked in the darkness.

"Yeah, now what?" Marilyn repeated.

"Just watch," Sydney answered. "He'll make it look like a UFO."

"He's so awesome," Bailey remarked. "He can make the D-94 do just about anything."

Offshore, Drake turned on the signal light. It flashed bright white in a series of dots and dashes. "He says, 'Watch this, Dad,'" Sydney heard Mr. Wright say as he stood nearby. "I'm so proud of you, son," Mr. Wright said, although Drake couldn't hear him.

The Wright D-94 Wave Smasher lit up like a Christmas tree, first with red lights chasing around its middle, then with multicolored lights flashing on and off. As the crowd watched,

Drake made the craft shoot like a bullet across
the water. Its lights provided the only clue as to where it was.

To make things even more interesting, Drake sometimes
turned off all the lights and then changed places before turning
them back on.

"He's over there!" someone in the crowd shouted.

"No, he's over there!"

"Look at how fast that thing can move."

"You can't tell if it's on or above the water!"

Drake put on an amazing show before bringing the craft
back to shore. As he approached the beach, Captain Swain
flipped the spotlights back on. The D-94 sailed to the water's
edge and lifted off the sand with a puff of air. It scooted across
the beach to where the bus was parked, and then Drake set it
down to rest in the sand. He killed the engine and pulled back
the cover on the cockpit.

"That was more wonderful than anything I could ever have
imagined," said Bailey.

"Wow, that's saying a lot," Sydney replied. "You have the
wildest imagination of anyone I've ever known."

"Ladies and gentlemen," the captain shouted. "Let's give
a big round of applause to our resident inventor, *Mr. Drake
Wright!*"

Everyone on the beach applauded, and many tried to get
past the yellow tape. "Stay back!" Mr. Wright shouted.

"That's all for tonight," the captain announced. "There will
be plenty more opportunities for you to see the Wright D-94
Wave Smasher in action. And before long, you might even have
one of your very own." He shut off the megaphone and climbed
down the ladder.

"Drake," Captain Swain said, approaching the D-94, "you were incredible!"

"Yes, you were!" Bailey agreed.

"We think so, too," said Carolyn and Marilyn.

Drake climbed out of the cockpit, and Sydney shook his hand.

"You did that just like a pro," she said. "I was praying for you the whole time."

"Thanks, Sydney," Drake said with a lot more confidence in his voice. "I felt your prayers. I couldn't have done it without you guys—"

"And the Greatest Helper of them all," said the captain, pointing up at the sky.

"He means God," Sydney whispered to the twins.

Mr. Kessler had climbed down from the bleachers and was walking toward them.

"Here comes our dad," said Marilyn.

"Drake," Mr. Kessler said in a serious voice. "My associates and I would like to have a word with you and your dad. Over there, please." He motioned to the bleachers where his friends were waiting. The Wrights followed Mr. Kessler through the sand.

"What do you think will happen?" Sydney asked.

"They're going to set him up," Carolyn said.

"Huh?" said Bailey.

"We overheard our dad talking on the phone this morning," said Marilyn. "He said that if Drake's demonstration went well tonight, his company will start manufacturing the Wright D-94 Wave Smasher."

"And there's more," said Carolyn. "He's going to set up a

dealership right here in Corolla, and Drake's dad will run it, and everybody on the Outer Banks will come here to buy their D-94s."

"Before long, there will be dealerships up and down both coasts," Marilyn added. "And Drake and his dad will own them all."

Captain Swain beamed. "Praise our God! His deeds are wonderful, too marvelous to describe."

"You really need to meet our friend Beth," Sydney told him. "You two could have a contest to see who knows the most scripture verses."

"Why, Sydney Lincoln," said Captain Swain, "I'd be honored to meet your friend. Maybe she can come with you the next time you visit your grandparents."

A few yards away from them, they heard Drake Wright let out a joyful whoop! Mr. Wright threw his arms around his son and hugged him.

"Watch that boy," said the captain. "This is only the beginning."

Camp Club Girls

Alexis
AND THE
ARIZONA
ESCAPADE

Erica Rodgers

The Bridge in the Desert

The noon sun shone bright in a sapphire sky. But twelve-year-old Alexis Howell wasn't paying attention. She stood on the bridge and watched the Arizona heat warping the hills of sand and sagebrush in the distance.

She had never been so afraid in all her life.

Alexis made herself look at the clouds to try to keep her mind off her fear. She liked their shapes, but mostly she was keeping her mind off the water. A crowd of tourists clamored past, and a tall man bumped her into the rail. Her eyes were ripped from the sky as she caught her balance. . .and looked down.

It seemed like forever to the water below. The wind blew, lifting her brown ponytail. The bridge swayed. It rocked beneath her feet.

Maybe it will flip over and throw me off, Alexis thought in sudden panic.

Why had she promised to meet Elizabeth *here* of all places? Why?

Like most children, Alexis had grown up singing the song "London Bridge is falling down. . ." She'd certainly been surprised to learn that the London Bridge wasn't in London at all. It was here in Arizona.

Another group of tourists nudged past. A large purse landed with a thud against Alexis's back, and before she knew it, she had flipped forward. She screamed. She was falling. . . falling. . .falling. . . .

"Alexis?"

The vision evaporated. Alexis turned toward the voice that had said her name.

"Elizabeth! I'm so glad you're here!" She hugged her friend but then couldn't seem to let go. She clung to her friend like a life preserver.

"I'm glad, too," said Elizabeth in her soft Texas twang, not seeming to notice the tightness of the hug. "This place is beautiful! The water is so calm and peaceful, and the bridge is magnificent! I *did* think it would be bigger though."

"Sure," said Alexis, who thought the bridge was quite big enough. She released Elizabeth but then held her arm until they reached the sidewalk at the end of the bridge.

The sounds of vacation echoed off the lake. Laughing children, scolding parents, and the sputter of motorboats. Vendors called out, advertising their wares.

"Cotton candy!"

"Funnel cakes here!"

"Hot dogs! Fresh, cold lemonade!"

Alexis had stopped shaking. Now she was simply trying to keep up with Elizabeth. This was not always easy, since her friend's legs seemed twice as long as hers. Elizabeth kept pulling on the bottom edges of her shorts, like they were too short.

"How was the trip?" said Alexis.

"Long," said Elizabeth. "We drove. We just got here, but I needed a break from my brother. Mom said I could meet you and hang out until dinner."

"Great! I'll take you to my hotel. You won't believe it. . . . It looks like a *castle*! It has an amazing pool, too. And Grandma got our room for free!"

"Wow!" said Elizabeth. "How'd she do that?"

"She's teaching some classes about British history," said Alexis. "It's a new addition to the London Bridge Days Festival." She gestured to all of the tourists.

They had entered the area of Lake Havasu City that looked like an old English village. People everywhere were dressed up. They all wore a lot of clothes for such a hot day. The women dressed in bright, heavy, velvet clothes. Some wore tattered dark clothes to look like beggars and paupers, poor people. Others were dressed regally to look like princes and queens. They reminded Alexis of the scenes and actors from movies like *Robin Hood* or *The Princess Bride* or even a few of the scenes in *The Chronicles of Narnia.*

Elizabeth turned and looked again at the bridge. She pulled her cell phone out of her pocket and took a picture. "That's really the London Bridge, huh?" asked Elizabeth.

Alexis glanced over her shoulder and shivered.

"Yep. The city of London had to replace it because it was so old, but they didn't want to throw it away, so they sold it to Lake Havasu City."

"I thought the London Bridge was tall, you know? With towers at the ends," said Elizabeth.

"You're thinking of the Tower Bridge," said Alexis. "My grandma told me that people always get them mixed up."

This bridge definitely didn't have towers. It was wide and low to the water, with five long arches supporting its weight.

The top of the bridge had a stone rail that held a few old lampposts and a flagpole.

"It's so weird to see something called the London Bridge in the middle of the Arizona desert!" said Elizabeth.

Alexis laughed as she led her friend toward the London Bridge Resort, where she was staying. She was so excited to be on fall break. She had a whole week off from school, so her grandmother had invited Alexis to join her at the resort. Alexis was happy already, but she became super-excited when she found out that Elizabeth was coming, too. Elizabeth's dad came to Lake Havasu every year for the bass-fishing tournament. This year he brought the whole family.

Alexis couldn't wait to spend an entire five days with the oldest of the Camp Club Girls! Who knew? Maybe they would get a chance to solve a mystery. Something was bound to happen when crowds this large got together.

"Wow! You're staying *here*?" Elizabeth cried. They had turned into the entrance of the London Bridge Resort. Two huge towers guarded the doors. Every time Alexis looked at them, she expected to see a princess waving from the top or a dragon at the bottom, clawing to get in.

"Hey, stand by the entrance and let me get a picture," Elizabeth directed. "Then I'll send it to the rest of the Camp Club Girls."

Alexis posed until Elizabeth said, "Okay. That'll make them wish they were here."

Then Alexis led the way through the front doors, and a huge scarlet lobby glittered before them. To the left was an expanse of marble floor, which led over to the check-in desk, and to the right was—Elizabeth gasped.

"I know," said Alexis. "Isn't it awesome?"

An expanse of soft red carpet was surrounded by gold stands and scarlet ropes. Inside the ropes was a gigantic carriage. It looked like it was made of gold. The roof of the carriage was held up by eight golden palm trees, and at the very top sat three cherubs. They were holding up the royal crown.

The girls were leaning in to get a closer look when a boyish voice snapped behind them.

"Can't you see the ropes? No touching!"

Alexis spun around. An officer in a brown sheriff's uniform stood at the edge of the carpet, crossing his arms.

"We weren't going to touch it, sir," said Elizabeth. "I promise—"

"I know troublemakers when I see 'em," said the young man. He couldn't have been much older than twenty.

"Hi," muttered Alexis. She glanced at his badge. "Um, Mr. Dewayne."

He pointed to his badge and said, "*Deputy* Dewayne to you."

"Nice to meet you," said Elizabeth, but it came out more like a question.

"Don't get smart with me, little girl!" said Deputy Dewayne. Alexis smiled. Elizabeth was easily as tall as the officer. "This is my town! I won't have tourists making a mess of things!"

Alexis and Elizabeth simply nodded.

"If I see you even put one finger over those ropes"—he pointed toward the carriage—"I'll clap you in irons!"

Alexis couldn't help it. She sniggered. *Clap us in irons? Whatever that means.*

"You think this is funny?" asked the deputy. Alexis was about to say no, but they were interrupted by a waitress carrying a paper bag.

"Here's your lunch, *Deputy*," she said with a smile. "Grilled cheese with no crust—just the way you like it." She winked at the girls and handed the officer his bag. . .which had cartoon animals all over it.

Deputy Dewayne saw the girls hide a laugh as they looked from him to the bag.

"The kiddie menu is cheaper!" he exclaimed. "And I *like* it! You just remember what I said. This is my town. Don't get on my bad side!" With that, he turned and marched out of the lobby.

"No way!" said Elizabeth.

"I know!" said Alexis. "Kiddie menu?"

"Clap us in irons?"

Elizabeth shot some pictures of the carriage, and then the girls laughed all the way up the stairs to the room where Alexis's grandmother was giving a speech on British literature. When they reached the door of the room where Mrs. Windsor was teaching, Alexis put a finger to her lips to tell Elizabeth to be quiet.

"And *that*," said Alexis's grandmother's voice, "is how the famous Gunpowder Plot was discovered."

The people applauded lightly and then stood to leave. Alexis had to wait for the group of people around her grandmother to clear before introducing Elizabeth.

"This is my grandma, Molly Windsor."

"It's nice to finally meet you," said the short lady, shaking Elizabeth's hand. Her hair was a powerful shade of red, and her face was covered with a smattering of freckles, just like Alexis's. "I hope you two have been enjoying the scenery!"

"We've only just begun," said Elizabeth. "But we *have* been to the bridge."

Alexis shuddered again.

"Really, Alexis!" said her grandmother. "That bridge is hardly twenty feet tall and made out of solid concrete and steel! It's perfectly safe. You need to work on that fear of yours!"

"You're afraid of bridges?" cried Elizabeth.

"It's nothing," said Alexis, changing the subject. "Want to go sightseeing with us, Grandma?"

"Sorry, girls. I have two more lectures today. Why don't you explore together? You're bound to find some fascinating things."

She bustled around her podium, taking out another set of notes. Just then, an older man approached the front. Had he been sitting in the back all that time? Or had it just taken him that long to walk up the aisle?

"Interesting topic, Dr. Windsor," he said. His voice sounded like sandpaper under water—scratchy and wet at the same time.

"Thank you," said Alexis's grandmother. "Girls, this is Dr. Edwards. He is speaking this week as well."

The skinny, slouched man reached out to shake hands but pulled back quickly. He yanked a square white piece of fabric out of his front pocket. He held the handkerchief up to his nose and sneezed into it. The violence of the sneeze did not mess up his perfect mustache, which was a glimmering white, like his short hair.

"Forgive me," he said. "The air here is dusty."

"This is my granddaughter, Alexis," said Grandma Windsor. "And her friend Elizabeth. Alexis is staying with me for the week."

The man eyed the girls and frowned.

"Well, hopefully you two will find something better to do than bother the people attending our conference," he said. "The bed race, for example, usually interests the *loud* youth of the city."

"Bed race?" said Alexis. "What's a bed race?" It sounded so interesting that she forgot Dr. Edwards had just insulted them.

"Ask the crazy lady at the front desk," said Dr. Edwards. With that, he bowed to Grandma Windsor and left.

"Don't mind him, girls," said Grandma Windsor when he was out of hearing range. "He's old and grouchy. Gets along better with books than with people."

Another audience began flooding into the room, so Alexis and Elizabeth fought against the tide and left, waving good-bye over their shoulders. They walked back down to the lobby and saw the woman Dr. Edwards had called "the crazy lady" at the front desk.

Of course she wasn't really crazy. She *did* have a streak of purple hair though. Alexis was sure that someone like Dr. Edwards would call that *crazy* instead of *creative, interesting,* or *fun.*

They waited at the desk behind a man who had lost his room key and a woman who needed more towels. When it was their turn, Alexis spoke up.

"Hi," she said. "We're visiting here, and we heard something about a bed race. Could you tell us what that is?"

"Of course!" said the lady. She wasn't old, but she wasn't too young either. The color in her hair made it even harder for Alexis to tell her age. "It's exactly what it sounds like—a bed race!" she said brightly.

Alexis and Elizabeth exchanged a confused look. The lady behind the desk explained further.

"The race happens on Saturday, before the parade. Each team decorates an old bed with wheels on it. Then the teams race the beds through town. Someone pushes or pulls the bed, and the others ride on it. You sign up over *there*." She pointed to the wall a few feet away. There was a large poster with a picture of a zooming four-poster and a scribbled list of names.

Alexis looked at Elizabeth and could tell she was thinking the same thing: This could be quite the adventure! A cloud passed over Alexis's smile.

"Where are we supposed to get an old bed?" she asked.

"You'd be surprised," said the woman behind the desk. "I'd start looking around the shopping area. Try the older shops—and don't hesitate to ask around."

The girls turned to leave, but the desk lady called out.

"I'm Jane, by the way."

"I'm Alexis, and this is Elizabeth."

"Well, good luck! The same team has won two years in a row. Maybe you can show them up, huh?" She waved at the girls and gave them a cheerful smile.

The girls waved back and walked across the lobby toward the front door and the sunshine.

Suddenly the lobby door flew open, and a short, round man with messy gray hair stumbled through it. His face was red beneath a bushy mustache, and sweat poured down his cheeks. Everyone in the area stopped moving and talking. The only sound in the room was the slap of the man's polished shoes as he crossed the marble floor.

"Mr. Mayor, what is it?"

The mayor, thought Alexis. *What could be wrong?*

"Mayor Applebee, can I help?" Jane came out from behind the front desk. The mayor stopped. A bead of sweat flipped off the end of his chin. He raised his hands in the air, as if he were about to make an important announcement.

His breathing was still labored, but it seemed that he couldn't wait any longer. He gulped at the air and spoke.

"The bridge. . .is. . . It's. . ." He almost fell over, but Jane rushed to support him. After a moment the mayor regained his balance. He drew in a breath—steadier this time—and managed to finish a whole sentence.

"The London Bridge is. . .*falling down*."

Falling Down!

Falling down, falling down.
   London Bridge is falling down. . .
   Alexis half expected the mayor to finish the old nursery rhyme.

   But there was no "my fair lady." Only a winded man standing in the silence of the lobby and looking distressed. No one spoke, because no one knew what to say. Was this some sort of joke? If so, it wasn't a very good one. No one was laughing.

   "The commissioner!" wheezed the mayor. "Where is he?"

   "In the restaurant," said Jane. "Eating lunch."

   Mayor Applebee took off through the lobby.

   "Who is the commissioner?" Alexis asked.

   "The bridge commissioner," answered Jane. "He's in charge of the committee that oversees the bridge. Something must really be wrong."

   Alexis and Elizabeth followed the flow of people out of the hotel lobby and toward the canal. A large group was already gathering on the shore, and it was difficult to see the bridge. They could only see a herd of people being shown off the nearest end of the bridge. The food stands that had been selling treats moments earlier were piling everything into boxes. Over the entrance to the bridge, the sign reading TASTES OF HAVASU had been removed, and a police officer was replacing it with yellow caution tape.

There must really be something wrong with the bridge, thought Alexis. "Come on, Elizabeth. Let's see if we can get closer."

The girls edged their way to the front of the crowd and then carefully walked along the water's edge toward the bridge. Eventually they saw it. A crack—about eight feet long— climbing out of the water and reaching toward the arch in the second bridge support. Even as they watched, a bit of mortar crumbled and plunked into the channel.

The crowd gasped.

Voices chimed together, striking chords of worry and fear.

"It couldn't really fall, could it?"

"The middle will go first, if it does."

"I guess that's what happens when you buy a used bridge!"

"What about the parade?"

What about the parade? thought Alexis. She had been so excited about the festival, but could it go on if the bridge was threatening to collapse? Suddenly a voice from the back of the crowd rose above all the others.

"It's the *curse*." The voice was solid but wavy—like an aged piece of oak. The people on the bank all turned. Their eyes locked onto an old woman. She was wearing a ragged brown dress and a cloak, even though it was hot. Her tin-colored hair hung tangled to her waist, and she was leaning on a warped walking stick.

Alexis couldn't tell if it was a costume or not. The lady definitely looked like some kind of medieval hag. The woman reminded her of the old hag in *The Princess Bride*, who cursed Princess Buttercup in her dreams for giving away her own true love.

"What curse?" someone called from the crowd.

"Don't you people keep up on your history?" asked the old woman. She was speaking from the top of the little green hill near the bridge. Everyone could see her as she lifted her hands to speak over them.

"History!" the woman repeated. "The London Bridge never remains whole for long, no matter how you rebuild it. From the time of the Romans, it has always sunk, burned, or *crumbled*!" She pointed toward the crack with her stick.

The crowd began to murmur. Some were nodding. Alexis made a mental note to ask her grandmother about the bridge's destructive past. The old woman continued.

"When the bridge was brought to Lake Havasu, the curse of the River Thames followed. Now it will prey on two cities instead of one! London and Lake Havasu City are sisters in destruction!"

The people began talking among themselves again. Some wandered back to whatever they had been doing before the commotion. Some called after the woman, asking her questions, but she was already out of reach. She walked toward town singing softly in a croaking voice, *"London Bridge is falling down, falling down, falling down. . ."*

When the crowd had thinned out, Alexis and Elizabeth wandered closer to the bridge. From the grassy slope they could easily see the crack. It looked strange—harmless and menacing at the same time. Elizabeth sat on the grass and crossed her lanky legs. Alexis plopped down beside her.

"Do you think a crack that small could really bring a whole bridge down?" Elizabeth asked.

"I have no idea!" answered Alexis. "I'm just glad nothing happened while we were up there this morning." Alexis ran her hand through the short grass.

"I just don't get it," she said, picking a small clover. "This bridge shouldn't just fall down. I read about it before I came. The outside layer of stone is from the real London Bridge, but everything underneath is solid steel and cement. It shouldn't be crumbling, Elizabeth."

Alexis was puzzled. What could possibly bring down such a huge structure? The bridge wasn't old—barely thirty years. And it wasn't like Lake Havasu got a lot of severe weather or anything. That only left one possibility.

"The curse," said Alexis, almost in a whisper.

"Alexis, come on," said Elizabeth. Now her gangly arms were crossed as well as her legs. "You can't really believe what that lady was saying. Curses aren't real!"

"I know," said Alexis. "But it sounds like a mystery, don't you think?" She looked sideways at her friend and raised her eyebrows. Elizabeth's mouth stretched into a wide smile.

"Mmm, I was hoping something like this might happen. . . . I mean, not the crack!" she apologized to the bridge. "You know what I mean. Do you happen to have that little pink notebook of yours?"

"What do you think?" said Alexis. She drew the notebook out of her back pocket and started scribbling as Elizabeth listed people they should try to talk to.

Problem: There's a crack in the London Bridge.

Plan: Track down more information. Start by talking to

the old woman—maybe there's more to this curse thing than we realize. Maybe it's a stunt for the tourists.

Alexis thought back to the conversation surrounding the bridge only moments before.

"Elizabeth," she said. "What if they cancel the parade? No parade means no bed race! That would be a total bummer!"

"I know," said Elizabeth. "But it's even worse than that. No London Bridge means no Lake Havasu. They built this town around that bridge, Alexis. How many tourists will come to see a pile of rocks?"

"Who knows," said Alexis. "It works for Stonehenge, doesn't it?"

Elizabeth didn't laugh.

"Stonehenge is a pile of big rocks in England that were propped upright sometime way before Jesus was born," Alexis explained, in case Elizabeth didn't know. "They don't know who put them up or why they're standing in a circle in the middle of a field. . . ."

"Oh, I know about that," Elizabeth said. "I saw a program about it on the History Channel. I was just thinking."

"Look!" Alexis whispered. She pointed across the road to where a short, slouched figure was walking quickly away, leaning on a stick. It was the old woman.

"Come on! Let's go talk to her!" Elizabeth exclaimed.

Both girls jumped to their feet and dusted off their backsides before jogging across the street. They wanted to catch up and ask her a few questions about the bridge and this so-called curse, but it wasn't that easy.

The closer they got to the woman, the faster she seemed to walk. Soon she was almost running. She zigged and zagged through the streets of Lake Havasu City, leading the girls deeper and deeper into the teeming crowds of tourists. The old woman took a sharp left into an alley behind a bakery, and the girls almost lost her.

They stood panting on the sidewalk, being jostled by purses. Alexis noticed that some of the purses had small dogs in them. She would never understand what made people carry their dogs around everywhere they went.

"It's like she knows we're following her and is trying to lose us!" panted Elizabeth. "She must be up to something devious, or she wouldn't run."

"I know," wheezed Alexis as a Pomeranian nipped at her elbow from inside its rainbow-colored Louis Vuitton. "Can you see anything?"

Elizabeth used her height to peer over the heads of the crowd.

"There!" she cried. The old woman emerged from an alley farther down the street. She bent low, as if she didn't want to be seen.

The girls resumed the chase.

"Maybe she's late for an appointment," said Alexis, fighting against the pressure of bodies as they weaved through yet another crosswalk. At that moment the woman turned around. The girls emerged from a clump of people, and they made eye contact.

The woman ran.

Now Alexis knew that the woman was definitely avoiding them. But why? It didn't make any sense. She was the one who had stood near the bridge yelling about a curse. All they wanted was a little more information, for goodness' sake! And for a rickety, old-looking woman, she sure ran fast!

They ran for half a mile or more, making three left-hand turns and four to the right. Then Elizabeth stopped.

"She's gone," she huffed.

"Are you sure?" asked Alexis.

"Sure." Elizabeth bent over to catch her breath. "I haven't seen her for a few minutes. She got away."

Alexis slumped against the nearest window. It was cold to the touch. The store must have had the air-conditioning going full blast. *Well*, she thought, *there's nothing left to do now but go back.* She looked around. . .and recognized nothing.

"Elizabeth, do you know where we are?"

Her friend only shook her head. Great. They were alone in a strange city, and they had followed the old woman without even thinking about how they would get back. Alexis thought of *Hansel and Gretel*.

"Those two were smart," she said.

"What?" asked Elizabeth.

"Hansel and Gretel were smart. They left a way to get back home."

Elizabeth laughed. "Sure. I'll keep a few bread crumbs in my pocket for our next high-speed chase through a strange town!"

"I guess we can go in a shop and ask someone," said Alexis.

Elizabeth was about to answer when they both jumped.

Hundreds of screams ripped through the streets of Lake Havasu City.

CHAPTER
3

Imposters

The air was quiet for a moment or two. Then it happened again. Hundreds of people screamed.

Alexis looked at Elizabeth. By the fear on her friend's face, she could tell that Elizabeth was also worried. They were two young girls alone in a strange place. Frantic screams filled the air. They did the only thing two Camp Club Girls would have done. They ran. . .toward the screaming.

When they rounded the last corner, the screaming finally made sense. Alexis and Elizabeth stood facing a huge building. Glittering letters on the side of it told them it was Lake Havasu High School, home of the Fighting Knights. The noise was coming from inside the gym. A few straggling students made their way through a pair of double doors.

"Look, Alexis." Elizabeth pointed to another sign. It was splashed bright with purple and gold poster paint: PEP RALLY TODAY! GO KNIGHTS!

"Want to take a look?" asked Alexis. She had been to one pep rally at her middle school, but it had been pretty lame. It hadn't been for a sport or anything. Just an assembly meant to encourage the students to do their best in school this year. Who had ever heard of a "Yay for Homework!" rally?

Alexis had never even been inside a high school. How cool would it be to tell her friends she'd seen a high school pep rally, even if it was from the outside?

The girls edged toward the doors, trying to get a peek before they closed. A voice behind them made them jump.

"Hey! Get in there, or you'll miss it!"

The man ordering them into the building was obviously a teacher. Elizabeth tried to explain that they were tourists, but the man held up a thick pink pad of paper.

"Please," he said. "Don't make me give out two more detentions."

At that point the girls figured it was useless to protest. He lightly nudged them through the doors, followed them in, and closed the doors with a snap.

Immediately the girls' senses were overloaded.

The horns of the marching band wailed what must have been the school song. The rhythm of the drums was constant and violent, like the heartbeat of an enormous beast. The bleachers exploded with a chant, "Go, Knights, go! Fight, Knights, fight! Go! Fight! *WIN!*" Then more of the screaming the girls had heard from the street.

Alexis didn't know whether to be afraid of high school or extremely excited to be a part of it. Just then she saw something that made up her mind. Five of the cheerleaders, dazzling in purple and gold, gathered in a small clump. The girl in the center disappeared for a moment, and someone yelled, "One, two!"

The cheerleaders moved down together, and when they rose, the tiny girl in the middle exploded toward the ceiling. She completed a backflip before slamming her hands out to meet her toes and falling gracefully back into her teammates' waiting arms.

Alexis's mouth hung open in shock. She had never seen a stunt go that high. Sometimes the girls throwing her in practice barely got her above their heads. She was sure this cheerleader had almost hit the rafters of the looming gym. And she knew that she was going to fly like that one day. No matter what it took.

Someone nudged her. It was the teacher again. He pointed over to the bleachers labeled Freshmen, and Alexis and Elizabeth squeezed into the front row.

"Hey, you don't go to school here." The voice came from a blond boy next to Elizabeth. It wasn't accusing, just amused. "I've never seen you before. You're imposters! I would have noticed you," he added, winking at Elizabeth. The girls ignored him.

A tall girl with purple face paint walked to the center of the gym. She was holding a microphone.

"Attention, Fighting Knights! It's time for the class competition! Now we're going to pick one member from each class. Who will win? The freshmen? Sophomores? Juniors? Or seniors?"

The students roared, and before Alexis realized what was going on, the blond boy had shoved her from her spot on the bench.

"Alrighty! I have a freshman volunteer," the tall girl said, grabbing Alexis by the hand.

Alexis looked at Elizabeth frantically, but Elizabeth just shrugged in a hopeless "What can I do?" expression.

The tall girl with the purple face dragged Alexis onto the hardwood. Alexis stood in front of a thousand teenagers, petrified.

Didn't they know she didn't belong here? Surely it was

painted on her like one of their posters. The blond boy had known right away.

Whether or not they knew, nobody said anything. Three older students joined her in the middle of the floor: one sophomore, one junior, and one senior. Cheerleaders pulled two red wagons into the middle of the floor.

"Here, you two work together," the tall girl commanded as she placed Alexis next to the sophomore—a short, chunky boy with glasses. The girl holding the microphone gave Alexis a broomstick and then spoke to the crowd.

"Since this week is the London Bridge Festival, our competition today is the wagon joust!" The gym erupted. "Each team will have two chances to collect as many rings on their broomsticks as possible. As always, seniors and juniors first!"

The other team got ready. One got in the wagon with the broomstick, and the other got ready to pull. Small hula hoops hung from fishing string down the middle of the gym. The person with the broom was supposed to grab them by passing the broom through the middle as they raced past.

All at once, the wagon took off. It was more than a little bit wobbly. The person pulling the wagon had a hard time steering, and the team missed the first three hoops because they weren't close enough.

They weaved some and grabbed two hoops before getting tangled in the third and tumbling over. The students in the gym laughed as the competitors got up and tried their second run. They got three more hoops, giving them a total of five. The older students roared their approval and booed as Alexis climbed in her wagon.

"That's probably a good idea that they gave you the broom,"

her partner said with a laugh. "I don't think I would fit in that wagon! And if I could, I don't think you'd be able to pull me!"

"Just keep us going straight, okay?" said Alexis. She took a deep breath. How on earth had she gotten herself into this?

They were off. The boy was pulling Alexis a lot faster than she had expected to go. How long had it been since she had been in a wagon anyway? No time to think about it. The first hoop tore by before she realized it, but the next three slid easily onto the end of her stick.

Cheers erupted from the younger side of the gym.

When she picked up a fourth hoop, the broomstick got heavy, and it slipped off before she could lift the handle. They reached the end of the gym and turned around. Alexis only needed to get three more hoops to win.

They tore back down the way they had come, and Alexis aimed for the three hoops left behind. Two slid on easily, but the third spun round and round on the handle, threatening to fly into the audience. The wagon stopped suddenly, and Alexis flew out.

The crowd gasped.

Alexis was lying on her back. She lifted her broomstick in the air, and the girl with the microphone counted out loud.

"Six!" she cried. "The freshmen and sophomores win, probably for the first time in ten years!"

The boos of the older students were drowned out by the higher-pitched cheers of the freshmen and sophomores. Alexis scooted back to her seat, blushing like crazy.

"Alexis, you're amazing!" said Elizabeth.

"Thanks," said Alexis. She elbowed her way in next to the blond boy. "Thanks to you, too," she said, pushing him playfully.

"It wasn't that bad, was it?" He laughed.

The microphone girl called for silence.

"Now," she said, "it's time for the reason we're all here in the first place! Let's give it up for your Lake Havasu High School swim team!"

Again the crowd went wild.

"The swim team?" said Alexis and Elizabeth together. Elizabeth leaned over Alexis and addressed the blond boy.

"Aren't pep rallies usually for football or something? I've never heard of a pep rally for the swim team."

"I know," replied the blond boy. "This is the first time the school has had a pep rally for the swim team. But this is more for one guy than the whole team. You see those?" He pointed up to the gym ceiling, and Alexis noticed a collection of banners for the first time. They were purple satin lined with gold. Each one had STATE CHAMPION embroidered along the top with a different event underneath. *100 m Butterfly, 100 m Freestyle, 400 m Individual Medley*. All six of them were labeled with the same name: *David Turner*.

"That's him," said the blond boy. He pointed across the gym to where one member of the swim team stood a little behind the others. "He's only a freshman, too. He won all of those last year, before he was even in high school. The guy's a machine. So they decided that the swim team is worthy of being honored this year with a pep rally."

"Wow," said Elizabeth. Alexis was speechless. Something about the swim champion bothered her. Everyone in the school was clapping and screaming for *him*, but he didn't seem to like it. He was off to the side, the hood of his sweatshirt pulled in front of his face and his lanky shoulders stooped. Alexis got the feeling that he wished he were invisible.

The coach who was with the team grabbed a microphone and announced that the team would have a swim meet the following afternoon. It would be held at four o'clock at the Aquatic Center in town.

From the noise and excitement of the screaming crowd, Alexis guessed that just about everyone would be there. She thought it was kind of funny. She wondered if the schools in her area even *had* swim teams. She made a mental note to check when she got back to Sacramento.

The gym began to empty, and students filed out of the gym to go back to their classes. Alexis and Elizabeth slipped out the door to the street, making sure to avoid the teacher who had led them inside. They walked back the way they had come.

Soon they were melting in the heat. A sign up ahead rocked in the breeze. It had a triple-scoop ice cream cone on it.

"What do you think?" asked Alexis. "We can ask for directions to the hotel and get a snack at the same time."

"Perfect!" said Elizabeth.

The girls walked into the shop and sighed with delight as the cool of the air-conditioning mingled with the warm smell of fresh waffle cones. Alexis ordered a scoop of chocolate and a scoop of rainbow sherbet.

"Those don't go together!" said Elizabeth.

"Of course they do!" said Alexis. "What am I supposed to do when I can't decide between chocolate or fruity?"

The girls sat in a squishy booth near the front window and watched the tourists amble by. Their conversation shifted back to the Lake Havasu swim champion.

"I can't believe that!" said Alexis. "He must be really good to have won all of those championships."

"I know!" said Elizabeth. "And he beat a bunch of older swimmers to get them!"

The bell on the ice cream shop door jingled.

The mayor walked through the door and up to the counter, followed by the bridge commissioner and a crumpled old man sniffling into a hankie. Alexis choked on a bite of her rainbow sherbet.

"Elizabeth, look! What is Dr. Edwards doing with Mayor Applebee and the bridge commissioner?"

"Shh!" said Elizabeth. She motioned to Alexis, and the girls slumped down in their booth. The three men sat in the next booth over.

"You sure you don't want anything, Dr. Edwards?" asked the mayor. The only answer was another sneeze. "I suggested the ice cream shop just to get out of the office," continued the mayor. "All I've heard about all day is that silly curse. My phone has been ringing off the hook!"

"I can assure you, Mayor," said Dr. Edwards, "there is no such thing as the curse of the Thames. History never mentions it. It's just a story someone has made up to scare the tourists."

A deeper, calmer voice broke into the conversation. Alexis knew it had to be the bridge commissioner.

"Curse or not, something's wrong with our bridge. The engineers are flying in tomorrow. If there is any structural damage, the parade can't happen."

"Aren't you being hasty, Commissioner?" said Dr. Edwards.

"Are you trying to tell me how to do my job, Doctor?"

"Gentlemen, gentlemen," said the mayor. "Let's get along, shall we?"

"We can't let years of tradition be stopped by a tiny crack!" Dr. Edwards pounded the table.

"Have you ever seen an avalanche, Doctor?" asked the commissioner. "It all starts with a tiny crack, and then. . .*boom!* Everything goes down, and there's no stopping it.

"To take a chance on the parade would be totally foolhardy. Can you imagine the bridge collapsing with dozens or even hundreds of people on it? Imagine the injuries and even deaths."

"But the chances of that are probably slim," Dr. Edwards said, his voice rising. "If we have to cancel the parade this year, many people probably won't return next year. Our tradition will be lost. *That* would be foolhardy!"

"Yes," said the commissioner. "And imagine how many people will never return and what will happen to the tradition if a tragedy should happen."

"All right, all right!" said Mayor Applebee. "No more fighting! We all want the parade to go on as planned, but safety must come first. If the bridge is okay, it will happen. If something is wrong. . ." He sighed heavily and stood up, carrying the last of his now dripping ice cream cone. The other two men followed him out of the shop, still arguing.

"Why is Dr. Edwards so concerned about the parade?" asked Elizabeth.

"I have no idea," said Alexis. It didn't make sense. "The mayor might have asked him about the curse, since the doctor is an expert in English history. But why did Dr. Edwards get so angry about the idea of canceling the parade?"

"I wouldn't have thought Dr. Edwards was the type of person who would even enjoy a parade," said Elizabeth. "Actually, I can't imagine him enjoying *anything*."

"That's what I was just thinking," Alexis said.

"Well," said Elizabeth, "do you want to walk back to the hotel? We could hit the pool and go swimming before dinner."

"Sounds good," said Alexis. They got directions and walked the streets silently. Alexis was still trying to figure out why Dr. Edwards cared so much about the problem with the bridge. It sounded like the bridge commissioner was pretty worried. Alexis couldn't stop thinking about one thing he had said. *"It all starts with a tiny crack, and then. . .boom!"*

The more Alexis thought about it, the more she realized the commissioner was right. But not just about the bridge. Sometimes the smallest things could cause the biggest problems. Like this summer, for instance. Her friend Jerry had wanted to help Miss Maria save her nature park in Sacramento. Her business had dropped, and she'd brought in mechanical dinosaurs. But what Jerry had thought was harmless fun ended up as a huge news story and a mystery for the Camp Club Girls to solve. But feelings had gotten hurt, and Miss Maria even got injured because of Jerry's little idea.

"Elizabeth," said Alexis. "Isn't there something in the Bible about small things causing big problems?"

"Well, there are a few things," said Elizabeth. "A verse or two talks about little foxes spoiling the vineyards, which means small things that we tend to ignore can bring destruction. And in the book of James, we're told that our tongue, even though it's so small, can do big-time damage."

Alexis and Elizabeth walked in silence for a few minutes. Then Alexis suddenly turned to Elizabeth.

"What did you say?" she asked.

"Huh?"

"I thought you said something," said Alexis. She looked around. Not too many people were outside now since it was the hottest time of the day. They were near the alley where they had lost the old woman earlier. Alexis strained her ears and heard it again—a hurried whisper.

She edged toward the alley but didn't look around the corner. The words were muffled, but she heard them loud and clear.

"We have to steal the whole carriage."

A second voice began to argue.

"How are we gonna get it out of the hotel?"

The hotel? Alexis thought. Were these people seriously talking about stealing the golden carriage from the London Bridge Resort?

Elizabeth let out a quiet gasp, and the girls looked at each other.

"Don't worry," said the first voice again. "It'll be easy. And smile—this job is worth millions."

CHAPTER 4

The Golden Coach

Suddenly Alexis heard rustling, as if the people who had been speaking were moving toward them.

Elizabeth grabbed her arm and motioned for them to leave.

Alexis hated to go without at least getting a look at the whisperers. But the rustling seemed to draw closer.

The girls fled. They didn't know what else to do. What would happen if the people in the alley knew Alexis and Elizabeth had heard their plan?

They had run close to two miles when they finally saw the London Bridge Resort. Alexis was grateful to see its towers.

This must be how retreating armies felt once they had left the danger of the battlefield and found the safety of their castle walls again, she thought.

Alexis and Elizabeth stood in the lobby, panting and trying to catch their breath. Their eyes were drawn toward the carriage. It was absolutely huge. Could anyone really think they would be able to steal this thing?

Alexis walked over to a sign standing near the ropes protecting the golden masterpiece. It gave a brief history of the original carriage and the replica.

The Golden State Coach was built in London in 1762. King

George III commissioned it and meant to ride in it on the day of his coronation. The greatness of the coach, however, kept it from being finished until three years later. Nonetheless, King George III and his family used it as the Coach of State. Recent monarchs have used the coach once a year in their customary parade to open Parliament. The last time the coach was used was by Elizabeth II in 2002.

This priceless replica is the only full-size model of the original coach. It was built for the use of the London Bridge Resort and Hotel.

Alexis looked around the hotel lobby. It was filled with people. Tourists were on their way to dinner. Bellhops ran for the elevators with teetering piles of suitcases. Jane, with her purple hair, was busily checking people in and getting fresh towels or extra pillows.

Alexis knew she wouldn't be able to get near the carriage unnoticed. If she tried, she probably wouldn't make it over the ropes before someone yanked her out. How did anyone expect to *remove* the carriage from the room entirely? It just didn't seem possible.

Alexis felt a bony elbow digging into her side. She looked up at Elizabeth, who pointed across the carriage to a row of red velvet chairs. Dr. Edwards sat in one, not seeming to even be aware of the hustle and bustle all around him. His head was bowed over a notebook in his lap. His arched hands supported his forehead.

Curious, the girls watched him. Within a few minutes he shook off his daze, stood up hastily, and dashed out of the lobby more quickly than the girls thought he was even capable of moving.

A piece of paper fluttered out of his notebook and onto the floor.

The girls ran over and picked it up.

"Dr. Edwards!" called Alexis. "You dropped something!"

But the man was already in an elevator, and he didn't hear her. Alexis glanced at the paper in her hand, and her eyes opened wide. The paper was thick and unlined with frayed holes along one side, like it had been torn from a sketchbook. On it was a perfect pencil sketch of the Golden State Coach.

"Man," said Elizabeth. "He's a pretty good artist. Look, he even drew the swirly detail on the dolphin's tail! What's that writing say?" She pointed to the bottom corner where a sentence was scrawled. Alexis pulled the paper closer to her face. She had assumed the writing was just the artist's name or something, but it wasn't. It was a question, written in perfect cursive.

Where could it be hiding?

" 'Where could it be hiding?' That doesn't make any sense," Alexis said.

"The carriage isn't hiding at all. It's in plain sight," Elizabeth added. "So what does that mean?"

"I don't know," Alexis said. "I think maybe we'll have to think about it. For right now I'll put this in my notebook. Do you have your computer here?"

"My dad has his MacBook. I can use that," Elizabeth said.

"Good. I don't have a notebook computer, and Grandma's practically in the Dark Ages—she only has a big old desktop back home," Alexis said. "Why don't you go online tonight and set Kate or Sydney busy seeing if they can find anything about the coach being in hiding."

"Will do," Elizabeth said.

"I think we also need more background information than we have," Alexis said. "The sign was helpful, but we need more."

"I can ask the girls to dig up everything they can on the coach," Elizabeth said.

Alexis grinned at her. "You forget that we have an expert right here. I'll ask Grandma about it tonight while you're filling the girls in. There isn't much about English history that she doesn't know. And I know she brushed up on the carriage and everything pertaining to the London Bridge before she came here."

"Perfect," said Elizabeth. "It's about time for me to get back for dinner anyway. See you tomorrow?"

"Definitely. We'll have a lot to look into. Maybe we'll have time to see the swim meet between investigations." Alexis smiled. Why was she so interested in swimming all of a sudden? It must have been the pep rally.

Elizabeth hugged her and left the hotel.

Alexis stood in the crowded lobby waiting for an elevator to take her to the top floor, where her grandmother and she were sharing a suite. Their suite was amazing. It had two bedrooms with king-size beds, a dining room, a living room with a big-screen TV, and its own kitchen. They didn't really use the kitchen, except to store some drinks in the fridge. Most meals they got for free from the hotel—another one of Grandma Windsor's perks.

Alexis entered the room and saw piles of food on the small table in the living room. Grandma Windsor was on the couch, already in her pajamas and fluffy slippers.

"I thought we'd do room service tonight!" she called

through a mouthful of pizza. Alexis laughed, imagining what her mom would say if she spoke with her mouth full like Grandma Windsor had.

"Perfect!" said Alexis. She changed into boxer shorts and a tank top and plopped down next to her grandma in front of the TV. They watched a bit of the news, and Alexis saw that Elizabeth's dad had caught the largest fish on the first day of the bass tournament. She was surprised to see no news of the bridge. She guessed the mayor was keeping everything quiet until they found out what was going on.

After the pizza was gone, Alexis popped open a Mountain Dew and got comfy.

"So that coach thing downstairs is pretty cool," she said, acting just a little bit interested. For some reason she didn't want to come right out and say, "Someone's trying to steal the coach!" She didn't have any evidence besides a whispered conversation in an alley. And what if the people had only been joking?

"Yes," said Grandma Windsor, "the coach is an amazing replica. The real one was part of a very historical reign in England."

"You mean King George the Third?" asked Alexis, remembering the name from the sign in the lobby.

"Yes, Alexis! I'm proud of you!" Grandma Windsor muted the TV, excited to talk about her favorite subject. "King George the Third was famous for two things, mostly."

"What were they?" asked Alexis.

"Losing the American Revolutionary War and going crazy."

"He went crazy?" Alexis had never enjoyed history class, but for some reason she loved it when her grandmother told her stories like this. The characters seemed so much more real than the ones in her schoolbooks.

"Well, yes," said her grandma. "That's what they say. It may have been the pressure, of course. Being a king isn't easy. Scholars today, however, believe that he was probably genetically predisposed to mental illness and that he had a blood disease."

"What?" asked Alexis.

"It means that his mind might have always been a little fragile. He might have always been mentally unbalanced. If he had been in charge of the country while it was peaceful and wealthy, maybe he wouldn't have snapped. But he didn't live during peace, and he *did* finally snap." Grandma Windsor clicked the TV off.

"How did people know he was crazy?" asked Alexis. She felt sad for this king who had collapsed under the weight of his crown.

"Well, he didn't really lose his mind until his later years. They say it happened after his youngest daughter died. Her name was Princess Amelia, and she was his favorite. In fact, the king was so protective of his daughters that he didn't want them to marry. There were rumors that the young Amelia had fallen in love with someone below her rank. A princess would never be allowed to marry a horse trainer."

"That's awful!" said Alexis. She imagined a beautiful young princess locked in a tower, while her crazy father kept the key on a chain around his neck. The wonderful and extremely handsome boy who wanted to marry the princess stood beneath the tower, day and night, waiting.

Alexis was becoming what her mother called a "romantic type" of person.

Alexis forgot about the mystery surrounding the carriage as Grandma Windsor told story after story about crazy King George III. Alexis learned that Princess Amelia had sent secret letters to the one she loved. Then she had become ill and died without ever getting married.

Alexis asked what happened to the letters, but her grandmother didn't know.

When Alexis and her grandmother stopped talking, she called Elizabeth and passed along what she'd learned.

"The girls all said to tell you hi," Elizabeth said. "McKenzie thought it was a rip-off that you had to ride a wagon instead of a real horse to joust today. Sydney wanted more information on the swimming team since she's so into sports. Kate wishes she would have sent you a prototype her dad has of a new iPad clone so we could keep them posted every minute. Kate is going to look up information. She said anytime we have news to text her and she'll circulate it to the rest of the girls.

"Bailey is really proud of you for winning the contest in the school today. She wants to know if either of us are going to try to be the pageant queen. And dear little Biscuit the Wonder Dog even woofed. I think he was saying if he'd been with us today he would have caught the old hag for us!"

Alexis laughed. The messages sounded so much like the Camp Club Girls! Count on the Camp Club Girls to be there with them in spirit, in thought, and in prayers!

"Can you text Kate and ask her to check into letters Grandma mentioned that were written by Princess Amelia?" Alexis asked.

"Sure," Elizabeth replied. "I think I'll also ask her to check into curses surrounding the London Bridge."

With that, the girls said good night.

When Alexis finally climbed into bed, her mind was swimming with pictures of royalty: beautiful gowns, golden coaches, and lost letters of love. Eventually she fell asleep to the sound of water slapping the bridge outside her window.

And she dreamed.

She was walking along the London Bridge again, only this time she was not afraid. Halfway across she stopped to look over the rail. The reflection of the full moon sparkled brightly in the night, rippling with the small waves. Suddenly she heard a voice. A sweet voice, singing a familiar tune.

"London Bridge is falling down, falling down, falling down. . ."

It was a girl not much older than Alexis—maybe fifteen or sixteen. Her dress looked old-fashioned but gorgeous. Silver silk sparkling in the starlight. Pearls were strung throughout her long waves of dark hair. They matched the necklace around her delicate throat. The girl's liquid eyes didn't see Alexis, but she stopped to look over the rail, too, farther down the bridge.

The young girl took something from the inside of her gown—a folded piece of paper. She hugged it to her chest. Then she kissed it and let it drift down into the lake. She turned away and kept walking toward the other side of the bridge. She kept singing.

"London Bridge is falling down, my fair lady."

The bridge rumbled. The girl disappeared as a thick fog rolled up from the water to engulf everything. Her sweet voice vanished as well and was replaced by an older voice.

"My fair lady!" it shrieked, and then it laughed. The long, dry cackle was all too familiar. It was the voice of the old crone Elizabeth and Alexis had seen earlier in the day. Alexis could see the outline of a bent form through the fog. The figure lifted a

walking stick high into the air and brought it down hard onto the stonework of the bridge.

The bridge rumbled again, and this time it rocked. The rail in front of Alexis broke away and fell toward the water. . .and she followed it.

Alexis wanted to scream, but her voice was caught in her throat. Stone and cement surrounded her as she plummeted into the water. It was icy, and the stabbing cold stole her breath. She fought to swim, every moment expecting a piece of the London Bridge to crush her and push her to the bottom.

A few feet away something white was floating on the surface. It was the girl's letter, and it was soaked through. With what? Alexis wondered. Tears or water?

One more breath, that's all she could take. Her arms hurt. They couldn't support her anymore. She was sinking.

An arm. A long, thin arm reached out and grabbed her. Alexis was pulled to the safety of the shore by the powerful sidestroke of a swimming prince.

The Message of the Moon

The next morning, Alexis met Elizabeth outside her hotel. There were loud voices coming from the area of the bridge, so naturally they drifted in that direction. When the bridge came into view, Alexis's dream came flooding back. She shuddered.

She almost told Elizabeth about it but decided not to. It had really been weird, and she didn't think she could remember it all anyway.

"Look," said Elizabeth. "The bridge is still closed."

The bridge looked different than it had the day before. It was still decorated with yellow caution tape, but now there were big men in hard hats crawling all over it. They were all using strange instruments that looked like levels. A few of them were even in the water near the closest pillar. It was only up to their waist.

"That's funny," said Alexis. "I thought the water was a lot deeper than that."

"Those must be the engineers," said Elizabeth.

"Good. It shouldn't take them long to figure out what's going on." Alexis led Elizabeth farther down the grassy slope, and they sat on the little beach, about twenty feet from the yellow tape. "Hopefully the festival can pick up where it left off."

The men in the water were pointing toward the second

pillar, where the crack had grown overnight. They seemed to be arguing about something.

"That's strange," said Elizabeth.

"What?" asked Alexis.

"The crack. It's reaching *up* the arch of the bridge. See? It's climbing closer to the top every day."

"I know," said Alexis. "That means whatever is causing the crack is under the water."

"I wonder what it could be," said Elizabeth. She shot Alexis a sneaky look. "We could check it out, you know."

"What? You mean under the water?" Alexis's heart began to pound. Not only was she afraid of bridges, but last night she had also dreamed of this particular bridge falling on top of her. "That's crazy! The engineers aren't even getting close to that crack!"

"It's not crazy," said Elizabeth. She leaned forward and shielded her eyes from the sun. She squinted, looking toward the middle of the river where the crack loomed. "The channel under the bridge is only eight feet deep in the middle. A lady at my hotel told me."

"Okay," said Alexis. "Keep in mind that I am barely five feet tall. You, my giant friend, may be able to tiptoe out there, but I. . ." Alexis shivered again. Her dream had been way too realistic.

"Oh come on, Alexis! All we need is a couple pairs of goggles. We brought our swimsuits, right? We can walk out most of the way, swim the last few feet to the pillar, and dunk our heads under to check out the crack."

Alexis was just about to say, "I'll think about it," when a noise behind them made them jump. Chipper whistling. . .to the tune of "London Bridge."

The girls spun around where they sat and saw the old woman dressed as a hag coming toward the bridge. She spotted them, but she didn't run away this time. Instead she turned a little so she was heading right for them. The spring in her step told Alexis the old lady was in a good mood and that maybe she wasn't as old as they had thought. She kept whistling as she reached the bench near the sidewalk. Alexis moved to get up, but a sharp whistle made her freeze.

She looked up, and the old woman raised her eyebrows and shook a finger at her. Then she sat on the bench and looked around, much like a tourist just enjoying the view. *What in the world is going on?* thought Alexis. She watched the woman for almost five minutes before anything else happened.

The lady reached into the pocket of her ragged robe and drew out a small yellow envelope. She held it in front of her for a moment and looked at the girls to make sure they saw it. Then she placed it beside her on the bench, got up, and left— whistling her tune again.

Alexis and Elizabeth looked at each other. They both asked the same question.

"What was that all about?"

When they could no longer see or hear the old woman, Alexis got up and approached the bench. The little yellow envelope lay facedown on the seat. Alexis picked it up and flipped it over. Three words were scratched on the front:

For the Curious

Alexis looked at Elizabeth and shrugged her shoulders. She tore the envelope open and pulled out a matching note card. The twiglike handwriting said:

442 Lakeview Avenue, 7:00 tonight. Don't be late.

That was all. No name. Nothing.

The girls exchanged glances again. What on earth did this mean?

"I guess she wants to talk to us," said Elizabeth.

"Yeah," said Alexis. "But why tonight? At. . .four hundred and forty-two Lakeview Avenue? Why not here and now? Wouldn't that have been more convenient?"

"Maybe," said Elizabeth. "But maybe there's more to it. Maybe she wants to talk where no one can overhear."

They glanced over their shoulders to where the engineers were still investigating the bridge.

"Or," said Alexis, "maybe she wants to lock us in a cage, fatten us up, and throw us into her giant oven."

"Enough with the *Hansel and Gretel* stuff, okay?" said Elizabeth. "Do you want to investigate this stuff or not?"

"Of course I do!" said Alexis. "I think my imagination keeps running away with me." Alexis had no idea why she had been so freaked out lately. Maybe the dream and the bridge had her on edge. Whatever it was, she needed to get over it. She had never thought of herself as a chicken before.

"It's okay, Alex," said Elizabeth. "It's easy to let that happen here. Half the town thinks it's back in seventeenth-century London. You know what you need?"

"Huh?"

"A little water to wake you up."

Alexis took a fearful step back and pointed to the channel. "I'm not going in there."

"Not the lake, nerd! The swim meet! It will give us something to do until we go meet Miss Creepy."

Alexis lit up. "Yes! Let's go!"

Again she asked herself the question: Why was she so excited about a swim meet? Maybe it was just the allure of something new. She'd never been to one before.

The girls walked across downtown to the Aquatic Center. Alexis thought it looked like a giant concrete ice cube. They were greeted by more purple and gold signs and a gaggle of giggling girls. It looked like the entire female population of Lake Havasu City had shown up.

Other schools were there, too. Alexis could tell by the many different colors on the swimming caps of the swimmers. Yellow and black, green and silver, red and blue—just like her school colors back home.

She and Elizabeth found seats halfway up the bleachers. From this place they could see everything. Swimmers were warming up or cooling down in a smaller pool at one end. The huge pool in the middle was divided into eight lanes. Small platforms lined one end.

Within minutes the crowd was on its feet screaming. Alexis and Elizabeth stood, too, so they could see. A woman with huge hair was standing right in front of Alexis. Elizabeth looked over and laughed.

"Here," she said. "Trade me spots!" The girls swapped seats, and Alexis saw the reason for the insanity. The Arizona swimming champion was making his way to one of the platforms at the edge of the pool.

"In lane five," said an intercom voice over the crowd, "David Turner!"

The crowd roared. All the other swimmers had waved and smiled up at the crowd when their names were called. Turner kept his eyes on the water in front of him. The swimmers bent forward, ready to enter the water, and the gun went off.

One swimmer on the end had been late jumping off, but everyone else was already gone. In the middle of the pool Turner hadn't yet broken the surface. He powered through the water, moving his body like a dolphin, until he was almost halfway across. Then his arms came up at the same time, propelling his head and shoulders out of the water as they pushed back under.

It looked as if he were flying.

"So *that's* why they call it the butterfly," said Alexis. She had always heard of the butterfly stroke but had never seen what it looked like.

Turner was at the end of the pool, diving underwater to turn around. When he finished, the person in second place was still in the middle of the pool. The crowd cheered. Turner didn't even look up at the board that showed the swimmers' times in bright lights.

The crowd settled a little as the other swimmers filed out of the pool. The other competitors were greeted by warm hugs from family and the excited smiles of friends. Alexis saw David Turner receive a wet slap on the back from his coach before he slipped away to the locker room. Alone.

His fans, who were still cheering for him, hadn't even noticed he was gone.

"He always looks so sad," said Alexis out loud.

"What?" said Elizabeth, who was watching another race that had already started.

"Nothing," said Alexis. But she couldn't help thinking about the champion. How could someone be so popular—so adored—and still look so alone?

●—●—●

The girls watched the rest of the meet and then went to meet Elizabeth's family for dinner. They ate at a little café near the square, where the jousting tournament was taking place. The sound of clashing metal and pounding hooves made it easy to ignore Elizabeth's little brother, who kept pretending to pick his nose.

"Talk about little things that spoil stuff," Elizabeth said to Alexis, nodding at her brother. "He's a case in point!"

Alexis's reply was drowned out by the thud of hooves. Every few minutes gigantic horses charged each other. The men on their backs wore real armor and held shields and lances.

Alexis was about to ask why they had to wear the armor when two knights clashed. The lance that the blue knight was holding slammed into the green knight's shield, snapped in half, and then slid up and landed with a crack on the piece of metal protecting the man's throat.

That was why they were wearing real armor.

"Hey, this isn't any game!" she exclaimed to Elizabeth.

"What, jousting?" Elizabeth asked.

"Yes, I guess I thought they were like stuntmen. I didn't realize they were really fighting," she said.

"Jousting is a big hobby all over the United States," Elizabeth said. "A lot of regions have jousting clubs where they're really into it. A lot of cities have Renaissance festivals where jousting is part of the action."

"Do people often get hurt?" Alexis asked.

"I don't know," Elizabeth admitted. "I guess they sometimes have accidents, but I haven't really paid attention or heard much about it."

Alexis had no idea that people still did this kind of thing. Her heart was beating so fast she could hardly eat.

After dinner the girls began wandering through the streets of downtown. Alexis had gotten a map at her hotel that showed them how to get to 442 Lakeview Avenue. They followed the tiny red lines that indicated where streets were block after block. Finally they ended up in a small neighborhood.

The houses were perfect. Each one was small and built of stone or brick. Short fences surrounded each front yard, and wild—but beautiful—English gardens were in full bloom. The fall flowers filled the air with a smell that reminded Alexis of the honeysuckle back home in Sacramento.

When they finally reached number 442, it was getting dark.

"It doesn't look like anyone is home," said Elizabeth.

The girls walked up to the porch, and sure enough, no lights were on inside the house. The flicker of a light with an electrical short licked at the darkness, throwing shadows against the front door.

"Maybe she forgot," said Alexis. "Let's take a look around to be sure she's not home."

Elizabeth knocked, and Alexis left the porch to peek into the first window. The other side was in absolute darkness. There was no way to tell what was inside. That didn't matter, really, but Alexis found that she was very interested to see how this woman lived.

"Do you think this woman is really creepy, or is she pretending?" she asked Elizabeth.

"I don't know," Elizabeth said. "Does she dress up and walk around town cackling to entertain the tourists? Or is there more to her?"

"It's awfully dark around here," Alexis said. "Reminds me of a scary movie."

" 'People loved darkness instead of light because their deeds were evil,' " Elizabeth quoted. "John 3:19. Sometimes the Bible just has the perfect words!

"I don't think anyone is home," Elizabeth added.

"Yeah, maybe we'd better leave," Alexis said. "It's too much like a scary movie."

"Yep. It's after dark. Two young girls out alone. Supposed to meet someone at a house, but the house is empty," Elizabeth said.

"And the light is flickering," Alexis added.

"Now all we need is—" She abruptly stopped talking as the girls heard footsteps.

They heard the footsteps turn off the sidewalk and enter the gate of 442 Lakeview Avenue. The girls spun around, expecting to see the old woman. Instead, a tall man raised something over his head. It looked like a short baseball bat.

He was coming toward them!

Alexis tried to scream. Elizabeth covered her head.

Then the object in the man's hand blinded them.

It was a flashlight.

"What are you doing poking around people's houses?"

"Oh no," groaned Alexis. It was Deputy Dewayne, the officer the girls had met on their first day in Lake Havasu City.

"I got a call about some trespassers, so I came to *investigate*."

"We're not poking, really, sir," said Alexis. "We had an appointment. We were supposed to come see this woman at seven."

"*This woman?*" asked the deputy. "And what is *this woman's* name? Huh?" The girls looked at each other. He would never believe them. "That's what I thought," Deputy Dewayne said. He put his hands on his hips.

"I have half a mind to take you in," he said.

"But sir, we weren't doing anything," said Elizabeth. "I promise!"

"Well, get out of here then. If I find you out here again, I won't be so forgiving." He shined his flashlight in their faces, and Alexis turned around to get out of the glare. That's when she saw it. A sentence, scribbled in pencil on the white paint of the front door.

Watch beneath the moon when the bridge calls out.

●—●—●

Deputy Dewayne gave the girls a ride back to their hotels. Alexis didn't dare bring up the writing in the police car. The deputy hadn't noticed it, and she wanted to keep it that way. She didn't want him blaming them for graffiti, too. When the officer dropped off Elizabeth, Alexis waved good-bye. She would have to call Elizabeth later.

There was a note from her grandmother when she got to her room. Some old friends from Europe had come to the conference, and Grandma Windsor was going to be out with them until late. Alexis watched some old detective shows on TV Land for a while. But her mind kept going back to the things that had happened that day. Since she had so much to think about, she got in her pajamas and climbed into her bed.

Watch beneath the moon when the bridge calls out.

What on earth did that mean? *Watch beneath the moon* was easy enough. Alexis suspected it meant to watch when the moon was shining, which would mean at night. But what about the last part? What did the woman mean, *when the bridge calls out*? Stone and cement didn't talk, as far as Alexis knew. Bridges definitely didn't *call out*.

Whatever. The lady was obviously a little crazy. And who knew? Maybe the message wasn't for the girls anyway.

Alexis looked at her clock. Too late to call Elizabeth. She would run the clue by Elizabeth tomorrow and see what she thought. She wondered if Elizabeth had gotten any e-mails from the Camp Club Girls.

Alexis rolled over onto her side. She had left the curtains and the window open to let in the fresh, cool evening air. The desert smelled wonderful at night—like cooling sage. She drifted in and out of sleep as she watched the moonbeams dance on the wall. And then she heard it: the distinct ringing of metal hitting stone, followed by a splash.

Alexis sat up, looked toward the window, and heard it again. *Ring, thump, splash.*

Was the bridge calling out?

Moonlight Sonata

Alexis pushed the covers away and scooted to the edge of her bed.

Ring, thump, splash!

What could that sound be? It was strange and muffled, as if it were coming from under a pillow. . .or water. Could this be what the writing on the old woman's door was talking about? Did she know something was happening to the bridge during the night? Alexis inched her feet down into the soft hotel carpet and tiptoed toward the window. Her grandma hadn't come back to the room yet. This and the darkness made Alexis feel very alone.

When she reached the window, the breeze stiffened and blew her unruly, bed-head hair out of her face. It was dark outside. The moon was hiding behind a large cloud. The noise had also stopped. Maybe it hadn't been the bridge. Maybe some tourists had been out late playing around the water.

Ring, thump, splash!

Alexis leaned out the window to get a better look. The strange noise was definitely coming from the bridge. The streets were empty. All the tourists and engineers were at home in their beds. She couldn't see anyone. So who—or what—was making the noise?

Alexis heard another splash, so she focused on the water. She couldn't see anything along either shore. No one was skipping rocks or taking a stroll along the water's edge. Eventually she looked at the bridge again. If it was dark outside, the areas beneath the bridge were pitch-black. There was no way to see anything without some light. Alexis jumped from the window and grabbed her backpack. She rummaged through it and found what she was looking for: a flashlight.

Alexis carried the flashlight to the window and turned it on. She aimed it across the water toward the bridge. It didn't help much. The beam of light was small, and it didn't penetrate very far into the darkness under the bridge.

Splash.

Alexis turned the light toward the sound. Under the second arch, near the crack, the water rippled. Had someone thrown something into the water? She looked to the top of the bridge, but still she saw no one. So what had dropped into the water? Alexis moved the light back toward the water, but it went dark.

Alexis hit the flashlight with the palm of her hand. The batteries were dead.

"Oh come on!" she whispered furiously. "You have to be kidding me!" The light flashed back on but only long enough to blind her before it went dark again.

"Kate would tell me I should have a solar-powered or hand-crank flashlight for emergencies," she muttered, almost hearing the voice of the most techno-savvy of the Camp Club Girls in her mind. "But a lot of good that does me now!"

She dropped the light and leaned out the window again, trying as hard as she could to see without it. She couldn't.

Alexis sighed and was about to go back to bed when the

wind blew again. The clouds drifted out of the way, and the brilliant rays of the moon lit up Lake Havasu like it was day. Alexis couldn't believe what she saw under the bridge. Bobbing up and down on the water was a small, wooden rowboat.

That shouldn't have been surprising, since it was a lake. People rowed small boats around Lake Havasu all the time. Even at night. What confused Alexis was the fact that the small boat was empty. Had it come untied from the dock and drifted to the bridge on its own? And she still had no way to explain the noises.

Then. . .

Splash. A head emerged from the water.

Thump. Something heavy fell into the boat.

Ring. Something else fell in on top of it.

Alexis gasped. A long, dark shadow pulled itself out of the water and slid into the boat. Then it began to paddle in the opposite direction and out of sight. Alexis left the window and grabbed her notebook and a small camera she had brought for the trip. She left the room and sprinted down the hallway to the elevator.

When it opened on the first floor, Alexis ran toward the front doors. The coolness of the marble under her feet made her realize she had forgotten to put on her shoes. *Oh well*, she thought. *I've had dirty feet before.*

But when she saw the automatic doors swing open, she stopped in her tracks. Deputy Dewayne was sitting just outside in his patrol car, as if he was just waiting for her to do something like this. Alexis didn't want to cross his path for the second time in one night, so she turned around and trudged back to the elevator.

On the ride up to her floor, her mind raced. How did all of this fit together? Was it a coincidence that someone was diving in the dark beneath the bridge right where it happened to be cracked? Or could something more sinister be going on?

Alexis was sure the old woman had been trying to tell her something. Maybe she knew it wasn't really a curse. The curse could be a story made up to scare the tourists, like Dr. Edwards had said. In that case Lake Havasu City was in real trouble. Someone was trying to bring down the London Bridge. But *why*?

●—●—●

The next morning Alexis told Elizabeth everything she had seen. First about the scribbled note on the door. Then about the incident with the bridge.

"Do you really think that note was meant for us?" asked Elizabeth as they walked toward the bench near the bridge.

"I guess there's no way to know for sure," said Alexis. "We can ask the old lady the next time we see her. I really think she meant us to get it, though. I mean, she knew we were coming to see her, right?"

"Yeah," said Elizabeth, folding one long leg beneath her as she sat down. "But why on the door? Why didn't she leave another envelope or note like yesterday?"

"Well, she is a little dramatic," said Alexis. "She dresses like a medieval peasant, for goodness' sake! She's secretive, too. Maybe she was worried that an envelope taped to the door would be too obvious and that someone else would read it."

"Maybe," said Elizabeth. "We won't know until we talk to her again. So you really saw someone under the bridge last night?"

"Yep. And I just know they were banging on the bridge with some tools. Maybe a hammer or something."

"Did you see the tools?" asked Elizabeth.

"No, but I heard the banging. I saw the person drop them back into the boat when he came up, too."

"When he came up?"

"Yeah," said Alexis. "From under the water." Elizabeth looked back at the channel where dozens of engineers were busy at work again. A shifty smile spread across her face.

"You know what that means, don't you?" she said.

"What?" asked Alexis.

"It means that there really *is* a reason for us to check out the bridge! You know, like I said yesterday. We'll get some cheap goggles, and—"

"No way!" Alexis jumped off the bench. "You're crazy! The public isn't supposed to be anywhere near the bridge! And if you haven't noticed, Elizabeth, *we're the public.* Besides, it's just plain stupid to go swimming around under a bridge that's about to collapse!"

"It's not about to collapse," said Elizabeth. "It just has a tiny crack."

"You sound like Dr. Edwards," said Alexis. "Don't you remember what the bridge commissioner said about tiny cracks? They start avalanches, Elizabeth!"

"Okay, okay! Don't freak out. You're right." Elizabeth took a deep breath and looked around. "It really isn't a good idea. So what do we do today?"

Alexis caught sight of a purple flyer taped on a lamppost.

"We haven't thought any more about the bed race," she said. "Are you still interested?"

"Of course!" said Elizabeth. "We need a little something to distract us."

"We'd better get working on it, then. The first thing we'll need is a bed."

"Good job, Einstein!" Elizabeth elbowed Alexis playfully, and the pair of girls walked toward the shopping area of downtown Lake Havasu City.

They passed a mattress shop, and Elizabeth stopped.

"This place sells beds," she said. Alexis pointed to the price tag of the small bed that was sitting in the window.

"Six hundred dollars," she said. "I think we'll need a used one."

They kept walking and turned into an older part of town. The street was narrow, more like an alley than a road. It was lined with antique shops on both sides, with a couple of coffee and pastry shops snuggled in between.

The first store they walked into was called Betsy's Boutique. It was crowded with crystal vases and candleholders and lace doilies. The girls had taken two steps into the shop when a thin woman with a birdlike nose and her hair pulled back into a tight bun stepped out from behind an ancient polished dresser.

"Where are your parents?" she asked.

"Um, back at the hotel," answered Elizabeth. The woman pointed toward a sign in the window that read No Unattended Children Allowed. Then she coughed and nudged them toward the door.

Back outside on the sidewalk the girls laughed.

"Well, I guess we'd better find a shop that doesn't have a problem with *unattended children*," laughed Alexis. "What about that one?" She pointed across the narrow street to a whimsical sign that said Bill's Tarnished Treasures. Its windows were crowded with all kinds of things, from worn-out lamps to old bicycle seats.

"Looks good to me," said Elizabeth. They looked both ways and crossed over to the opposite sidewalk. A large jingly bell on the door announced their arrival, but nobody greeted them. In fact, the store looked empty.

"Maybe they're in the back?" said Elizabeth.

"Let's look around," said Alexis. The girls didn't see a bed anywhere, but they saw plenty of other amazing things in the piles of junk. Alexis was sifting through a huge crystal bowl full of ancient brass buttons when a voice from behind her made her jump.

"That one is from a World War II naval jacket."

Alexis spun around and faced a large man in glasses. His voice was low and gentle, and his smile was warm and genuine.

"Oh," said Alexis, looking at the button she was holding. It had an anchor etched into it. "That's really neat," she said. "That makes it about. . .sixty years old."

"Just a little older, actually," said the man. "But good job! My name's Bill. This is my shop." Bill stuck out his hand, and Alexis grasped it. This was awkward, since he had a crutch under his arm.

"Nice to meet you, Bill. I'm Alexis, and this is my friend Elizabeth." Elizabeth emerged from a pile of tattered books and waved.

"It's good to meet the two of you," said Bill. "What brings you in here today? Anything in particular?"

"Well," said Alexis, "actually we're looking for a bed. We want to enter the race this weekend, but we're from out of town, and we don't, um. . .have a bed." Alexis looked around the shop. "And it doesn't look like you have one either."

Bill's face lit up, his smile stretching so wide that his glasses bounced on his large cheeks. "We're both in luck!" he said. "Follow me." He turned and hobbled past the cash register, and Alexis saw that he was wearing a full cast on one of his legs. She wondered how such a large man managed to move on crutches through such a crowded store without breaking everything in sight. Bill led them to a curtain at the back of the shop and started through it. Alexis and Elizabeth hesitated, and Bill turned around.

"Don't worry," he said. "Mary!"

"Yes, Bill?" A lovely voice floated into the room from beyond the curtain, and a pretty face followed it.

"Mary," said Bill, "this is Alexis and Elizabeth. Girls, this is Mary, my wife. They're interested in the race, so I'm going to show them the castle!" Bill sounded like a little kid at Christmastime. Mary nodded and pointed through the curtain. The mention of a castle made the girls even more curious. They followed Bill behind the curtain, leaving it open so they could still see the door. Some of her friends called Alexis paranoid, but she got uncomfortable when she couldn't see an exit.

"Whoa," said Elizabeth.

Alexis turned around to see a huge contraption filling the tiny back room. It really was a castle! Bill had built a tower at the head of the bed, where the pillow usually went, and a low wall surrounded the rest of the mattress. At the foot, a real wooden drawbridge was closed, and a blue bed skirt fell to the floor like a rippling moat.

"This is amazing!" cried Alexis.

"Do you think so?" asked Bill. "It's taken me almost a year to build. Go ahead. Climb up and take a look!" He gestured to the back of the tower where a trapdoor revealed an entry onto the bed itself and a couple of stairs leading to the top of the tower. Alexis climbed right up.

"It feels so stable," said Alexis. "But the tower is so tall. Why doesn't it tip over?"

"Well, that's why I used real wood for the drawbridge. The tower makes the back of the bed really heavy. I needed something just as heavy to even out the weight in the front. Otherwise it would topple over the first time it went around a corner. That's also why I put *these* on it." Bill raised a corner of the bed skirt, revealing knobby tires.

"Those things look big enough to go on a tractor!" said Elizabeth.

"Close," said Bill. "They came from a riding lawn mower. The old wobbly bed wheels weren't going to work for something this huge. I also put brakes in it—something most beds in the race won't have. Once this baby gets going, it would be impossible to stop otherwise."

"I see the pedals," said Alexis. "And there's even a steering wheel!"

"Wow," said Elizabeth. "You sure put a lot into this bed. It's amazing, but I don't think we could afford to buy it from you."

Alexis sighed. She knew Elizabeth was right. There was no way they could afford a bed this cool for the race.

"It's not for sale," said Bill. "I'm giving it to you. Just for the race, I mean."

The girls were stunned.

"But why?" asked Alexis. Bill pointed to his broken leg.

"Racing is against the doctor's orders. But I'd hate to see this thing sit back here unused. And I always like to have a bed in the race representing the shop. Instead of my charging you rent, how about if you just finish the work on it and represent us? It still needs to be painted. I've got the paint. It probably wouldn't take you two very long. What do you say?"

Alexis was speechless. They hadn't even been looking for an hour, and they had found the most amazing racing bed *ever*. And they weren't going to have to pay a dime.

"Wow, Mr. Bill. I don't know what to say," said Alexis.

"Just say you'll race her hard. I'd love to be part of a winning team, even if it's just to cheer you across the finish line."

Alexis laughed and shook Bill's hand. "It's a deal!" she said. "Where are the paintbrushes?"

Alexis called her grandmother, and Elizabeth called her parents to tell them what was going on and where they were. Then they painted until late afternoon. Mary brought them turkey sandwiches for lunch and filled plastic cups with iced lemonade every twenty minutes or so.

By the time the girls began to rinse their brushes and close the cans of paint, the bed had been transformed. The walls of the castle were gray stone. White and gray paint had been sponged over it in spots to make it look real. The drawbridge was dark brown. Bill had come in with a hammer and beaten it up a little. The effect made it look weatherworn and very old. He also brought two lengths of chain and attached them to either side of the wooden bridge and then to the castle walls. They hung limp, like real chains that would allow the bridge to fall open.

A few finishing touches still needed to be done, so the girls would have to come back later in the week.

"In the meantime," said Mary as the girls prepared to leave, "Madame Brussau's is a wonderful costume shop. Your costumes should match your bed, Your Highnesses." She curtsied as if the girls were royalty.

"We will visit the shop, Madame Mary," answered Alexis. She and Elizabeth curtsied in return. "Thank you for all of your help."

All the way back to the hotel, the girls talked about their bed. Hardly any other bed would have brakes or a steering wheel, so they really felt they had a good chance of winning. That was if they could get the hang of driving the bed when they had never done it before.

Elizabeth's parents told her she could stay the night with Alexis at the London Bridge Resort. They were going to watch the bridge. Alexis hoped the person in the boat would show up again. Maybe this time they could sneak down to the water and take some pictures.

When they entered the shining lobby of the hotel, an unusual crowd surrounded the front desk. Dr. Edwards was standing across the counter from Jane. He seemed to be introducing her to two strange men in canvas work suits. They looked like painters.

Alexis motioned to Elizabeth, and the two of them slowed down. Alexis wanted to hear what they were saying as they walked past. Dr. Edwards spoke first.

"These men are Jerold and Jim," he said to Jane. "They have been hired to create a float that will represent the conference and hotel in Saturday's parade. Please allow them unlimited access to the hotel's premises, even though they are not guests. I believe your manager has left you a note to that effect."

Jane dug around on the desk in front of her. She picked up a piece of paper and studied it.

"Yep," she said. "You're good to go! This says he's set up a workroom for you near the ballroom," she said to the workmen.

"Thank you very much," said the larger of the two. The hairs on the back of Alexis's neck stood on end. That voice. It was so familiar. Alexis waited for the man to say something else so she could place his voice, but he didn't. He only nodded and then turned and followed Dr. Edwards around the corner toward the ballroom.

Oh well. It probably just reminded her of someone back home. The two girls went upstairs, ate room service with Grandma Windsor, and went into Alexis's room to get ready for bed.

As Elizabeth opened her backpack and reached inside, Alexis saw a flash of white.

"Is that what I think it is?" she asked.

"Yep. Dad's MacBook," Elizabeth said, pulling the computer out of the canvas bag. "He said I could bring it with me tonight."

The girls put on their pajamas and then sat side by side at the computer desk in the room. Elizabeth turned on the screen, and a glowing apple appeared while the machine booted up.

When she entered the Camp Club Girls chat room, she and Alexis saw that the other girls were already there.

Bailey: *Hi Bettyboo and Lexy.*
Elizabeth: *You know I hate that name. And Lexy?*
    That's a new one. =0
McKenzie: *We were just talking about you. Kate*
    was telling us the stuff you texted her all day.
Elizabeth: *Did Kate send you the photos of the*
    bed, too?

Sydney: *Yeah, that thing's amazing. I wish I was there to push it for you!*

McKenzie: *I don't see why they don't just race horses. Beds don't make sense. If you guys go back there next year, maybe I could come down with my horse. There's a jousting club not too far from here. Maybe I could learn to joust.*

Elizabeth: *That would be cool. Did you guys find anything out?*

Kate: *I looked up Princess Amelia. I found out that she was in love with a stable hand.*

Bailey: *Maybe he's the one who taught her to ride horses.*

Kate: *Maybe. Tradition is that she wrote him letters. After she died, the stories say he couldn't find her last letter. He spent the rest of his life looking for it.*

McKenzie: *What happened to him?*

Kate: *Well, actually he died not too long after Amelia. Of some sort of plague.*

Sydney: *That happened a lot in those times. People died suddenly. He might even have died in the saddle!*

Bailey: *What are you going to do next?*

Elizabeth: *As I texted you earlier today, Alexis saw weird stuff at the bridge last night. We're going to try to keep an eye on the bridge tonight.*

Kate: *Do you have your automatic recording camera with you that you used at Miss*

> Maria's nature park? You know—when you
> were trying to catch the dinosaurs in action?
> If so, you can set it up to try to catch any action.

Elizabeth: *No, we don't have one of those.*

Kate: *Do you want me to overnight a spycam
to you?*

Elizabeth: *I think we'll be okay.*

●—●—●

When the girls got off the computer, they weren't tired at all. On the contrary, they were quite excited. They sat at the window for hours waiting for the mysterious person in the rowboat.

He didn't come.

It was one o'clock in the morning, and both girls were asleep on the windowsill. Suddenly Alexis jumped.

"What?" said Elizabeth, immediately awake. "Did you see something?"

"No," said Alexis. "That man in the lobby! I just remembered where I've heard his voice before!"

"Oh. Where?" asked Elizabeth. She relaxed back into her chair.

"Elizabeth, I heard it in the alley! Remember? The two voices were talking about—"

"No way!" Elizabeth sat straight up again.

"Yes way! I have no idea how they are going to do it, but those two men are going to steal the golden coach!"

Priceless or Useless

The girls had breakfast in the hotel restaurant with Alexis's grandma. Alexis still didn't feel the girls had enough information to tell her grandmother what was happening. Still, she was nervous about the speculations she and Elizabeth had. The fact that the con men had gotten jobs at the hotel would make it easier for them to steal the carriage. She had *no* idea how they could do it, but it still worried her.

Alexis knew her grandma would know what to do, but she still didn't feel confident enough to tell her everything. She wondered what she would say about the *idea* of the carriage being stolen.

"Grandma," said Alexis, as the waitress filled her glass of orange juice. "Why is there so little security around the carriage? What would happen if someone tried to steal it?"

Grandma Windsor chuckled.

"Darling, that carriage is huge! No one would be able to get it out of the hotel unnoticed. But even if they could, what would they do with it?"

"Well, it's valuable, isn't it?" asked Elizabeth.

"In its own way, yes," said Grandma Windsor. "But I don't see why anyone would want it. It's the only replica of its kind, so you couldn't sell it to anyone. It would be too easy for the police to track it down again."

"Well, what about a collector or something? Someone like you, who really likes history and stuff?" asked Alexis. She was remembering the many old trinkets her grandmother brought back from her travels. Her house was full of them. Again Grandma Windsor laughed.

"A *real* collector or historian wouldn't want a replica. Deep down, it's only a fake. Would a literature professor be content with a new version of Shakespeare, if there was a possibility they could hold the original? No. Anyone can walk into a bookstore and get a copy of *Romeo and Juliet* for less than five dollars. But the original? Priceless."

"So replicas are worthless?" asked Alexis.

"Now, I didn't say that," said Grandma Windsor. "Take Michelangelo's statue of David, for instance. If you walk up to the statue in the plaza, you will enjoy its beauty. You may take pictures and go on your merry way, but if that's as far as you went, then you missed the truth. You have only seen a replica—a smaller shadow of the true art of Michelangelo. The real statue is inside, hidden away from the damaging elements. But the replica is not worthless, Alexis. It is still beautiful; it's just not *as* beautiful. It does not have the same history."

The waitress was back, refilling Grandma Windsor's glass of tea this time.

"So, besides the fact that it is almost impossible to get the coach out of this building unnoticed, I simply don't see why someone would want to steal it in the first place. That is why there isn't much security around it. The hotel has never felt that it was threatened."

But it is *threatened!* Alexis wanted to scream. But after all Grandma Windsor had just said, she thought it would sound silly to voice her thoughts.

After they finished eating, the girls left Grandma Windsor and walked toward Bill and Mary's shop. The bridge was still crawling with engineers, and they would have to wait until night before looking for the rowboat again. So no matter how tempting the mystery surrounding the bridge was, Alexis was going to focus on the carriage for a while.

Alexis knew Jerold and Jim were the same people she had overheard in the alley earlier in the week. But she was starting to have doubts about other things. Would it really be possible for Jerold and Jim, those silly-looking "float builders," to steal the golden coach? There was *no way* they could remove it without someone noticing. As soon as it was missing, someone would sound the alarm. They wouldn't make it very far.

And *why* were they planning to steal it in the first place? They had said it was worth millions, but Grandma Windsor claimed the carriage wasn't worth much at all. Sure, it was probably expensive to make, but you could always build another one. It wasn't like the original coach back in London, which was covered with real gold.

"There's only one way to know for sure if they are going to steal the carriage," said Alexis as they turned down the narrow street to Bill's. "We have to *investigate* these two guys."

"You mean spy on them?" asked Elizabeth, smiling.

"Well, yes," laughed Alexis. "*Investigating* just sounds a lot better! We'll work on the bed for a bit and then go back to the hotel. They're making the float near the ballroom. It shouldn't be too hard to find them."

In the back room of the antique shop, the girls admired their castle. It only needed a couple of touch-ups. Alexis was attaching fake fish to the bed-skirt moat when the bell on the front door jingled. She heard a girl's voice say, "Hello, Uncle Bill."

The voice didn't sound friendly.

Alexis and Elizabeth poked their heads through the curtain and saw a slim brunette standing with her hands on her hips.

"Hello, Emily," said Bill. "Shouldn't you be in school?"

"I heard you have someone driving your bed," the girl said, ignoring his question. Her face was scrunched up, like she smelled something gross.

"Yep, sure do," said Bill. He sounded friendly, but his stiff shoulders told Alexis he had put his guard up. "What brings you down here? Need something for a costume?"

"Eew, gross! Like I would use any of this junk for my costume!" Emily picked up a silver teaspoon with her forefinger and thumb, like it was covered in grime.

"I don't understand what makes you love other people's old stuff so much. Like this spoon." She held it up to the light and then looked around the table where it had been sitting. "It's all dingy, and there's only *one*. What on earth would anyone do with only one spoon?"

"Actually, if you look at the handle—"

But Emily didn't. She rolled her eyes and tossed the spoon toward Bill. He fumbled, and it fell to the ground. Alexis stepped through the curtain to pick it up and hand it to him.

"Who are *you*?" asked Bill's demanding niece.

"This is Alexis," said Bill. "She's the one racing my bed this Saturday."

Alexis smiled and waved. Emily's eyes narrowed to tiny slits.

"Well, she'd better be careful," she said, stepping closer. "The driver who tried to beat me last year ended up in the hospital with a broken arm. And I *don't lose*."

Emily turned and stormed out of the shop. Alexis was sure she would have slammed the door if it hadn't been for the automatic spring that caught it and made it close gently.

"What was that all about?" asked Elizabeth.

"Oh, don't mind Emily," said Bill. "She's just mad because I wouldn't let her use my bed in the race. She thought I would for sure, since she's family. My brother's kid. Ever heard the term 'spoiled rotten'? Well, that's Emily for sure."

"Why wouldn't you let her race it?" asked Alexis.

"You heard her, didn't you?" said Bill. "She put a guy in the hospital last year—slammed into his bed on the last turn and sent him flying into the crowd. You're not supposed to touch anyone else's bed. Emily told the judges it was an accident, and they believed her and gave her the prize."

"But you didn't believe it was an accident?" asked Alexis.

"Do you, Alexis? I can't have anyone representing my shop doing risky things that might bring bad publicity."

Bill was right. Alexis had just met Emily, and she was pretty sure Emily would have broken someone's arm to get what she wanted.

"Well, she can have the prize for all I care," said Alexis. "I just want to race!"

"That's right," said Elizabeth. "It's like Psalm 37:1 says, 'Do not fret because of those who are evil or be envious of those who do wrong.' No matter what happens, we'll have a blast."

"*And* you'll have the best bed out there!" said Bill. "That thing should be in the parade! It'll be better than any other float!"

Bill still held the small spoon that Emily had tossed at him. He placed it on the table, but Alexis picked it up.

"What were you about to say about the spoon, Bill—before Emily interrupted you?" asked Alexis. Bill smiled. It reminded Alexis of her grandmother's smile when she asked her about history.

"Look at the handle," he said. Alexis held the spoon up in the light, and Elizabeth came close to look as well. A small pink stone shaped like an oval was mounted on the end of the handle. Upon the oval stone a face had been carved. It was the silhouette of a young beautiful woman.

"Who is it?" asked Elizabeth.

"Princess Amelia, the youngest daughter of—"

"King George the Third!" gasped Alexis.

"You've heard her story, then?" asked Bill.

"Pieces of it," answered Alexis. "My grandmother told me some of the stories surrounding her. Something about Princess Amelia and a young man she was forbidden to marry."

"That's what she is most known for," said Bill. "They say the law would have allowed her to marry him after she turned twenty-six, but that was pretty old to be married back then. Her letters may have told him that she would wait. If she hid a letter to give him, no one knows if he ever found it. This spoon is a rare piece. Since Princess Amelia was never a queen, it is quite strange for silverware to have her picture on it. Maybe she really was her father's favorite."

"Wow!" said Alexis. "That means this spoon is more than two hundred years old!"

"Why do you keep that out on a table?" asked Elizabeth. "Shouldn't it be locked away somewhere?"

Bill laughed.

"Probably. A lot of the stuff in my store is more valuable than people think. Like Emily, many think it's just junk—like an indoor yard sale."

"Well, I think it's brilliant," said Alexis. She looked at the spoon again. Was it just her imagination, or did the picture on the spoon look like the girl from her dream? Her imagination was running wild again.

"Hey, look!" cried Elizabeth. Alexis followed her pointed finger toward the large window. Outside, three familiar figures were walking through the alley.

"It's Dr. Edwards—and those two workmen from the hotel!" Alexis looked at Elizabeth and lowered her voice so Bill couldn't hear. "If we follow them, we might find out more about their plan for the carriage."

"They probably won't talk about it with Dr. Edwards around," said Elizabeth. "Maybe he'll leave."

Alexis nodded. "See ya later," she said to Bill. "It's getting to be lunchtime."

"I'm getting hungry myself," said the shop owner. "See you girls later."

Alexis and Elizabeth waved good-bye and left the shop. They were just in time to see the end of Dr. Edwards's walking stick disappear around a corner. They followed, and after a couple of turns their prey entered a small deli.

"Well, it *is* lunchtime," said Alexis. "Feel like a sandwich?" Elizabeth smiled. The girls allowed a couple more people to enter before they did. They didn't want to be directly behind Dr. Edwards in line in case he recognized them.

After ordering turkey sandwiches and grabbing a couple

bags of chips, Alexis led Elizabeth to a booth that hid them from the three men but was still close enough so they could hear everything that was being said.

"I thought you said this job was going to be easy," said the taller of the two men.

"I thought the job was going to be easy, Jerold," said Dr. Edwards. "But circumstances have changed."

"Well, I hope we're getting paid more," said Jerold.

"Yes, yes," said Dr. Edwards testily. "Don't worry about the money! It will come!"

"I don't know what you want with that thing anyway," said another voice. It must have been Jim. "It's a fake. How can it be worth much money?"

Dr. Edwards sighed. Alexis was sure that if she could see him, his eyes would be bulging in exasperation.

"It's not the carriage itself that is priceless," he said, dropping his voice to a whisper. Alexis had to stop chewing her chips so that she could still hear him. "It's something hidden within it."

Alexis stared across the table at Elizabeth. She, too, had stopped chewing. They sat still, straining to hear every word.

"I have reason to believe that an original document, hundreds of years old, has been hidden somewhere within the carriage. The *document*, my dear fellows, is what's priceless. The carriage just happens to be the hiding place."

The thieves seemed to be happy with the doctor's explanation, because all Alexis and Elizabeth heard after that was the chomping and slurping of the two men eating.

The girls finished their food and slipped out the front.

"So *that's* why Dr. Edwards wants the carriage! He thinks

something is hidden inside of it!" said Elizabeth.

"Yeah," said Alexis. "A priceless document. What if it was Princess Amelia's letter?"

"Why would Princess Amelia's letter be hidden in a *replica*?" asked Elizabeth. "The real carriage, maybe, but there's no reason for it to be in Arizona. Your imagination's running away with you again, Alex."

"You're right," said Alexis. "But wouldn't it be cool? No matter what the document is, it's obviously worth a lot of money. *And* it has a rightful owner. I bet if Dr. Edwards were the rightful owner, he wouldn't have to steal it."

"I know," said Elizabeth. "We have to keep him from stealing it. But how are we supposed to do that when we don't know where it is?"

"Easy," said Alexis, smiling wide. "We just have to find it before he does."

Encounter in the Costume Shop

"How on earth are we supposed to do that?" asked Elizabeth. "You saw how that deputy guy reacted when we were just looking at the carriage. What do you think will happen if we actually try to *touch* the thing? Or search it for an ancient letter?"

"We'll just have to be careful," said Alexis. "It might be difficult, but we don't have a choice. If the document exists, it belongs in a museum—not in Dr. Edwards's personal collection."

They walked toward the hotel, thinking about how best to search for the hidden paper. Alexis was so deep in thought that she ran right into a sidewalk display in front of the costume store. She and Elizabeth struggled to dust off the white, curly wigs and hang them back up before anyone noticed.

"Let's go in here," said Alexis. "We need costumes for the bed race and parade, don't we?"

"Definitely!" squealed Elizabeth. They walked in and were immediately hidden in a maze of silk dresses, old-fashioned shoes, and jesters' hats.

"It looks like it's almost all medieval," said Elizabeth.

"Good," said Alexis. "We have to match our bed. It's a castle.

What do you think we should be?"

"We could be knights," said Elizabeth, walking over to a suit of armor. "This looks so real!"

"It also looks like it weighs a hundred pounds!" laughed Alexis. They continued through the store, yelling back and forth whenever they found something interesting. Before long they were trying on everything they could reach, making each other collapse in fits of giggles. Alexis grabbed a garish jester's hat with six floppy tentacles and jingle bells everywhere. She smashed it onto her head and spun around.

"Classy, huh?" she asked Elizabeth. But the person behind her wasn't Elizabeth.

It was David Turner, the Arizona state swim champion.

"Very classy," he said, raising his eyebrows and giving her an amused smile. Alexis blushed. It was the first time she'd ever seen David smile. He was twice as cute when he did. She wondered why he never smiled at swim meets or in front of his school.

Alexis yanked the hat off her head but was instantly aware of how messed up her hair must be.

"Um, sorry," she said. "I thought my friend was standing there."

She looked around frantically. Where was Elizabeth anyway?

"Don't apologize," said David. "I wouldn't expect any less of someone visiting a costume shop." He was still smiling, as if whatever bothered him at other times was now forgotten.

"I'm Alexis," she said, holding out her hand. David had to rearrange the things he was holding to shake her hand. He dropped a large sword, and they banged heads as they both reached to pick it up.

347

"Ow!" said Alexis.

"Sorry!" he said, rubbing his head and wiping his long hair out of his eyes at the same time. "You look familiar. Have I met you before?"

"No," said Alexis. "My friend and I went to the swim meet the other day."

"No, that's not it," he said. "Dude! You're the girl from the pep rally!"

Alexis turned crimson. "That was an accident," she said hastily. "My friend and I don't even go to school here!"

"Oh," said the boy. "You don't?" Was Alexis imagining things, or did he look disappointed?

"It's a long story," she said. "We just ended up in the building by accident."

"Well, you're a legend anyway. The whole school's talking about you."

"Great," said Alexis. They both laughed. Then there was an embarrassing silence. Alexis twisted the jester's hat in her hands, and David placed the sword back in a display.

"Not going to get it?" Alexis asked.

"Nope," he said. "I think I'm going to go with the dragon." He held up the head of a costume that was piled under his right arm.

Just then a horrible screech came from outside, followed by a loud crash. Alexis turned and ran to the sidewalk with David just behind her. Elizabeth wasn't far behind. Right in front of the store, two cars were stopped. Apparently one of the drivers hadn't been paying attention and had slammed into the car ahead. Both bumpers were crushed, and the back car was smoking a bit.

The drivers stumbled out of their vehicles and began yelling at each other. No one was hurt, but neither person wanted to take the blame. Within minutes two police cars showed up and a sheriff approached the arguing drivers.

Someone tapped Alexis on the shoulder.

"Trespassing wasn't enough?" a voice said. "Now you have to shoplift, too?"

Alexis spun around to see Deputy Dewayne inches from her face.

"What? Shoplifting?" she stammered. The deputy pointed to her arms. Alexis was still carrying the jester's hat. She looked side to side. David still had his dragon costume, and Elizabeth was holding a pink dress and had a matching crown on her head. None of the items had been paid for.

"Oh, this," said Alexis. "We were just looking inside the store when the crash happened. We ran outside to see what happened and forgot we were holding it all."

Deputy Dewayne didn't move.

"Really, Deputy," said David. "She's telling the truth. We were just about to pay."

The officer's eyes narrowed, and then he spun around as the sheriff called his name. Alexis, Elizabeth, and David took that opportunity to slide back into the store and head for the cash register.

Elizabeth had found a great princess costume. Alexis found a crazy outfit that matched her jester's hat. She had wanted to be a princess, too, but she loved the hat too much to part with it. They paid and turned to go.

"Uh, see you later?" said David from behind them. His dragon costume was on the counter.

"Yeah, later," said Alexis. She turned and led Elizabeth out the door.

"Um, Alexis?" said Elizabeth.

"Yeah?"

"I think that was a question."

"What do you mean?" asked Alexis.

"What David said just now—I think it was a question. Like, *Can I see you later?* Not, *See ya later.* Get the difference?"

Alexis stopped in her tracks, blushing from her neck all the way up to her ponytail. Her eyes were dinner plates.

"No way!" she said.

"I could be wrong," said Elizabeth. "But it seemed like he liked you."

"What do I do?" said Alexis, frantic. "I don't want him to think I was rude!"

"Go talk to him. He's coming out of the store right now."

Alexis turned around. "David!" she called. He spun around, yanking a pair of earbuds out of his ears so he could hear her.

"Yeah?"

"Um, do you want to hang out with us? I mean, we're not doing anything really, just walking around."

"I've got swim practice now. Maybe later?"

"Tomorrow, maybe," said Alexis. "If not, we'll be in the bed race. Look for the amazing castle."

"Okay," said David, smiling shyly. "See ya."

This time she was sure it was "see ya later." Alexis waved and turned back to Elizabeth, smiling like she had just won a million dollars.

"Chill out!" said Elizabeth. "Take a deep breath. He's a boy, not Superman!" Alexis laughed.

"So what now?" she asked.

"We could try to find out more about the piece of paper Dr. Edwards is looking for," said Elizabeth.

"That's a good idea," said Alexis. "We should check out the area at the hotel where those guys are building the float. We might overhear something else—or at least get an idea of where to look."

Back at the hotel the girls asked Jane for directions to the ballroom. As they approached it, they heard the *tick, tick, tick* of someone shaking a can of spray paint. It was coming from a door across the hall. Fumes and voices drifted out to where the girls were standing.

The door was open a couple of feet, so the girls walked up and peeked inside. Jerold and Jim were working on what Alexis guessed was the float. It was a perfect model of the carriage in the lobby, except that it was white. Alexis waved a hand at Elizabeth to get her to follow, and then she ducked inside and hid behind a tower of empty buckets.

No one saw them come in.

Jerold put down the spray paint he had been using and turned to call across the room.

"Oy! Jim! Hurry up with that stuff, eh? We ain't got all day!"

"I'm a-comin', I'm a-comin'! Hold yer horses!"

Alexis and Elizabeth held their breath. Jim's voice was just on the other side of the buckets. They heard him rustle around some more and then tromp off toward where the carriage and Jerold waited in the center of the room.

Relieved, Alexis looked through a gap between two buckets so she could see what was going on. Jim had a large roll of something in his hand. It looked like aluminum foil, except that it was gold instead of silver.

"Be careful, dimwit!" yelled Jerold. "You're making it flake! We can't have pieces of gold missing!"

"Why are we doing this, anyway?" asked Jim. "If the boss wants some old paper, why doesn't he just get it out of the carriage while everyone's asleep? We could do that easy!"

"Because it's not just lying on top of the velvet cushion, stupid. It's in a hidden compartment, and he doesn't know where it is. He needs more time to search."

"So how is a carriage float going to help?" asked Jim.

"Are you really that dim?" said Jerold, smacking Jim upside the head. But he didn't say anything else. Alexis and Elizabeth hid for almost an hour, but the conversation was over. Both men were intent on covering the carriage float with the golden foil.

Alexis was with Jim. She didn't see how this float was going to help Dr. Edwards find the document he was looking for. They needed more information. Alexis felt like she had a lot of clues, but none of them seemed to fit together.

Were the Camp Club Girls at a dead end?

CHAPTER 9

David's Story

Bailey: *Lex, I really like your court jester hat.*
   Are you and Bets going to be in a costume contest?
Alexis: *How do you know about my costume?*
Bailey: *K8 forwarded the photos of you trying on*
   the hats.
Sydney: *Who was that hottie standing*
   behind you?
Alexis: *Beth? How could she be standing behind*
   me if she was taking pictures? And since
   when do you call her a hottie?
Sydney: *Not her, goofy. The dude.*
Bailey: *Was he the Man of La Mancha or whatever?*
Sydney: *What's that?*
Alexis: *Oh, I saw that old movie. It was about*
   Don Quixote.
Sydney: *Who's that?*
Alexis: *Some knight in search of adventure.*
Kate: *I believe that was during the Spanish*
   Inquisition—in a different country and a
   different century than King George's time.
Sydney: *Well, he may not be the Man of La*

Mancha, but I definitely think he's the man of la macho!

Alexis: *He is cute. And he was really nice in the costume store. You'd like him, Sydney—he's a champion swimmer. But he's been kind of surly the other times I've seen him.*

Bailey: *Surly? What's that?*

Alexis: *Grouchy.*

Kate: *Beth just texted me that you're blushing bright red when you're talking or writing about Daaaavvviiiddd.*

Bailey: *Wait, where's Bettyboo? And who's David?*

Alexis: *She's right here. But I have control of the keyboard, and I'm not giving it up. . . . Mwah-ha-ha. . . (That's an evil laugh, Bailey. And you better be glad she doesn't have control of anything if you're calling her Bettyboo again. She hates that.) And David's the guy in the photo.*

Bailey: *Oh, Groucho—the guy who's the swimmer.*

McKenzie: *So. . . Don't avoid the subject. Why do you blush when the guy's around? Are you and he going to the festivities dressed as Princess Amelia and her horse trainer?*

Bailey: *Do you think Groucho has anything to do with the mystery?*

Alexis: *Oh no. I'm sure he doesn't.*

Bailey: *But you saw someone in the water a couple of nights ago. If he's a swimmer, could that have been him?*

Alexis: *That late at night? It was a school night.*

What would a kid not much older than
us be doing out at that time of night?

Bailey: *Well, if he's the swim-meister of the century. . .*

Alexis: *I don't think so. I think it has something to*
do with Dr. Edwards and with the cursing woman.

Bailey: *She uses bad language?*

Alexis: *No, she is the one who was saying there's*
a curse on the bridge. I think adults are
running this thing.

Kate: *Well, I researched Dr. Edwards, and he's*
legit. I couldn't find anything suspicious
about him. I even checked his photo from the
past against one Beth snapped and sent to us
the other day, and it was definitely the same
guy who's listed all over the Internet with all
kinds of credentials.

Sydney: *I asked my aunt—you know, who works*
with the park services—if she knew anything
about any funny business in that area. She says the
rangers in the region have never mentioned anything.

Alexis: *We're stuck. I keep trying to think of what*
Sherlock Holmes or Hercule Poirot or
MacGyver or Jessica Fletcher would do.

Bailey: *Who are they?*

Sydney: *They're fictional detectives.*

Bailey: *Oh. Or Scooby-Doo, Shaggy, Velma,*
and Daphne.

Alexis: *Yeah or even them. I'm sure I've seen*
something on one of those mystery shows that
should ring a bell and remind me of one of

*their plots, but I'm stumped. Ebeth just
reminded me we have to go. Have to do a
final check on the bed. Will send more photos
later. Keep thinking. . . .*

●—■—●

As Alexis and Elizabeth walked back to Bill's shop, they kept
trying to figure out what was going on. No matter how exciting
the investigation was getting, they had to admit that they were
stuck.

Then they were at the shop. As Alexis looked at the bed, she
paced back and forth biting her nails.

"I wish we could test-drive it!" Alexis said. She was more
than a little nervous about driving in a race when she had never
even sat behind the steering wheel of a go-cart.

"I'll push," said Elizabeth. "You can steer. My legs are longer,
so I can push and ride at the same time—almost like a scooter."

Alexis almost protested, but when she stopped pacing, she
realized that the back of the bed came up to her waist. There
was no way she'd be able to jump on when the bed got going
very fast.

She was going to have to steer.

Bill climbed up into the front of the bed and called her up,
too. Since they had been here last, Bill and Mary had made a
driver's seat. It was an old recliner painted gold to look like a
throne.

"This is the steering wheel, obviously," said Bill, pointing.
Alexis sat on the edge of the throne and grasped the wheel so
hard her knuckles turned white.

"Mr. Bill," said Alexis. "I would love to be able to say that I
drive on a regular basis, but I'm twelve." Bill laughed.

"Well, have you ever played one of those racing video games? The huge ones with wheels and pedals?"

"A couple of times," said Alexis.

"You'll be fine then. There's only one pedal on this one though. That's the brake." He pointed his foot below the chair, and Alexis saw the black pedal. It was as big as her foot. *Good*, she thought. *There's no way I'll miss it.*

Alexis turned the steering wheel and pressed the pedal over and over. If she could just get used to it, maybe she wouldn't be so afraid in the morning. She wished she had more strength in her legs.

Maybe I should take up swimming or something, she thought. That reminded her of David.

"Hey, Mr. Bill, do you know David Turner?"

"Yes, I've met him," Mr. Bill replied. "Good kid."

"It seems like he doesn't smile too often," said Alexis. "And I noticed at the swim meet the other day that other people had family members around to congratulate them, but he didn't. He just stood there looking grouchy."

Mary walked into the room with some glasses and a pitcher full of lemonade for the girls.

"Poor kid," she said. "David lost his parents and sister a year or so ago in a car wreck." She handed each of the girls a glass and started pouring out the cool yellow treat. "David wasn't in the car because he was at a swim meet. He lives with his uncle Jeff. Jeff is a good man, but he isn't married and doesn't know what it's like to be a parent. He works a lot of hours, so David's left alone a lot. Often at night, even," she explained. "I understand money is a problem for them, too. I've noticed that David is smiling more lately. It's tough to lose your parents.

"I know David's coach, too. He told me meets are really hard for David sometimes. Especially when he wins. His parents were on the way to his meet when they had the wreck. It was hard for him to keep swimming. But he does love it and is so good at it. They've thought about training him for the Olympics even if he is a little old for starting that," she added.

"The swim-meister," Elizabeth murmured.

The front door jingled as someone entered. Seconds later, Emily's better-than-you voice drifted through the curtain.

"Hey, Uncle Bill," she called. "You ready to lose tomorrow?"

Bill sighed and walked into the shop. Alexis and Elizabeth climbed off the bed and followed.

"We're ready to race, if that's what you mean," said Alexis. She smiled, hoping to get a similar reaction out of Emily.

"'Do not answer a fool according to his folly, or you yourself will be like him,'" Elizabeth murmured.

Alexis smiled. "Proverbs?"

"Yep, 26:4."

Emily did smile at Alexis's comment all right, but it was not a smile of kindness.

"Mmm," she said. "Where's your third, anyway?"

"Our what?" asked Elizabeth.

"Your third. You know, your other person." Alexis and Elizabeth looked at each other, confused. "Don't tell me you don't know!" squealed Emily. Alexis thought she sounded a little too pleased. Emily dug a folded purple paper out of her back pocket. As she unfolded it, Alexis recognized it as one of the bed race flyers.

"Didn't you read the small print?" asked Emily. She pointed to the very bottom of the flyer. "All teams must be made up of three or four people. No more, no less." She refolded the flyer and looked at them with a smile.

"See you in the morning!" Emily chirped, then she turned and left.

Alexis looked back and forth between Elizabeth and Bill. What were they going to do?

"Mr. Bill, can you ride with us?" asked Elizabeth. "I'm sure we could make it safe enough. We'll go slow!"

"No way, girls," he answered. "That's kind of you, but if you went slow enough to keep my leg from getting hurt, you'd have no chance at winning."

"We'd rather race slowly than not race at all!" said Alexis.

"You'll find someone else," said Bill. "There are tons of people in this town willing to jump on a bed just for the ride."

"What about Miss Mary?" asked Elizabeth.

The woman's voice floated from behind the cash register. "Someone has to keep the store open for the tourists," she said.

Alexis and Elizabeth couldn't believe their luck. They had worked so hard on finishing this bed and had been so excited to race. Now it looked like they might not even be able to. Alexis took a deep breath. There was no way she was giving up this easily.

"Come on, Elizabeth," she said. "We've got to find a partner."

"Well, you know what Matthew 7:7 says," Elizabeth pointed out. "'Seek and you will find!'"

The girls waved at Bill and Mary. "We'll see you bright and early," said Bill. "Don't worry. Not only will your bed race, but it will win if I can do anything about it!"

The girls practically ran back to the hotel. But before long they were sitting outside on the curb sulking. They had run out of options. Grandma Windsor was riding on the hotel float with Dr. Edwards. Elizabeth's dad was riding on the bass float, since he won third place in the tournament. And Elizabeth's brother had eaten too much cotton candy and was sick. That meant her mom was staying with him at their hotel. Alexis even asked Jane, the lady at the front desk, but she had to work.

Alexis was trying to be upbeat, but she was really disappointed.

"Excuse me, ma'am!" Alexis called to a complete stranger walking past them. "Would you like to ride with us in the bed race tomorrow?" The lady gave her a funny look and shook her head. Then she walked away mumbling something in a foreign language.

Elizabeth laughed.

"Well, at least I tried!" said Alexis. She couldn't help but laugh, too. Something would come up; she just knew it would. There was no way they weren't going to race tomorrow.

After twenty minutes or so the girls decided to take a walk before dinner. They headed toward the bridge and were surprised to find that no one was there. The caution tape was still up, but the engineers were all gone.

"I wonder where they all went," said Elizabeth.

"Me, too," said Alexis. "Why aren't the engineers working? Don't they care if the town has to cancel the parade?"

They were walking past the bridge to the harbor when Alexis saw him. David Turner. He turned onto the street a few blocks ahead of them, hands shoved in his pockets and his hood pulled up over his head.

"Elizabeth, look! It's David!"

"Okay, okay! Calm down! Remember, Alex, he's just a boy."

"No, it's not *that*!" said Alexis, blushing. "The race! I bet he'd ride with us. Come on!" Alexis pulled Elizabeth by the elbow and walked even faster.

"David!" Alexis called, but he didn't turn around. "I bet he has his earbuds in." They sped up even more, trying to catch up, but wherever David was off to, it seemed like he was in a hurry.

"That's odd," said Elizabeth. "Is he pulling a wagon?"

"I think he is," said Alexis. Sure enough, David was pulling a red metal wagon behind him. "What could he possibly be doing with that?" asked Alexis.

David came to a stop near the harbor. He turned onto the wooden pier, wheeling his wagon along with him. When the girls caught up, he was on his knees digging around in a rowboat that was bobbing up and down in the water.

"Hey, David," said Alexis. "How are you—"

Alexis almost screamed. She was looking over David's shoulder into the small rowboat. When he moved an old tarp aside, she saw a chisel and a hammer along with some snorkeling gear. Next to the tools was a large pile of stones from the London Bridge.

CHAPTER 10

Rocks in the Boat

"What is all of this?" squealed Alexis. The music from David's earbuds thrummed. He couldn't hear her. Alexis reached out and tapped him firmly on the shoulder. He spun around so fast that he almost lost his balance and fell in the water.

"Alexis!" he yelled, pulling the device from his ears. "I didn't see you there. You scared me."

David looked between the two girls. Elizabeth's mouth hung open in shock. Alexis's face was scrunched up in fury.

"Bailey was right! It's been you the whole time!" she yelled, pointing her finger in his face. David's mouth opened and closed like a fish out of water. It looked like he wanted to say something but couldn't quite find the words. "You've been the one tearing the London Bridge apart! You're responsible for the crack!"

"What are you talking about?" asked David. "I'm not tearing the bridge apart."

"Then where did those stones come from?" asked Elizabeth. David looked over his shoulder to the pile of stones in the rowboat. There was no doubt—they were the same gray, weathered stones that built the bridge.

"These are from the bridge, but they're just samples," said

David. "One of the engineers asked me if I could gather some of the stones for testing. He was supposed to come down here and get them this afternoon."

David seemed like he was being completely honest, but Alexis didn't like the sound of his story. Why would an engineer ask a teenager to take apart a bridge? Didn't they have their own people to do that stuff? Well, the story might sound shifty, but Alexis thought David was telling the truth. He believed he was helping, not hurting the bridge. There was one way to find out for sure.

"When did this *engineer* ask you to do this?" asked Alexis. Her face softened, and she was no longer glaring at him.

"About two weeks ago. It takes about two days for me to get one stone loose."

"And didn't you notice you were causing a crack to appear in the bridge?" said Elizabeth.

"I do my work at night, because I'm so busy during the day. And I wanted to make some extra money to help my uncle pay bills. I wanted to surprise him, so I've been working at night, while he's at work. I never saw the crack until earlier this week, when people started making such a fuss. I asked the engineer about it the last time I saw him, but he said not to worry about it." David turned to Elizabeth. "Why are you looking at me like that?" he asked.

Alexis turned around and looked at her friend. Elizabeth was still looking suspicious. Her eyes were narrow, and her arms were crossed. One of her feet at the end of a long leg was tap, tap, tapping on the wood of the dock.

"No offense, David," Elizabeth said, "but your story sounds crazy. You said you were supposed to meet this engineer today?

Well, where is he?"

David looked up the street toward town.

"I'm not sure." He glanced at his watch. "He's late."

"Well," said Alexis, "the engineers who are taking care of
the bridge are staying at my hotel. We could go see if he's there.
Then you could give him the stones, and we can clear all this up."

"Sounds good to me," said David. "You wanna help me put
these things in the wagon? I doubt we'd be able to carry them all
the way."

One by one they piled the old stones into the wagon. They
were as gentle as possible. The last thing they wanted to do
was break one of them in half. Twenty minutes later they were
pulling the wagon into the lobby of the London Bridge Resort.
The tourists and workers alike turned to watch them wheel the
wagon toward the front desk.

"Hi, Jane," said Alexis. "Do you know where the head
engineer is right now?"

"I believe the engineers are eating a late lunch," she said,
pointing toward the restaurant at the front of the lobby. "What's
in the wagon?"

Alexis didn't answer. She turned and led Elizabeth and
David toward a nearby table where a team of men in jeans and
white polo shirts were eating.

"Um, excuse me," she said. The men stopped chewing and
looked at her. One of them sat frozen with his sandwich halfway
to his open mouth. "We're looking for one of your engineers."

The men looked back and forth at one another, surprised.
Then the one with his sandwich halfway to his mouth answered
her.

"I'm the chief engineer, name's Cliff. Which one of my men are you looking for?" Alexis looked at David, since he was the one who knew whom they were looking for.

"I don't remember his name," he said, "but I think it started with a *J*."

"I'm John," said a thin man at the end of the table with a bowl of pasta in front of him.

David looked at Alexis and shook his head. The man he was looking for was not at the table.

"This is all of us," said Cliff. "Is there something I can help you with?"

"Well," said Alexis, "some engineer told David that he would pay him to take samples from the bridge for testing. They're right here." She gestured toward the wagon, and Cliff's sandwich dropped onto his plate with a splat.

"These are from the bridge? The *London Bridge*?"

David nodded.

"Where did you take them from?" asked Cliff, excited. He jumped up and flew to the wagon, picking up the stones one by one.

"The second pillar, under the waterline," said David. "That's where the engineer told me to take them from."

"Let's get one thing straight," said Cliff. "A true engineer would never tell a kid to remove stonework from a bridge— especially an historical bridge like this one. I think you got duped, kid."

"I don't understand," said David. "The guy was so—"

"Wait!" yelled Cliff. "Did you say you took these from the second pillar?"

"Yeah," said David.

"Right under where the crack appeared?" said another

engineer with gravy all over his chin. David nodded.

Cliff jumped out of his seat.

"John, Matt—finish eating, then check this out. I believe this explains the crack. If so, then there's no real damage. These stones can be replaced, and the crack can be filled. It's only surface damage!"

Cliff called over to where Jane was standing at the front desk. "Call the mayor! Tell him the parade is on!" Everyone in the restaurant and hotel lobby erupted in applause. After a minute, David's voice broke through the commotion.

"Excuse me, sir," he said. Cliff turned back toward the three young people. Alexis and Elizabeth were glad that the parade would go on, but David looked troubled.

"I feel stupid," he said. "I should have known that pulling chunks off the bridge wasn't right, but the guy was so convincing. Why would he want these rocks anyway?"

"Don't worry, son," said Cliff. "I believe that you didn't mean to cause any harm. You're no danger to anyone. The person who is a danger is that man who talked you into this. If you see him around, don't let him know we're on to him. You come find me, and we'll get the sheriff. As for why he wanted them, well, maybe he was trying to tear down the bridge for some reason. He might be one of these kooks who wants to get on the news. If he wasn't a kook, he was probably a crook bribed to do it—or he was doing it for money for some reason. You'd be surprised at how much people will pay for pieces of history."

Alexis elbowed Elizabeth. She was thinking of Dr. Edwards. All of this came down to history.

Cliff ran off to help his crew get the bridge ready for the parade and left the three of them standing staring at the floor.

"Well, I guess I'd better get home," said David.

"Yeah, it's almost dinnertime," said Elizabeth. They all walked toward the front doors. All at once, Alexis stopped and yelled.

"Wait!" cried Alexis. David and Elizabeth spun around in surprise. "David! What are you doing tomorrow?"

"Uh, watching the parade, I guess."

Alexis and Elizabeth exchanged excited glances.

"Do you want to ride with us in the bed race tomorrow?" Alexis asked.

"Please! You have to!" said Elizabeth. "I'm going to push, and Alexis is going to steer, but we don't have a third person!"

"You need a shifter," said David.

"A what?" said the girls together.

"A shifter—someone to sit in the middle of the bed and shift from side to side as you go around corners. It keeps the bed from flipping over. You're in luck. I happen to be the best shifter in Lake Havasu. Been on the winning float two years in a row."

"But that means you raced with Emily!" said Alexis.

"Yeah, I did. Until she broke that guy's arm anyway. She's a good racer, but she's too brutal. She'll do anything to win."

"So you'll ride with us?" asked Elizabeth.

"Of course!" said David. "Where should I meet you?"

"Outside of Bill's Tarnished Treasures first thing in the morning," said Alexis. "Don't forget to wear your costume!"

Alexis walked David and Elizabeth to the sidewalk, where the two of them peeled off in opposite directions—David to his home and Elizabeth to her hotel. Alexis turned to go inside and was almost bowled over by a round man in a flapping suit.

It was the mayor.

"Sorry, girl! Sorry! Didn't see you in all the excitement!"

Then he turned and continued running toward the bridge, yelling at anyone who crossed his path. "Did you hear? Did you hear? The parade is on! There's no curse after all!"

Alexis watched him disappear around the corner, half expecting him to do a hitch kick on his way.

The Great Race

The sun was barely up, but the people of Lake Havasu City were already gathering. A variety of beds were ready at the starting line. Racing teams were making final adjustments and getting into position.

Alexis was reattaching a sequined fish that had fallen off when David leaned out over her head from his seat on the bed.

"You almost done?" he asked. Alexis looked up. David's dragon costume was hilarious. It was a glittery blue, and the hood was shaped like a horned dragon's head, complete with three-inch fangs on the front of the snout.

"Yeah, almost," said Alexis. "This fish won't stay put!"

"Well, maybe if your decorations weren't so cheap, they wouldn't fall apart," said a nasty voice from behind them. Alexis spun around and found Emily's knees in her face. They were covered in sparkly tights. Alexis looked up and saw that Emily was dressed like a fairy. Even her makeup was gorgeous, and she had pointed ears and wings.

"Don't you have your own bed to attend to?" asked David.

"Oh," said Emily to Alexis. "I see you had to pick up last year's leftovers to get a third. Well, good luck, *girls*."

She curtsied to David with her last word and traipsed back

to her own bed.

"Don't worry about her," said David as he helped Alexis climb over the wall and onto the bed. "She wouldn't even be talking to us unless she was afraid we might beat her."

"And I think you just might!" It was Bill. He came out of the crowd and hobbled one last time around the castle-bed. "This thing really has a chance with a crew like you three!"

Bill pointed at David and spoke to the girls."You know this guy's the best shifter in Lake Havasu, right?" he said. "Mary takes the credit. She used to go with his mom to ride go-carts, and she taught him how to take the corners!"

David bowed, his dragon's tail flying up in the air and knocking off Elizabeth's tiara.

"Be careful where you swing that thing!" she said. "Everybody ready? They're about to start!"

Alexis scrambled to the front and sat on the throne. She twisted her jester's hat so she was looking between two of the floppy arms. There was no way she was going to let a couple of jingle bells keep her from seeing where she was going.

Elizabeth climbed out of the bed and took up her station behind the tower, on the ground. She would be the one to start pushing when the gun went off. David plunked down in between the tower and Alexis's throne. There he would squat, ready to shift to one side or the other each time they took a corner. Hopefully he could keep the bed from tipping up or— even worse—from falling over.

"Alexis! Hey, Alexis!"

Alexis looked over and saw her grandmother's shocking red hair bobbing up and down in the crowd. She was waving frantically, elbowing Dr. Edwards in the side as she did so. He did not seem the least bit interested.

"Hi, Grandma!" called Alexis.

"Drive that thing well, baby!" called Grandma Windsor.

"I will!" cried Alexis. "And I'll meet you at the end of the parade!"

Their conversation was interrupted by the mayor's amplified voice. It roared over the noise of the crowd, causing a hush that was unnatural for so many people. The air hummed, as if the noise was just waiting for the right moment to explode again.

"Ready! Set!" called the mayor, the cap gun raised high over his head. *Snap!*

And they were off.

Along the starting line, beds began to roll forward. All of them were slow at first, but after a few seconds they picked up some speed.

"Come on, Elizabeth!" yelled Alexis. Just then David's head appeared over her shoulder.

"Alexis!" he said. "Just around the first corner is a hill! When I tell you to, lean forward as far as you can without falling out!"

"What?" Alexis cried. "What for?"

"You'll see," he said. Alexis didn't like the grin on his face.

The corner came faster than Alexis had expected. They were in the middle of the road with beds on either side. The street curved a little to the right, and David crouched down along the right wall of their castle.

"I'm on!" cried Elizabeth. She had stopped pushing and was now standing on the back of the bed.

"Now!" cried David. Alexis leaned forward, keeping her hands on the steering wheel. To her surprise, David was beside her, adding his weight to hers at the front of the bed. Soon she

saw why they were doing it.

At first it was only five inches, but soon their castle-bed was a good twenty feet in front of everyone else. Their weight was forcing the bed down the hill faster than all the others!

The wind in her face made Alexis whoop in excitement. *This is how it must feel to fly*, she thought. The road continued straight at the bottom of the hill, so Alexis just sat back in her seat and held tight to the vibrating steering wheel. David returned to the middle of the bed, and Elizabeth got ready to jump off and push—but they were going too fast. She didn't need to.

"Woo-hoo!" cried Elizabeth. Her head peeked up over the top of the tower. "You guys are doing great!"

"Here comes another corner!" said David. "Alexis! Tap the brakes once, then lean into the turn!" Alexis did as she was told. She tapped the pedal with her foot—but she did it twice. The bed lurched and took the turn at a crawl. They had lost most of their momentum, and two beds flew past them.

"Push, Elizabeth!" called David. Alexis felt the pressure from behind as Elizabeth struggled with the weight of the bed. She could see that the road up ahead dropped off in another hill, and she hoped they could catch up on the way down.

"All right!" shouted David. "Let's do it all over again! Elizabeth—get on! Alexis, lean forward and, no matter what you do, *don't touch the brakes!*"

Once again they were flying. In no time at all they had overtaken two teams. Now only one bed was ahead of them. Alexis looked up and recognized the sparkly wings of Emily's costume.

"We're going to pass her on the curve at the bottom!" said

David. "Put our bed on the inside of the turn! Between her bed and the curb! If we lean left, you won't need the brakes! Plus," he said with a smile, "even if we tip, all we'll do is bump her a little. Ready? *Lean!*"

And she did. Alexis leaned to her left with everything she had. The force pulling the bed to the right was crazy. Alexis thought for sure they were going to topple over. Once, their left wheels lifted into the air, but David's weight put them back on the ground.

They came out of the turn just ahead of Emily's bed. An angry screech came from behind them. Then there was a jolt, and their castle-bed almost flew off the road and into the watching audience.

Cheers turned to boos, and after she got control of her bed, Alexis looked over to see Emily passing her.

"Oops!" said Emily. "Guess I got a little close. Sorry!" And she kept rolling.

"No way!" cried Alexis. "She cheated!"

"She always does," said David. "One more curve, then it's a slight hill to the finish. Don't pass her yet. Stay behind her on the turn, and we'll lean down the hill again, okay?"

Alexis nodded. Elizabeth joined them up front. They were going so fast there was no way she could push anymore. The last turn behind them, Alexis gripped the wheel and leaned. David and Elizabeth leaned forward, too, one on either side of her.

They were even with the back of Emily's bed—they were at the middle—they were nose and nose—

The finish line was feet away. Without warning, David put his feet on the castle wall and leaped forward, grasping the finishing ribbon in his hands before falling and rolling beneath the bed with a crash.

Cheers erupted from the crowd. Alexis slammed on the brakes as the medical staff ran out to pull David from under the bed. He was fine, except for some minor scrapes, and one of his dragon's teeth had been knocked out.

"Dragons have tough hides!" he said with a laugh as Alexis and Elizabeth ran up to him.

"That was *crazy!*" said Elizabeth.

"Why did you do that?" asked Alexis.

"I couldn't let her win," he said. "Not like that."

Alexis noticed there was quite a commotion near the side of the finish line. Most of the beds had finished, but the judges seemed to be fighting over something. Alexis led the way over to the judges, her jester's hat flopping in her hands.

"Where's the picture? We have to have the picture!" called one of the judges. He was a short man with a huge mustache.

"It's coming, Wilbur," said another judge. She was tall and was looking around the crowd. "Where's the photographer?" she shouted.

"I'm right here!" called a man in a tweed coat. He was running as fast as he could, huffing from the exertion. A digital camera was around his neck. He stopped near the judges and played with the buttons for a few seconds. Then he passed it to the judges. After a few moments of silence the tall judge spoke.

"I just don't believe it!" she said.

"Me neither," said the little man with the mustache. "But the rules say—"

"The rules say what, exactly?" said Emily. She had abandoned her bed and was stalking toward the judges. "They had better say that I won!"

"Well, actually, young lady," said the man, "you didn't."

He showed her the camera. Emily's mouth dropped open, and she shoved the camera at Alexis. Alexis grabbed the camera. There was the proof, clear as day. David's long arms outstretched, grasping the finish line and beating the front of Emily's bed by a good six inches.

"But their bed didn't cross before mine!" argued Emily. "He jumped off!"

"The rules state that each team member is considered a part of the bed as long as they are touching it," said the lady judge. "And as you can see, his feet were still on the wall when he crossed the finish line."

Emily looked ready to argue, but the mayor burst past her, shoving her to the side.

"Congratulations!" he said, shaking hands with Alexis, Elizabeth, and David. "Great job! New winners!"

He squeezed them all in close, and the photographer took a picture. Then, without a moment to spare, the mayor was gone again.

"The parade!" he called. "Ten minutes until the parade!"

Alexis couldn't believe it. Not only had they been able to race, but they had also won!

"I can't believe we beat Emily!" Alexis exclaimed. "She's so mean that I was sure she'd win!"

"Well, I guess when we do the right thing and try hard, well, maybe the good guys don't always finish last," Elizabeth said. "It's kind of like 2 Samuel 22:25 says, 'The Lord has rewarded me according to my righteousness, according to my cleanness in his sight.'"

The three winners walked through the crowd and found

a grassy spot on a hill to watch the parade pass. People kept stopping to congratulate them, and many shop owners told them to come by later for something or other "on the house." They made a plan to get free ice cream and chocolates but *not* to visit the taxidermist who had promised a special surprise.

The parade was all they had hoped it would be. The school marching band opened up, and not far behind them was the golden float from the hotel. Dr. Edwards sat in the driver's seat, accompanied by Grandma Windsor. They were both dressed in authentic costumes from the era of King George III, and Alexis thought it looked like her grandmother was having the time of her life.

You know, she told herself, *Dr. Edwards even looks happy. He looks like a gentleman driving his lady.*

Alexis gasped and stood up.

"What?" asked Elizabeth and David at the same time.

"A gentleman driving his lady," she murmured. "A gentleman. . .driving his *lady*!"

Without explaining, Alexis tore off through the crowd. Elizabeth and David followed, catching up outside the London Bridge Resort.

"What's going on?" Elizabeth panted.

"I think I know where the letter is hidden!" said Alexis. She ran through the automatic doors and stopped. The lobby was empty. Even Jane was nowhere to be seen. Alexis turned toward the golden coach.

"I think I know where it is!" she said again. As she went to cross the red ropes, she tripped, putting out a hand to stabilize herself on the coach. When she touched it, a huge sheet of golden foil came off in her hand.

"Wow," said David. "I thought the replica was sturdier than that!"

Alexis and Elizabeth looked at each other in horror.

"It is," they both said. Then they took off running back out the doors.

"Wait!" called David. "What's going on?"

"It's Dr. Edwards!" said Alexis. "He's stealing the replica from the hotel!"

"How?" asked David. "What are you talking about?"

"You saw the foil slip off," said Elizabeth. "He must have replaced the real carriage with his phony 'float' while everyone was watching the bed race."

"Right now, he's driving the actual replica of the golden carriage through Lake Havasu City!" said Alexis. "And everyone just thinks it's a float!"

The three teens ran across the street and down a couple of blocks. They stopped outside the Lake Havasu City Sheriff's Department. Inside, they met a bored-looking woman sitting at the front desk.

"Excuse me, ma'am," said Alexis. "We have an emergency."

"What is it?" said the woman, sitting up a little straighter and looking alert.

"Someone has stolen the golden carriage from the London Bridge Resort!" said Elizabeth.

The woman behind the desk burst out laughing. She laughed so hard that she began crying. Alexis tried to explain, but the lady just kept laughing and showed them out the door.

Alexis was stupefied. If the police didn't believe them, who would? They walked back slowly to the parade. Grandma Windsor hollered to them, and Alexis pushed her way through the crowd to get to her.

"You're already done, Mrs. Windsor?" asked Elizabeth.

"Yes," Grandma Windsor said. "Dr. Edwards and I were leading the parade, so we were done first. Hey! Why's everybody so glum?"

Alexis didn't think her grandmother would believe her, but there was no reason to hold back anymore. She told her the whole story, from hearing Jerold and Jim in the alley to finding the fake carriage in the lobby only minutes earlier.

"The police don't believe us," Alexis finished. "There's nothing we can do."

"What do you mean, nothing?" cried Grandma Windsor. She disappeared into the crowd, and within minutes honking filled the air. People parted as it came closer. Grandma Windsor was behind the wheel of her cherry-red convertible, motioning for Alexis to jump in.

"I don't want to leave you two behind," she said to David and Elizabeth, "but we haven't asked your parents, and we don't have time. I just saw Dr. Edwards loading the carriage into a semitruck. He's already on the interstate, heading west!"

With that they were gone. Alexis buckled her seat belt as Grandma Windsor hit the gas pedal.

"I called the sheriff," said Grandma Windsor. "Told him he'd better listen to me, since he ignored my granddaughter. They should be on their way."

When they got on the freeway, Alexis could barely make out the shape of a truck in the distance.

"It's time to see what this baby can do!"

The engine thrummed as the car went faster. . .and faster.

A siren wailed behind them, and Alexis saw the red and

blue of flashing lights in the rearview mirror. *Thank goodness!* she thought. *The sheriff will catch Dr. Edwards in no time!* The car pulled up next to them but didn't drive past. Alexis looked over and gasped.

It was Deputy Dewayne, and he was motioning for Grandma Windsor to pull her car over.

CHAPTER 12

Busted!

"What is he doing here?" hollered Alexis over the noise of the car's engine.

"Well, I did call the sheriff," said Grandma Windsor. "Maybe he wants to question me." She coasted to the side of the road. When the car stopped, Deputy Dewayne pulled in right behind them, lights still flashing and siren blaring.

Grandma Windsor rolled down her window, and Alexis spun around in her seat to watch the deputy approach. He swaggered up to the car and stood with his hands on his hips. The look on his face reminded Alexis of a starving lion that had just found something to eat.

"Ma'am," said Deputy Dewayne to Grandma Windsor, "do you have any idea how fast you were going back there?"

"I'm sorry, Officer," said Alexis's grandma. She put on her best smile. "I must have gotten carried away. I didn't want the fugitives to get away." Alexis leaned over so she could see Deputy Dewayne's face.

"She's telling the truth, sir," she said. "We were trying to catch up to Dr. Edwards before he gets away with the golden coach."

Deputy Dewayne's eyes narrowed.

"So it's you!" he said. "I should have known!"

"Now Deputy," said Grandma Windsor. "There's no reason to talk to my granddaughter that way." The deputy took off his sunglasses and leaned through the window.

"Now ma'am, you need to understand something," he said. Alexis wondered why he was suddenly talking to her grandmother like she was a five-year-old. "Every time there's been a disturbance this week, I've found this girl in the middle of things."

Grandma Windsor was still smiling, but Alexis could tell that it was getting harder for her to keep it up.

"I'm sure there have been a few misunderstandings," she said, "but that is not the issue right now. Right now we are trying to keep a thief from—"

"I don't think you are qualified to tell me what is or is not the issue, ma'am," said the deputy.

"Maybe not, but if you would just radio the sheriff, he'll tell you—"

Deputy Dewayne stepped back and yanked the car door open.

"Step out of the car, ma'am," he said. Grandma Windsor's mouth dropped open. Alexis dropped her head into her hands with a sigh.

"Don't fight it, Grandma," she said. "This is a losing battle."

Grandma Windsor huffed in anger and got out of her car. Deputy Dewayne spun her around and pulled out his handcuffs.

"Molly Windsor, you're under arrest for obstruction of justice and failure to comply."

Alexis was about to complain when more sirens filled the air. She turned to see four sheriff's cars blow past them on their way to catch Dr. Edwards. Deputy Dewayne stared after them, stunned. He fumbled with Grandma Windsor's handcuffs and ran toward his car. Alexis had a sudden thought. She had to be with the police when they caught Dr. Edwards. She was the only one here who really knew what was going on. But how was she going to get there? Grandma Windsor couldn't drive with her hands cuffed behind her back, and it would be too far to walk. She glanced at Deputy Dewayne and got an idea.

"Um, you'd better take me with you," she said.

"Why would I do that?" he asked suspiciously.

"Well, you said it yourself—I've been involved in every crazy thing that's happened this week. Don't you think I have something to do with this, too?" The deputy opened the passenger door to his car.

"Get in," he said. Alexis smiled at her grandmother as she jumped in the front seat of the police car. She was about to say something when Deputy Dewayne jumped in the other side and took off, siren blazing—and left Grandma Windsor standing in handcuffs on the side of the road.

Neither of them said a word during the drive. Within five minutes they were pulling up behind a gaggle of red and blue lights that had surrounded a huge semitruck. They were just opening the back end when Alexis and Deputy Dewayne walked up.

Alexis saw that Jerold and Jim were already in handcuffs. Alexis watched two officers lead them into one of the patrol cars in front of the truck. The sheriff was near the golden coach, talking to Dr. Edwards. Alexis edged nearer so she could hear what they were saying.

"I just don't understand it, Doc," said the sheriff. "Why would you steal this thing? What on earth could you do with a replica of a golden coach?"

"Well," said Dr. Edwards, "it's very pretty. Thought it would look good in my garage." He pulled out a handkerchief and blew his nose.

"You expect me to believe that?" said the sheriff. He kept ranting, adding question after question. Dr. Edwards kept answering with one or two words. It was as if he wanted to keep the sheriff talking as long as possible. Alexis got the impression that he was biding time.

"Good, they got him!"

Alexis turned around to see David and Elizabeth standing near her. She looked back and saw Elizabeth's parents wave at her from their car fifty yards behind everyone else.

"How did you know where we were?" Alexis asked.

"When we saw the deputy taking off after your grandma onto the highway, we knew the direction you were going. I called my parents, and they agreed to bring us out."

"So we could be in on the catch!" David said with a big smile.

"Well, *catch* is the right word." Alexis turned to Elizabeth. "Jim and Jerold are up in the front patrol car," she said. Then she explained to David, "Those were the two men who were building the float for Dr. Edwards, the ones we heard talking about the robbery in the alley."

"So what's going on here?" Elizabeth asked, motioning at Dr. Edwards and the sheriff.

"The sheriff's asking questions, like why the doctor stole the carriage, but Dr. Edwards isn't answering them very quickly. I was just thinking that it's almost like he's stalling," she said. And then she realized why he was stalling.

Every few seconds Dr. Edwards scooted a little bit closer to the carriage. He must have known this was his last chance if he wanted to find the document.

"Wait!" cried Alexis. The sheriff spun around, surprised to see her. Dr. Edwards noticed her and gasped. She had never seen his ancient face look so angry.

"Little miss," said the sheriff, "what are you doing here?"

"My grandma was the one who called and told you about the theft," Alexis said. "But it's not really about the carriage at all, is it, Dr. Edwards?" The old professor wiped his nose again.

"Of course it is," he sniveled. "I have no idea what you're talking about, little girl."

Alexis turned toward the sheriff.

"Sir," she said, "Dr. Edwards believes that there is a priceless letter hidden somewhere in the carriage. He came to Lake Havasu City so he could look for it, but when he couldn't find it, he decided to steal the whole carriage instead."

"Is this true?" asked the sheriff, turning toward Dr. Edwards.

Dr. Edwards's lips tightened into a flat line. He was obviously trying not to say anything. When there was no answer, the sheriff turned to Alexis again.

"This is an interesting story," he said. "But there's no evidence that it's true. We've still got him on the theft charge though."

He turned back to Dr. Edwards as Elizabeth nudged Alexis and showed her something on her cell phone.

Alexis read the words that were texted there and looked up at Elizabeth in amazement. Elizabeth grinned and nodded.

"Sir," said Alexis, touching the sheriff on the elbow. "I know where the letter is hidden—at least I think I do."

Dr. Edwards smirked. "Little girl, I have been searching this carriage for years—visited London Bridge Resort every vacation. There's no way *you* would have been able to find the document after four days in town!"

Alexis ignored him. "May I?" she asked the sheriff.

"Be my guest," he said. Alexis climbed up into the back of the trailer and made her way toward the front of the carriage. A golden wave of water hid the driver's seat from view. When she was level with the seat—where Dr. Edwards had been only this morning—she turned and spoke to the crowd of curious police.

"There's a story that the princess Amelia, King George the Third's youngest daughter, hid a letter for the man she loved in her father's coach. Dr. Edwards was probably looking throughout the inside of the coach, since that's where the princess would have sat, but one of our other mystery-solving friends who loves horses, McKenzie, thought of somewhere else to look. The man the princess loved worked with the horses. In that case she probably would have hidden the note where he would have found it while harnessing them to the carriage."

Alexis grabbed the golden post that was meant to hold the horses and slid her hand into the hollow end. She pulled out a thin box and opened it. The hinges creaked in the silence.

And there it was—a small, folded package, yellowed with age.

"'For the Son of Man came to seek and to save the lost,'" Elizabeth murmured. "Luke 19:10 doesn't quite fit the situation, but I think God must have nudged McKenzie's brain!"

"No!" hollered Dr. Edwards. "That's mine! Mine by right!"

"How do you figure that, Doc?" asked the sheriff. "And what on earth is a priceless letter doing here, in Lake Havasu City? Shouldn't it be in the real coach in Britain?"

"I did all the research decades ago, while I was in college," said Dr. Edwards. He spoke to the sheriff, but he was glaring at Alexis.

"I finally figured that the letter was probably in the carriage," he continued, "so I wrote to the royal family and got permission to search it from the queen herself. But before I could save the money to go back to Britain, my professor stole my permission letters and went himself. He found the letter, but he told me he had hidden it from the royal family so he could keep it for himself. He died in a train accident on his way to southern California, and it took me fifty years to figure out that he'd hidden it in the carriage. So you see? I did all the work! It's rightfully mine!"

The sheriff smiled sadly.

"It's a sad story, Doc," he said. "And I wish I could take your side, but the truth is that you committed a crime when you stole the replica. Why didn't you just ask permission to search the carriage? We could have helped you take it apart if need be."

Dr. Edwards looked crestfallen. Alexis felt bad for him, but the sheriff was right. Dr. Edwards had committed a crime, and they couldn't reward him by giving him the letter now. Another deputy handcuffed the doctor and led him toward another car with flashing lights.

"I guess we'd better figure out what to do with this," said the sheriff. He stepped forward and reached into the box that Alexis was still holding.

"Stop! Don't touch anything!"

Everyone spun around to see Grandma Windsor leap out of yet another police car. Her wrists had been freed from the cuffs, and she strode toward the back of the truck trailer with purpose, her costume dress flapping behind her.

"You can't just go and grab a two-hundred-and-fifty-year-old document like it was a letter from your mother!" she yelled at the sheriff. The man smiled and stepped back.

"Of course, Professor Windsor. I'm glad you're here. Would you mind helping us out with this?"

"Not at all," Grandma Windsor said with a smile. She slipped a white glove onto her hand and reached into the compartment. She lifted the letter out with a flat hand and slipped it into a large plastic Ziploc bag. "It's not perfect, but it will do," she said.

● — ●

The next morning Alexis was sad because it would be her last day in Lake Havasu City. At least for now. David and Elizabeth met her in the hotel lobby after breakfast. David was carrying three neon-colored rubber duckies.

"What are those for, David?" asked Alexis as he handed her a pink one. He gave the purple one to Elizabeth and kept the green one for himself.

"You'll see," he said. "Follow me!"

They left the hotel and made their way toward the bridge. Alexis noticed quite a crowd gathering along the railings.

For a moment she was afraid that something was wrong, but then she realized the people were smiling.

"What's all the commotion?" she asked. "I thought the festival was over."

"Not quite!" said David. "We close it out with the duck race!"

Alexis looked at the bridge again and saw that everyone at the railings had a rubber ducky in their hands. They were passing the sheriff's department when Elizabeth grabbed Alexis's arm.

"Look! Wonder where they're taking Jim and Jerold?" she said.

Alexis looked across the street. Two police officers were putting Jim and Jerold into the back of a police car.

"Hey!" said David. "That's the engineer I told you about! The one who wanted the stones from the bridge!" He was pointing to Jim.

"It doesn't surprise me," said Alexis. "Those two were helping Dr. Edwards, but I don't imagine that's the only shady deal they were involved in. I wonder what they wanted them for, if not to destroy the bridge or ruin the race."

"Bet I know what they wanted the stones for," Elizabeth said. "I updated the girls last night on what was going on. Awhile ago Kate texted me that she'd done a search on London Bridge artifacts and found someone selling stones from the London Bridge on several Internet auction sites."

"You mean like eBay?" David asked.

"Well, I'm not sure if it was eBay, but there are a lot of sites out there like that now," Elizabeth said. "One of the sites she saw them on that requires a selling location listed Lake Havasu City. And the sellers' names were words like Jerold, and J and J Auctions."

"We'll have to tell Grandma so she can let the sheriff know. Then he can look into it," Alexis said.

"Has your grandma found out what's going to happen to the letter from Princess Amelia?" Elizabeth asked.

"Yes, she called the British Museum, and they are super-excited about finally having the letter. They even offered to let Lake Havasu City borrow it each year during the festival," Alexis explained.

Elizabeth looked at David and frowned. "You know there's one other thing I don't get. If it was you making the crack in the bridge, then what was the thing with the old hag cursing the bridge?"

"I know which woman you mean," David said. "That one dressed up to be really ugly? I heard her saying something about the bridge."

"Do you mean Meghan?" Suddenly the young teens realized that Grandma Windsor had joined them. "Are you talking about my friend Meghan?" she asked, linking arms with Alexis.

"I don't know. She was some old lady who looked like she stepped out of the movie *The Princess Bride*," Alexis explained.

"Oh yes, that's Meghan!" Grandma exclaimed. "She's actually not old. She's quite young. She's a drama student who likes to come to the festival dressed up as an old woman. She seems to have a talent for that kind of voice and for living in character. She's great at curses."

"Grandma!" Alexis exclaimed.

"Well, not real curses, silly. They're all make-believe," Grandma said. "She is convincing, isn't she? If she can't make it as an actress, I'm sure she has a future as a makeup artist."

"But she left a message for us," Elizabeth said. "And why would she run away from us if she was your friend?"

"Well, that's just it, dears," Grandma Windsor explained. "I had told her about this fabulous Camp Club Girls group you have and all the mysteries you solve. I'm quite proud, you know. She was so afraid you'd be bored that she said she was going to try to stir up a bit of a mystery for you. Secret messages, anyway. She thought it would just be a spot of fun for you."

"You mean you knew all along?" Alexis asked.

"Oh yes, dear. I meant to tell you about it before you thought there was a real mystery there, but it seems like you found your own mysteries to solve without Meghan's help. I think she had a couple of more messages planned, but she had to leave town and go back to where she normally lives—Tuscon, I think. Her mother got ill and needed her," Grandma Windsor said. "Now Alexis, I need to scoot for a few minutes. I'm on my way to the sheriff's office. Have to see him about that silly ticket his silly deputy gave me. I'll see you at the hotel in a bit."

Grandma Windsor trotted off.

"Well, at least that answers that!" said Elizabeth. "Oh, you know, I decided I'm going to talk to Mr. Bill about buying that spoon with Princess Amelia on it. Mom gave me some money this morning. Alexis, I guess I'm as much of a romantic at heart as you are. I'm going to run and get it and will meet you at the bridge in about ten minutes. Here, hold my ducky for me, will you?" she said as she thrust the purple duck in Alexis's hand.

"So you're a romantic at heart, hmm?" David asked, with a tender smile on his face.

Alexis blushed and shrugged.

"So any chance your grandma will be back in Lake Havasu?" asked David. "Maybe this winter?"

"I don't think so," she said.

"Oh," said David. "I just know some old people like to come to Arizona in the winter. I mean, not like she's old!"

Alexis laughed.

"No, she's not really old," she said. "And I think she's coming to visit us for the holidays. Dad mentioned a trip up to Tahoe, but I don't think I'll be back down here anytime soon."

"Do you have an e-mail address, then?" asked David.

"Better than that," said Alexis. "The Camp Club Girls have a website!"

"The *what*?"

"It's a long story," said Alexis. She and David walked to the bridge while she explained to him about the Camp Club Girls and their mysteries. Then Elizabeth joined them, and all three leaned over the railing of the bridge and dropped their ducks into the water.

Alexis didn't know if it was because she had solved two cases, because she was with such good friends, or because God had just erased her fears. But for some reason, she wasn't scared of the bridge anymore.

The Camp Club Girls
are on the case!

Don't miss these other exciting
3-in-1 story collections. . . .

Get a Clue

Secrets and Surprises

Available wherever books are sold.

Introducing God ♡s Me

A brand-new series
for girls ages 10 to 14

Check out the entire series. . .

God ♡s Me: The New Life™ Bible for Girls

God ♡s Me: A Bible Promise Book for Girls

God ♡s Me: A Devotional Journal for Girls

God ♡s Me: Daily Devotions for a Girl's Heart

the
S.A.V.E.
Squad

Since they can't save the whole world, what about
a small piece of it? Sixth-graders Sunny, Aneta,
Vee, and Esther join together as the S.A.V.E. Squad
and set out to rescue homeless dogs, dumpster cats,
retired thoroughbreds, and injured owls.

True Story! ...

These pages from EJ Payne's diary will have
you ROTFL as EJ records her thoughts about living in little
old Spooner, Wisconsin (*snooze!*), eventually leaving her
hometown to do *big* things when she's all grown up (*oh
glorious day!*), and having to star in the role of lead angel in
the Vine Street Christmas pageant (*are you kidding me?*).

EJ's story continues with *Church Camp Chaos*...
available March 2014!